More Praise for
An Eye for Murder

"The kind of mystery that I am searching for in the stacks and on the bookshelves. It is not 'just a mystery,' but a story—about reality, about human beings, about life, a story believably told. The plot propelled me forward, kept me 'turning the pages' and reached a satisfying, believable, and surprising conclusion."
—Eleanor Taylor Bland,
author of the Marti MacAlister mystery series

"A terrific writer . . . I love the Ellie Foreman character and I want more books about her."
—Barbara D'Amato, winner of the
Mary Higgins Clark Award

"Intelligent and gutsy, the protagonist is someone I'd like to have as a friend. The author knows Chicago, and, more to the point, catches it on the page. *An Eye for Murder* is a wonderful book. Read it!"
—Michael Allen Dymmoch,
author of *Incendiary Designs*

"What a joy to watch Ellie Foreman become a take-charge woman who investigates the past to solve crimes of the present. *An Eye for Murder* is a remarkable debut mystery."
—Judy Duhl, Scotland Yard Books

"*An Eye for Murder* is my favorite kind of mystery—a secret from the past snowballs into the present, creating an avalanche of problems for the protagonist who is witty, resourceful, and determined to dig her way out."
—Jacqueline Fiedler, author of *Tiger's Palette*

W9-CPQ-969

AN EYE FOR MURDER

LIBBY FISCHER HELLMANN

BERKLEY PRIME CRIME, NEW YORK

AN EYE FOR MURDER

A Berkley Prime Crime Book / published by arrangement with the author

PRINTING HISTORY
Berkley Prime Crime mass-market edition / December 2002

Visit our website at
www.penguinputnam.com

ISBN: 0-425-18739-X

Berkley Prime Crime Books are published
by The Berkley Publishing Group,
a division of Penguin Putnam Inc.,
375 Hudson Street, New York, New York 10014.
The name BERKLEY PRIME CRIME
and the BERKLEY PRIME CRIME design
are trademarks belonging to Penguin Putnam Inc.

PRINTED IN THE UNITED STATES OF AMERICA

10 9 8 7 6 5 4 3 2 1

For my Mother
who started it all

ACKNOWLEDGMENTS

A writer never does it alone.

I had help from talented people, many of them experts in their fields. Any errors in the text are mine.

To Irving Cutler, whose book *The Jews of Chicago* was so helpful; Linda Juhasz, who really is the resident steel historian in Chicago; Don Whiteman; Howard Preis; Paul Horowitz; Peter and, especially, Barbie Mehler; Kathy Smith; Rick Felt; Sue Maier; Robert White; David Wechsler and all the folks at RDR; Lucy Zahray, the "Poison Lady"; Catherine Mambretti; and Sandy Tooley, my heartfelt thanks.

Also to Deputy Chief Mike Green of the Northbrook Police Department; Detective Mike O'Malley, also of Northbrook; Bill Lustig, Northfield's Chief of Police; and Sergeant Dave Case of the Chicago Police Department, all of whom took repeated calls from me.

To Teri Mathes and the Red Herrings: Dave, Michael, Eleanor, Bruce, Steve, Dave, and Gordon—where would I be without you? And to Nora Cavin: you are—quite simply—my North Star.

To Jacky and Samantha, thanks for the start of a "beautiful friendship."

Finally, to Mark, Robin, Michael, Deane, Steven, and Susan: I love you all. Thanks for putting up with me.

History is made out of the failures and heroism of each insignificant moment.

—FRANZ KAFKA

PROLOGUE

Prague: August 1944

The evening air was heavy and damp. Summer kept hanging on. The smell of rotting fish mixed with exhaust fumes as trucks cut through the narrow streets of the city. Nothing seemed clean anymore. It was hard to imagine Prague was once the crown jewel of the Hapsburg Empire.

He'd spent the afternoon checking the route. Strolling past Panska and the office that had housed the Prager Tagblatt until the Nazis shut it down. Past the castle, the palace, and the basilica, with their jumble of Romanesque, Renaissance, and Baroque architecture. Trying to look unobtrusive. Just another Czech citizen out on a late summer day.

The city made him uncomfortable. Back home before the war, he'd prowled dark streets and alleys, courting danger, practically daring it to appear. But now, danger meant death if he was caught. He was careful to avoid people and crowds.

The restaurant smelled of stale beer, and the tables were coated with grime. Maybe it was the European tolerance for a state of clean that would make Westerners cringe. Or maybe it was the only way the people in occupied countries had to rebel against Nazi discipline. A few patrons had come in, old men mostly, their bodies shriveled with age. One hobbled on a cane.

After observing the place for an hour, he decided it was

safe to enter. He leaned in at the bar, a glass of beer in his hand, but his gut twisted every time someone glanced his way.

The door squeaked as someone came in. He turned around. The new arrival ordered a schnapps. The bartender, busying himself with a glass and the bottle, didn't look up. The man tossed his drink down in one gulp and thumped his glass on the bar. The bartender refilled it.

"The Kinski gardens are beautiful now, yes?" the new arrival said in German, looking down the bar.

The American replied in heavily accented German. "I prefer the park this time of year."

The new arrival shifted slightly, almost imperceptibly. "Yes. It is cooler there."

After ten minutes and another schnapps, the new arrival dug deep in his pocket, tossed a few coins on the bar, and walked out. The American stayed a few more minutes and then left also, turning toward the river. Dusk was upon him, dark shadows softening the edges of buildings. He was careful to make sure he wasn't followed. Three streets north and two streets east. Just another citizen out for a walk.

As he passed the narrow cobblestone alley behind the museum, a voice from the shadows said softly, "Good evening, Comrade."

The American looked up, startled.

"Sorry. My little joke." His contact smiled. "We will speak in English. But we whisper."

The American managed a nod. "What should I call you?"

He paused. "Kafka. And you?"

"You can call me Joe."

"GI Joe." Kafka's smile faded. "It is unusual to see an American so far from home. Especially here. How did it come about?"

"I had work to do."

"You have had a long journey."

"I have been in Berlin. The East before that."

"A freedom fighter. We honor you, Joe."

Again he shrugged.

"So. I understand you have information for us?"

"How do I know it will get to the right place?"

"There is no guarantee. But we both know you did not agree to this meeting without—how do you say it—checking us out."

Kafka was right. Joe had heard about the intelligence unit formed by the British and the Americans. Fighting the Germans by stealing codes. Infiltrating their ranks. Kafka worked for them, he'd been told. He took a breath. *"You've heard of Josef Mengele?"*

Kafka's jaw tightened. *"The Butcher of Auschwitz."*

"Yes." Joe had learned for himself one sunny day not long ago. He remembered wondering how the sun had the nerve to keep shining.

"We have heard the rumors. Obscene medical experiments. Inhumane. Vile," Kafka said.

Joe nodded. *"We thought the insanity belonged only to Hitler, Mengele, and the madmen here in Europe. But now . . ."* He reached into his jacket and pulled out a sheaf of papers tied together with string. He untied them and handed them to Kafka.

Kafka stayed in the shadows, angling the documents toward a light that spilled into the alley. Joe couldn't see them in the blackness. He didn't need to. A report detailing experiments. Sent with a cover letter to Reichsführer Himmler, Carl Clauberg, and someone named Rauscher. And one other person.

Joe waited while the agent read what he knew by heart: *". . . and to our friends on the other side of the ocean, whose financial and moral support has sustained us. We are united in working toward the same goals. May this research aid your efforts as well."*

Kafka looked up. His eyes glittered in the shadows. *"How did you come by this?"*

"I can't tell you," he said. It had been Magda's doing.

She had "intercepted" the courier. He owed her. "But I will vouch for its authenticity."

"The name on this letter . . . he is—"

"I know who he is."

"Do you know him?"

"No."

"I do. He is involved in the war effort. My superiors speak well of him."

Joe squinted. "What are you trying to say?"

"They will not believe this."

A chill edged up his spine. Everything he'd worked for was suddenly in jeopardy. "Does that mean you're not going to pass it through channels?"

Kafka shrugged. "They will think it is disinformation. Calculated to make us respond."

He opened his hand. "Give it back, then. I'll handle it myself."

Kafka moved the letter beyond his reach.

The American's hand crept to his pocket, his fingers gripping the barrel of his forty-five. "I haven't risked my fucking neck to see this buried. Not now."

Kafka kept his eyes on the American's pocket. "I have an idea," he said slowly. "Where are you from, Comrade?"

Joe tilted his head. "What the—what does that matter?"

"You are from Chicago, yes?" Kafka moved away from the light.

"How do you know that?"

"Do you think we did not check you out as well?" Kafka smiled. "What is it you Americans say? It is a small world, yes?"

He glared. "What does that mean?"

"I live there, too. Since I left Germany."

Joe kept his grip on the gun.

"Where can I find you in Chicago?"

"Listen, pal, I'm not gonna—"

"Trust me. Your journey has not been in vain."

*Just then, he heard the click of boots on the pavement.
A group of Waffen SS troops, full of drink from a nearby
tavern. He tried to grab the report, but Kafka edged behind him and slipped it inside his shirt. He heard Kafka's
whisper.*

"Well, Comrade?"

*The American stiffened. Then he whispered hoarsely,
"Miller's. Davy Miller's."*

*He made himself small as the soldiers stumbled past
the alley. When their beery laughs faded into the night,
he turned around. Kafka was gone.*

Chicago: The Present

The old man lifted his head at the sound. It was probably the dog sniffing outside his door, waiting for a treat.
He folded the newspaper and pushed himself up from his
chair. His landlady got the mutt last month. For security,
she said. Some guard dog. He never barked and always
wagged his damn tail when he saw the old man.

He didn't mind. The dog was better company than its
owner. He shuffled to the door, stopping to pull out a box
of Milk Bones he'd stashed in the closet. He pictured the
animal wriggling in pleasure as he waited for his treat.
It struck him that the dog was his sole link to a life of
warmth and affection. Well, life had always handed him
the bent fork. But he'd survived. Like a sewer rat always
on the move, he'd foraged what he needed, sometimes
getting more, sometimes less.

But now survival wasn't enough. His eyes moved to the
newspaper. He'd somehow known it would come to this.
You could never destroy the evil; it always grew back,
like one of those lethal viruses, more virulent and dangerous than its previous incarnation. He had to act. Soon.
He would launch a surgical strike, precisely timed for
maximum impact. And this time, he would get results.

Clutching the dog treat in one hand, he opened the
door with the other. Two men pushed their way in. One
had a ponytail and wore sunglasses; the other wore a

fishing hat pulled low on his forehead. The man with the
hat grabbed him in a hammerlock while the other pulled
something out of his pocket. A syringe. The old man struggled feebly, but he was no match for them. Ponytail
plunged the needle into his chest. The old man's hands
flew up. The dog biscuit fell from his hands and skittered
across the floor.

ONE

I DIDN'T GET the mail until late. Rachel and I were in the car driving home from school. "Honky Tonk Woman" was blaring out of the speakers, and I was thumping my hand on the wheel, thinking I had just enough time to chop onions and celery for a casserole before her piano lesson, when my twelve-year-old asked me about sex.

"Mom, have you ever had oral sex?"

"What was that, sweetheart?"

"Have you ever had oral sex?"

I nearly slammed on the brakes praying for something—anything—to say. But then I stole a look at her, strapped in the front seat, her blue eyes wide and innocent. Was she was testing me? Friends had been warning me sixth grade was a lot different these days.

I turned the radio down. "Who wants to know?"

"Oh, come on, Mom. Have you?"

I glanced over. Somehow her eyes didn't look as innocent. I might even have seen the hint of a smirk. "Ask me again in about twenty years."

"Muhtherrrr . . ."

Her face scrunched into that exasperated expression only preteen girls can produce. I remembered doing the same thing at her age. But I was behaving just like my mother did, so I guess we were even. I changed the subject.

"How was school?"

She wriggled deep into the front seat, stretched out her

arm, and turned up the radio. She punched all six buttons in turn, ending up at the oldies station it had been tuned to originally. "Two guys got into a fight at lunch."

First sex. Now violence. This was a big day. "What happened?"

"You know Sammy Thornton, right?"

"Sure." Everyone knew Sammy Thornton. A few years ago, his older brother, Daniel, had rampaged through a predominantly Jewish neighborhood on the north side of Chicago and shot six Orthodox Jews. He shot two more people downstate before turning the gun on himself. Afterward, it was discovered he had ties to a neo-Nazi group in central Illinois. I remember huddling in front of the TV that Friday night, watching the horror unfold with Rachel, who, at nine, was asking the one question I couldn't answer: Why? I remember feeling sorry for Sammy at the time, knowing that no matter how hard he struggled to rebuild his life, he would never escape being Dan Thornton's brother.

"Joel Merrick is a friend of his."

"I don't think I know Joel."

"He lives over on Summerfield. Has a sister in fourth grade."

I shrugged.

"Well, Pete Nichols started calling Sammy a Nazi. Joel stuck up for him and told Pete to shut up. Then Pete called Joel a Nazi too, so Joel decked him."

I turned onto our block. "Was anyone hurt?"

"Pete got a bloody nose, but he didn't go to the nurse's office."

"What did the teachers do?"

Rachel was silent.

"Didn't anyone say anything?"

She shook her head.

"Maybe someone should."

"You can't!" She wailed in dismay. "Mom, if you say anything, I'll die."

I parked in the driveway. "Okay. But I want you to

know that Pete's behavior was totally unacceptable. No one has the right to lash out at people like that."

She looked over.

"Hate is hate, no matter who it's coming from."

Rachel gathered her backpack and climbed out of the car. "Pete's a jerk. Everyone knows that. And no one believes Sammy is a Nazi."

I relaxed. Maybe I worried too much. Rachel was a resilient, self-assured kid. Despite her messy upbringing. I unloaded a sack of groceries and took them into the house.

"So, Mom, have you had oral sex?"

Damn. That always happens when I get complacent. I set the groceries down on the kitchen table. Then I heard a giggle.

I turned around. "What's so funny?"

"JK, Mom."

"Huh?"

"Just kidding." She grabbed a can of pop from the refrigerator and dashed out.

Later that night after she went to bed, I called two friends to analyze how I'd handled the situation. Susan thought I'd done a great job, but Genna wasn't so sure. She wanted me to call the Parent Hot Line. Genna is always telling people to open up to strangers. She's a social worker.

By the time I settled down with a glass of wine, it was almost midnight. That's when I remembered the mail. We live in a bedroom community twenty miles north of Chicago. I'd intended to remain an urban pioneer forever— until the day Rachel and I walked to the park from our Lakeview condo. Strolling by a sidewalk Dumpster at the end of our block, my bright, curious three-year-old pointed to it and exclaimed, "Mommy, look, there's an arm!" Sure enough, a human arm hung motionless over the edge. We moved to the suburbs six months later.

I sometimes think about moving back to the city, but the school system, despite the occasional incident, is one

of the best in the state. And while the village I live in has
minimal charm and less personality, it is safe enough to
go outside at night. Even to the park.

The problem is that I don't like getting the mail.
There's never anything besides bills. But tomorrow was
Friday, and if I got the mail tonight, I could rationalize
avoiding it again until Monday. I threw on a jacket—it
was late April, but spring is just a theoretical concept in
Chicago—and sprinted to the mailbox.

In between statements from ComEd and the gas company was a large white envelope from the Chicago Special
Events Bureau, a client for whom I'd produced a videotape. When I opened it, a smaller pale yellow envelope
tagged with a Post-it fell out.

*Ellie: This came for you. Probably yet another
piece of fan mail. The mayor says to quit it.
You're stealing his thunder. Dana*

I smiled. The mayor's office had commissioned an hour
documentary for the city's Millennium Celebration, and I
was amazed when I won the bid. *Celebrate Chicago*
turned out to be the best show I've ever produced: a lyr-
ical, descriptive piece that traced the history of several
city neighborhoods with stock footage, photos, and interviews. The show debuted at a city gala and is still running
on cable. Though the stream of complimentary notes has
dwindled to a trickle, Dana Novak, the special events director, graciously forwards them to me.

I turned over the yellow envelope, noting the floral design embossed on the border. My name, Ellie Foreman,
was handwritten in ink, in care of *Celebrate Chicago*. The
return address said Lunt Street, Chicago. Lunt was in
Rogers Park. I slit the envelope with a knife. Small,
cramped writing filled the page.

*Dear Ms. Foreman,
I hope this letter reaches you. I didn't have your
address. My name is Ruth Fleishman. We've never*

*met, but I didn't know where else to turn. For the
past two years, I rented out a room to an elderly
gentleman by the name of Ben Sinclair. Unfortunately, Mr. Sinclair passed away a few weeks ago.
He doesn't have any family that I know about.
That's why, when I found your name on a scrap
of paper among his possessions, I thought you
might be a relative or a friend. If you are, I would
appreciate a call. I don't think Mr. Sinclair left a
will; however, there may be some sentimental
value to the few things he did leave behind. I
hope to hear from you soon.*

Under the signature was a phone number. I poured another glass of wine. Ben Sinclair's name wasn't familiar,
but we'd spoken to hundreds of people in dozens of
neighborhoods during *Celebrate Chicago*. I should probably check with Brenda Kuhns, my researcher. She keeps
meticulous notes.

Still, I was curious why a dead man would have my
name. Despite the show, I'm no VIP, and I couldn't imagine how my life intersected with that of a solitary old man
who died alone in a boardinghouse.

THE CLOCK READ four-fifteen, and I couldn't sleep.
Maybe it was the wine. When alcohol turns into sugar, I
get all geeked up. Or maybe it was the handful of chocolate chips I ate just before turning in. Or possibly it was
a lingering unease about the letter. I rolled out of bed,
checked on Rachel, and took the letter up to my office.

My office used to be the guest room before the divorce.
It's not big, but the view more than compensates for its
size. Outside the window is a honey locust, and on breezy
summer days, the sun shooting through the leaves creates
sparkles and shimmers that humble any man-made pyro-
technics. If you peek through the leaves, you can see

down the entire length of our block. Of course, nothing much happens on our block, but if it did, I'd be there to sound the alarm—my desk is right under the window. The only trade-off is a lack of space for overnight guests.

Works for me.

I booted up and ran through my show files, using the Search command for "Ben Sinclair." Nothing popped up. I opened Eudora and did the same thing with my E-mail. Nothing. I E-mailed Brenda and asked if the name meant anything to her.

I went into the bathroom, debating whether to take a sleeping pill. A fortyish face with gray eyes and wavy black hair—the yin to my blond daughter's yang—stared back at me in the mirror. I still had a decent body, thanks to walking, an occasional aerobics class, and worrying about Rachel. But the lines around my eyes were more like duck's webbing than crow's feet, and gray strands filigreed my hair.

I decided against a sleeping pill. Back in my office, I reread Ruth Fleishman's letter, then logged onto a white pages site, which promised to give me the address and phone number of anyone in the country. I entered Ben Sinclair's name. A mouse-click later, fifteen Ben Sinclairs across the country surfaced, each with an address and phone number. When I tried Benjamin Sinclair, another six names appeared. None of the listings were in the Chicago area. I printed them out anyway.

A set of headlights winked through the window shade, and the newspaper hit the front lawn with a plop. I yawned and shut down the computer.

TWO

AFTER RACHEL LEFT for school the next morning, I checked my E-mail and found a reply from Brenda. She's either the most efficient person on earth or suffers from insomnia like me. She'd reviewed her files but had nothing on Ben Sinclair.

Sipping a cup of coffee, I checked my Day-Timer. I owed a script to Midwest Mutual, one of my bread-and-butter clients, but it wasn't due until the following week. I picked up the letter and dialed Ruth Fleishman's number.

"Hello?" The voice was somewhere between a bleat and a foghorn. I pictured a woman with too much makeup, dyed hair, and lots of jewelry.

"Mrs. Fleishman, this is Ellie Foreman. I got your letter yesterday."

"Oh, yes. Thank you for calling. This entire situation has been so upsetting. I've had boarders over twenty years, ever since Maury died, of course, but I've never had to bury one before. It's been a very stressful time."

Add extension nails. With bright orange nail polish. "I understand. But I'm afraid I don't know Mr. Sinclair. In fact, I have no idea who he is. Or was."

"Oh dear. I was hoping you knew him."

"Why is that?"

"Well, because of—well—we saw your show, of course."

"My show? *Celebrate Chicago?*"

"That's right."

I waited for her to say how much she loved it.

"I can't afford the really good networks like HBO or Showtime, see. Maury left me just enough to get by. So I make do with the basic cable." Her voice had an annoying nasal pitch to it. "It was good," she added. "Your show."

"Thanks." For everything. "Did Mr. Sinclair say how he knew me?"

"Well, see, you have to understand. Mr. Sinclair didn't spend much time outside his room. Except for going to the library, of course. He was old, over ninety, see, and he pretty much kept to himself. Not that he was a problem. He always paid his rent on time. Never made a fuss, either, even when we had that terrible storm and the power was out for two days. He didn't have his own television, of course, so sometimes I invited him down to watch a show with me. But he did like to take Bruno out for a walk."

"Bruno?"

"My dog. My guard dog. I need protection, of course. Since the . . . the problem a few summers ago." Rogers Park was the neighborhood through which Dan Thornton had run riot. "So you see, Miss Foreman . . . uh . . . it is Miss, isn't it?" Somehow her voice sounded too eager. Could there be an unmarried son or nephew hanging around somewhere?

"It's Mrs., and I have a twelve-year-old daughter."

"Oh," she said regretfully. It had to be a male relative. "Well, anyway. Where was I?"

"You were watching *Celebrate Chicago* with Mr. Sinclair."

"Yes. I made a coffee cake that morning, and I was just slicing it up. I could tell Mr. Sinclair liked it. The show, I mean. Especially the part about Lawndale." Lawndale, one of the neighborhoods we'd featured, is on Chicago's West Side. During the '30s and '40s it was center of Jewish life in Chicago. "At the end, you know, when they say who made it and everybody who was in it—"

"The credits."

"Of course, the credits. Well, when he saw your name, he got this look on his face."

"A look?"

"That's right. One of those—it was as if he knew you. And was surprised that he did. He said your name out loud."

"Ellie Foreman?"

"That's right. That's what he said. With a kind of question mark after it."

"Go on."

"That's it."

"That's all he said? Just my name?"

"He went upstairs right afterward."

"He never said anything else, I mean, later on?"

"I asked myself the same thing after . . . afterward. But no, he didn't. In fact, I forgot all about it, until I found your name and the picture."

"Picture?"

There was a beat of silence. "It's one of those old snapshots. You know, a black-and-white. The kind with the scalloped edges, of course."

"Of cour—What was the picture of?"

"Well, dear, that's what I was hoping you could tell me."

THE AREA OF Rogers Park that Ruth Fleishman lived in hasn't changed much in fifty years. Small bungalows and two-flats hug sidewalks veined with cracks. Closer to the lake, regentrification is flourishing, but over here, even the canopies of leaves fail to mask the quiet air of neglect.

I parked and walked south to 4109, a narrow brick building fronted by a porch. Underneath the porch was latticework, partially hidden by a scrawny forsythia bush. A few daffodils, braving the cold spring, studded the ground around it. I climbed three wobbly stairs and rang the bell. A large window covered by white curtains gave onto the porch. I was trying to peek through the gap between the panels when the door opened.

Ruth Fleishman's face was thick with powder, and her arms jangled with bracelets, but her hair wasn't dyed. A brown bouffant wig in a young Jackie Kennedy style covered a seventy-year-old head. She was either a cancer survivor or an Orthodox Jew who still wore a *sheitel*. Most likely an Orthodox Jew. This part of Rogers Park has replaced Lawndale as the center of *frum* life in Chicago, and she looked too vigorous to have suffered a round of chemo.

As she led me through a cluttered living room, a mop of black and white fur on the couch lifted its head and sniffed. Then, as if deciding I was a new scent worth investigating, it jumped off the sofa.

"This must be Bruno," I said, as he ran up, his tail wagging so hard I thought it might fly off. "Your guard dog."

Mrs. Fleishman hiked her shoulders and eyebrows resignedly. I bent down to pet him. Part beagle, part mutt, he ducked his head under my hand, forcing me to pet him. I ruffled his ears with my hands. When I stopped, he jumped up and pawed my pants leg, as if to say, "I'll decide when you're finished."

"So. Come upstairs. I'll show you his room." Her voice made the thought of fingernails on a blackboard sound attractive.

We climbed the stairs, Bruno trotting behind us. "When did Mr. Sinclair die?"

"April twelfth."

"How?" I asked.

Her voice dropped. "They think he mixed up his Inderal and Lanoxin. I was out walking Bruno, and when I got back, Bruno ran upstairs and started barking to beat the band. That's how we found him. Such a sad thing. He was over ninety, of course, but you hate to see someone leave this world before their time."

She opened a door at the front of the house. The air inside had a sour, musty scent. A double bed, the mattress stripped, was wedged against one wall. A five-drawer captain's chest leaned against another. A small desk took up space under the window. The closet, aside from a few wire hangers, was empty, but several cardboard cartons were stacked on the floor.

Mrs. Fleishman crossed to the window and opened it. A wave of frigid air floated in. "Everything's in there." She pointed to the cartons. "The first two are his clothes . . . I was going to give them away. His personal things are in the other." Turning around, she saw me hovering at the door. "Come in, dear. They won't bite."

Reluctantly, I stepped in and helped her move two cartons aside. She gestured for me to sit on the floor. I sat cross-legged and raised the flaps of the third carton. A plastic bag closed with a twist-tie sat on top. Inside were a razor, a package of blades, shaving cream, and two brown plastic prescription bottles. I checked the labels. Lanoxin and Inderal.

"Were these the ones . . . ?" I asked.

"No. The people who picked him up took them. Those must have been from an old prescription."

I studied the bottle through the plastic. "An accidental overdose, you said?"

Mrs. Fleishman nodded. "He was supposed to take Inderal four times a day and Lanoxin once a day, but they look so much alike, it's easy to get confused. It even happens to me. I keep a chart down in the kitchen. Of course, then I have to remember to fill it in."

I've glimpsed the decline that aging brings with my own father, who's over eighty himself. But like most boomers who cling to their youth, I'm more or less blind to the burdens of elderly people. Aging gracefully is an art form I've yet to master.

Underneath the plastic bag was a stack of books, including an Artscroll Siddur, the Orthodox version of the Jewish prayer book. The others looked liked they were from the public library. I lifted out *Untold Stories of World War Two*, *The Nazi Doctors*, and *Shadow Warriors: Origins of the OSS*. There were also a couple of le Carré paperbacks.

"He took the bus to the library almost every day," she said. "They opened a new branch not far from here."

I flipped to the back of one book. It was overdue by several months. I handed one to Mrs. Fleishman. "They need to be returned."

"Oh dear." She sighed. "I hope they won't make me pay."

Near the bottom of the carton was a beige metal box, about twelve inches square and three inches deep. It looked like it could hold fishing tackle. I lifted it out.

"I couldn't get it open," Mrs. Fleishman said. "Why don't you try?" I held it in my hands. "Oh, come on, dear," she said conspiratorially. "Don't you want to know what's inside?"

I bit my lip. The man was dead; I felt like a vulture. She took the box from me and jiggled the clasp with her fingers. It didn't move.

"You know, I might have something in my room." She put the box down and walked out. I heard a door across the hall open and close. A minute later, she was back. "Here." She handed me a metal nail file. "See if this works."

"Mrs. Fleishman, I don't know. I mean, I didn't know Mr. Sinclair, and it seems—"

"Don't worry." She waved her hand in the air, her bracelets jangling. "Mr. Sinclair doesn't care anymore. And if there's something inside that tells us who he was and where he came from, well . . ." She shrugged, as if no further explanation was necessary.

Reluctantly, I took the nail file. Using it as a lever, I tried to pry open the lock, but it didn't budge. Then I inserted the pointed tip of the file and wiggled it around, thinking that might dislodge the clasp. It didn't. Figuring gravity might make a difference, I turned the box upside down and repeated the levering action, but nothing shook loose.

Mrs. Fleishman watched impatiently. Finally, she grabbed the box and threw it back in the carton. "I give up."

At the bottom of the carton lay a small gray velvet bag with a drawstring tie. I loosened the string and drew out a shiny silver cigarette lighter. An insignia showed the profile of a man with a jaunty hat leaning against a lamp-post. On the back were three initials engraved against a blue background: SKL. I flipped up the cover and rolled the flint. Sparks flew.

"Look at this." I held it out for Mrs. Fleishman.

"I don't have my reading glasses on, dear."

"It's a lighter. And it still works." I snapped the top back and inspected the initials. "The initials say 'SKL.' " I frowned. "Shouldn't they be 'BS'?"

"I would think so." She knit her brow. "But, then, Ben Sinclair was a man with secrets."

"Secrets?"

"When you get to be my age, you don't ask too many questions. It's enough just to spend time with someone. Mr. Sinclair never talked much about himself. Frankly, I had the feeling he might have had ... uh ... a shady background. If I hadn't needed the money, well, who knows? But, like I said, he was a good boarder."

I ran my finger over the lighter. Maybe it belonged to one of his friends or a relative. And somehow came into his possession. I wondered how. There was a story here somewhere; everyone has one. That's why I became a filmmaker, to help people tell their stories.

"Which reminds me." Ruth went to the desk and opened a drawer. "Take a look at this, would you?"

She handed me an old snapshot, the sort that fill my parents' photo albums. Shot with a wide lens, probably a Brownie, the picture was of a couple posing on a cobble-stone path at the side of a bridge. Edged in a low stone wall, the bridge was flanked with statues and overlooked a building with the kind of tiled roof you see in European countries. On the far side of the bridge were more buildings, and in the background, high on a hill, the graceful Gothic spires and towers of a castle. A narrow river flowed underneath.

The man in the picture was young, wiry, and compact, with dark, piercing eyes. He held a snap-brimmed fedora. The woman, dressed in a sturdy suit with padded shoulders, had thick dark hair piled on top of her head. She cradled an infant in her arms. Despite their stiff poses, the couple smiled into the camera.

"Is this Ben Sinclair?"

"I think so," Ruth said, touching her brow. "The eyes."

I turned the picture over, hoping for a name or date but knowing I wouldn't find anything. "When was it taken, do you think?"

"Judging from the clothes, during the war. Or soon after." Ruth plucked the bracelets on her wrist, moving one in front of the other. "I asked him when he first moved in whether he had any family, but he said no. I didn't press it."

I handed the picture back. "Mrs. Fleishman, I did some research last night. I found a number of Ben Sinclairs around the country. I've got the list in my purse. Let me get it for you."

"Why?"

"Well, you might want to call some of them. You never know. One of them may turn out to know him." A queer look crept into her eyes. Figuring she was concerned about the cost of calling long distance, I added, "There were only about twenty listings."

She shrugged and looked at the floor. I stood up and dusted off my hands. My reflection in the window, sharpened by the overcast outside, showed dark hair against light skin. Like the woman in the picture.

"Hold on," I said slowly. "Do . . . do you think I have something to do with this picture?" She reddened. "My God. You think I'm the baby in the picture."

"I . . . I wasn't sure. We watched your show, and he seemed to recognize your name. And then, after he died, I found your name and the picture—"

"And you figured I might be his daughter." I gestured toward the snapshot. "A long-lost daughter. Possibly from Europe." Damn. Did I really look that old? "I'm sorry, Mrs. Fleishman. I was born right here in Chicago, well after the war, and my father is alive and well. I never knew Ben Sinclair."

Her face crumpled. "I knew it was a long shot." Sighing, she dabbed her fingers on her wig, as if to soothe her nerves. "Well, I do appreciate you coming all this way. I'm sorry it was all for nothing." She gazed at the cartons. Her eyes brightened. "Well, actually, there is something else. Could you do me just the tiniest favor?"

"What's that?"

"I'd like his clothes to go to *Or Hadash*, but I don't have a car, and they don't pick up. Would you mind taking his things over there? It's not far from here."

Or Hadash was the Jewish charity agency in Chicago. Figures. She'd just met me an hour ago, and she was already asking me to do her errands. I should say no. I'd done enough. I looked over; she was plucking at her bracelets, looking helpless and vulnerable. I glanced at my watch: barely three. Rachel wouldn't be home from soccer until five. I sighed. "Okay."

"Oh, that's lovely. The books, too?"

I pursed my lips. A pleased smile fluttered across her face.

As we started to tape the cartons shut, Ruth's eyes fell on the lighter. She lifted it out of the box. "You know, *Or Hadash* doesn't need this. Do you smoke?"

"No."

"How about your boyfriend? Or your father?"

"Well, as a matter of fact, my father does."

"Why don't you take it for him?"

"Oh, I don't know. I don't like to encourage him."

She forced it into my hand. "Now dear, he is a grown man."

I looked at the lighter. It *was* a curiosity. I slipped it into my bag. "Thanks."

As I hauled the cartons out the front door, I noticed two men parked in a car near mine. The driver, who had long hair pulled back in a ponytail, was fiddling with the radio, and the other man slouched in the seat, head down, as if searching for something on the floor. Too bad. I could have used some help. But judging from their studied inattention to my plight, they were probably the type who got off on watching a woman struggle: the "you asked for it, you got it, lady" types. I stowed the boxes in the trunk. As I slammed down the trunk, Mrs. Fleishman called out from the house.

"When you're done, dear, come in for a nosh. I've got coffee and Danish."

I headed back in. She wasn't that bad, once you got used to her. Anyway, how many people have Jackie Kennedy serving them Danish in Rogers Park?

THREE

OR HADASH WAS wedged between a Korean dry cleaners and a tamale stand on Touhy Avenue, the commercial street that cuts a wide swath through Rogers Park. It looked well-stocked, cheerful, and closed. A sign on the window said donations were received on alternate Thursdays or by appointment. A phone number followed. "Just my luck," I muttered, jotting down the number. At least I hadn't taken the cartons out of the car. I climbed back into the Volvo.

The Rogers Park library on Clark Street practically shouts new construction. A neat red-brick building with white trim, it clashes with the crumbling apartment building next door and the dilapidated American Legion hall across the street. Inside, though, it was filled with after-school activity, and the cheerful buzz contrasted with the funereal silence of most libraries.

The crowd, a mix of white, black, and Hispanic kids, sat at long red tables in the center of the room, all apparently content to share space together. I waited at a counter of faux marble while the librarian, a gnarled, gray woman with a *pince-nez* around her neck, helped an Asian boy find a periodical. She reminded me of Miss Finkel, the strictest teacher in my elementary school. I set the overdue books on the counter.

"Oh, Mr. Sinclair," she said, when I explained why I was there. "We haven't seen him in a while. He's all right, isn't he?"

"No, he's not." I told her what happened.

The lines in her face deepened. "I'm sorry."

I nodded. "I'll pay for these, if necessary." I picked up *Shadow Warriors* to show her the due date stamped in the back. As I riffled through the pages, a scrap of paper floated to the floor. I bent down to pick it up. The Internet address www.familyroots.com was scrawled on it in pencil.

"Hey," I said. "Look at that." I showed the paper to the librarian. She inspected it and gave me a puzzled glance.

"It's a web site." She frowned as if I'd somehow intruded into her well-ordered universe.

"I know. I just never thought a ninety-year-old man would be surfing the net. Not that there's anything wrong with it. But . . . uh . . . my father still thinks that computers are nothing more than fancy pencils."

She threw me a chilly look.

"I mean, I didn't see a computer at his home."

"Mr. Sinclair was on-line here nearly every day." She pointed to the computers on some of the tables.

"You're kidding. What was he doing?"

"Oh, I couldn't tell you, even if I knew. We have strict privacy rules here." Her face softened. "But I can tell you he was usually here first thing in the morning, sometimes before we opened up. It's a good time to go on-line. Less traffic."

"Was this one of the sites he went to?" I pointed to the scrap of paper.

Her face was noncommittal.

"Did you teach him how to log on?"

She peered at me through her *pince-nez*. "It isn't difficult, if you follow instructions. You could learn."

I didn't correct her. She looked past me, her expression tight. I turned around. Several people had formed a line behind me.

"Well, considering what happened," she said briskly, "I think we can waive the fines. Thank you for returning the books." She slid them toward her and looked at the person behind me. I had been dismissed.

I WAS ALMOST out the door when I felt a tug on my sleeve. I whipped around to see a young teenage boy with dark brown skin and wooly hair. A blue Georgetown baseball cap cocked to the right covered most of his head. Over his shoulder was a backpack decorated with black markings.

"You know Sinclair?" he asked. His voice was accusatory, almost belligerent. If I hadn't heard the crack in it, I might have felt uncomfortable.

"Kind of," I answered.

"You say he dead?" He fingered his ear. A gold post protruded from it.

I nodded.

The kid didn't flinch.

"Were you a friend of his?"

"Yeah." He looked as if he was trying out the concept and liked it. "He was cool with me."

"I'm Ellie Foreman." I stepped through the door. "What's your name?"

"Boo Boo."

I got a clear view of his backpack. The markings on it were Jewish stars.

"He be your friend, too?"

"To be honest, Boo Boo," I said, staring at his backpack, "I didn't really know him. But I think he knew me." I looked at him. "I . . . I know the lady he lived with."

"Aww, man. The old lady?" The boy grinned. "Shit. She used to dis him all the time. Rag on him, too. Least that's what he say."

I smiled. "Did you meet him here? At the library?"

"Yeah." He straightened up. "I teached him things." His chest puffed out. "Computers."

I opened the outside door, and he followed me out. I saw the trace of a swagger.

"You taught him how to go on-line?" I raised my voice above the afternoon traffic, already crawling down Clark.

His turn to nod.

My eyes strayed to his backpack. "Boo Boo, you're not Jewish, are you?" I pointed to the backpack.

He took it off his shoulder and offered it to me for inspection. Two pitchforks formed an X behind some of the stars. Above the designs were the initials "GDN."

"What's that?" I pointed to the letters.

"GDs," he said, and then added impatiently, "Gangster Disciples, man. Gangster Disciple Nation."

"Oh," I said, instinctively tightening my hold on my bag. "Are you a member?"

He drew himself up. "Sinclair done ask me the same thing." We eyed each other carefully. "My brother is. I be one soon."

I relaxed my grip. What kind of gang-banger spends time at the library?

"Ben was Jewish." I cleared my throat. "I am, too."

"Damn." His brow wrinkled.

"Did you teach him how to surf the net? The lady at the desk said he taught himself."

He threw a cold look back inside the library. "She don' know shit."

We walked past a building with a disintegrating façade and a blue and white 'Medicos' sign out front. I wasn't sure what to make of this kid. Part geek, part gangster. A modern-day centaur.

"Hey, Boo Boo," I said, "you can help me with something." I pulled out the scrap of paper. "Was this one of the sites you helped him log on to?"

He glanced at it and shrugged.

I searched for the right words. "Look. I don't want to make trouble for you, but Ben had my name on a piece of paper. Mrs. Fleishman, the lady he lived with, found it. I'd like to know why."

"You one of dose people he E-mailed?"

"E-mail?" I raised an eyebrow. "He had his own E-mail?"

A grimace shot across his face, as if he realized he'd said too much.

Two doors past the Medicos building was a small Middle Eastern eatery. "Boo Boo, how 'bout a Coke?"

He nodded, and I ducked inside. A man with a dirty apron and sweaty brow grunted at me from behind a counter. I ordered a falafel pita with cucumber-yogurt sauce and two Cokes.

Ben Sinclair had his own E-mail account. He'd been sending messages. Probably through the library. Funny. I wasn't sure the library allowed that kind of thing. I didn't even know how you did it without the right software. I paid for the food and took it outside. Boo Boo was gone.

FOUR

I DUMPED THE drinks but wolfed down the sandwich. I kept glancing in the rearview mirror, hoping Boo Boo would reappear, but after twenty minutes with no sighting, I started back to Lunt Street. It was nearly four-thirty; I had to get home. Ruth Fleishman would have to dispose of Ben Sinclair's things after all.

There was no answer when I rang the bell. I peeked through the front window, expecting to see two floppy ears and a wet black nose poke through the curtains, but there was no hint of dog or human. Maybe they were out for a walk. Rummaging in my bag for a pen, I found a gas station receipt and scrawled a quick note. I squatted down to nudge it under the door when something caught my eye.

At the bottom of the doorframe was a line of brass weather stripping that had been hidden by the screen door. Behind it I saw empty space. The door was ajar. I straightened up and tried the doorknob. It twisted freely in my hand.

I debated what to do. I didn't know Mrs. Fleishman well enough to barge into her house, but I didn't relish the idea of coming back again just to drop off two boxes.

"Mrs. Fleishman?" I called out. "It's Ellie Foreman. You there?" There was no answer. Then I remembered the dog. "Bruno? Here, Bruno. Come here, boy." I whistled. Nothing.

I stepped across the threshold. The house was still, but

there was a predatory weight to the silence, as if something had been disturbed, and tranquility had not quite been restored. Even the dust motes seemed lethargic. Intuition told me to leave. To take the cartons and go home. But something else tugged at me, too; curiosity perhaps, or the same sense of obligation that made me take the cartons in the first place. I slowly climbed the stairs to Ben Sinclair's room.

Ruth Fleishman was sprawled on the floor.

WHEN THE COPS arrived, I was on the porch steps taking big gulps of fresh air. One of the cops was young, with a leather jacket, crisp uniform shirt, and a pencil-thin mustache that looked pasted on. His partner, older and more rumpled, wore an expression that said he'd seen it all. After asking me a few questions, they went inside.

A few minutes later, they came back out. The younger cop dug out a cell phone and started tapping in numbers.

The older cop grabbed it away from his partner. "Don't waste your minutes." He yanked his thumb toward the house. "Use hers. She won't be needing it."

The younger cop slipped his phone into a pocket and headed inside.

"Is she . . . ?" I asked shakily.

The older cop, whose shield read Mahoney, nodded.

I gripped a stake on the porch railing. "But I was just with her an hour ago, and she was fine. What happened?"

Interest flickered on Mahoney's face. "You were here earlier?"

"I left around three."

"Powers. Get back out here." The younger cop reappeared. "Why don't you tell us about it."

Midway through my first sentence, the older cop raised a hand, cutting me off. "Notes, Powers. You gotta take notes."

Powers lowered his chin and pulled out a notepad. He wrote furiously as I told them how I'd come down to

Rogers Park at Mrs. Fleishman's request. How we went through Ben Sinclair's things. How she persuaded me to take the boxes and how, when I came back, she was on the floor.

Mahoney stopped me. "You say she wrote you a letter?"

"Yes." I told him about *Celebrate Chicago*.

"You did that show?" He looked me up and down. I tensed. "I saw it. I grew up on the East Side." His face melted into a grin. "You hit it right on the money." I relaxed.

The medical examiners' car pulled up, and Mahoney cut short our interview. I heard snatches of their conversation as they moved into the house: ". . . no cuts, abrasions or evidence of trauma" . . . "maybe an hour or two" . . . "place seems to be in order." When he pointed to me, I stood up, felt the world spin, and sat down again.

By the time the paramedics brought Ruth out on a stretcher, a small crowd had gathered. Among them was an elderly woman in a shapeless dress and sweater, hugging herself against the cold. Tan stockings were rolled at her knees. She walked over and introduced herself as Shirley Altshuler, Ruth's neighbor and friend.

"What happened, dear?"

The only other dead person I've ever seen was my mother, but that was in a hospital after she died of cancer. I started to answer, but tears unexpectedly stung my eyes. Mrs. Altshuler laid a hand on my arm. Then she spied Powers ambling out, notepad in hand.

"Officer, what happened to Ruth?" Mrs. Altshuler asked. Powers studied his notes as if she wasn't there. "Officer, what happened to my friend? I had coffee with her, not even an hour ago."

He looked up. "You did?"

She told him she'd come over about three-thirty, a few minutes after I left. They visited for half an hour. Powers started scribbling again.

"What happened?" Mrs. Altshuler asked again.

"Looks like heart failure, ma'am."

"That's *meshuga*. Ruth was as healthy as a horse."

"She was in her seventies, Mrs. Altshuler," I said.

"It's Shirley." She turned back to Powers. "I've known her thirty years, and she always took her medication. Walked every day. She had the stamina of a woman half her age."

I looked at Powers. "Are you sure about heart failure? The front door was open when I came back. Maybe—"

Powers cut me off. "There's no sign of forced entry. And the place is clean." He glanced at Shirley. "Old people forget to close their doors."

Shirley's face tightened.

"But this was so soon after Mr. Sinclair," I said.

"It happens," Powers said. "One goes and the other doesn't want to go on. I've seen it a million times."

"But they weren't . . . I mean, she and he weren't—"

Powers stopped me. "Sure they weren't."

"Officer." Shirley drew herself up. "There was nothing unseemly in their relationship."

Powers shrugged. As I glanced from one to the other, something occurred to me. "What about the dog?"

"The dog?" He frowned.

"Bruno. Mrs. Fleishman's dog. He's not here. He was earlier."

He frowned. "Our priority is people, not animals."

Thinking about Bruno wagging his tail and wiggling all over at his first sight of me made me start blinking again.

"Young man," Shirley cut in. "My niece lives in an apartment building in Skokie. Someone broke into her neighbor's home and killed her neighbor's dog. Dismembered it, she said. Turned out it was a Russian street gang. The Russian Mafia."

Powers's jaw twitched. "This isn't Skokie, ma'am. And there's no evidence of foul play. The dog probably ran away." He gestured toward the door. "Especially with the front door open. But I'll tell the ME about the coffee.

Maybe the caffeine . . ." He closed his notepad. I took it as a signal he was ready to move on.

Mahoney joined us and gestured for Powers's notepad. Powers offered it to his partner. Mahoney glanced at it, then asked Shirley about next of kin. Ruth had a nephew in the western suburbs, she said. She thought he was divorced.

Despite everything, I felt a tug at the corners of my mouth.

"We'll get in touch with him," Mahoney said.

"Where are you taking Ruth?" Shirley asked.

"Evanston Hospital."

She dipped her head and started back across the lawn. Suddenly Mahoney, still holding Powers's notepad, pointed, and jabbed his elbow in his partner's side.

"Excuse me," Powers said, traipsing after Shirley. "What was your name again?"

I drove home thinking about the fragility of life and the permanence of death. Rachel was camped out in front of the TV. I hugged her longer and tighter than usual. Then I stowed Ben Sinclair's things in the basement. I let Rachel fall asleep in my bed where I listened to the steady whisper of her breathing until the birds began to sing.

FIVE

"HEY MAC, HOW'S it going?" I stuck my head in his office the next day.

Mac rolled his eyes toward the phone, cradled between his neck and his shoulder, and waved me in with his free hand. "They undercut us by how much?"

MacArthur J. Kendall III, my director on *Celebrate Chicago*, owns a small production studio in Northbrook. He started out doing sweet sixteens, bar mitzvahs, and weddings but quickly parlayed that into corporate videos. Over the years, he's established a solid reputation for high quality and low prices. But today, apparently, they weren't low enough.

"Does that include all the post?" Silence. "Graphics, too?" He started doodling with a pencil. "I can't compete with those rates, Fred. All I can tell you is to make sure you're comparing apples to apples." Another pause. I dug the lighter out of my jeans. "I understand. Well, if things don't work out, we're here for you." He hung up the phone and shook his head.

"What?" I sat down, scanning his face. The only thing that prevents Mac, with his crew neck sweaters, button-down collars, and insufferable name from being a caricature of himself is an ugly scar running down his left cheek. When I first met him, he said he got it running drugs out of Mexico. It wasn't until we made our first video together that he admitted to being in a serious car accident as a teen. Whenever he's upset, the scar flares up in angry red streaks. Now it was blazing.

"We're dinosaurs, Ellie." He pointed the pencil at me. "Washed up."

"What happened?"

"Last week I bid on a big project for Comway—you know, the network and modem guys—"

I nodded.

"I thought it was in the bag. I mean, we've done work for them before. Then I get this call. Evergreen underbid us by fifteen grand."

"Evergreen? That's the kid who set up shop with Daddy's money, isn't it?"

Mac threw the pencil down. It skipped across the desk. "Everybody thinks they're a fucking Steven Spielberg."

I turned over the lighter in my hand. As video equipment gets more sophisticated, prices drop, which encourages anyone with a camera and edit bay to think they're a player, especially if they watch MTV. The sad part is that there are clients who don't know the difference. "There's nothing you can do?"

"Get real. I can't drop my prices that much."

"Well, at least you'll have the satisfaction of cleaning up after they screw it up."

He shot me a look. "Yeah, that's me, the old clean-up-their-shit-ster."

"It could be worse."

"Save it for the jury." He rubbed his eyes. "Sorry, Ellie. You walked in at the wrong time."

"Story of my life." I shrugged.

That brought a smile. "Good one." He leaned forward and looked at me. "So, what's happening, my little chickadee? You look tired."

"I'd rather be in Philadelphia."

He shook his head. "Bad one."

"You're right. I guess I'm not up to par today."

"How come?"

I told him about yesterday.

"God, Ellie, finding a dead body . . . That sucks."

"It isn't something I care to repeat." I turned the lighter over in my palm. "But listen. I'm doing another show for Midwest Mutual. They're going to shoot and off-line it in-house, but I'd like to use you for the online."

"You got it. When?"

"Four to five weeks, I hope. Can I have Hank for the edit?" Hank Chenowsky is the best editor I've ever worked with. Not only is he highly talented, but he's got the personality of a placid lapdog, a prerequisite for a type A like me.

"Don't see why not. Doesn't look like we'll be doing much else."

"Stop playing victim, Mac. It doesn't suit you."

"A direct hit!" He laughed, then pointed to the lighter. "You take up smoking again?"

"I got it yesterday. At Mrs. Fleishman's." I told him how most of Ben Sinclair's things were now in my basement.

"Lemme see that," Mac said.

"That's right." I handed it over. "You and Sharon do some collecting."

All you have to do is visit their house. Mac's wife keeps her Lilliputian dollhouse collection in a floor-to-ceiling glass case with ornate wooden moldings. It's the only piece of furniture in their living room.

Mac carefully inspected both sides. "You may have something here, my friend."

"What is it?"

"A Zippo. An old one, too."

"That's good?" When God gave out genes for antiques, he skipped me, an oversight for which I am grateful. Otherwise, there'd be nothing but collectibles in my house, too.

He nodded. "They started making these things in the thirties, I think. Gave them to GIs during the war. People have huge collections of them." He snapped it open and twirled the wheel. Sparks flew. "Man. Sixty years, and it sparks on the first try. They made things right back then."

"You think it's worth something?"

"I don't know, but I could find out. Interested?"

I shrugged. "How much?"

"A few hundred, maybe."

"I was thinking of giving it to my father."

"Nice gift." He smiled. "Tell you what. Lemme make a copy of the graphic and do a little surfing tonight. At least I can tell you how much we're talking about."

A few hundred dollars was more discretionary income than I was used to these days. "You got it."

Mac nodded. "By the way, I got a bootleg of the new Scorsese flick. You want to borrow it?"

"Uh-duh."

While he was making a copy of the man and the lamp-post on the Zippo, I wandered into the master editing suite. Hank was hunched over two monitors. Gangly, with strawlike hair, his pasty complexion attested to years spent in the glow of a computer screen rather than sunshine. He moved the cursor back and forth, adjusting a bank of numbers on one monitor and highlighting a series of menus on another. Then he double-clicked the mouse, rolled his chair back, and clasped his hands behind his head.

Video rolled on the monitors, and the image cut from a wide shot of a man walking toward the camera to a medium close-up of the same man stopping in front of the camera.

"Seamless," I said.

Hank twisted around, saw me, and shook his head. "Watch it again."

He reran the edit. This time I saw it. In the first image, the man was gesturing, and his left hand was approximately at waist level. In the second image, the hand had jumped to his chest. "You're right. You need a few extra frames."

"Except I don't have them."

"Can't you cut into him earlier?"

"Nope. Audio's too tight."

I nodded. No matter how carefully you anticipate

everything, problems always crop up in postproduction. The difference between a good show and a great show is your editor's ability to fix them.

Hank's eyes lit up. "Got an idea."

Bending over the keyboard, he worked for almost five minutes, adjusting, clicking, and previewing. Then he reran the scene. This time the man's hand naturally rose from his waist to his chest.

"Amazing. What did you do?"

"I interpolated. Added a frame here and there."

"But you didn't have them."

"I created them."

"How?"

"I can't tell you all my secrets, Ellie. You'd think I was a mere mortal."

Mac came back in. "Don't believe him. It's all in the software. As a matter of fact, I'm thinking of trading Hank in for a programmer and a first round draft choice."

"Watch yourself, Mac," Hank said.

Mac tossed me the lighter. "I'll take my chances." He handed me a cassette in a white cardboard sleeve. "Enjoy."

I dropped the tape and the lighter into my black leather bag. "I'm a happy woman."

"If that's all it takes, you're way too easy," Mac said.

I practiced my over-the-shoulder Veronica Lake smile and exited stage left.

SIX

ON SATURDAY MORNING you can't drive past any open spaces around here without seeing packs of young people, in brightly colored shirts, shorts, and knee socks, scrambling up and down the field after a ball. Organized soccer has become one of those rites of passage kids can't afford to miss. Parents come out for it, too, armed with deck chairs, coffee, and attitude.

One man, the father of one of Rachel's teammates, gives meddling a new name. He insinuates himself into every play, barks instructions to his daughter, and belittles her when they don't work out. The kid's the best player on the team, but I have visions of her in a few years with blue hair, black lipstick, and multiple rings piercing every inch of her body.

Most people assume this guy is acting out his fantasies through his kid. Or that the boomers have taken competition to absurd heights. But I think he's still suffering the effects of the Vietnam War. Really. Our generation never got the chance to feel good about combat. There weren't any battles like Verdun or Normandy that called forth the sanctity of war. Instead, there was this seedy guerilla war where our boys were sitting ducks for the VC. Plus a war over whether we should be there at all. Thirty years later, all that pent-up frustration is leaching out of guys like him. Too bad it hasn't made him less obnoxious.

A gloomy fog hung over the field, and slivers of cold rain stung my face. The ground was partially frozen, but chunks of earth had broken free and were starting to ooze mud. I brought a thermos of coffee, but my fingers were numb by the end of the quarter.

Rachel played halfback. After a particularly fierce encounter, she stole the ball and passed it to a forward, who dribbled it down the field and scored. Our side erupted in cheers. I whooped along with the others, all thoughts of unseemly parental behavior forgotten. Then I felt a tap on my shoulder.

I turned, instantly unnerved by the pleasurable shiver that ran through me. Damn it. I wish my ex-husband didn't look so much like Kevin Costner. I'm doomed to a Pavlovian response for the rest of my life. I smiled.

Barry returned the smile with the one that says, *I know I look like a million bucks.* And he did look good in his fleece vest, turtleneck, jeans, and work boots. In fact, his only physical imperfection is his nose, too long and narrow. But even that keeps him from being too pretty.

"How's she doing?" He turned toward the field.

"She just made an incredible play." I described it.

"That's my girl."

I ignored the proprietary vanity. "Where are you going after the game?"

"We'll probably head back to my place."

"No big plans?"

Barry shrugged. I shifted my feet. Usually he can't wait to impress me with the weekend marathon he's planned for Rachel, as if we're competing for her affection, and the winner is whoever has exhausted her most by Sunday night. "What about you?"

"I'm going down to Dad's."

"Oh."

I peered at him. "Are you okay?"

"Fine." His eyes darted from one goalie to the other.

I wrapped my hands around the lukewarm thermos. He always was a lousy liar.

Then, "There is something I need to talk to you about."

Prickles shot up my spine. I'd heard rumors he was

seeing someone. I tried to play it cool. "Shoot."

"I may not be able to meet Rachel's child support payments for a while."

Here it comes. "Why not?"

"I'm . . . I'm temporarily short of cash."

I looked past him, expecting to hear about weddings, condos, and honeymoons, but cheers on the other side of the field distracted me. The other team scored a goal. A collective sigh went up from our side. Barry studied the ground.

"What's going on?"

He hesitated. "One of my stocks fell out of bed."

I wasn't sure whether to be relieved or incensed. "I didn't know you were trading again." Before we broke up, we'd opened an account to trade on-line. A minor-league version of day trading, it wasn't a lot of money, but the therapist suggested it was something we could do together. We closed the account and divided the assets when we split up. "How much?"

Another hesitation. "About a hundred."

"Grand?" My voice spiked. The noise from the sidelines was suddenly hollow, as if it was being funneled through an empty tube.

"It's a high-tech incubator," he went on. "They buy pieces of technology start-ups. But it wasn't their fault," he said defensively. "It's a good VC firm. I did a lot of research on it, and the fundamentals are there. It's just this lousy market. They're switching over to bricks and mortar. It'll come back."

The little girls on the field bobbed and weaved like buoys in a muddy sea. "Come back? What are you saying, Barry?"

"It's bottomed out. It's gonna turn around, and I want to be there when it does."

"Hold on. You've just lost a hundred thousand dollars, you can't make child support payments, and you're buying more stock?"

His jaw worked. "Now's the time to get in. Look, Ellie.

You can get by for a couple of months. I'll make it up to you."

"Barry, aren't you forgetting something? What if the stock doesn't go up? What if it goes down even more?"

"It's not going to. We—I got burned, but it's over now. I promise. Anyway, it's just a few months."

It was an old tape. He'd promise and cajole, paint the most seductive pictures, and I'd believe him. Except we weren't married anymore, and I didn't have to play the tape. "Barry, I can't do it. You know how tight things are for me."

The warmth disappeared from his eyes. "Christ, Ellie. Ease up. It's not like you'll have to file for welfare."

Typical response. Attack me. Soon it would be my fault the stock went down in the first place. "You don't get it, do you? I don't have to ease up. The judge said so. You need to make sure the check's in the mail."

I watched the rest of the game from the end zone. Alone.

SEVEN

MY FATHER LIVES in a colonial-style retirement home in Skokie with a big lounge off the lobby and an acre of garden plots in the back. They call it assisted living, and it comes with daily maid service and meals. No beds to make, no meals to cook, no vacuums to push. I keep begging to be put on the waiting list, but Dad says you have to make a fortune first, so you can give it away to these *gonifs*.

I parked in the lot later that afternoon and pushed through a glass door. In the lounge a cloud of blue cigar smoke hung over a card table where Dad and his buddies were playing five-card stud. His shiny round head, freckled with age spots, gleamed in the fluorescent light as he scooped up a pile of chips. Somehow he looked frailer than he had just a week ago.

"Ellie, sweetheart," he called from across the room. "How's my Hollywood bombshell?" Since *Celebrate Chicago*, he'd taken to calling me that, half in jest, half in pride.

"I keep telling you, Dad. Hollywood's for losers. It's Lina Wertmuller."

"So, come here already, Lina."

He introduced me to the other players, forgetting I'd met them before. Al was puffy all over, like an aged Pillsbury Doughboy. Marv was long and lean, the Laurel to Al's Hardy, and Frank's thick glasses obscured a wizened face.

"Sorry for interrupting. I'll wait."

"No. I'm losing anyway."

"Not with that pot, you're not, Jake," Marv grumbled.

"She your shill, Snake?" This was Frank. "She sure showed up at the right time."

"You're just jealous that I got the beautiful girl." Dad winked at me and collected his chips. He's never been tall, and age has stooped him, but there is a gentleness about him that radiates trust, and his eyes disappear into folds of wrinkles when he smiles, which is often. He guided me to the elevator. "Thank you, gentlemen. It's been profitable."

We rode to the third floor and walked down the hall, skirting a housekeeping cart near his door. Inside his apartment, a neat one-bedroom with a large living room, he punched in a Benny Goodman CD and poured himself a scotch. "You can't listen to Benny Goodman without a drink," he said.

"Dad, you shouldn't be drinking in the middle of the afternoon."

"It's a little late to worry about it now." He dropped three ice cubes in his glass. "What about you?"

"Diet Coke, please."

While he fixed my drink, I glanced at the newspaper, spread out in sections on the couch. A front-page article reported that Marian Iverson, the GOP candidate for the Senate, was making inroads against the Democratic incumbent. A moderate conservative in the Liddy Dole tradition, Iverson was saying all the right things. She'd even come out pro-choice.

Dad handed me my soda and settled in his old wing-back chair, a brown leather piece with gold tacking on the edges. Humming the chorus of "Sing, Sing, Sing," he spread his hands when it ended. *"Nu?"*

That's a Yiddish term that can mean anything from "what's new" to *"oy vay"* to "why are you bothering me."

I debated whether to tell him about the money. He's never liked Barry, mostly because we're German Jews and Barry, whose family came from somewhere east of Krakow, isn't. In Dad's day, that kind of thing was important. When my father looked at Barry, he never saw a successful real estate lawyer. He saw a two-bit hustler who couldn't possibly bring his daughter happiness. I could already hear the "I told you sos." I kept my mouth shut.

"I'm good, Dad. How about you?"

"Marv got a new cache of Havanas from his son."

"Dad, you've got to be careful—"

"*Sorg sich nicht,* Ellie. You'll put me in the grave with your worrying."

"You never smoked before you moved here."

"So? I should move out because I can finally smoke a decent cigar?" He inspected me. "How about I move in with you?"

"Okay, okay." Stubborn cuss. I wasn't allowed to worry about him.

He settled himself in his chair. "How is Rachel?"

"You should see her on the soccer field." I filled him in.

"You women are definitely taking over." He smiled. "Your mother would be proud."

Mother had been a white-gloved liberal, practically a rebel, given that she grew up in Washington, D.C., which, despite its pretensions now, used to be a sleepy Southern town. Her only flaw was her insistence on courtesy. Power to the people, but don't forget your manners. Please.

Dad got up and put on Sinatra with Basie, snapping his fingers to the brush on the snare drum. My eyes drifted back to the newspaper. "Not just sports," I said.

Dad looked puzzled.

"Women taking over." I pointed to the newspaper. "What do you think of her?"

"She's a politician." He sniffed. "With money."

We sat for a few more minutes, while Frank crooned about having me under his skin. I looked at my hands. I could use some nail polish.

"What's the matter, sweetheart?"

I looked up. "Nothing. Why?"

"You look like you've just lost all your money. Or your best friend."

He's getting much too perceptive in his old age. I searched for something to say. "Um, well . . . actually, a sad thing did happen the other day."

"What?"

I blurted out the story of Ruth Fleishman's letter and my trip to Rogers Park. By the time I'd finished, the sun broke through the clouds. The late afternoon rays slanting through the window picked out Dad's stricken expression.

"Oh, Dad. I'm sorry." I scrambled up guiltily. An old man and woman had died alone, with no family to grieve for them. Of course he'd be upset. "Daddy, that won't ever happen to you." I wrapped my arms around him. "And it wasn't as bad as all that," I said. "Mrs. Fleishman gave me something of his. A lighter. Turns out it might be worth something."

"Yeah?" His face perked up.

"Mac's looking into it for me. Here." I rooted inside my bag and pulled it out. "Mac says it's a Zippo." I handed it to my father.

He frowned at it. Then he took his reading glasses out of his shirt pocket, put them on, and examined the lighter at length. When he looked up, the color had drained from his face. "Tell me again where you got this."

I told him.

"Ben Sinclair, you say?"

"That's right."

His eyes were bright with something I didn't recognize.

"Why? What's the matter?"

"I've seen this lighter before. There's only one person this could have belonged to."

"Dad, stop kidding around." I saw from his face he wasn't. "Are you telling me you know—knew—Ben Sinclair?"

He scratched the back of his neck. "When I knew him,

his name was Ben Skulnick—Skull for short. See?" He showed me the monogram: SKL.

"Skull? You knew a guy named Skull?"

"It's what everyone called him."

"What kind of a name is that?"

"I think it came from the fact that he could bash your head in if he didn't like you."

I glanced at the lighter, then at Dad.

"I remember when he got this. It was one of the first Zippos ever engraved. He was so proud of it. He always had it with him. Used it to light the ladies' cigarettes." Dad flicked the wheel with a flourish.

"Hold on," I said doubtfully. "How do you know it's the same lighter?"

"Take a look." Dad pointed to the insignia of the man leaning against the lamppost. "They called this 'The Drunk.' It was one of the first engravings you could get. Came out in thirty-six, I think. Skull bought one for all the Miller boys. You know, because of the bar." He leaned forward. "Anyway, how many people do you know have the chutzpah to put their nickname on a lighter? It's got to be Skull's."

The music ended on cue, and the air in the room thickened.

EIGHT

"YOU KNOW I used to spend time in Lawndale when I was young," my father said, settling himself in his chair.

"In the late thirties, wasn't it?" I curled up on the couch. He'd told me the stories: how he hung out at a pool hall and bar called Davy Miller's; how he called himself Jake the Snake; how he his buddy, Barney Bow-Tie, ran errands for sharks and hustlers. He refused to let me interview him for *Celebrate Chicago*, but a few of his memories ended up in the show anyway.

"My best friend was Barney Teitelman. His parents ran a rooming house and restaurant off Douglas Boulevard." He paused. "My parents never approved of Barney."

"How come?" I asked.

"We were German Jews from Hyde Park." He shrugged. "The Teitlemans weren't. Of course, I didn't put much stock in it back then."

I squirmed. Things change.

"Barney and I did our best to ingratiate ourselves with the guys at Davy Miller's. Skull was one of those guys."

He took a sip from his drink; most of the ice cubes had melted. "Skull was tough. Not big. But wiry. Strong. And a hustler. The man could charm the birds out of the trees." He grinned, clearly savoring the memory.

"Where did he come from?"

"Someone said New York. Somebody else thought he

moved over from Maxwell Street. No one really knew.
I'll tell you one thing, though. Skull was one of the best-
dressed men I ever saw. Always wore the toniest wool
suits. Silk ties, too. And a snap-brimmed fedora."

I thought of the picture Ruth Fleishman had shown me.
"I saw a picture of a man and a woman at Mrs. Fleishman's. The man was holding a snap-brimmed fedora."

Dad canted his head. "I'd like to have a look at that."

"I don't have it," I said. "It's still at Mrs. Fleishman's.
So, what did he do, this Skull?"

"He ran numbers, greased palms, took payoffs." Dad
cleared his throat. "Not the sort of activity I condone, you
understand."

"Of course not."

"But I'll tell you, Ellie. He did it with such style the
ladies practically stood in line to give him his take."

"Learned a few tricks from him, huh?"

My father's forehead puckered. "All I did was run errands. Relay messages."

"You were hanging around with gangsters."

A sigh escaped my father's lips. "It was different then,
sweetheart. You gotta understand. It was Davy Miller's
gang who opened up Clarendon Beach in the twenties. It
was restricted before that. And it was his boys who kept
all the Yeshiva-*bochurs* safe from the Irish street gangs.
And there were the stories about the Nazis."

"What stories?"

"People said Davy Miller and his pals were going after
Nazi Bund members on the North Side."

"Were they?"

My father looked past me. "There was this actress at
the Yiddish Theater one summer. Her name was Miriam
Hirsch; I had a crush on her. Followed her around all
summer. That's how I met Skull. The two of them were
crazy about each other." He cut himself off and looked at
me sideways, as if weighing whether to go on.

First Rachel. Now Dad. Every generation has their secrets. "Dad. This happened over sixty years ago."

He rubbed his nose. "You're right. Well, the bottom line was that Miriam was killed, and Skull went after the guy who did it. Who happened to be the head of the Nazi Bund."

"She was killed?"

"They caught her spying on the Bund and passing it back to Skull."

"God. What happened?"

"Skull killed the head of the Bund. Then he disappeared. Skull, I mean." He pushed himself up and stepped into the kitchen.

I followed him in. "Where did he go?"

"He claimed he ran off to Europe and worked for the underground."

"The Resistance?"

"That's what he said. But who really knows? Skull always had a story."

"Did you ever see him again?"

Dad shook pretzels into a bowl. "Once. After the war. Before I left for law school." He offered me the bowl. "Barney and I were having a beer at Miller's. I didn't see him come in, but all of a sudden, he was there. He sat with us for a while. Not long, I recall. He had *shpulkes*; he kept looking around the room, peeking through the window. I found out afterward he was on the lam."

I took a pretzel. "What did you talk about?"

My father hunched his shoulders. "This and that. I'd been in the service myself, and I was—" He stiffened, suddenly uncomfortable. "Well, I was trying to figure out what to do with my life. So we talked. A few days after that, they arrested him for the murder of the Nazi Bund officer."

"Was he convicted?"

"Oh, yes. They gave him life."

"And you never heard from him again?"

"Not a word." Dad walked back into the living room and bent over his CDs.

"I don't get it. Why would this Skull, or Ben Sinclair, have my name on a piece of paper?"

Dad frowned. "I don't know."

"Was there any unfinished business between you two?"

"No." He dropped in another CD. "Maybe he wanted to congratulate you on the show. He did live in Lawndale."

"Maybe." I washed down the pretzel with pop. "Or maybe when he saw my name, it reminded him of you, and he thought about getting in touch with you."

"So why didn't he pick up the phone and call?"

"You're not listed anymore since you moved, remember?"

"That's true."

"His things are sitting in my basement. Maybe I should bring something down for you to check out. You know, to see if it's really him."

Dad sat back down in his chair. "What have you got?"

"A couple of cartons. Clothes mostly. But there is that snapshot at Mrs. Fleishman's. A man and a woman on some bridge. With a baby. It looked like it was taken in Europe. Did Skull ever marry?"

"I don't know."

"There was also this metal tackle box. But it was locked." I shook my head. "She sure wanted to get that thing open. She even had me try a nail file on it. Didn't work, though."

"I don't know, Ellie. If this man really was Skull, he wasn't the type of man—"

I cut him off. "But you knew him, Dad. It's quite a coincidence. Aren't you curious?"

"Yes, but—"

"Well, you see?" I took my empty glass into the kitchen.

When I left a short time later, the housekeeping cart

was still in the hall. I pocketed a couple of the little soaps that were stacked on the side. As the elevator doors opened, the first measures of "My Kind of Town" wafted out of Dad's apartment.

NINE

BY THE TIME I got home it was dusk, and the driveway, flanked with shrubs just now starting to bud, was shrouded in shadows. I pulled into the garage, listening to the last verse of "Miracles," wishing I could come back as Grace Slick in my next life. As the last note faded, I noticed the door leading out from the basement was open. I thought I'd closed it before I left. I parked, turned off the engine, and headed inside, thinking about the bottle of unopened white wine in the kitchen. But when I got upstairs, I gasped.

Cabinet doors were ripped open; several dangled at precarious angles. Broken china covered the counters. Drawers had been pulled out, and silverware had been flung everywhere. A sheaf of papers that I normally keep in neat files lay in a heap on the floor, with mops and brooms piled on top. The pantry had been ransacked, too, cereal boxes smashed under cans of soup.

I registered the chaos in rapid-fire images, like a pulsing strobe light, and ran into the family room. The base of the couch was slashed in several places, and the cushions were a mass of tears and wadding where someone had pulled out the stuffing. The coffee table lay upside down. My good pieces of silver had been hurled into the corners of the room. Then it hit me. Whoever did this might still be in the house.

I bolted out the door, threw myself into the car, and backed out of the garage. At the end of the block I stopped. My hands shook as I tapped 911 on my cell. The police dispatcher told me to stay where I was, and not, under any circumstances, to go back inside. They didn't have to worry. I gripped the wheel. What if Rachel hadn't been with Barry? What if she had been home—alone— when this happened? I swallowed.

A few minutes later, two patrol cars with flashing lights turned down the block and slowed in front of the house. Two officers, a man and a woman, hurried out of each car, their hands over their holsters. As they disappeared inside, I tried to think good, safe thoughts. I tracked their progress as lights flipped on in various rooms. There was no sound of gunshots.

The officers came back out to the Volvo. I rolled down the window. "No one's in the house, ma'am," the young man said. His shield read Officer North. "You can come back in."

I tightened my grip on the wheel.

"You can come back in now," he repeated. "The house is empty."

I nodded and stayed in the car.

The female, whose shield read Fletcher, reached for the door handle. "You're going to have to figure out what's gone. And we need to ask you some questions." I dragged myself out of the car.

As we walked from room to room, I tried to focus on what was missing, but I felt oddly distanced from the scene, as if a gelatinous curtain had dropped in front of my eyes. I sank down on the steps while North went over when I'd left, where I'd been, and when I got back. He asked if I knew anyone who might want to break in. I shook my head.

"No recent arguments or fights with family members?"

"No."

"Any disagreements with coworkers?" North asked.

"I work alone. Upstairs." The officers exchanged glances. "Why—what did they do?"

I raced upstairs. In my office, file cabinets were flung off their tracks, their contents scattered everywhere. Scissors, pens, files, and diskettes littered the floor. The computer was on, and my screen saver, a series of stills by famous photographers, flashed malevolently.

"I didn't leave it on." I pointed. "The computer. It wasn't on this morning."

"Are you sure?" Fletcher squinted at me. "People leave them on all the time these days."

"I'm positive."

She examined the keyboard and mouse. North disappeared downstairs, returning with a canvas bag in his hand. "We could try to get some prints," she said, more to her partner than me.

North fished out a camera and started taking pictures. When he had shot the office from every possible angle, he motioned to Fletcher. "All yours." He went back downstairs, where I heard him moving around in the family room.

Fletcher took a small case out of the bag and extracted a brush and jar of what looked like dark powder. She put on a pair of latex gloves, then started to brush my keyboard and mouse. "Aren't the evidence techs supposed to do that?" I asked.

"I swear, if one more person tells me I'm supposed to do it like they do on TV, they can have my job. Truth is, most cops do it themselves."

"Really?"

"Unless you're in a big city; there isn't enough staff or budget."

"Oh." A thick coating clung to the keys. "Uh . . . that powder won't screw up the computer, will it?"

The look on her face told me to back off. She worked her way around the room, methodically brushing the handles and edges of drawers, file cabinets, and doorknobs, then checking to see what surfaced. When she finished, she packed up her equipment. The office looked worse than before. "I lifted a lot of impressions. We'll see who they belong to." She straightened up, wiped her hands on her pants. "Now. What about that list?"

I dropped my bag on the chair and poked halfheartedly through the clutter. "I can't tell. I think some of my silver might be missing. And maybe some jewelry. But I don't know for sure."

"You should write it down now, while everything's fresh." She picked up her bag.

Panic rose in my throat. "You're not leaving, are you?" They couldn't leave me alone.

She ignored my distress as we headed down the steps. "We'll hand this over to a detective. He'll want your fingerprints, your daughter's, too. To compare. There have been a string of break-ins on the North Shore recently."

"So this is just a random burglary?"

North joined us at the foot of the stairs. "Junkies. From the city. You were lucky. They didn't get much."

"Oh." I wrapped my arms around myself. "So . . . so what do I do now?"

He considered it. "Might as well start cleaning up. I think we've got everything."

"They . . . they won't be coming back, will they?"

"No way." He chuckled, shooting an imaginary hypodermic into his arm. "They're a million miles away."

I didn't react.

His grin faded, and he awkwardly touched the brim of his cap. "You have someone who can stay with you tonight?"

I couldn't call Dad; he would worry himself into a heart attack. And I wouldn't call Susan or Genna; they were probably out anyway. "No."

"Well, you might want to check into a hotel. You'll feel better in the morning."

*   *   *

AFTER THEY LEFT, I picked my way through the kitchen, reached above the refrigerator, and pulled out a bottle of bourbon, which, happily, hadn't been ripped off. I poured an inch into a juice glass and tossed it down, trying to ignore how much it burned. Then I did it again.

After the third shot I decided not to take North's advice. No faceless intruder was going to run me out of my own house. I managed to find the phone book under the mops in the kitchen and called a twenty-four-hour locksmith. While he installed new double locks on every door, I walked from room to room, running my hands over my belongings, as if touching them could somehow brand them as mine and weld them permanently in place.

A strand of pearls and matching earrings were missing, but the diamond tennis bracelet Barry gave me as an anniversary present was still in my jewelry box. So was the emergency cash I keep under the mattress. Although the computer had been booted up, my files were all there, including the diskette I left in the drive. To my surprise, Rachel's room was untouched. I felt unaccountably grateful.

Downstairs, my sterling silver fruit bowl and coffeepot were gone, but the matching tray was still there, along with the sugar bowl and creamer. It was odd. Things I assumed a junkie would want, like a TV, VCR, or microwave, hadn't been ripped off. Other things were.

The furnace clicked on while I was rummaging for trash bags in the kitchen. As warm air began to circulate, I realized I hadn't checked the basement. I don't keep anything of value down there: mainly an old exercise bike that Barry bought when he'd decided to build a home gym. An early model, he'd only used it for about a month, and it was now obsolete. He left it here when he moved.

I took the steps down. The bicycle was still collecting dust. So was a bag of toys Rachel had outgrown, a table on rickety legs, and some unmatched chairs. Nothing seemed disturbed. As I headed back up, I glanced at the garage door, behind which I'd stacked the cartons of Skull's clothes. They were gone.

TEN

VILLAGE DETECTIVE DAN O' Malley was at my door by
nine the next morning. Tall, fair, and freckled, he looked
like Howdy Doody on growth hormones. I led him into
the kitchen, where he leaned against the doorframe and
surveyed the room. A trash bag heaped with broken china,
food, and papers occupied the center of the room. Silverware covered the table.

"Sorry." I cleared off a section of table.

He sat down gingerly and took me through last night's
events, jotting down notes as we talked. I pulled on a lock
of hair. Hadn't he read Fletcher and North's report? But
when I got to the missing cartons, he frowned. "Cartons?
Those weren't on the report."

What's that they say about making assumptions?
"Er . . . I didn't realize they were gone until later."

"What was in them?"

I explained.

"So you had two boxes that belonged to a man you
never knew." He angled his head. "How long were they
in your house?"

"A couple of days."

"And the man they belong to is dead."

"That's right."

"Do you know where was he living?"

"Rogers Park. But the woman he was living with died
of a heart attack a few days ago, a month or so after him."

"What about relatives?"

I shrugged.

He looked around, his fingers smoothing a carroty mustache that was longer on one side than the other. Then he dropped his hand, as if he'd considered and rejected whatever he'd been thinking.

"Did you get any prints?" I asked. "The officers dusted." And left a grimy residue over everything, Fletcher's denial notwithstanding.

"I wouldn't hold your breath. They're probably yours." He wiggled his fingers. "Even junkies wear gloves these days."

"So you don't need my prints? Or my daughter's?" I had a set of Rachel's prints from one of those Kid-Safe programs they held at the mall years ago.

"I'm not going to lie to you, Ms. Foreman. Very few home burglaries end up in an arrest. You got off easy. Consider yourself lucky." That was the second time a cop had told me I was lucky.

"You're convinced it was druggies?"

"You have any workmen here recently?"

"No."

"Maids? Landscapers?"

"Not anymore."

He checked his notes. "What about your ex? Any arguments over visitation, alimony, that kind of thing?"

"Doesn't everyone?" He looked up. "I'm sure it wasn't him," I added hastily. "He has my daughter this weekend. And there's nothing here he wants. Anymore."

I saw the trace of a smile. "You change your locks?"

"Last night."

"How about an alarm system?"

"I can't afford it."

"Try to. It'll give you peace of mind."

Before he left, he gave me some brochures on home security, part of the Police Are Your Partners program. As he pulled away from the house, I realized that I'd dealt with more cops in one week than I had in thirty years. They'd evolved from pigs to pals. Which probably goes to prove what my father always said: I would become more conservative when I had something to lose. I hate it when he's right.

I WAS HAULING bags of trash out to the curb when Susan showed up. A willowy redhead who, even in sweats, manages to make me look shabby, Susan Siler considers herself an outcast in a village where all the women are blond and wear Birkenstocks and pearls. Together. She cast an appraising look around the kitchen. "It doesn't look that bad."

"I've been cleaning up since dawn."

"Then it's time for a break. Come on, let's walk." She held the door open for me. "What's the final tally?"

"Besides what I already told you, nothing. The jewelry, two pieces of silver, and those cartons."

"Strange."

"I know." We jogged over to Happ Road, the north end of our circuit. A weak sun penetrated the heavy overcast, but the air was still somewhere between Fairbanks and Seattle on a good day. Susan was in a teal warm-up jacket that made her hair look incandescent. I was in scruffy gray sweats with paint stains on the legs.

We fell into step, and I summarized O'Malley's visit. "His attitude was basically 'Get over it, lady.' I don't think they're going to find the assholes who did it."

"What else is new?"

"He left me some brochures on home security." I said. "Part of the Police Are Your Partners program."

She rolled her eyes. "So what's your next step?"

"I don't know. Call my insurance company. Move on. Try not to take it personally." I glanced at her. "Nice jacket."

"Twenty-four dollars at TJ Maxx." Susan and I first met at a discount shopping outlet when she pointed out a mint green Garfield and Marx suit marked down 80 percent and said it was my color. We became friends over coffee when

I confessed to smashing Rachel's fingers in the car door, and she admitted she'd once sat on her daughter and broke her collarbone. But I knew she'd be my friend for life when she told me she had actually seen Grace Slick on a Marin County beach watching sea otters.

"I don't think I'll be shopping much for a while," I said.

"Not even discount?"

I shook my head. "It's not just the break-in. I should never have kept the house." I told her about Barry's stock. "When we split up, I bought the concept that Rachel should have as little disruption in her life as possible. I should strive for continuity. That's why I fought so hard to keep the house."

A couple of kids on bicycles flew past us, barely swerving in time to avoid a collision.

"Most women do," Susan said.

"We were sold a bill of goods. Everything I make goes for the mortgage, utilities, and food. God forbid the water heater blows, or the air conditioner breaks down, or the roof starts to leak. I'm always struggling. Now I'm supposed to install an alarm system. The house is a goddamn albatross around my neck."

Susan didn't say anything. She's a good listener.

"Now compare that with Barry. Okay. For a few months, right after the settlement, he was strapped. Maybe even a year. But now he's got his condo, a grand or so in child support every month, and no other obligations. Nada. He even has enough to play the market." I stepped up my pace. "Tell me. What's wrong with this picture?"

"You made the best decision you could at the time."

"It was shortsighted."

"You're being too hard on yourself. How could you predict the future?"

We reached the Catholic church at the end of the road. The parking lot was a sea of cars, with a white limo bearing a Just Married sign in front. Pink and white streamers floated from the bumper. "Where's Dustin Hoffman when you need him?"

"Huh?"

"Someone should break up the wedding while there's a chance." I pointed to the limo. "They only have a fifty-fifty shot anyway."

Susan's other eyebrow arched. After eight years of friendship, we can sense when one of us is dissembling, even if we are just trying it out on each other. "My, we are bitter today."

"What if Barry doesn't come through with child support, Susan? What am I going to do?"

"Don't you think you might be overreacting just a bit?"

"With Barry?"

"Whatever happens, you will survive. At the very worst, you'll borrow money. People do it every day. They have these places called banks."

"Assuming my credit rating isn't in the tank. Which it probably is. It takes years to sort out your credit after a divorce. And with Barry's track record—"

"You know, sometimes I get the feeling you like to obsess about things, Ellie. You know what they say. If you fixate long enough, you can actually cause it to happen. A self-fulfilling prophecy."

"I'm not obsessing. I just want to be able to . . . to manage the situation. Control it."

"Aha. Now we get to the root of the problem. Except that last I heard, random break-ins and ex-husbands are beyond ex-wives' control." I started to cut in, but she overrode me. "Look, Ellie. I know it's frustrating. You want answers right now. For all the right reasons. And you've had a rough time. But you're going to have to ride it out. You never know. Maybe the detective will catch those thieves. Maybe the stock will come back."

"And maybe there's a tooth fairy."

We turned west past Rachel's school. We were into a rhythm now, hiking at a good clip. The bicyclists who passed us earlier were now crisscrossing the playground.

Susan changed the subject. "Marian Iverson's having a fund-raiser up in Lake Forest in a couple of weeks."

"That's nice."

"Doug's supporting her." Susan's husband, a village trustee, is involved in local politics. "Why don't you come with us?"

I wrinkled my nose. When I was young, I joined the revolution, confident that we would topple the fascist pigs corrupting the system. I read the *Revolutionary Times* and studied my 3 Ms: Mao, Marcuse, and Marx. It didn't last. I was told I was hopelessly bourgeoise. The most I could aspire to was running a safe house. Since then, I've tried to eschew politics.

"She's a woman, Ellie. And she came out pro-choice."

"I suppose for a Republican that takes courage."

Susan giggled. "Come on. Compared to some of the candidates you've supported, this one might even win." I shot her a look. "And you never know. The man of your dreams might be there."

I broke into a jog and left her in my dust.

ELEVEN

THAT AFTERNOON I made a trip to the store to restock my cabinets. At the end of one aisle was an eye-catching display of smoking accessories, including pipe cleaners, butane lighters, and flints. Festooned with colorful ribbons and signs, it wasn't there to attract young smokers, of course. I picked up a small can of lighter fluid.

As I pulled into the garage, I got the shakes. I thought about the bottle of bourbon above the refrigerator. That wasn't a solution. Neither was weed. Or cigarettes. Or any of the other substances I abuse from time to time. I sat in the car until the trembling stopped, wondering if that was going to happen whenever I came home now.

Barry dropped Rachel off at the end of the driveway around four but sped away before I could talk to him. After she unpacked, I poured two glasses of fresh lemonade and opened a box of cookies. She eyed me suspiciously. "What's wrong?"

"What do you mean?"

"You never make lemonade and cookies. Something's wrong."

"Okay." I leaned across the table. "Here it is. Someone broke into the house last night." When I finished explaining, she jumped up and threw her arms around me. "Oh, Mom, are you all right?"

"I'm fine, honey." I buried my face in her neck. Her skin was smooth and warm. Still little girl's skin.

"Were you scared?"

"I wasn't here when they broke in. But yes, I was scared."

She released her grip and helped herself to another cookie. "What did they get?"

"That's just it," I said. "Not much. A few pieces of silver, some jewelry. Nothing of yours." I took a sip of lemonade. I didn't mention Skull's cartons.

She stroked her jaw with her fingers, just like Dad. "Probably someone on drugs."

I nearly choked on my lemonade. "How do you know that?"

"Everyone knows drug addicts steal to feed their habit."

"Oh yeah?"

"Mom, even Officer Friendly warns kids about stuff like that."

Part of the Police Are Your Partners program, no doubt. "Well, the police agree with you. They're doing what they can, but there is a chance they'll never catch the people who did it."

She grabbed the last cookie off the plate and crammed half of it in her mouth. "That's okay." She chewed thoughtfully. "I've got you to protect me."

From her mouth to God's ears. I bit into the other half of the cookie.

THAT NIGHT I pulled out the vacuum cleaner and tried to restore order to my office and my life. We live on a cul-de-sac, and I'd always thought ours was the safest house on the block. After all, what burglar in their right mind would risk driving past seventeen houses, twice, just to rob my house? If they had been on foot, they might have cut across a few backyards, but, given that they made off with heavy cartons, that seemed unlikely.

Which meant that whoever broke in was pretty hard up or strung out. But then, why leave the cash and the jewelry? Wasn't that exactly what junkies wanted? I finished vacuuming and bent over to unplug the cord. As I did, I came across Skull's Zippo underneath the desk, wedged between the hard drive and the wall. It must have fallen out of my bag when Fletcher was here. I picked it up, its silver casing glinting in the light. As I straightened up, the image of two men watching me lug Skull's cartons out to the car outside Ruth Fleishman's sprang into my mind. Were they the addicts who broke into my house? Did they follow me home, thinking those cartons somehow contained the mother lode?

I palmed the lighter. Maybe I should call O'Malley. No, that was stupid. Drug addicts don't lurk in front of old ladies' homes on the off chance that someone might emerge with cartons. Susan was right. I was getting obsessive.

I took the Zippo down to the kitchen. The lighter fluid was sitting on the counter. I unscrewed the small bolt on the bottom, filled the cottony cavity with fluid, and reattached the screw. I flipped open the cap and rolled the flint. A steady orange flame leapt up. Who was Ben Skulnick? And why did he have my name? I knew practically nothing about him except that he changed his name, spent time at the library, and knew my father sixty years ago.

Capping the flame, I ran my fingers over the bumpy engravings of the S, K, and L. This lighter could be the only tangible proof that the man ever existed. Ninety years of life reduced to a Zippo. For some reason, Dorothea Lange's series of poor migrant workers drifted into my mind; stoic faces staring into a desolate future.

No. My hand closed around the lighter. There was something else. The scrap of paper that fell out of his library book. With a web site scrawled in pencil. The web site had meant something to Skull—enough to write it down. I searched my memory, willing the URL to come into my mind: www.familyroots.com.

I went back upstairs and logged on, waiting impatiently while the computer downloaded information that, like a mosaic, gradually merged into a series of images. At the top of the page was a sepia-toned photo of a woman with a baby in her arms. The baby was in an old-fashioned sailor suit, and the woman's hair was coiled in braids around her head. Below that were more images: a Davy Crockett lookalike in buckskins and coonskin hat; a line of immigrants at Ellis Island; a little boy in knickers rolling a hoop. A paragraph of text in the center described the web site as a free exchange of genealogical information with over fifty thousand topics in its database.

I hit an icon, and a page of topics materialized: everything from Icelanders in the Dakotas to descendants of the Mexican revolution. A flashing cursor urged me to type in the topic or surname I wanted to search. I typed in "Foreman" and was promptly informed that there was a family tree for the name Foreman. Did I want to search through all the posts for that name?

I clicked, and twenty messages popped up on the screen, each requesting information about a specific Foreman. Dad was an only child, but Roses, Simons, and Leopolds ran through his family tree. I scrolled through the messages looking for those names. I didn't find anything.

Hitting the link to a new page, I was invited to upload my branch of the family tree to the Internet. I declined and clicked onto a site that claimed it could search through four hundred million names for relatives. Half a billion names. Why would anyone spend that much time chasing down a few of them? Were people that isolated? Maybe finding a distant cousin or great-uncle somehow elevated your family's status. We'll call your folk hero and raise you an eccentric or two.

I typed in the name "Skulnick," imagining the computer culling through four hundred million names. The results came back. No match. I tried again. Nothing. There was no family tree for the Skulnicks.

No clothes, no boxes, no web site. I had struck out. I shut down the computer and changed into my bathrobe. I should have tried harder to open the box at Mrs. Fleishman's. Now it was too late.

I turned off the light and pulled the covers under my

chin, thinking how ironic, even sad, it was that Skull and
Ruth died so close together. Maybe Officer Powers was
right. Maybe they had been more than just landlord and
boarder. I curled on my side. At least they had each other.

Some pair. I smiled, recalling how hard Ruth tried to
open Skull's metal box. How frustrated she was when she
couldn't. How she threw it back in the carton with an
exasperated sigh.

I stopped smiling. Something about that nagged at me.
Something about the box. I mentally replayed the scene.
Ruth put the metal box back in the carton. I found the
lighter. Then she asked me to take Skull's clothes to *Or
Hadash*, and I carried two of the cartons down to my car.
No it wasn't the box itself. It was the carton the metal
box had been in. The third carton. I had taken two cartons
downstairs. But there was a third. And now that I was
thinking about it, I didn't recall seeing the third carton
when I got back to Mrs. Fleishman's.

I propped myself up on my elbow and turned on the
light. Ruth had been sprawled on her side in the middle
of the floor. One arm was extended as if she was raising
her hand. Her other arm was bent across her middle. The
bed was against the wall, the desk under the window. The
closet door was open. But there was no carton in the
room. I was sure. Mrs. Fleishman was lying on the spot
where it had been.

I got up and shuffled into the bathroom. Ruth had probably moved it herself. She said she wanted to get rid of
it. Except that she'd watched me lug the other cartons
downstairs without lifting a finger to help. Why would
she suddenly decide to move the third one by herself?
Moreover, given her age and condition, how could she?
Maybe the strain was what triggered her heart attack. But
then, where was the carton?

I picked up my hairbrush. Maybe someone else moved
it for her. I ran the brush through my hair. That was it.
Her neighbor, Shirley Altshuler, had come over for coffee
after I left. She and Ruth probably shoved it across the

hall into another room. Possibly even downstairs. I got back in bed and slipped a pillow over my head. Problem solved.

Seconds later, I lifted the pillow off. Why hadn't Ruth asked me to move the carton along with the others? She wasn't shy about asking for favors, and she'd watched me carry the other two downstairs. It was odd that she felt compelled to move the third carton after I left. Unless she was planning to have another go at the metal box.

I kicked out my legs, tangled in the sheets, and felt cool air on my feet. What if she and Shirley had managed to open the box while I was driving around Rogers Park? Maybe they had discovered something important about Skull, something that made Ruth go back up to his room after Shirley went home. That would explain why Ruth had collapsed in Skull's room. Maybe I should call Shirley in the morning. She'd given me her number. I curled up on my side. Good idea.

No it wasn't.

Shirley was a lovely person, but she'd probably think it odd if I asked whether she'd moved her neighbor's boarder's possessions. I would. And what would I say when she asked why I wanted to know? I wasn't sure myself. And what if it turned out she and Ruth hadn't moved the carton? Or opened the box? Where was that third carton?

I thought about the cartons that were stolen from my house. I thought about the carton that was supposed to be at Ruth Fleishman's. I thought about the two men in the car, and the family roots web site, advising me there was no family tree for the Skulnicks. Something wasn't right.

TWELVE

MONDAY MORNINGS ARE full of hope. I've got my own version of the nursery rhyme that tells you what to expect from life depending on the day you were born. Monday is my favorite. It's a clean slate, a chance to begin again, avoid mistakes, start a diet.

The weather finally broke. As if to apologize for the past few weeks, balmy sunshine bathed everything with a warm glow, and all the little green things that poke their heads out of the ground seemed to sprout overnight. Even the ground smelled earthy and fresh. The lawn would need attention soon. Barry used to handle the yard, investing lots of time and money to make sure our lawn measured up to everyone else's. I used to tease him about his "greenis" envy.

I showered and brought a glass of orange juice up to my office. The Midwest Mutual script was due today. An internal marketing video on how well the company handled catastrophes, or "cats," it wouldn't win an Oscar. Nonetheless, I felt obligated to find a creative approach, as much to keep my own interest up as to deliver a good product.

I haven't always done corporate videos. I discovered Edward R. Murrow in college, and his work inspired me to study film. I, too, would produce hard-hitting documentaries that changed the world. Along the way, though, I was seduced by the artistic challenge of telling a story in images, not words, and I started to flirt with feature films. Unfortunately, I was already seeing Barry at the time and kept postponing a move to New York or L.A. To work in Chicago back then meant making industrials or commercials, but I drew the line at commercials. Now, of course, I make twenty- to thirty-minute commercials to pay my bills, but we call them corporate identity films.

I did land a job at Channel Eleven for a couple of years before Rachel was born, and I worked on a few documentaries that are still occasionally rolled out when they need to fill airtime. And one day in the future, when I'm financially stable—well—who knows?

Now, for some reason, a version of *The Tempest* kept sneaking into my mind. The shipwreck could be the cat, and Ariel the metaphor for the internal system that gears up at the first sign of trouble. But I wasn't sure how to deal with Caliban or the love story between Miranda and Ferdinand. I took another sip of juice. Maybe it would come.

The phone rang an hour later. I jumped at the sound.

"Ellie, it's Mac. How's it going?"

Reaching for my juice, I told him about the break-in.

He was quiet. Then, "You've had one lousy week."

"Tell me about it."

"If there's anything I can do—"

"There isn't. The police think it was a random thing. Junkies."

"What did they take?"

"Not much." I filled him in.

"They left the TV and VCR?"

"Yeah."

"The dope must have fried their brain cells."

"Thank God."

"Yeah. Well, listen. I may have some good news for you. That Zippo you have? It could be worth a thousand bucks."

"No way."

"That's what they're quoting on eBay."

I rolled my neck muscles, which have been stiff for the

past several years. Poor ergonomic posture. "Lose some pearls, gain a lighter."

"I guess you could—" The beep of my call waiting interrupted him. "Hold on, Mac." I tapped the switch hook. "Ellie Foreman."

"Ellie, my name is Roger Wolinsky. I'm campaign manager for Marian Iverson." It was a cool, confident voice. All business.

"Hello. Hang on a second, will you?" I tapped back to Mac. "Call you back." I put on my professional voice. "Sorry. What can I do for you, Mr. Wolinsky?"

He cleared his throat. "The candidate wanted me to call you." The candidate? "We're planning a campaign video, and we'd like to explore the possibility of having you produce it. You come highly recommended."

Me? I felt my cheeks flush. "I'm flattered, but I have to tell you I don't do political work."

"Oh?" He sounded surprised. I picked up my orange juice, swirled it around, watched flecks of pulp coat the glass. "You did *Celebrate Chicago*."

"That wasn't political."

"Everything's political in Chicago."

Touché. I set the glass down.

"How about you at least meet her? She's having a fund-raiser this week; she'd like you to come as her guest. It's a great opportunity. This candidate is going places."

Susan had mentioned a fund-raiser for Marian Iverson. "I don't know, Mr. Wolin—"

"She'll be working the donors the first hour or so, but she should have time for you after eight."

"Look, as I said, I'm flattered but—"

"I should also mention that we compensate our vendors very competitively. Up front, too."

I kept my mouth shut.

I'D JUST E-MAILED the script to Midwest Mutual when I heard the whine of a broken-down muffler. Seconds later a Dodge Ram pickup pulled into the driveway. The door-bell rang, and a tall man with black hair grizzled on the sides smiled through the screen.

It was my former landscaper, Fouad Waleed Al Hamra. Fouad took care of our lawn when I was married. I remember how Barry would issue commands, and Fouad, who emigrated from Syria thirty years ago, replied respectfully, like a servant addressing the British potentate. It was only when Barry's back was turned and I caught the sly, mocking look in Fouad's eyes that I decided he was worth getting to know.

The first time we talked, I asked how he'd become a landscaper, growing up with nothing but desert around him. He replied that the Fertile Crescent runs through northeast Syria and contains some of the richest land in the world. His family had farmed it for generations.

"Of course."

He pretended not to see my burning cheeks.

His family had sent him to public school in England, he continued, before a Western education turned into a liability in that part of the world. He dutifully moved back when told to, but he never fit in. He moved to the States just before the Six Day War.

Fouad's a devout Muslim, and pro-Arab, but we get along. I figure it's because we're all busy trying to snatch our piece of the American dream, and the quest for the good life tempers one's ideals. Fouad's had a good quest. In addition to his landscaping services, he owns a garden supply store.

"Fouad. What a surprise." I opened the screen, hoping he wasn't going to pressure me into hiring him back. I couldn't afford him.

"Ellie. How are you? You have survived the winter?"

"I'm fine. And you?"

"Ahmed is finishing his first year at Duke, and Natalie starts Johns Hopkins next fall."

He *was* trolling for new customers.

"How's Rachel?"

I smiled. "Twelve, going on twenty-two. Look, Fouad—"

"Ellie—"

We exchanged sheepish smiles. "You first."

"Ellie, I hope you won't take this the wrong way, but, since you—since I—" he fumbled.

"Since the divorce, you mean."

"Yes. Since then, your lawn and your garden, well . . . they—"

"Look like nuclear winter?" I opened the screen door and stepped outside. "I know. But I don't have much disposable income these days. And I'm not much of a gardener."

He followed me out. "That's why I'm here."

"Fouad, I can't—"

"No, no." He shook his head. "I want to make you a proposition." He smiled tentatively. "I hate to see all the work I've done over the years go to waste. What if I come by once in a while and help you out a little? At no charge. Maybe teach you a bit about gardening."

I couldn't believe this. Was he offering to work for free?

"I won't be here every week. And I can't fix everything. But little by little, maybe we can turn this place around. With your help, of course."

"Fouad. What a generous offer." I couldn't remember the last time someone had been so, well, selfless. "Why? You have plenty to do without taking me on as a charity case."

A shy look spread across his face. "I don't . . . I . . . The Koran says that dead land is a sign for us. We must give it life and bring forth from it grains, so that many may eat of the fruit thereof. That is the way we give thanks to Him who created all that which the earth produces."

I made lines on the grass with my shoe. Even after thirty years in the West, Fouad sounds like a person displaced, his temperament better suited to simpler times, when faith was woven into the fabric of life. I run from anything requiring a belief I can't see, touch, or taste, but I try to be tolerant, in case there really is a God.

"Come," Fouad said.

Together we inspected the grounds, like the master of the hounds before the hunt. "Grounds," of course, is a euphemism; my lawn is about the size of two parking spaces. Fouad suggested I buy a weed-killing fertilizer right away. He would put it down. I should also invest in a box of Miracle-Gro for the perennials.

"Perennials?"

He bent his head, as if he was going to say something but thought better of it. Then he patiently explained the difference between perennials and annuals. He pointed out daylilies, dianthus, and hydrangeas, all of which grew, or soon would be, in varying states of profusion, and promised to bring some annuals next month. I agreed to everything. Maybe greenis envy is contagious.

SPRINGTIME ALWAYS BRINGS out the crazies. The local news that night featured Jeremiah Gibbs, leader of the Church of the Covenant, who was pledging his support for a neo-Nazi march through Skokie. The church, in reality a thinly veiled white separatist organization, counted as one of its members Dan Thornton, the brother of Rachel's classmate, who shot his way through Rogers Park. Gibbs, a slippery character who operated on a razor-thin edge of legality, was said to use a state-of-the-art web site for recruiting.

When it started years ago, many people, both Jews and Gentiles, were enraged by the thought of Nazis marching through a community with a large proportion of Holocaust survivors, and though there were vitriolic counterdemonstrations, small bands of fierce-looking thugs with swastika armbands and flags *did* goose-step through the streets with only a few incidents, mostly of the rock-throwing variety. Of course, that might have been due to the thick phalanx of police officers lining the route. Since then, they've marched every year, but, like a deformity you learn to live with, no one, Holocaust survivors included, seems to pay much attention.

The story cut to file footage of Gibbs at the time of the Rogers Park shootings. He was a handsome man, with slicked-back blond hair, a sparse mustache, and cold blue eyes, and he wore a good-looking suit befitting a banker or lawyer, which I gather he was, though he'd never been admitted to the bar.

"I feel bad that an illegal activity occurred," he was saying in a sound bite, "but our charter mandates that we not feel compassion for the other races." A spit of fury kicked through me. What right did he have to look so telegenic? To speak in crisp ten-second sound bites?

The bathroom door opened, and Rachel came out wrapped in a towel. Wisps of steam rose from her skin, and damp curls framed her face like a halo. "Mom?"

"Yes, honey?" I snapped off the TV.

"When can I shave my legs?"

"Shave your legs?"

"I'm the only girl in the whole class who doesn't. Everybody thinks I'm a dork."

"Does Katie?"

"Well, no, but her mom—"

"Does Callie?"

"No, but—"

"What about Sarah?"

"Mom. Everybody's doing it. I don't want to be the last one."

"Tell you what."

"What?" She raised an eager face.

"I guarantee you'll shave before your wedding."

She groaned and stomped off.

THIRTEEN

THE FORSYTHIA IN front of Mrs. Fleishman's house was flowering, and purple blossoms clustered on Mrs. Altshuler's rhododendron. It's remarkable what a few warm days can do. I climbed the steps and rang the bell.

As Shirley opened the door, recognition lit her face. "How are you dear?" She was wearing the same housedress and sweater as the day Ruth died. "I thought about calling you the other day. It was a lovely funeral. Her nephew made all the arrangements. Simple. But dignified."

"I hope it gave you some peace," I said.

"As much as anything could."

"Did Bruno ever show up?"

She shook her head, her eyes clouding. "I've been keeping an eye out. But it's been over a week." She opened the door wide. "Please come in."

I caught a glimpse of lace doilies, a dark sofa, a gloomy room. I stayed on the porch. "This is going to sound trivial, given everything that's happened." I began. "But I think I lost an earring when I helped Ruth with Mr. Sinclair's cartons." I fingered my ear. "I wouldn't bother you, but they were a gift from my daughter."

Her hand rose to her chest. "Oh dear."

I cleared my throat. "I was just wondering . . . Do you by any chance have a key to Ruth's house?"

She nodded.

"Could I . . . I mean, do you think I might be able to take a look for it inside?"

"Of course." She patted my arm. "Let me get the key." I started back down the steps. "Should we call Ruth's nephew and tell him? I'd hate for him to think I was trespassing."

"Oh, don't worry about him," Shirley said. "He said to use my judgment. He hasn't even been here himself."

"So, he hasn't gone through her things?"

"No. In fact, no one's been here since . . . since . . ." She pressed her lips together. "I'll just get the key."

I felt like a heel.

Lowered shades blocked most of the light inside, and a musty smell wafted over us. I pretended to look for my earring. "It might have come off when I brought the cartons downstairs." I dropped to my hands and knees, inspecting the floor near the steps. "Do you see anything?"

Shirley bent over and squinted. "What did it look like?"

I pointed to my ear where I'd clipped a small blue and white Wedgwood-style earring. Its mate lay on the front seat of the Volvo. But they *had* been a gift from Rachel. Really.

"I'm sorry, dear. I don't see a thing." She straightened up.

I sighed. "Me neither. I'll just take a quick look upstairs, if that's okay."

"Go ahead. I'll be in the kitchen."

Skull's room was as I remembered it. Bed, dresser, desk, closet. The floor was bare. There was no carton, no metal box. I opened the desk drawers. Empty. I checked the closet. Nothing. I lay on my stomach and peered under the bed frame. Dust balls but nothing else. I wiped myself off. "I can't find it." I called down to Shirley.

"What a pity," she called back.

"Would it be okay if I peeked in her bedroom? Maybe—"

"By all means."

I crossed the hall to Ruth's bedroom and opened the

door. Drapes blocked the light, a damask spread covered the bed, and a silk upholstered chaise occupied one corner. Norma Desmond's boudoir. I hunted through her closet, her drawers, even checked under her bed. I found old issues of *JUF News*, a spool of white thread, and a bottle of red nail polish, but no carton. And no metal box.

There was one other room upstairs, not much bigger than a closet. It held an ironing board, two empty laundry baskets, and a vintage black Singer sewing machine with the wheel on the side. The carton wasn't there, but a spider was lazily making its way across the floor. I went back downstairs.

"Any luck?" Shirley opened the blinds in the kitchen. A bright sun flooded through the slats. Her pinched face made me realize how hard this was for her.

I shook my head, feeling even guiltier.

"That's a shame. But, you know, I bet if you tell your daughter the truth, she'll understand."

She reached underneath the sink and pulled out a sponge and can of cleanser. Sprinkling cleanser into the sink, she turned on the water and started scrubbing the bowl.

"You're probably right." I hesitated. "Unless . . ."

"Unless what, dear?" She wiped down the sides of the sink, then splashed them with water.

"Unless someone came in after I left and found it."

"You mean the day Ruth died?" I nodded. She stopped wiping and wrinkled her brow. "I was here myself."

I leaned against the table. "That's right. I forgot. You came over for coffee."

She turned around to face me. "Yes, but I didn't see your earring. Of course, I wasn't looking for it."

"Was anyone else here?"

"Not that I recall." She held the sponge carefully; even so, a few drops of water dribbled onto the floor. "No. I do remember. Nobody was here. Nobody at all." She turned back to her task.

"So, if I left with the cartons around three, you got here

just after that and stayed—what—till about four?"

"That's right." She dried her hands on a dish towel, folded it, and put it away in the cabinet.

"Then I came back and found Ruth about four-thirty," I went on. "Which means unless someone came in during that half hour—"

"That earring must be very important to you." Her face softened.

I blinked. I couldn't take it anymore. "You know something? It's just an earring. Let's get out of here."

She smiled and looked around Ruth's kitchen as if this was the last time she'd see it. That's when I got it. The cleaning, the picking up: it was her final tribute to her friend.

BACK IN MY car, I twirled a lock of hair. From the time I left until the time I got back and found her dead, no one except Shirley had entered Ruth Fleishman's house, with the possible exception of a half-hour window between four and four-thirty. And no one had been in the house since. But two men had been lurking outside Ruth's house when I left. And Ben Skulnick's carton had disappeared. And Ruth Fleishman was dead.

I've read that Carl Jung says there is no such thing as coincidence. That the more unusual the coincidence, the more probable it is that something other than chance is responsible. I can't speak for Jung, but it seemed to me that the break-in at my house was looking less random. And the half-hour window when Mrs. Fleishman was alone more significant. Someone wanted Ben Skulnick's things badly enough to break into houses to get them. Ruth Fleishman had been inside when they did; an hour later, she was dead.

I tried to remember the car that the men outside Ruth's were sitting in. A light color, I thought. Older. Maybe a Cutlass. I dug out my cell phone and started to punch in

O'Malley's number. Then I disconnected. He'd want evidence, which I didn't have. I couldn't even provide a solid description of the car.

I called in for my messages instead. There was one from Karen Bishop, my client at Midwest Mutual. Their server must be acting up; she'd received my E-mail that said the script was attached, but it wasn't there. Could I E-mail it again?

I depend on E-mail to send scripts, proposals, transcripts, even invoices. In addition, I do almost all my research on the Net. And aside from a few bumps getting started, I've managed to avoid the horrors of technology hell. Still, I've heard the stories, and I have a cautious relationship with cyberspace, kind of like a lover you suspect has a dark side but haven't yet seen. I hoped that wasn't the case now. I started the car and headed north to Touhy. As I turned west toward the Edens, an image of Boo Boo, Skull's friend from the library, came into my mind. "Were you one of dose people he E-mailed?"

Ben Skulnick had been E-mailing people. With Boo Boo's help. Maybe Boo Boo knew something about his activities. I made a U-turn.

The librarian was behind the marble counter, chatting to a white-haired man with a cane in one hand and a stack of books in the other. The wall clock said it was just after three. I looked around. There was no sign of Boo Boo. The librarian finished a dissertation about the weather. The old man limped past me.

I approached the counter and asked politely, "Have you seen Boo Boo today?" She lifted her *pince-nez* and gazed at me. There was no sign of recognition on her face. "Who?"

"The kid in the Georgetown baseball hat with the gold earring. Likes computers?"

"Oh, you mean Clarence." She let the pince-nez drop. "He hasn't been here today." Subject closed. I stood for a moment, wondering if she might at least reward me with

a comment about the weather. She didn't. I gave her my
phone number and asked her to give it to Boo Boo the
next time she saw him. She gave me her back.

Outside the lemony aroma of marinated lamb drew me
down to the corner. I bought a *souvlaki* pita, added onions
and tomatoes, and dug in. I was wiping grease off my
hands when a black kid in a warm-up suit, Georgetown
baseball hat, and backpack stepped between two cars. I
ran out of the restaurant, waving my napkin like a flag.
Boo Boo darted in the opposite direction as if he'd just
figured out I was trouble he didn't care to meet.

"Boo Boo, wait up." I snaked around the traffic and
crossed the street. Uncertainty splashed across his face. I
had to think of something. Fast.

Swallowing hard—there went a thousand bucks—I
pulled Skull's Zippo out of my bag. "I have something
for you." I held it up. "You know what this is?"

Silver glinted in the sunshine. His eyes narrowed. "A
torch, man."

"Yeah, but not just any torch. Take a look." I handed
it to him. "You see the engraving of the man against the
lamppost? How he's leaning against it for dear life?"

Boo Boo frowned.

"They call this 'The Drunk.' It's a Zippo lighter, the
best ever made, and this design is one of the first they
ever put on the lighter. It's over sixty years old." I pointed
to the initials. "Now look at these letters."

He squinted. "SKL."

"You know who this belonged to?"

He shrugged.

"This was Ben's. Your friend, Ben Sinclair. His real
name was Skulnick. People called him Skull."

"Skull?"

I tapped my head. "He used to bash people's heads in."

"Damn." He snapped it shut and extracted a crumpled
Kool from a pack in his pocket. Then he flicked the Zippo

and touched the flame to his cigarette. "You say he in the mix?" He inhaled deeply.

"Huh?"

"You know. His own gang?" He blew smoke out in my direction.

I nodded. "That's what I'm saying."

He cupped the cigarette in the palm of his hand. "Where at?"

"Lawndale."

His frown deepened.

"It's on the West Side. South of here. But that was a long time ago."

"Who he run with?"

I hiked my shoulders noncommittally.

He threw the cigarette down and ground it out with his foot. "You come down here to gimme this?"

"I thought you'd appreciate having it. I know you were his friend. It's worth a lot of money."

He cocked his head as if he knew there was a catch. "What you want?"

"Well . . . there is something." I admitted.

"Uh-huh."

"I need your help." I reminded him what he'd said about Skull E-mailing people.

He was backing away before I finished. "No way. I ain't no snitch."

"Boo Boo, I know that. But things have happened. Mrs. Fleishman, the lady he lived with, died. The same day I was here." He looked away. "I had his clothes in my car. It's a long story. Anyway, I took them home. A few days later, my house was broken into. They took his things."

He played with the lighter.

"I have no idea who took them or why. But I think it has something to do with Ben."

A car horn blasted nearby. Boo Boo jerked his head up. A moving van passed by, and then a tan Cutlass with two figures in it. My stomach turned over. I followed it with my eyes until it turned the corner.

"Why you tell me this shit?"

I took a breath. Stop, I scolded myself. You're getting paranoid. "I . . . I remember you saying he'd been E-mailing people from the library, and I thought maybe you might be able to help me."

Palming the lighter, he inspected it carefully. Then he looked at me. "I don' know shit, lady. An even ifin I did, I wouldn't tell you." But something new edged into his voice. Defiance. Or fear.

"Look," I said, "I know you're not supposed to send E-mail from the library. I'm not going to rat you out. But I need to know what's going on."

He hoisted his backpack and started walking away.

"Please. Don't go. I'm scared, Boo Boo. I live with my daughter. It's just us. Whoever broke into my house broke into Ruth's. They might have had something to do with her death. They know where I live. What if they come back?" I heard the desperation in my voice. "I have to do something. The cops aren't doing shit."

"You got dat right." He kept walking.

"Boo Boo, I don't expect you to care about me. Or my daughter. But Ben was your friend. And whatever he was doing was important to him. So important that he learned how to E-mail and surf the net. And now, well, I don't know, but I keep thinking he needs our help. Your help."

He stopped. A metallic tanker drove past, its cylinder reflecting a wavy image of blue and black and boy. He turned around. "I don't know what the fuck he into," he said. "But I know he scared."

I read the fear on his face. "Scared of what?"

"He say they catch him, they take him out."

"Someone was going to kill him?"

"He say he don't have much time."

I stared at the American Legion hall across the street. The old man I'd seen in the library hobbled inside, his books still crooked under one arm. "Are you saying some-one was after him because of the E-mails he was send-ing?"

He wouldn't meet my eyes.

"Who was he writing?"

He shook his head.

"Okay. How about one name? Just tell me one person he was E-mailing."

He shot me a sidelong glance. "The CIA."

"Skull was E-mailing people at the CIA?" Was this kid messing with my head? "I don't believe it."

He shrugged.

"Prove it. Help me get into his E-mail."

He stiffened. "You crazy?"

"Look. If you're telling the truth, that's serious stuff. And if you're not, well . . . I still need to know who stole his things. And why. Then I'll have something to take to the police."

He thrust the lighter in his pocket and spun away from me.

Damn. I said the wrong thing again. "He was your friend, Boo Boo. He needs your help. What was his user name?"

Another truck thundered by on Clark Street. A couple of kids passed us. One of them said, "Who let the Erkle out?"

The other kid laughed. "What you say? Where his glasses at?" They looked at Boo Boo, slapped themselves high fives, and disappeared down the street. Boo Boo's mouth stretched into a grim line.

"Boo Boo?" I asked.

He looked in the direction the kids had gone. "BENS," he said slowly. "Like his name."

"And his password?" I whispered.

"GIJoe."

I slumped against a car. "You want to do it with me?"

He shook his head. "No way. She catch me—" he nod-ded toward the library. "I be out for good."

I understood. The library was his refuge, his ticket out. He wasn't ready to throw it away. "Thank you," I said and held out my hand. He looked around to see if anyone was watching before he took it.

FOURTEEN

I THREW TOGETHER grilled cheese sandwiches for dinner and went on-line as soon as I could. After finding the web site that hosted Skull's free E-mail account, I clicked to the log-in page and typed in "BENS" as my user name, and "GIJoe" as my password. A dozen messages instantly blinked on the screen. I studied the list. Most were ads and too-good-to-be-true offers, which I moved to the trash. One message remained. The return path said DGL@Premier.com. I opened it.

I may have the information you're seeking. But I need identification. Who are you and why do you want to know about Lisle Gottlieb?"

Lisle Gottlieb?

The only Lisle I'd ever heard of was the young Austrian girl in the *Sound of Music* whose heart was broken by her Nazi boyfriend. I swung the chair around and looked through the window. Some neighborhood kids were blading down the middle of the street. I watched as Rachel flew past. Without elbow or knee pads.

Who was Lisle Gottlieb? I tapped my fingers on the desk. Suddenly it came. The snapshot of Skull and a woman on a bridge in Europe at Mrs. Fleishman's. Lisle Gottlieb could be the woman in the picture. I squinted at the screen. Dad said Skull claimed to have worked with the Resistance. What if he'd met this Lisle over there,

fallen madly in love, had a baby? Then, one day, after a
quiet walk on the bridge of whatever city they were living
in, Nazi thugs stormed their home and seized Lisle. Or
Skull, while he was on some mission for the Resistance.
Then, having been taken to different camps, they never
found each other after liberation. It was a possibility; you
still see an occasional story like that on the news.

I flicked a pen back and forth between my fingers. I
should check Skull's out box. Perhaps if I read the message that he originally sent, I'd learn something. I clicked
on the icon to Skull's out box. A white screen bordered
in blue appeared on the screen. Inside were the words:
"There are no items in your out box."

I frowned. Most people keep their outgoing messages—
at least for a while—if only as a record of their correspondence. But Skull's box was empty. Unusual. Especially if he was E-mailing people regularly.

Unless. I picked up the pen again. Mrs. Fleishman said
Ben Sinclair was a man with secrets. Maybe Skull erased
his outgoing mail to protect himself. Hide his cybertracks.
Boo Boo said Skull thought someone was after him. If
Skull thought his E-mail might be under surveillance, it
did make a kind of paranoid sense. He might not have
known, given his rudimentary knowledge of cyberspace,
that a record of his messages was stored on various serv-
ers anyway.

But if he was searching for his long-lost love, why keep
his efforts secret? If I was trying to track down someone,
especially someone close, I'd cast as wide a net as possible. The more people who knew, the better. Evidently
Skull didn't agree. Unless a long-lost love was not what
he was searching for.

I backtracked to Skull's in box, wondering if the messages he'd received prior to today might reveal a clue.
But aside from DGL's message, his in box was empty,
too. I checked his trash, hoping he might have transferred
but not deleted them. Nothing except the ones I'd moved
a moment ago. He had been thorough.

The screen door slammed and footsteps thumped on the steps.

"Rachel?"

"Yeah, Ma?"

"You have homework tonight?"

No answer. That meant yes. The door to her room closed smartly.

I could always write DGL myself and ask about his or her connection to Lisle Gottlieb. Then I reconsidered. DGL, whoever he or she might be, might misunderstand the situation. It *was* confusing, and DGL was under no obligation to tell me a blessed thing.

I opened my browser thinking I'd run Lisle's name through a couple of search engines. At the bottom of the menu was the family roots web site. I'd forgotten I tagged it the other day. Seeing it now gave me an idea. I slid the mouse over and clicked.

The same web page appeared. I scrolled past the pictures and entered the name "Gottlieb" in the search box. Seconds later, over a hundred messages popped up. A prolific family. I skimmed through queries about Heinrich, Emily, and Alfred Gottlieb, but came up blank for Lisle. When I got to the end, I rolled my neck muscles, hunched my shoulders, and started to scroll backward. I was almost back to the top of the page when I saw it.

Looking for any information about Lisle Gottlieb or Lisle Weiss. She lived in Chicago during World War Two.

I brought up the full text.

Looking for any information about Lisle Gottlieb or Lisle Weiss. She lived in Chicago during World War Two. Moved away in forty-five. All replies confidential. BENS@webmail.com.

Goose bumps broke out on my arms. BENS@webmail.com was Skull's E-mail address. He had written this

post. I read it again. The second sentence was the most
revealing. If Lisle Gottlieb or Lisle Weiss lived in Chicago during the war, the odds that she was the woman in
the European snapshot were low; the photo I'd seen had
been shot around the same time. So who was she? And
why was Skull looking for her? Did it have anything to
do with the theft of his things?

I scrolled up to the date of Skull's post. April 5. Skull
died April 12, I recalled. I checked the date of DGL's
reply. It had been sent April 13. The day after Skull died.
Skull never saw it. But someone in cyberspace did, and
they knew Lisle Gottlieb.

FIFTEEN

COTTONY CLOUDS SCUDDED across the sky as I turned into Midwest Mutual's corporate park. A low-rise complex with several wings sticking out of its core, the building was surrounded by grassy fields dotted with geese. At the side of one field was a man-made pond with small dinghies that employees could use. Several people were paddling around now, making lazy circuits. I parked and headed in the opposite direction.

I waited in the glassed-in lobby for an escort to my client's office. Karen Bishop is a working mother like me. Well, not exactly like me; she's still married, and she's worked out a deal where she's off every Friday. I always assumed she spent it catching up on errands until I asked her about it one day, and a sly look came into her eyes.

"Are you kidding?" she purred. "The kids are in school, and Sam works freelance. I spend Fridays in bed with my husband." Now that's a woman with her priorities in order.

But today wasn't Friday, and Karen looked hassled. Cradling the phone on her shoulder, she was trying to persuade her client, the managing director of the Cat Teams, that our video was worth the cost. After repeated promises to shave as much off the budget as possible, she slammed down the phone.

"The jerk!" she fumed. "He claims he didn't know how much it was going to cost."

I sat down.

"Ellie, I told him from the get-go he was looking at close to thirty grand. I even have the E-mail to prove it."

I made sympathetic noises. "Are we still on?"

"Of course we are. He needs the video for his managers' meeting. He just wanted to yank my chain." She shook her head. "You know, if I were a man, this conversation would never have taken place." She riffled a stack of papers on her desk, as if that would clear the air. "Did you bring the shooting schedule?"

"I E-mailed it last night again. Along with the script."

"I'm sorry. Jared's baseball team is in the playoffs. I got in late."

"No problem." I rooted around in my bag and fished out a hard copy.

I had budgeted an out-of-town trip to shoot a catastrophe or the aftermath of one, but after we discussed it, Karen didn't think it was necessary. "We've got plenty of B-roll on file. Hurricanes, forest fires, the Mississippi River floods."

"But is it utter devastation and tragedy?" I asked.

"Sure."

"You have shots of people clinging to each other, grateful to be alive, even though they've lost everything?"

"You bet."

"You have sound bites of people saying they'll rebuild, no matter what it takes, thanks to Midwest Mutual?"

"We can probably dig some up."

"What about the close-up of the kid's teddy bear swirling down the river?"

"Oh, come on. You can shoot that yourself."

"Deal."

We moved on to the script. I'd dropped the concept of *The Tempest*; I couldn't justify the love story of Ferdinand and Miranda. But I consoled myself with dramatic tension in the sound track: lots of sirens, crashing thunder, and gale force winds. Karen said she liked it. Then, in her understated way, she made massive revisions.

We decided to shoot the interviews at headquarters over

the next two weeks. We would edit the rough cut in-house, and finish the online at Mac's place.

This would work out well. The project would be finished within a month, it wasn't a tough job, and I could prebill for the first half.

SUSAN AND DOUG picked me up that evening, and we barreled up 41 while Crosby, Stills, Nash & Young sang about moving forward. As we wound through the shady, well-bred streets of Lake Forest, a breeze rustled the thick canopy of trees. Already it was ten degrees cooler, as if the village elders had decreed that the quality of life here must be better than anywhere else. East of the railroad tracks, the houses grew larger and the driveways grander. By the time we were on Lake Road, we had passed an Art Deco mansion, a Moorish-style home, and several versions of Tara.

We arrived at a huge stone estate that sprawled over ten acres. The landscaping alone—hostas and impatiens, which, thanks to Fouad, I now knew were shade plants— probably cost more than my mortgage. Ivy obediently hugged a brick wall, and a break revealed a fountain with porcelain water nymphs poised for a dip. Three gravel driveways led to separate wings of the house. Valets in red vests were busy parking and reparking BMWs, Mercedes, and the occasional Cadillac.

"I'm glad I wore my Donna Karan," I said, as we made our way to the front entrance. Susan didn't answer. Even she seemed intimidated.

A heavy, paneled door was open, and a butler greeted us in the foyer. After placing our business cards on a silver tray, he ushered us through a dark hall lined with tapestries and oil portraits. I heard the distant tinkle of laughter and glasses.

"Da steel been bery, bery good to me," Doug whispered.

"I'm Marian Iverson, and I'm running for Congress," I shot back.

"It's the Senate," Susan said dryly.

We passed through a large drawing room with a set of French doors to a flagstone terrace. People milled about, drinks in hand. Beyond the terrace was a manicured lawn that sloped down to a narrow beach. In the distance a sloop bobbed on the lake. Two gulls played tag with the sails.

My eyes swept back to the terrace, where guests clustered in small groups. The women were dressed in casual springtime chic, the men sporty but moneyed. There was more moussed hair than at the Academy Awards.

"We can still make a getaway," I grumbled, increasingly aware that my pants suit was four years old.

Susan took some hors d'oeuvres from a passing waiter. The waiter turned to me, but I passed. I've never taken the course where they teach you to balance a plate of food in one hand and a drink in the other.

"It's black caviar," Susan said, nibbling on a toast point, her plate perfectly balanced. "Beluga, I think. Or Osetra."

"Must be nice," I sighed.

"What?"

"To throw yourself a party like this."

"I guess."

"The problem is you keep on spending money like water, people will think you don't need to raise any."

"Oh, I don't know," Susan said, her eyes on Doug, who was chatting up a portly man in a golf shirt and madras pants. "I guess it depends on the type of funds you want to raise."

A guffaw went up from madras man, and Doug came back to round up Susan. I scanned the crowd. I recognized some Chicago VIPs and their sycophants, a few North Shore politicians, even a couple of reporters. But judging from their appearance, most of the guests epitomized what

I call "loose money." Not old. Not new. Loose. As in freely thrown around.

I eased my way toward the bar and nearly collided with the back of a blond, Scandinavian-type woman. She turned around. It was Dana Novak, my former client from the city's Special Events Bureau.

"Ellie, what a surprise." She wrapped one arm around my neck and gave me an air hug, the Midwest version of the air kiss. "What brings you here?" she asked. "I thought your politics ran to the other side."

I shrugged. "What about you? Does the mayor know you're here?"

"He sent me," she laughed. At my puzzled look, she added, "I'm coordinating a Labor Day rally she'll be appearing at. I'm here as a courtesy."

"Labor?" I frowned. "But she's a Republican."

"A new Republican. They're compassionate now."

"But the mayor isn't. Republican, that is."

"It's a family thing. Turns out the mayor's father worked for her father once upon a time."

"You're kidding."

Dana nodded. "The mayor's father was a shop steward at Iverson Steel. There's been this mutual respect between them for years. It's all very cozy. But what about you? Why are you here?"

I told her about Roger Wolinsky's call. She punched me lightly on the shoulder. "You go girl. You did it."

"Did what?"

"Cracked the old boy's network."

"Uh, Dana, last time I looked, Marian Iverson was a woman."

"A powerful woman. There's a difference." She gestured to a group of people behind us. Several men were laughing with a well-preserved woman. Honey blond streaks disguised whatever gray ran through her hair, and she wore a crisp Armani suit, accessorized with pearl earrings and matching bracelet. Her makeup was as flawless as her hair. She could have been anywhere from fifty to seventy.

"Come on, I'll introduce you." Before I could protest, she simultaneously waved to a man in the group and plucked a crudité off a passing tray. Dana had clearly passed the plate-balancing course. She would go far in politics. "Roger Wolinsky, meet Ellie Foreman, the genius behind *Celebrate Chicago*. I hear you want to steal her away."

A man with thick, dark hair that covered his arms as well as his head detached himself from the group. Not particularly tall, his foot kept up a fast tap on the flagstones. He took my hand briefly, then rubbed his thumb and index finger together in tiny circles. Humphrey Bogart in *The Caine Mutiny*. Without the steel balls.

"Nice to meet you." I felt like a lamb being led to slaughter.

"She's not ready for you," he said and promptly returned to the inner circle. I wheeled around, looking for Dana, but she had disappeared. Roger stationed himself a discreet distance away from the candidate, but I had the feeling he was mentally recording every person who shook her hand, evaluating their worth as potential donors. I lifted a glass of wine from a waiter. Naturally, that's when Roger made his move.

"Marian, I want you to meet someone."

Suddenly I was in front of a bright smile, a firm handshake, and probing gray eyes. I fumbled with my glass. Roger whispered in her ear. Her face softened. "You're the woman who did the show for the mayor. An excellent piece of work."

"Thank you."

"It must have taken a lot of effort."

"It was a labor of love."

"It showed." She smiled warmly. "I learned a lot from your film." *Film*. Not *movie*. I smiled back. "Roger tells me you do political work as well?"

"As a matter of fact, I don't, Ms. Iverson."

"No?" Her eyes flicked to Roger. "Why not?"

Because I don't want to run a safe house. "I don't want to get a reputation for being too close to the process." I switched my wineglass to my other hand. "And politicians have this habit of forgetting to pay their bills."

Her smile broadened. "Good point. I wouldn't get involved, either."

"Really?" I countered. "Well, that seems to beg an obvious question." I waved a hand.

"You mean why I left this privileged life for the world of politics?" Her eyes twinkled. "Well, first of all, this is my mother's house, not mine. She insisted we have the fund-raiser here."

"But you grew up here. These are your roots."

"Everyone comes from someplace, don't they? In my case, the operative word is *from*."

Roger sputtered and rubbed his fingers together.

"I'm sorry." She laughed. "Forgive me for straying off-message. That is what you call it, isn't it, Roger?" She laid a hand on her deputy's arm. "In all seriousness, though, I do realize how fortunate I am to have been given so much. I suppose this is my way of giving back."

I gestured at the opulence around us. "To whom?"

Roger winced.

Marian seemed unperturbed. "Don't be naive. You know that money attracts money."

"I don't mean to be naive. Or disrespectful, but what can a tea-party Republican offer the people on the South Side? Or the people downstate who still live in tin shacks?"

She didn't miss a beat. "Another good point," she said smoothly. "And that is the challenge, isn't it? I do want to represent all the people. Not just—what did you call us—tea-party Republicans? I like that, by the way. I might steal it." Roger laid a hand on her arm. "I hope we'll meet again, Ellie."

Roger succeeded in pulling her away, but it was only because she allowed him to. "And I hope you'll give us tea-party folks a chance." She fingered a strand of pearls around her neck, then turned away, on to the next conquest.

I watched her drift away, surprised that I liked her. I was threading my way back to Susan and Doug when the French doors opened, and a woman in a wheelchair emerged. A study in gray, her skin was withered and ashy, and her thin, wispy hair was the color of storm clouds. As a nurse pushed her forward, the crowd on the terrace separated as if she was Charlton Heston dividing the Red Sea. This woman knew how to make an entrance.

"Who is that?" someone in front of me asked.

"That's Frances Iverson, Marian's mother," someone else answered. I edged closer. Her eyes were the same iron gray as her daughter's, but not as warm. I felt a chill.

SIXTEEN

FOUAD CAME BACK on Saturday with dahlias, begonias, and ageratum, and showed me how to space them so they would bloom in clumps. He pruned the yews, which were so overgrown they obscured my front door. Then he planted some impatiens on the ground underneath them, and the contrast between the peppermint pastels and the dark green needles was dazzling.

After he left, I watered everything as he'd directed, then wondered what to do. Soccer was over. Rachel was with Barry. I was alone. Back when my marriage was collapsing, and despair cut through the air like a knife, I remember wishing Barry and Rachel would just leave me alone in peace. Now, every other weekend, they do, and I mourn the silence. A human being, even an irresponsible, self-indulgent one, is better than no one at all. At least someone is there to acknowledge your presence, to register the fact that you exist.

I cued up the Scorsese bootleg and watched for a few minutes. Despite bits of sharp comedy, it was a dark film, full of the urban chaos he likes to explore. I turned it off. I made my way into the kitchen and started to toast a frozen bagel. Halfway through the cycle, I had an idea. I flicked up the switch, grabbed my bag, and headed out to the car.

*   *   *

THIRTY MINUTES LATER, I showed up at Dad's with a dozen fresh bagels and a pound of lox. My father, convinced that only a baker's son knows how to buy bread, carefully inspected them while Ella Fitzgerald warbled on about satin dolls.

I told Dad about Marian Iverson's fund-raiser and the possibility of doing a video for her. He wiped his hands on a dish towel. "I didn't know you were a Republican."

"I'm not." I carried a plate of onions and tomatoes to the table.

A lifelong Democrat, he brought out the bagels, peering at me over his glasses. "Well, it's your life."

We sat down, and I reached for a bagel. "You know, there is something I've been meaning to ask you."

"What's that?"

"I came across the name of a woman that I think Ben Skulnick was trying to find, and I wondered if by any chance you'd ever heard of her."

"I thought you were going to forget about him." He slathered his bagel with cream cheese.

"I got curious. Anyway . . ." I kept going. "Does the name Lisle Gottlieb mean anything to you?"

Dad's hands froze. "What did you say?"

"Lisle Gottlieb. Skull was trying to find a woman named Lisle Gottlieb."

His face turned a pale shade of parchment, and he gripped the knife so hard that veins protruded from his arm.

"Dad?"

He didn't say anything.

"Are you all right? Shall I call someone?"

He shook his head.

I ran into the kitchen and filled a glass with water. "Drink." I set it down in front of him.

He waved the glass away, then carefully put the knife back on his plate.

"Daddy, what . . ."

He slowly pushed himself up from the table, held up a

finger, and shuffled into his bedroom. I heard the bureau drawer slide open. It closed a minute later. He came back out, holding a picture.

"What's that?"

Sitting down, he cleared his throat. "This happened a long time ago." He studied the picture. "Frankly, it's not the kind of thing I ever thought I'd tell my daughter." He took a sip of water, looked at me. "But . . ." He passed me the picture.

It was an old black-and-white snapshot. Two young men in army uniforms sat at a small table in what looked like a coffee shop. Grinning at the camera, they both had an arm draped around a young woman. One of the soldiers was my father. The other was a young Barney Teitelman, Uncle Barney to me. I didn't recognize the girl, but her smile was so dazzling it made me want to smile back. She had a delicately boned face, a small straight nose, and Clara Bow lips. Her hair was a mass of curly blond ringlets. She was beautiful.

"That's me and Barney. After we enlisted," he said softly.

"And the woman?"

He hesitated. "I want you to know that this happened before I ever met your mother. I never gave your mother anything to worry about, you know what I mean?" His eyes moved to the picture. "Lisle Gottlieb was my girlfriend back in Lawndale."

I laid the picture on the table.

"She was a German refugee. Came over in the fall of thirty-eight. She was sixteen. She had blond hair and blue eyes. Like an angel." He poured us both a cup of coffee. "She was living at the Jewish Orphans Home, but she cleaned houses for a living. She hardly spoke a word of English."

I curled my fingers around my coffee cup, remembering the string of cleaning ladies that had come through my house when I was married. How one of them, an immigrant from Latvia, sat down at our piano and played a

Beethoven sonata from memory. Flawlessly.

"Lisle was from Freiburg," Dad went on, "in the Black Forest. She was the oldest of three children. Her parents managed to get her out. A distant cousin here sponsored her. I got the impression they paid him a lot of money, but it didn't work out. Lisle never said much about him."

He picked up the picture. "When I met her, she'd managed to convince the home in Lawndale to take her in temporarily, but she worked over in Hyde Park. I used to walk her to the Cottage Grove streetcar after school. Then I'd see her on weekends when I went over to Barney's." He chuckled. "I remember she never wanted to talk in German, even though I could manage. She'd point to things, and I'd tell her what they were in English.

"A few months after the war started, she got a letter from her brother in Germany. Her father had been killed. Her mother and sister had been taken away in a truck. Her brother was hiding out at a friend's. He said he was going to try and pass. She never heard from him again."

I winced.

"After that I was her closest friend. I helped her move into a room at Mrs. T's. Helped her learn to read and write in English. Took her places."

"You dated?"

Dad nodded, looking past me. "I remember one night we went to see Benny Goodman at the Blackhawk. Gene Krupa was on drums, Teddy Wilson on piano. It was the tops. So full of magic neither Lisle nor I wanted it to end." His expression was dreamy. "We stopped for a drink on the way home; it was past midnight when we got back to Barney's.

" 'I'm going to run away from home and join the Benny Goodman Trio,' I remember saying.

" 'Yes? But what will you play?' Lisle teased me. She had this light, musical voice. Like bells tinkling.

" 'I can cover a comb with tissue paper pretty well,' I said.

"Then she grew serious. 'So Jacob'—she was the only

person who ever called me that—'what are you going to do when you grow up?'

" 'Marry you,' I said. 'And take care of you forever.' "

He blinked. "After Pearl Harbor, Barney and I enlisted," he said. "Lisle was scared. She said I should run away with the Benny Goodman trio." He put down the snapshot. "But then, one night, a few weeks before we left for basic, I took her to dinner. She was beaming. She'd gotten a job. 'A real job,' she said. She had read about it in the newspaper. I still don't know what she was prouder of—the fact that she got a job or that she could now read in English," he said. "The job was at Iverson Steel."

"Iverson?" I cut in. "As in Marian Iverson, the candidate?"

"Her father."

"That's a coincidence."

"They needed women. They trained her to be a riveter." He smiled at some private memory. "She loved it. I remember picking her up at the plant one day. There was some kind of war rally going on. Iverson himself led a procession of workers through the plant. They were all holding flags, blowing horns, singing songs. I'll never forget it; the man looked like a king with his entourage. Everyone treated him like one, too. When he passed us, Lisle waved her flag and curtsied.

"I was shipped off to California soon after that." He shifted. "Her letters stopped after a few months. I figured she was just insecure about writing in English. But when she didn't return my calls, I knew something was wrong. I finally finagled a pass, borrowed a car, and drove straight through to Chicago. Got to Mrs. T's at two in the morning. Joe, the headwaiter, was closing up.

" 'Jake, what are you doing here?' he said. 'Is she up there?' I asked. 'Don't go up there,' I remember he said.

" 'What are you, dizzy?' I didn't listen. I still had her key, you see. Wore it around my neck with my dog tags."

I closed my eyes. I knew what was coming.

"Lisle was in bed with another man." He looked over. "You know, the thing is . . . the thing I'll always remember . . . when she finally realized who had unlocked her door, there was no guilt. No shame. She didn't even flinch. All she said was, 'Hello, Jake.' In that light, breathy voice."

I watched the dust motes swirl in the air.

"His name was Kurt Weiss," Dad went on. "He was a German refugee, like she was. From Frankfurt. The SS shot his family, but he escaped. Somehow he made it over here and got a job as a delivery boy." Dad paused. "He and Lisle fell for each other like a ton of bricks. I suppose it wasn't surprising. They shared a language, a history, and a suffering too horrible for words. How could I compete?"

I pushed my coffee cup away, my heart breaking for my father.

"I got a letter from her a few months later. It was full of apologies. She knew she had caused me pain, and she prayed I would forgive her. I was the only one she could turn to. Kurt, it seemed, had been drafted."

"But he was an immigrant. How could that happen?"

"The government did what it had to back then. Remember, he spoke perfect German, and he knew the lay of the land. He was recruited into a clandestine operation, she said."

I took a sip of coffee. It was cold. "What clandestine operation?"

"The OSS."

The Organization of Secret Services. Forerunner of the CIA. Formed during the war.

"Apparently, Lisle hadn't heard from him in months, and she was afraid he'd been sent back to Europe. Behind enemy lines. She was frantic. She wanted me to do something, anything." He got up and started to pace. "Of course there was nothing I could do."

"What happened?"

He stopped pacing. "Kurt survived. He came back.

What he did during the war I don't know. He never said."

"You actually talked to him?"

He slipped back into his chair. "Naturally, he wouldn't speak to me until he knew I wasn't a threat. But I was a gentleman about the whole thing, and eventually, we did share a few beers. He turned out to be a pleasant guy." He folded his hands together. "Lisle stayed on at the steel mill. At one point, Kurt talked to someone down there, too, and I thought he might start working there, but nothing ever came of it.

"A few weeks after Kurt got back, Barney and I—he was home by then—went to a concert in Douglas Park with them. The Blue Notes, I remember." He sat back in his chair. "It was still hot, and we were lounging on a blanket when I heard a couple of pops. I thought the drummer was starting his own riff until Lisle screamed. When I twisted around, Kurt was slumped over, blood pouring out of him. He died a minute later."

I gasped.

"The police got there quickly, but in the dark and confusion, the killer got away. Lisle was hysterical; Barney and I took her home as soon as we could." He fell silent. Then, "It was a small funeral. Aside from Lisle, Barney, and me, the only other mourners were two of Lisle's friends from the mill and the detective working the case." He stirred his coffee with a spoon. "The case was never solved."

"How come?"

"I don't know. But I do remember thinking the cops weren't working too hard on it."

"Why not?"

"Some things you don't ask; you might not like the answers." He gathered up both coffee cups. "A week or so later, Lisle paid me one last visit."

"What did she want this time?"

"She was pregnant."

"Pregnant?"

He nodded. "She wanted to know what she should do.

I got the feeling she wanted me to fix it for her. Marry her, find a doctor to take care of it, whatever I thought."

"What did you do?"

"Nothing." He shrugged. *"Gnugch ist gnugch.* I told her I couldn't help her. I went east to law school. A couple of weeks later, she left Chicago."

SEVENTEEN

THE APARTMENT WAS silent except for the whoosh of cold air streaming through the vents. Dad took the coffee cups into the kitchen.

I followed with the plates. "So you have no idea why Kurt was killed?"

He shook his head.

"Did it have something to do with the OSS?"

"Who knows? I don't even know if that's who he was working for." He bent over the dishwasher.

Kurt had—potentially—worked for the OSS; Skull had a library book about the OSS. Years later, Skull was E-mailing the CIA. "Did Skull and Kurt know each other?"

Dad shook his head. "Skull was long gone by the time Kurt arrived."

"But he had to know Lisle." We walked back into the living room.

"I don't know about that, either. Skull disappeared in August of thirty-eight. Lisle didn't get here until October."

"Then why was he looking for her on the web site?"

"What web site?"

I realized I hadn't told Dad about my research. I explained, leaving out the part about the break-in. When I finished, he stroked his chin with his hand. "Don't you have better things to do with your time? The man was a gangster, Ellie."

I looked at the floor. "Not recently."

He bristled. "So now you're an expert on Ben Skulnick?"

"No. I just meant . . . he seemed to have some . . ." My voice trailed off. I wasn't sure what I meant. I picked up the snapshot from the table. Dad and Barney looked young and confident, convinced they would come home wearing the laurels of victory. Barney almost didn't; he was seriously wounded on Omaha Beach. "Did he know about you and Lisle?" I asked.

"Who?"

"Skull."

"If he did, it was only through hearsay."

Always the lawyer. "Hearsay?"

"Well, I did see him once or twice after the war. Before they arrested him. I might have mentioned her name. But it would have only been in passing."

A flimsy connection at best. But it was all I had. "I think that's why he had my name."

Dad turned a puzzled face to me.

"I think that when Skull watched *Celebrate Chicago* and saw my name on the credits, he connected me to you."

"Me?"

"Foreman. The name. He saw the name Foreman and figured we might be related."

"But that's crazy. There's gotta be hundreds of Foremans."

"Think about it. There was a segment about Lawndale on the show. You were there. So was he. So was Lisle. Suppose the show triggered all those memories in him and when he saw my name, he wondered if you and I were related. Maybe he figured he could contact me and, through me, track you down. And find out what happened to Lisle."

Dad sighed. "I guess anything's possible. But why? What motive would he have? There's nothing to indicate that he knew her."

I flipped up my palms. "I'm out of ideas. How about you?"

A stern look came into his eyes. "One. I don't want you getting too curious about Ben Skulnick, Ellie. He's nothing but trouble."

"But he's dead."

Dad's eyebrows shot up. "He should rest in peace."

THE LATE-DAY SUN washed everything with a rosy warmth, but I shivered as I pulled into the driveway. Inside the house a quick inspection assured me that everything was in its place, including the bagel I'd left in the toaster. Even so, I made sure the doors were double-locked before heading upstairs.

In my office I picked up the printout of DGL's message. Now that I knew who Lisle was, I was even more curious. Why was Skull looking for my father's girlfriend? According to Dad, they'd never met. The only connection between them, in fact, and that was tenuous at best, seemed to be through my father. Nevertheless, Skull was clearly trying to find this woman. And DGL, whoever he or she was, knew something about her.

Long dusky shadows crept across the lawn. I'd begun looking into Skull's background, hoping it would help me figure out who had broken into my house. Now that I knew about Dad's relationship with Lisle Gottlieb, it seemed I had more of a stake. I studied the message again. If DGL had a piece of the puzzle, I wanted to know what it was.

Dear Sir or Madam: I found your reply to BenS's post to the family roots site in his E-mail. I'm sorry to tell you that BenS passed away on April 12. Because your message to him was dated April 13, I am sure he never had the chance to read it. However, it turns out that my father knew Lisle Gottlieb as well, independently of Mr. Skulnick . . .

I backspaced and deleted "Skulnick." Skull hadn't revealed his identity to DGL. I wouldn't, either.

independently of BenS, and we would very much
appreciate any information you could provide
about her.

Okay. I was taking editorial license with the "we." But
everything else in my note was true. I leaned back, trying
to imagine how DGL would react to my message.

It sounded weak. DGL might decide I was a nutcase
and trash the note without replying. But I couldn't explain
my reasons for pursuing Lisle Gottlieb in an E-mail. Wild
stories about a break-in and stolen cartons would scare
anybody off. I needed to establish credibility. But that
would mean giving up some privacy. I chewed my lip,
curious about Lisle Gottlieb, but reluctant to make myself
more vulnerable. Curiosity won out.

I'm sure you have questions. I would be willing to
answer them by phone. I look forward to hearing
from you. 847-555-9876. Ellie Foreman

EIGHTEEN

WHEN I GOT home from the Midwest Mutual shoot a few days later, my answering machine was flashing. The first message was from Roger Wolinsky, Marian Iverson's campaign director. He left both his work and home number. The second message was from Barry, asking me to call him ASAP. I called Barry first.

"It's me. What's up?"

"Oh." There was a pause. "Ellie, I don't know how to say this . . ."

I mentally reviewed where my family was supposed to be. Rachel was at school; Dad was probably playing cards at his place. If something was wrong, they would have called my cell. If they could. My stomach twisted. "What happened?"

"I . . . I just lost a lot of money. The high-tech incubator I was telling you about . . . it tanked. The stock's in the toilet."

I sagged against the counter. It was only money. Still. It was money. I picked up a butcher knife. "How much, Barry?"

"It's this unstable economy, you know? There's no way we could have known—"

"How much, Barry?"

"Half a million. They want a chunk of it now."

I concentrated on my breathing and studied my shoes.

"I'm sorry, Ellie. I fucked up."

I concentrated hard on my breathing and studied my shoes.

"But I don't think you'll be involved."

I angled the knife above the cutting board. "What do you mean, you don't think I'll be involved?"

Barry didn't say anything.

"Except for child support, which I gather I'll never see again, I'm not involved."

Silence.

"Right?"

More silence.

"Barry, what are trying to tell me?"

I heard a long exhalation. "The account I was trading on was a joint account. It has your name on it."

"What are you, a comedian?"

"It's true."

"That's impossible. We closed the account when we settled. I got money. You got money. The end."

"They never closed it. Some kind of administrative snafu. When Arnie retired, instead of being closed, the account somehow went dormant. I tried to open a new one when I started to invest again, but they said I already had an account open. I meant to do the paperwork and get it straightened out, but I just never got around to it, and then—"

"Let me get this straight. You're telling me that technically, I'm liable for half a million dollars of your stock loss?"

"It's not going to happen, Ellie. I'll fix it."

A car crawled down the street, its movement distorted like a slow-motion film. The sun glinted off the chrome bumper, shooting out sparks of light. The engine chuffed noisily. Insects droned.

"Look, I know you're upset, but I'll call Gene. He'll get it all worked out." Gene Sherwood was his lawyer. The lawyer's lawyer. "Just hold on for a day or two, okay Ellie? Don't do anything stupid."

I stabbed the knife into the cutting board. He'd just lost

half a million dollars, made me a party to his debt, and was telling me not to do anything stupid. The stupidest thing I could do was stay on the phone.

MY LAWYER, PAM Huddleston, said not to worry. It had to be a clerical mistake. I wouldn't be held responsible; we had the paperwork to prove it. It was an aggravation, nothing more. Maybe for her. I've always had a love-hate relationship with money. I've yet to feel the love.

"Will this go on my credit rating?" I stared through the window. The car was gone.

"I don't know."

"What if I have to get a loan to tide me over?"

"Calm down, Ellie," she said. "It's not going to go that far. Let me see what's happening and call you back. In the meantime, here's what to do." I jotted down notes as she told me to round up the title to the house and make sure it was in my name, and to locate the rest of the divorce records. She also suggested this might be a good time to start organizing my money. She could refer me to a great financial planner. Great. All I needed was enough net worth to manage.

My next call was to Roger Wolinksy. We set up a meeting for Thursday.

NINETEEN

RIVER NORTH, JUST north and west of the Loop, is artsy without being bohemian, commercial without being crass. Marian Iverson's headquarters were squeezed into the third floor of a loft building at Franklin and Superior, above a graphic designer on the first floor and a furniture outlet on the second. An Italian restaurant was next door.

Inside, an enormous redwood desk with a mottled marble counter obscured the person behind it. I stretched up on my toes before spotting a young, blond woman with a pair of headphones and a tiny mike clamped to her head.

"May I help you?" she chirped, looking up from the latest edition of *Cosmopolitan*.

"Ellie Foreman to see Roger Wolinksy."

"Have a seat."

I sat down on a small, hard couch, the receptionist invisible again but her voice surprisingly clear as she repeated my name. The walls above her were bare except for a clock, and the odor of fresh paint was strong. Craning my neck, I peeked around the corner.

The office was essentially one huge room dominated by high ceilings. Two floor-to-ceiling windows with a fleur-de-lis pattern on the glass overlooked Superior. The glass looked new. In the middle of the room, eight desks, each with banks of telephones, were pushed together.

Three women and two men, all of them young, and all with the same headphones as the receptionist, huddled at the desks. Several murmured into their mikes. One of the women looked Hispanic. At the far end of room was a large conference table with a Starbucks machine on one end and an empty donut box beside it. Rimming the central area were a few private offices. Someone had made an effort to cheer up the place. Plants on laminated pedestals were scattered here and there.

Roger Wolinsky rounded the corner. I stood up.

"Ellie."

He was wearing a dark green polo shirt and jeans, and the dark hair on his arms gave him a swarthy but not unattractive appearance. He smiled when he realized I was studying him and did the same to me. I was in a long flowery skirt with a white T-shirt and sandals. My hair was gathered at the back of my neck with a butterfly clip.

As we shook hands, my eyes drifted to the people at the desks. Their voices were barely louder than the hum of the air-conditioning. The restraint and sense of order was disquieting.

"I thought campaigns were supposed to be crazy. Chaotic," I said. "People screaming, running around, gnashing their teeth over the latest polls."

He laughed. "It'll pick up. We'll be adding staff over the summer. But it's amazing what we've already accomplished with E-mail and the net. And don't forget, this is only one office. We have people all over the state."

"What are they doing?" I pointed to the people at the desks.

"The pit bulls?" He gestured. "That's our pit."

"Oh."

"They're doing advance work. Coordinating with the field. Planning where we're gonna be on the Fourth of July."

"But it's not even Memorial Day."

"That's been set in stone for months. We're working on the Fourth now." He caught me by the elbow and walked me back to the conference table. "We can do three, maybe four events downstate if we charter a fly-around."

"A fly-around?"

"A plane . . . so we can get to multiple events."

I flinched. I hate to fly.

"Everybody wants her," Roger continued, apparently oblivious to my reaction. "She's climbed seven points in the past two weeks. Which is phenomenal, given that she's running against an incumbent."

Her opponent, a downstate Democrat just finishing his first term, was likable but unremarkable. No hanging chads in this election. We reached the conference table.

"Coffee?"

I shook my head while he poured himself a cup, his eyes on the "pit bulls." Roger was definitely B-ship material, I decided. The B-ship, according to *The Hitchhiker's Guide to the Galaxy,* was one of three arks sent out to colonize a new planet when a giant mutant stargoat threatened to destroy the Golgafrinchams. The A-ship contained the planet's leaders, inventors, and scientists. The C-ship was filled with worker bees. But the B-ship, which was launched *first,* to prepare the way for the others, included hairdressers, middle managers, and marketing types. Five years after the launch, no one from the other ships had yet contacted the B-ship.

Roger gestured to a manila folder on the conference table. "I took the liberty of pulling together some background for you: Marian's bio, her legislative record, a few other things."

We sat down, and I opened the file.

"There's an article from the *Trib,*" he said. "It's a good interview."

I riffled through the papers and pulled it out.

"It's going to be a series. Kind of a campaign journal."

"Really?" I looked at the reporter's byline: Stephen Lamont. The name wasn't familiar.

"We couldn't pay for this kind of publicity." Roger's eyes gleamed. "Lamont is turning out to be quite a friend. You'll run into him."

I skimmed the article. A thumbnail sketch of Marian's

career, it covered her two terms in the Illinois Senate where, as chairman of the Agribusiness Subcommittee, she pushed through a major ethanol bill. It also mentioned her job as deputy administrator of DCCA, the state's commerce department, prior to her election. Before that, she was CEO of Iverson Steel.

"She ran Iverson's?"

"For ten years. Until it was sold."

"When was that?"

"The family sold it off in the seventies around the time imports started to strangle the industry," Roger said.

"I had no idea," I murmured. "She was so young."

Roger shrugged. "She doesn't talk about it much." He lowered his voice. "A rift in the family."

Rift or no rift, my admiration for her deepened. To be a young female CEO back then was rare enough. To be a female CEO during hard times for the steel industry was extraordinary. It must have shaped her character in ways I could only guess.

"Looks like there's a gap of several years here before she went into public service. What did she do?"

"Took a few years off. Traveled. Saw the world. When she decided to enter public service, the governor offered her a job in Springfield right away."

Easy for her. I closed the file. "So, Roger, what are your thoughts about the video?"

Roger lifted a Palm Pilot from his pocket and turned it on. "Marian was talking about the kind of thing they did for Clinton. *The Man from Hope* shtick. It worked well for him."

Not wanting to insult his taste, I said carefully, "Do you really think we need to copy him?"

"Why not? He copied us for years."

I was about to respond when someone shoved a piece of paper in front of him. I looked up. The Hispanic woman stood over him. "Excuse me, Roger," she said, "But I need a signature on this."

He looked up. "What is it?"

"It's the posters we ordered. I went ahead and got five thousand. We can distribute them in the precincts." The woman was striking, with dark, soulful eyes and long black hair that grazed her shoulders.

"Ellie. Meet Dory Sanchez," Roger said. The woman straightened up. She was dressed in a tailored suit that made my outfit look shabby.

"Nice to meet you," she said. "Did you just join the staff?"

"Not exactly. I'm producing a videotape for the campaign."

"I see." She eyed me thoughtfully before turning back to Roger. A look passed between them, and he signed the paper. As she returned to her desk, Roger followed her with his eyes.

"Where were we?" His hand started to twitch, and he started making little circles with his thumb and forefinger. Captain Queeg was back.

"The Man from Hope."

"Right." He cleared his throat. "How about something like that?"

"Frankly, Marian doesn't strike me as that kind of person."

"How does she strike you?"

I straightened my shoulders. "Intelligent. Straightforward. Confident. Determined, although she doesn't push herself on you."

"Go on." Tapping a metallic pen on the tiny monitor of his Palm, he made notes. "What about her politics?"

"It's interesting," I said. "She's almost a blend. I mean she's definitely a Republican, but she doesn't come off as rigid. She's traditional but modern. Almost liberal on some issues. It's almost as if there's something for everyone."

"Then it's working." Roger grinned.

"What's working?"

"We're targeting a broad base of support. You're confirming that our message is getting through. If we can keep up the momentum, the sky's the limit."

"Including the urban vote?"

Roger yanked his thumb toward the pit bulls where Dory and an African-American man were in deep conversation. "I'm not writing anything off. Like I said, the sky's the limit."

He suggested that I come up with a proposal—a "concept"—by the following week. We agreed to shoot during June and July and post during August. We would need some stock footage as well. I should plan on shooting over July Fourth weekend, he said and made a note to get us aboard the plane. I ignored the uneasy twinge.

When it came to the budget, I was surprised at his lack of concern. "It takes what it takes," he said. "We want to do it right. How much do you need up front?"

I swallowed. "Er, forty percent would be good."

"No problem. We'll cut you a check." He got up from the table, a signal that our meeting was over. "Send me an invoice. I'm glad you're on board, Ellie."

I stood up, and we shook hands again. As I pushed through the door, Dory Sanchez stared after me.

TWENTY

PAUL IVERSON CLAIMED to be from modest origins. Raised in the coal-mining region of Pennsylvania, he moved to the Midwest as a young man and married Frances Chandler, daughter of William and Marie Chandler. William Chandler owned a pharmaceutical company and was friendly with the Fords. Iverson and Frances had two children, a boy and a girl. I printed out the article and made a note. I'd thought Marian was an only child.

Iverson was ambitious. And smart. While Sam Insull was stringing up electric lines on the North Shore and the Armours ran the stockyards, Iverson, with the help of his father-in-law, bought a moribund smelting operation. Over the next few years, according to the article, he built it into a thriving specialty processing plant and repaid his father-in-law's loan with interest. At its zenith, Iverson Steel developed a reputation for agricultural applications and employed over three thousand workers. That surged to four thousand during the war when they retooled to produce military parts.

Iverson Steel was also the first Chicago mill to let in the union, with the proviso that they stay out of management issues. Despite regular disputes over what constituted "management issues," Iverson's gamble paid off. In 1938, a strike of seventy-eight thousand Chicago steelworkers erupted into riots, killing ten people at Republic. But Iverson's, just down the road, was untouched, and

Iverson himself ended up mediating between the mill owners and the workers.

Another article described Iverson's philanthropic activities. During the war, Iverson apparently contributed large sums of money to bring Jews out of Nazi Europe. Some of the money went to the Zionist organization to help Jews emigrate to Palestine. The rest went to help smooth immigration into the States, not an easy task with Cordell Hull at the State Department. Iverson's efforts won the respect of the rank and file, many of whom were immigrants from Nazi-occupied countries or had family there, and the article included a picture of Iverson with William Green, head of the AFL, hailing Iverson as "a hero, one of the few to stick out his neck when others were burying their heads in the sand."

I studied the picture I'd downloaded. Why would a tycoon from Lake Forest, whose in-laws were close to Henry Ford, stick out his neck for Jews? Iverson looked like a handsome man, somewhere in his forties, but the photograph was so degraded and blurred it was hard to tell. Tall, thin, elegantly dressed, he had dark eyes and a thick shock of what looked like white hair.

Reading on, I discovered that Iverson's place in history was guaranteed not because of his philanthropy or entrepreneurial success. When American soldiers went off to fight World War Two, thousands of women moved into factories and plants to take their places. The government, in fact, launched a huge propaganda campaign designed to push women into the workplace. Rosie the Riveter featured posters, songs, and photos of young women on the factory floor, happily riveting bolts onto tanks, airplanes, and other heavy equipment.

Although most of them quit after the war, it was a significant milestone for women's rights. Iverson Steel was thought to have hired more women more quickly than any other steel mill in the country. One historian speculated that the concept for Rosie the Riveter might well have originated on Iverson's shop floor. Was that how Lisle

Gottlieb got her job? I wondered. Unfortunately, Iverson
didn't live long enough to enjoy his place in history. He
died at the end of the war from a sudden heart attack.

The phone rang just as I finished the article.

"Ellie, this is Dory Sanchez?" Her voice rose on the
word "Sanchez," turning her statement into a question.
Women in the workplace do that often, I've noticed. It's
as if they're still seeking permission to be in the club, and
they're not brave enough to make an authoritative decla-
ration. Men don't bother.

"Hi, Dory." My voice brimmed with authority.

"I hate to bother you, but Roger wanted me to find out
whether you might want office space down here while
you're working on the video."

"Office space?"

"We have a couple of offices available—at least until
Labor Day. He wanted you to know you're welcome to
use one of them."

"That's kind of him. And you." I hesitated. "But I don't
think I'll need it."

"Oh." She sounded disappointed.

"I'll be on location quite a bit, and then in the editing
room. And . . . well . . . you know. . . ." I bit the inside of
my lip.

"I'll tell you what," she said cheerily. "We'll leave it
open. I'll put a phone in one of them. In case you change
your mind. By the way, would you mind giving me your
cell number? For emergencies."

I frowned. "I . . . I guess not. It's 847-904-5566."

"And your E-mail?"

I told her.

"Thanks. You know, I hope we'll be able to talk at
some point. I'd love to hear more about your work."

"Sure," I replied. "I'll be around."

"Great. I'll give this number to Roger."

After lunch I investigated the Rosie the Riveter story.
An hour of calls to various trade associations and libraries
unearthed the name of Linda Jorgenson, considered by

many to be the unofficial historian of the Chicago steel mills. Her family's been in the business for several generations, and she's collected all sorts of documents and records. When I got her on the phone, I asked if she knew anything about the Rosie the Riveter campaign.

"Oh, yes. That was quite a time for the steel industry."

"I've been doing some research, and one of the articles said that the campaign might have originated at the Iverson steel mill. Would you know anything about that?"

"Are you kidding? I'm surprised nobody told you. *Movietone News* came out from Hollywood to do a story about the women at Iverson's. It helped launch the Rosie campaign."

"Really. When was that?"

"Let me think. My father saw it. It would have been early forty-two, I think."

I straightened up like a pointer who's picked up a scent. *"Movietone News."* I made a note. "That's owned by Fox."

"If you say so."

"I wonder if they have a copy of it." Cradling the phone on my ear, I surfed over to Fox Movietone News and jotted down their number. I'd call them later.

"You know, I have some other things from Iverson's you might want to take a look at." She explained that when Iverson's was sold, the new owners didn't feel it was necessary to keep all the old records and handed them over to Linda. She had boxes of files stored in a warehouse.

I said I'd keep them in mind. "I've gotta ask you. How did you get into all of this?"

"My family owns a small steelyard on the East Side. It used to be part of Republic."

"Republic was one of the big ones."

"It was huge. My grandfather, my father, and my uncles worked there. But it got hit hard in the sixties along with the others. My cousins and I pooled all our money and bought part of it for a song. We turned it into a wire and cable operation."

"When was this?"

"Late seventies," she said. "We had to downsize, retrofit, streamline. But it has a happy ending. We're finally turning a profit."

Marxists be warned. The means of production had passed from the owners to the workers. Capitalism works in mysterious ways. "That's a great story." I made a note. After the campaign video, who knew?

"You know, it was really a shame the way everything ended up," she said.

"What do you mean?"

"With Mr. Iverson," she said. "No one ever understood why he did it."

"Did what?"

She hesitated. "Why he killed himself, of course."

Silence swirled around me. "Paul Iverson committed suicide?"

"Yes." She coughed. "I'm sorry. I thought you knew."

"I thought he died from a heart attack."

"That was the public version. I guess the family didn't want it to get out. But everybody knew."

MY FATHER CALLED that night to remind me that tomorrow was *Shavuos*, and I was expected to say *Yiskor* for my mother. *Yiskor,* an extra service tacked onto the liturgy to memorialize those who have passed on, comes four times a year, always in conjunction with another holiday. That's one of the problems with being Jewish. There are so many holidays during the year that it's entirely possible to spend all your time preparing to observe them, observing them, then recovering from observing them. Some Jews do little else. I hang on to a few traditions. I won't bring ham in the house, I don't celebrate Christmas, and I won't eat bread during Passover. I call it Kosher Lite.

*   *   *

FOUAD'S PICKUP WAS in the driveway when I got back. He was pulling the lawnmower from the bed of the truck. He eyed my skirt, long-sleeved blouse, and good shoes. "You are busy?"

I shook my head. "I was at synagogue. It's *Shavuos*."

"Would you like me to come back another time?"

"Not at all. Just give me a minute."

"You would have been proud of me, Fouad," I said after changing into cutoffs and a T-shirt. "I was up in Lake Forest the other night, and I was able to tell the difference between shade and sun plants."

He smiled at me.

"There had to be at least an acre of impatiens and hostas in front of the house I was at."

"Really." He pushed the mower over toward the grass.

"It's the old Iverson estate. On the lake. I'm producing a campaign video for Marian Iverson. She's running for the Senate."

"Ahh." He walked back to his pickup and retrieved a thick pair of canvas gloves. "And what did you learn today? In synagogue?" he asked pulling the gloves over his hands, evidently unimpressed with my new client.

"Learn? I didn't learn anything."

"That's hard to believe. Yours is a heritage of learning. Every time you observe, you give yourself the opportunity to learn." He sounded a lot like the rabbi I just heard, imploring people like me to come to *shul* more often to reacquaint themselves with the joys of Judaism.

I hooked my hands over the belt loops of my cutoffs. "I don't know if I'd call it learning, but when I was a little girl I'd go to services with my parents. Whenever *Yiskor* came, the kids were shooed out of the sanctuary. You weren't allowed to stay unless one of your parents was dead. It was all very grown-up and secretive, and I remember wanting to spy. Find out what the mystery was." I looked down. "Now I'm supposed to be there, and I don't want to be."

"Because of your mother."

My throat was suddenly tight.

"Everyone is going to taste death." He said. "The Koran says death is part of the cycle of life. We all have our turn. Your *Yiskors,* perhaps in some way, they are preparing you for that time. Teaching you how to accept death. Your loved ones, as well as your own."

I dumped my hands in my pockets.

"There can be great solace with those of your own faith."

He bent over the lawnmower. "Now, Ellie . . ." He ripped the cord, and the motor roared to life. "You will learn how to mow the lawn."

TWENTY-ONE

RACHEL WAS SUPPOSED to spend the Memorial Day weekend with Barry, but he never called. I left a series of messages on his machine, but by Saturday morning, I gave up.

"He must have gone on an unexpected business trip, honey," I lied.

Rachel nodded bravely and said she understood, but her lower lip quivered. I busied myself with cleaning the kitchen, trying to suppress my concern. Barry was rarely out of touch for more than a week at a time, and he never missed a weekend with Rachel. Should I call? No. He was a responsible adult. Well, an adult.

I opened the back door and emptied the trash, mentally casting around for last-minute plans. The sun spilled down, coating everything with a seductive layer of warmth. The newly mowed grass smelled fresh, and the lilac blossoms were so fragrant we might have been in a tropical paradise, not a windswept prairie.

"I have an idea." I transferred some money to a fanny pack and motioned Rachel out to the garage. We wheeled out our bikes and pedaled up to the Botanic Gardens, sniffing all the way.

After parking the bikes, we wandered through the Japanese garden, admiring the bonsai sculptures that stand guard over the tranquil lagoon. Then we headed over to the English walled garden, where Rachel meandered through trellised walkways, checkerboard box elders, and primrose hedges, and I studied water lilies in the goldfish pool, pretending I had nothing more pressing to do than to read Jane Austen. But my thoughts weren't on the British landed gentry. I was wondering how I would make it through the summer without child support.

That night we picked up a pizza and a video. We watched the video in bed, but Rachel lost interest and fell asleep halfway through. I was nodding off myself when the trill of the phone startled me awake. I scrambled for it. Barry, probably. With another lame excuse.

"Is this Ellie Foreman?"

I didn't recognize the voice. "Yes?"

"This is David Linden."

"Yes?" I rolled over. The clock read eleven-thirty. Was Barry hurt?

"I believe you sent me an E-mail a week ago."

A breeze bowed out the blinds. It smelled earthy and wet. "You're DGL," I breathed.

"I hope this isn't too late to call. I . . . I've been out of the country."

Sure. I always get calls from strangers at midnight on Saturday night. "It's okay."

A long silence followed, which I realized I was supposed to fill.

"Thank you for getting back to me. You're . . . you're probably wondering what this is all about."

"Yes."

"It's an unusual story."

Silence.

I swung out of bed and took the phone into my office. The locust tree, bathed in weak moonlight, threw spidery shadows through the window. "It started about a month ago." I took him through the letter from Ruth. How it turned out my father knew BenS. The scrap of paper from the library books. How I'd found the post about Lisle. I left out the part about the break-in. When I finished, there was more silence.

Then, "You keep calling him BenS. I understand that

was his E-mail moniker, but what was his real name?"

I didn't say anything.

"Ms. Foreman, I can't start to make any sense of this if I don't know his name."

A cloud moved across the moon, dimming the outline of the tree. I cradled the phone between my neck and shoulder. Why was I protecting Skull? He was dead. "His name was Skulnick. Ben Skulnick. But he called himself Ben Sinclair, at least for the last few years."

"Skulnick? That doesn't sound familiar. I don't think I have any relatives by that name."

"What about Sinclair?"

"I'm sorry. I wish I could help you." He sounded as if he was winding down, preparing to hang up.

"You can." I swiveled the chair so I faced the window. "Ben Skulnick was trying to locate Lisle Gottlieb. You know who she is, don't you?"

"But I don't know you, Ms. Foreman. And I'm not in the habit of releasing information to strangers. Especially ones who track me down by hacking into other people's E-mail."

I winced, thinking about Boo Boo. "Mr. Linden, I didn't hack into Ben's E-mail. It's true we don't know each other, and maybe I was wrong to contact you the way that I did. But I wasn't motivated by any desire to pry. I'm trying to find a connection between this man and Lisle Gottlieb." Again I skipped over the break-in. "I was also thinking about my father," I added.

"Your father?"

"Yes."

"Why? What does your father have to do with this?"

"He knew Lisle Gottlieb."

"Your father knew her?"

"Yes. I said that in my E-mail, didn't I?"

"Who is your father?"

"Jake. Jake Foreman."

"Your father is Jake Foreman?"

"Do you . . . have you heard that name before?"

The cloud moved away from the moon. The bark of
the locust shimmered like a white birch.

"My mother said . . . she said he was her only friend in
Chicago."

"Your mother was Lisle Gottlieb."

"Yes." For a heart-stopping moment, everything was
still.

"And she mentioned my father to you."

"Yes."

I swiveled in the chair. "So you know they were . . . I
mean . . . you know she lived in a boardinghouse for a
time."

"In Lawndale."

"The Teitelman's place."

"Right."

But this man's name was David Linden. Not Weiss.
"Your father . . . he wasn't—"

"My stepfather, Joseph Linden, adopted me. My father
died before I was born."

"Your father was Kurt Weiss."

His voice registered surprise. "How did you know?"

"My father told me. But he lost touch with your mother
after she . . . left Chicago. Where did she go?"

"She moved to Philadelphia."

Philadelphia. All I knew about the place was hoagies,
cheese steaks, and soft pretzels. And that W. C. Fields
considered it marginally preferable to death.

A sound issued from the other end. It could have been
a chuckle. "I take it you're not impressed."

"I've never been there. Do you live there now?"

A new silence pressed down on my skin. Had I over-
stepped some tacit boundary, asked one too many questions? I blew out my breath, fanning the hair on my
forehead.

"Mr. Linden, I'm not sure why Skull was—"

"Skull?"

"I'm sorry. Mr. Skulnick was sometimes called Skull
by his friends."

"I see."

I probably had about five seconds until he hung up. "Mr. Linden, Ben wanted to reach your mother. Do you have any idea why?"

"No. It's moot, anyway. She died a long time ago."

"I'm sorry." Shit. Now he would hang up. Do not pass go. Do not collect two hundred dollars.

Another pause. Then, "Ms. Foreman, I have no idea how you think I can help you." Here it comes. "But you may be able to help me."

I realized my mouth was open. I closed it. "Me? Help you?"

He cleared his throat. "You've realized, no doubt, that I am interested in tracing my family roots."

"Yes."

"As it happens, I'll be in Chicago next week on business. If your father really is the same Jake Foreman who knew my mother, I'd like to meet him."

"You want to talk to my father?"

"Very much." For the first time during the call, his voice seemed vulnerable, stripped of all artifice.

Butterflies dive-bombed my stomach. "I'll ask him. I don't think he'd mind."

"Good. I'll call you back in a day or two."

"I could E-mail you."

"I'll call," he said firmly.

Disconnecting, I almost skipped back to the bedroom. My efforts had paid off. Of course, there was the small problem that David Linden didn't recognize Skull's name. But there had to be a connection between his mother and Ben Skulnick. I was confident I'd find it.

As I undressed, it occurred to me that David Linden didn't know the exact nature of his mother's relationship with my father. Lisle considered Dad a friend, he'd said. I recalled Dad telling me how Lisle, pregnant and alone, came to see him after Kurt died. How she begged my father to take care of her. David Linden should only know how close he came to having Jake Foreman as his step-father. Some friend.

I WAS NEARLY asleep when the drum of rain against the window roused me. I got up and turned on the light. Rivulets of water dribbled down the glass and pooled on the sill. I closed the window, glancing out as I did. A car was inching down the street. I couldn't make out the model or color, but I thought I saw two people in the front.

When it slowed in front of my house, I lunged for the phone and tore it off the base. As I started to punch in nine and then one, I heard a car door close, its slam muffled by the rain. I dropped the phone and raised the shade high, flooding part of the lawn with light. The car pulled away, leaving a silvery spray of rain in its wake. My neighbors' spotlights threw a wash of light over the car as it passed; it was a tan, four-door sedan.

I forced myself to take deep breaths until the swishing sound of tires on wet pavement faded. I put the phone back on the base, instinctively knowing the police couldn't help me. Whoever was out there would make sure of it.

I crept downstairs, blood pulsing in my ears, and made sure the doors were locked. I went into the kitchen and grabbed the biggest knife I could find. When I got back upstairs, I stowed the knife under my bed and checked on Rachel. She was sleeping peacefully. Someone should.

TWENTY-TWO

MAC PICKED ME up on Friday, in the darkest, stillest part of the night when the hum of the insects had stopped, but the twitter of birds hadn't begun. We were heading out to shoot some B-roll before meeting Marian Iverson a few hours later. Mac had a friend with thirty acres of farmland near Harvard, Illinois, and we wanted to get a beauty shot of dawn breaking over the prairie.

Mac had dispensed with seats, stereo speakers, and cup holders in his oversized Ford Expedition. Filled with large metallic cases and not much else, the van reminded me of a stripped-down transport plane. I squeezed in beside camera cases and the sound man. Mac's cameraman handed me a cup of coffee.

"Bless you, my child." I took the paper cup from him. He crossed himself and folded his hands.

Once off the highway, we cruised down a rural road. The van's headlights swept across an occasional farm, barn, and roadside store, but the landscape was mostly fields of young corn and soybeans, which, in the darkness, seemed to extend forever, a series of expanding universes with infinite horizons. I kept turning around, half expecting to see a tan car behind us, but there was nothing but empty road. As we turned off at a dirt road bisecting a cornfield, the sky lightened from black to charcoal. A bird began a feeble chirp.

Mac and his crew unloaded the cases from the van. I

gathered up empty coffee cups and stowed them in a plastic bag.

"I hate to admit this." I wiped my hands on my pants. "But I'm not sure which way is east."

Mac didn't answer me.

"Mac?"

He finished bolting the camera to the tripod, then turned around in a wide circle. He faced me and flipped up his palms.

"You're kidding." I'd thought about bringing a compass but decided that would be too heavy-handed. A producer has to trust her crew. Damn. I should have listened to my gut. I started walking toward the van.

"Gotcha." Mac chortled.

I spun around. He dug out a compass from his jeans pocket.

"Don't do that again." I sagged against a fencepost.

"Oh ye of little faith." He handed me the compass. "Here. You're in charge of the sun. Make sure it comes up right—" he pointed across the cornfield—"over there."

I looked. Two trees of different heights framed an open space in the distance, their ebony branches etched against the horizon. There was an exotic, almost African feel to the shot. Ankle-high stalks of corn ran diagonally across the foreground. The symmetry in the shot was conscious but not extreme. "You scouted this ahead of time, didn't you?"

"Maybe." He shrugged.

He must have made a special trip just to find the right shot. "It's perfect."

He smiled. "And, before you ask, I *am* using a neutral density filter. Either a six or a nine."

The sound man told us to be quiet and began recording the birds and the stirrings of little creatures. A gentle breeze pushed through the grass. The sky brightened, and fingers of purple clouds above the trees became tinged with crimson. The chill in the air melted away, leaving wisps of mist that clung to the cornstalks. We camped on the dirt road and waited.

A few minutes later, a smudge of red broke through the horizon. Mac turned on the camera. Gold replaced the crimson-edged clouds, and the trees changed from pen-and-ink sketches to color. The sun crested the trees. We applauded.

An hour later, fortified with more coffee and donuts, we drove into town. A town of about six thousand, Harvard was a center for dairy farming in years past, especially during World War Two. Though the farming population dwindled after the war, a Motorola plant helped stem the community's decline, and every June, Harvard commemorates its past in a four-day festival called Milk Days.

We set up in the center of town, where instead of some obscure military figure, a statue of a Holstein named Harmilda graces a plaza. A small crowd had gathered, and Marian, impeccable in a navy and white St. John dress, cut a long white ribbon with a pair of giant shears. The crowd cheered, and a sea of balloons floated skyward. I tapped Mac on the shoulder. He panned up for a shot.

After the ceremony, during which Marian delivered the requisite platitudes in precise eight-second sound bites, she started working the crowd. We followed with the camera. At one point, she bent down to a little girl in shorts and a cropped shirt and clasped both of her hands around the little girl's. The girl smiled up adoringly. I turned around to Mac. He gave me a thumbs-up.

People were in high spirits: For farmers, it was the launch of a new season; for factory workers, a day off. Kids, happy to be out of school, jostled each other exuberantly. Marian was in her element, too, seeming to fuel herself with the energy of the crowd. Success must be rejuvenating.

*   *   *

WE TOOK A lunch break at the local McDonald's. The contrived cheerfulness of the place, with its splashes of yellow, red, and brown plastic, was a welcome break from the wholesomeness of Milk Days. Grabbing a booth, I massaged my jaw, sore from too many smiles, and unwrapped my Big Mac. Mac sat down with a salad and diet Coke.

I eyeballed his tray. "What's wrong with this picture?"

"I have to keep my girlish figure."

I stuffed fries into my mouth. "How much have we shot?"

"Including the beauty shot, five cassettes." At thirty minutes per cassette, that was over two hours of raw footage.

"I know tomorrow's Saturday, but do you think I can get window dubs?"

He dipped his hand into my fries. "You'll pay for it."

"What do you mean?"

"Buy me a shake. In honor of Milk Days."

I went up to the counter and ordered a chocolate shake, although it was doubtful anything in the chemical soup they gave me was real milk. Then I called to check on Rachel. School had ended two days ago, and she'd spent the night over at Genna's. She and Katie were now at the pool. When I got back to the table, the milkshake container was empty. So was my bag of fries, and Mac was nodding at a bearded guy in a safari shirt with a camera slung over his shoulder.

"So Customs stops the car and opens it up. Man, there had to be over thirty of 'em packed into this Ford Expedition. A new one, too. Just like yours. Uncles, aunts, cousins, kids, all of them desperate to get across the border."

"What happened?" Mac asked.

"They sent 'em all back to Mexico. I mean, that's what they were supposed to do, right? Can't contaminate our soil with illegals. Gave 'em a couple of bucks and put 'em back on the bus to *Cartagena*," he said.

But that's in Colombia, I thought.

"What about the van?" Mac asked.

"Bingo." The man pointed his index finger at Mac. "That's the real story, my friend. Customs kept it. Just appropriated it, said it belonged to the government of the United States. The Mexicans couldn't do a damn thing about it."

"No shit," Mac said.

"For all I know, it was ours to begin with. The wetbacks coulda ripped it off themselves." He shook his head. "Someone's probably running dope into Texas with it right now."

"I don't believe it," Mac said.

The man opened his palm. "Man. I swear to you. I saw it with my own eyes. Got the pictures to prove it." He tapped his camera.

Mac turned, saw me coming, and yanked his thumb in my direction. "Here she is. Talk to her."

The beard twisted around. "Hi. I'm Stephen Lamont. I'm with the *Trib*."

I guessed I was supposed to be impressed. We shook hands. "You're the one who's covering Marian."

"And you're the one who did the piece on Chicago neighborhoods." He looked me up and down. "Now you're doing a campaign video?"

I stiffened, resenting the implication behind the word *now*. As if I'd sunk to the level of a seedy huckster. "A Macababy's gotta do what a Macababy's gotta do." I shrugged. It was the signature statement from one of the kids' shows Rachel watched. Mac laughed. Lamont frowned; he obviously didn't have kids.

He spread his hands. "Sorry."

Sure you are. "So what can I do for you?"

"I was hoping you and I might be able to collaborate."

"On what?"

"My series. I'm covering Marian's campaign for the *Trib*. This could be an interesting sidebar."

My brow wrinkled. "The video?"

"It's a powerful tool. Part of the marketing arsenal. I'd like to explore how it's conceived. What your expectations are. You know." He grinned. "It could be a winner."

I emptied my tray in the trash bin. I wasn't anxious for any publicity. I didn't want the world to know I was working for a political candidate. And I resented journalists who felt entitled to insinuate themselves into the inner workings of peoples' lives just because they were the Fourth Estate. "You must be hard up if you think a campaign video is gonna make a good sidebar."

Lamont aimed a finger at me. "Bingo. There's slim pickins' out here."

"How come?"

"The lady's gonna win by a landslide. Everybody loves her. There's no contest. And we still have four months to go."

He didn't seem like the type to let a dull assignment stand in his way. "I'm sure you'll come up with something."

"Hey. I'm scratching the bottom of the barrel," he said. "Not your video, of course." His ears turned scarlet.

"No, of course not."

"Well, think about it." He fished out some keys from a shirt pocket. "Are you gonna do the fly-around with her over the Fourth?"

I nodded.

"Me, too." He looked up and down again as he pushed through the door. "We'll talk then. Ciao."

I wiggled my fingers at him. He waved his keys. I turned around. Mac was smirking. "What?"

"Getting pretty fine and fancy, aren't we? With reporters covering you and all? You'll be setting up your own digs in River North soon."

I shot him a look.

He shrugged. "Just kidding."

"We're doing a piece of fluff. Now he wants to do a

piece of fluff on our piece of fluff." I shoved my hands in my pocket.

Mac laughed. "He's gotta eat, too."

"Eat . . . or cannibalize?"

He pointed a finger at me. "Bingo."

TWENTY-THREE

"YOUR FATHER WAS very progressive," I said to Marian at the Clocktower Hotel in Rockford. "For a businessman of his time."

Marian was ensconced in one of the hotel's suites so she could repeat her Milk Days performance the next day. The sitting room included a pea-green sofa bed in a nubby worsted, two chairs in a flowery fabric, and chartreuse wall-to-wall carpeting. A bowl of fruit rested on the coffee table. Luxury by Rockford standards. Roger drifted in and out, Palm Pilot in hand, cell phone pressed to his ear. Very B-ship.

"We try to keep that a secret." She laughed. "It's not very Republican." She slipped off her shoes and leaned back on the couch. "God. That feels good." She rolled her ankles. "Talk about instruments of torture."

As she stretched her feet, I studied her. She had to be well in her sixties, but she cut a slender figure, with well-curved legs and ankles. Her honey blond hair was carefully streaked, and her patrician nose reminded me of the photos I'd seen of her father. She wasn't a beautiful woman, but she'd capitalized on her best features and was the type I'd call handsome. Her eyes were her most interesting feature: clear, dead-on pools of gray that flashed warm or cool at whim.

She looked at me now with a pleasant, slightly anxious expression. "It went well today, don't you think?"

"They ate you up," Roger called from the doorway.

She smiled. "But how many of them can we count on in November? Farmers are so ornery."

"Not to worry. This is Iverson country, ma'am," Roger deadpanned.

"Compared to what?"

"The inner city, for one."

"I thought we were making progress there."

"We are." Roger angled his head toward me. "We're riding the contract issue hard."

"The contract issue?" I asked.

"Over two billion in city bond issues and contracts were let out to minority businesses," he said. "But there were a few . . . snags . . . with the concept. You remember when that city contract was awarded to a female-owned firm, and it turned out to be a front for white men?"

I nodded. "The mayor was pretty embarrassed."

"Well, we want to make sure no one forgets."

"But that was city business, not state," I said.

"That's the beauty of it." Roger smiled. "It doesn't matter. It wasn't on our watch. They're Democrats."

"I thought the mayor was a friend."

"It's an election," he said cheerfully.

Marian lifted her shoulders in an apologetic shrug.

I looked at my notes. "I have a question."

"By all means."

"Okay." I leaned forward. "You came out pro-choice. You're attacking the mayor for not following through on minority contracts. And I understand you're going to appear at a Labor Day rally in the fall. None of that sounds very . . . very Republican. I'm confused."

Marian helped herself to a cluster of grapes, then tipped the bowl in my direction. I bit into a peach. "You're clearly a bright woman, Ellie." She settled back in her chair. "But you don't follow politics, do you?"

I shook my head.

She smiled. "That's one of the reasons I hired you. I didn't want someone too close to the process, either." I was impressed she remembered.

"The political situation in this country today is far more complex than labels suggest. Constituencies we used to count on don't support us anymore. Others, whom we have traditionally neglected, do." She plucked a grape off its stem.

"Take labor, for example. There are many socially conservative blue-collar workers today. Men and women who want to protect their futures by cutting down on imports and immigrants. They hate the Democrats for supporting free trade with China. They'd vote for Pat Buchanan in a heartbeat if they could. We want them under our tent."

I thought about it. "I can understand that. But what about coming out pro-choice? Don't you risk alienating a significant wing of your own party?"

Roger broke in. "Women go to the polls in higher numbers than men. They're a critical swing vote."

"Roger and I disagree about the women issue," she said, cutting him off. "Don't get me wrong. I do feel women should have control over their own bodies. But I don't expect them to vote for me just because we share the same plumbing. I want women to vote for me because they share my vision."

"Your vision?"

"How we're going to solve the problems they care about. Schools. Social security. Health insurance."

"You sound like a Democrat."

She set the grapes down on a napkin and folded her hands in her lap. "I strongly disagree, my dear. We may discuss the same issues, but our solutions are quite different."

Roger pounced. "Ellie, that's enough. Marian needs to rest."

She waved him off. Roger's cell phone chirped. He went out to the hall to answer it.

"So what is your vision?" I dug out a notebook from my bag.

She was silent a moment, her eyes clouding in concentration. "I believe that the real problem in our society is the loss of boundaries," she said slowly. "People don't know what to think, what to do, what to expect. Life has become too frightening, too complicated, too conflicted. Opportunities that used to be there are gone. Terrorists destroy our landmarks. Interest groups compete with each other . . . on a truly global basis now. Politics, in its own way, is reflecting this breakdown. That's why one sees such confusion over labels."

I scribbled furiously. "What's your solution?"

"I don't have all the answers. But I do believe people need strong leadership. Someone to help them find answers. Provide clear direction. I don't give a damn what color, gender, or nationality they are; everyone needs guidance. The most successful civilizations, the Greeks, the Romans, even the Jews, are ones whose leaders had the courage and authority to lift their people out of chaos, to steer them to a higher order. I'd like the chance to provide that leadership. If not me, then someone else. But it must be done. Civilization is dangling on the precipice."

I stopped writing. Her back was straight, and her eyes, now sharp and clear, were glued to mine. I saw ambition and determination in them. But there was something else in them, too, though it took me a moment to figure it out. It was conviction. And it was absolute. Marian Iverson couldn't possibly be wrong.

Her face softened, and the spell broke. She leaned back. I closed my notebook. Roger came back in the room, his cell plugged into his ear.

"Can we talk about the video for a minute?" I asked. "Please."

"I'd like to mention your father at the beginning of your bio sequence. To set the stage. In his own way, he was a pioneer, ahead of his time. Not unlike you."

Marian twisted. "What do you think, Roger?"

Roger removed the phone from his ear. "About what?"

"I may have a lead on some stock footage of Iverson's.

A riveter during the war. I'd like to use it in the video, if it turns out to be decent."

Roger frowned. "The video is supposed to be about Marian, not her father."

"I understand. But his experiences reflect the influence and traditions she grew up with." I shifted toward Marian. "And the fact that he allowed the union to organize, which of course we'll mention, couldn't hurt."

"That might be a desirable," Roger admitted, as if concepts could be bought and displayed like furniture.

Marian broke in. "There's actually film of my father?"

"I'm not sure, but it's possible."

I explained how I'd called Movietone Newsreel. "They claimed to have footage of Rosie the Riveter, shot in Chicago in the early forties, so I ordered it."

"How fascinating," she said. "I'd love to see it."

"I'll let you know when it comes in," I said. "Your father passed away at the end of the war, didn't he?"

"Yes." She rose and moved to a sliding door that opened onto a tiny balcony. A pigeon strutted across the railing. "A heart attack."

"A heart attack?" Linda Jorgenson said Paul Iverson committed suicide. Marian opened the door and stepped onto the balcony. I followed her out. Was it possible she didn't know? Maybe her mother had shielded her from the truth. She would have been quite young at the time, perhaps too young to understand. Or maybe Linda Jorgenson got it wrong.

A loud voice came from the hall. It sounded like Roger. Marian didn't seem to notice.

"Marian, one of the articles I read mentioned two Iverson children. Do you have a sibling?"

She gazed over the railing at the parking lot below, so still I wasn't sure she'd heard me. The pigeon flapped its wings and lifted off. I was about to repeat the question when she spoke in a low voice. "I had a brother." She turned around. "Gordon. He died at a young age. Before

I went into the mill. I was living in New York." The lines on her face deepened, and for the first time since I'd met her, she looked old.

"You lived in New York?"

"For a while during the fifties."

"I see. So there were just the two of you?" She nodded. She'd known a lot of pain, I realized, first losing her father, then her brother. All the men in her life. "Is that why you never married?"

The door to the suite opened, and Roger stomped in. Behind him in the hall, Dory Sanchez stood, her eyes swimming with anger. Roger slammed the door in her face.

Marian's eyebrows shot up, as if she was waiting for an explanation.

Roger slumped on the couch, his face a mask of studied indifference. His knee jerked up and down.

Marian turned back to me. "After Gordon died, I went to work for the mill. Then, after we sold it, I traveled. I suppose . . . I suppose I just never got around to marriage." Her eyes flicked to Roger. "Judging from the problems one sees in relationships these days, perhaps that wasn't such a bad thing." The hint of a smile played on her lips.

I met her smile with my own. "One other thing. We're going to need pictures of you as a young girl. Where I can find some?"

Her smile faded, and her mouth tightened. She stepped back in the hotel room. "Mother probably has some."

"May I call her for them?" I followed her back in.

She shrugged.

"I'd like to interview her for the video, anyway."

A harsh sound came out of her throat. "Good luck. Mother hates publicity."

"Maybe you can convince her."

"Mother? I can't convince her of anything. I don't mean to sound cruel," she added hastily. "My parents were—

are wonderful people. But they grew up in different times. Their values were tempered by depression and war. We need new approaches today. We don't always see eye to eye."

I could relate to that. I nodded.

"Yes." The sparkle came back into her eyes. "I knew you'd understand. But perhaps we should ask Roger." She looked over. "What do you think? Should we interview mother for the video?"

"Actually, I think it's a good idea," he said. "It helps build continuity. Between the past and the present. Couldn't hurt the senior vote, either."

"Really." She fingered the necklace at her throat, a thick gold chain. "Well, if you both agree, I suppose I'll have to persuade Mother."

I looked at Roger and mouthed the word *Thanks*.

Marian caught the interaction between us. "I am glad you're working with us, Ellie."

I felt a flush creep up my neck. "I'd like to tape your interview next week. At the studio so we have maximum control over the location."

She nodded.

"I won't take up any more of your time today." I held out my hand. "Thank you."

"I've enjoyed it."

Roger got up and walked me to the door, casually draping his arm on my shoulders. It felt like a steel band.

"How about dinner?" he asked, opening the door.

I looked pointedly at the ring on his finger.

"There are some things about the video I'd like to discuss," he said, clearing his throat.

"Sorry. I have plans."

"Okay. Another time."

The door closed behind me, and I headed toward the elevator. Dory Sanchez, her head down, arms folded, was pacing the hall.

"Dory," I called out. "Is everything okay?"

She waved me away without looking up.

"Dory?" She looked up then, and the misery on her face cut through me like a knife. I took the stairs.

TWENTY-FOUR

TIME ALWAYS SLOWS down in summer, as if the heat stretches minutes into hours and hours into days. It was past seven, but the sun was still hot, and cries of children filled the air. I met Rachel at the pool. I was tired, but it was a good fatigue, the kind you get when you've accomplished something. We swam a few laps and played Marco Polo until the lifeguard kicked us out. By the time we got home and finished eating, it was nearly ten. I peeled off my clothes and opened the windows. A breeze fluttered through the shades.

I turned on the news, hoping to compare the media's footage of Milk Days with ours. The anchor was in the middle of a report about three white supremacists who had been arrested by the FBI in Minneapolis for planning to explode a bomb at a federal building. One of the men arrested was a GS Fifteen who conspired with the militants from the inside, turning over blueprints of the building as well as peak traffic schedules.

As if to apologize for devoting so much airtime to a racist plot, the next story featured a young, pretty blond breathlessly summarizing a press conference called by LABOR, Latinos for a Better Order. According to Raoul Iglesias, LABOR's leader, Latinos would soon be the largest minority in the United States but were stuck on the lowest rung of the employment ladder.

"We are being starved out of the economic system," Iglesias said. "Many of us do not even get minimum wage. Of the twenty-five hundred minority companies that do business with the city, Latino firms have less than three percent of the contracts. We want our fair share." To focus attention to these issues, LABOR was asking Latinos to demonstrate at the rally planned for Labor Day at Daley Plaza.

The report cut to a sound bite of the mayor, who proclaimed in mangled speech that his goal was to give everyone a fair shake. "I come from a blue-collar family myself, and I know how important it is to have a rock-solid job. This administration will not exclude any deserving family from their share of the American dream."

This was a real Chicago story. Ethnic. Blue-collar. Political. Stephen Lamont must be eating his heart out.

Finally, the broadcast segued to twenty seconds of Milk Days. A close-up of the cow, a cutaway of the crowd, a short sound bite of Marian. Your typical quick and dirty TV fare. Our footage was better. I was spooning vanilla ice cream into a dish as a reward when the telephone rang.

"This is David Linden."

Dressed in T-shirt and panties, I looked for something to cover myself with. "Uh . . . hello."

There was a pause. Could he sense my disorientation? Then, "I'm sorry I didn't call sooner, but I was out of the country."

I rummaged in the broom closet and grabbed a dirty sweatshirt. "You travel quite a bit."

"Yes." Silence.

I wrapped the sweatshirt around my shoulders. "I've been busy, too."

"Oh." More silence. "I wondered whether you and your father still wanted to meet."

"Of course. When did you have in mind?" I should run up for my day book; it was in my office.

"How's tomorrow?"

"Tomorrow? Are you—"

"I flew in today for a conference."

"A conference?" The lights of a passing car winked in

the night, streaming ribbons of red in their wake. I pulled the arms of the sweatshirt more snugly around me. "On what?"

"The regulatory and tax implications of foreign currency exchange in the new millennium."

"Oh."

"I'm the head of foreign currency trading for the Franklin National Bank," he said impatiently.

Currency trading, day trading; they both seemed vaguely sinister.

"Ms. Foreman—"

"How about two o'clock?" I said. "Where are you staying?"

"The Ritz-Carlton."

SUNDAY MORNING I slipped into my good pair of white linen slacks and a black silk shirt. I hadn't worn the pants since last season, and now, of course, they refused to zip. Sighing, I changed into a dark blue pants suit. I looked like a linebacker for the Bears. I switched to a red dress with white polka dots. Now I was Little Red Riding Hood on speed. I changed back into the black shirt and white slacks and sucked everything in. If I sat down slowly, I might avoid splitting a seam. I put on makeup, pulled my hair back in a clip, and hooked my sunglasses down the front of my shirt.

A hot, hazy day, it was two-thirty by the time I found a parking space. As I hurried past Water Tower to The Ritz-Carlton, perspiration beaded my forehead. A blast of icy air hit me as I pushed through the door. Downtown Chicago is rife with luxury hotels, but The Ritz was one of the first and has managed to maintain its cachet. I rode the elevator to the twelfth-floor lobby and padded across a Persian carpet. The house phone was in a semiprivate booth near a large oil painting with a gilt frame. I sat down—slowly—on a white satin bench and picked up the receiver. He answered on the second ring.

"It's Ellie Foreman. Sorry I'm late."

"I'll be right down."

Getting up, I tugged at my shirt and strolled past a whispering fountain to a large dining room with an intricately designed marble floor. Potted palms peeked around trellises, and a live tree framed a picture-window view of the street. Though lunch was technically over, a busboy hefted a tray of silver-domed dishes to a station where a waiter stood at attention. The waiter presented the dishes to a blond couple and their three towheaded children, all of them in crisp summer whites. Jay Gatsby and Daisy Buchanan and their kids, if things had worked out differently. I wondered if David Linden had brought his wife and kids along. I pictured a sweet, demure wife. Cute, well-behaved kids.

The waiter set one of the domed plates in front of the little girl, but she elbowed him away, preferring to walk her Barbie along the edge of the table. Her mother leaned over and whispered to her, but the little girl sulked and shook her head. The mother repeated her request. The little girl issued a loud, whiny "No."

Then one of the boys threw a buttered roll at his sister, which hit her in her chest. The girl's scream was so shrill that everyone in the dining room momentarily froze, like those old E. F. Hutton commercials. When it became clear that the little girl wasn't hurt, movement cranked up again. The father scolded his son, the mother berated the father, and the little girl, fingering the grease spot left by the butter, burst into tears.

On second thought, I decided, if David Linden could afford to stay at The Ritz, maybe his children weren't so well-behaved. Maybe they were as spoiled as these brats. One of them might even be a future ax murderer. It was a comforting thought.

"Ellie?"

I spun around. In front of me was a man in a white polo shirt, navy slacks, and cordovan loafers. His broad shoulders and sculpted biceps said he worked out regularly. He had large cornflower eyes framed with tiny lines and a thin, aristocratic nose that gave him a slightly haughty expression. He had to be over fifty, but he looked much younger, partly because of the pair of Revo sunglasses pushed up on his crown, and partly because of a thick shock of prematurely white hair.

CANNED MUZAK SPILLED from speakers, cutlery clinked on china, but I couldn't speak. Except for his coloring and something around the mouth, the man in front of me was Paul Iverson's double.

His face, open and eager an instant ago, grew suddenly wary. "You are Ellie Foreman, aren't you?"

I shoved my hands in my pockets. Then I pulled one out and extended it. "I'm sorry. You . . . you took me by surprise."

A question crept across his face, but he apparently chose not to ask it. His handshake was firm; the feel of it resonated on mine.

"Shall we go in?" He motioned to the dining room.

"If you like."

He strode to the dining room. I trotted behind, my brain racing to complete its circuits. Lisle was his mother. Kurt was his father. Why did he look exactly like Paul Iverson?

When he reached the three marble steps that separated the dining room from the lobby, he turned as if he'd just remembered I was there. As he ushered me down the steps, his hand lightly brushed my back. It felt good.

The maître d' seated us at a small table away from the Gatsbys, who were now bickering like any other dysfunctional family.

"Have you eaten?" He opened a red leather menu embossed with gold letters.

"I . . . well, no, but I . . ."

He looked at me speculatively. "Well, I'm going to order a sandwich."

He closed the menu, and a waiter promptly appeared.

There must be a secret signal that sophisticated diners use to get a waiter's attention. I wish I knew it. David ordered chicken salad on toast and iced tea. I asked for a glass of wine. The waiter sniffed.

David unfolded his napkin and put it in his lap. I played with my knife, noticing the smooth blond hair on his forearms and how it grew in one direction. "You have your mother's coloring."

He looked puzzled. "You know what she looked like?"

"My father has an old snapshot of her with him and Barney Teitelman."

"Oh."

The drinks came. I took a sip of wine.

"Is he meeting us here?"

"Who?"

"Your father."

I winced. There was a slight problem with that. It hadn't gone so well when I told him about David.

"Are you *meshuga*?" he'd exclaimed. "You gave your number to a total stranger?"

"He isn't a total stranger," I said. "He's Lisle Gottlieb's son."

"That's what he says," Dad said and launched into an extended diatribe about my naïveté and propensity to accept people at face value. This man could be anyone, posing as Lisle's son. What did I know about him? How could I have given him my number and then, God forbid, agreed to meet him? Even the fact that David was staying at The Ritz didn't mollify him.

"Let me tell you something, Ellie. If I was looking to sucker you out of something, would I stay at some fleabag hotel? Of course, he'd be at The Ritz. You've got a lot to learn about human nature, sweetheart."

I let him rant, hoping he just needed time to get used to the idea, but he never called me back.

"Umm, Dad couldn't make it today," I said to David. "His . . . his arthritis is acting up. You know."

"Oh." A muscle in his jaw tightened.

"I'm sorry."

"No. It's all right." His nostrils flared, accentuating the air of haughtiness.

"So, you trade currency?"

"That's right."

"I see." I looked at him. "Have you always lived in Philadelphia?"

"Except when I travel."

"Which is often, I gather."

"Yes."

I picked up a spoon. "Where do you travel? When you travel, I mean?"

"Europe, mostly. Sometimes Tokyo."

"Have you been to Germany?"

"Yes."

"That's where your parents came from."

"Yes."

This was getting painful. I've never been very good at cocktail chatter. And I was desperately trying not to think how much he looked like Paul Iverson. Which was about as successful as trying not to think about a pink elephant.

The waiter brought his sandwich. David took neat, meticulous bites. Then he set the sandwich down on his plate and folded his hands in front of him. "What about you? What do you do?"

Finally. A question. He must have been embarrassed by the pathetic quality of our conversation. "I produce videos."

"Really?" An unexpectedly sweet smile lifted the corners of his mouth. "I've always wanted to direct a film."

Film. Not movie. He looked like he could afford a digital camera and all the gear. Even the editing software now on the market. "Why don't you? Everyone else does."

He shrugged.

"You can always experiment on your family."

He shook his head. "I don't want to do home movies," he said. "And I don't have a family."

No wife. No kids. No ax murderer.

"I don't do features," I said. "I make industrials. For corporate clients."

"But you know how."

Again a smile. Sunny. Open. Like the smile I'd seen on Dad's picture of Lisle. A twinge of pleasure shot through me. "Yes. I haven't always done corporate gigs. And one of these days . . . well . . . who knows?"

"The best memories I have of my childhood were at the movies. I worked in a theater during high school."

"No way. An usher?"

He nodded.

I closed one eye, trying to imagine him as a pimply red-jacketed geek. "Okay, what's your favorite film?"

He raised his palm. "Oh no. I'm not that dumb."

I grinned. "Top five then."

"Still tough." He looked past me, his sandwich forgotten. "Let's see." He held up his hand. "There's *High Noon. The Godfather.*" He ticked them off on his fingers. "*Citizen Kane. The Seven Samurai. . . . and . . . The Battle of Algiers.*" He spread his fingers, looking proud of himself.

I raised an eyebrow. "Impressive."

He picked up the last bite of sandwich and put it in his mouth.

"I'll give you three for five."

He stopped chewing, and his smiled faded. "What did I miss?"

"*Casablanca. Double Indemnity. Some Like It Hot.* Maybe *L.A. Confidential.*"

"Pretty Hollywood, aren't you?"

"Long live the studio system."

He leaned back and squinted. "You're not the type."

"Perceptive, too." I grinned. "I used to make documentaries. You know, getting back to our . . . I mean your family . . . I have a question. If you don't mind." He wiped his mouth with his napkin. "I told you about Skull—Mr. Skulnick—on the phone—"

"And I told you I didn't know him."

"I realize that. I was just thinking. I saw a snapshot of Skull, which was taken around the time of World War Two. He was standing next to a woman. She had dark hair, and there was a baby in her arms. I assumed the woman and the baby were his family. The picture was taken someplace in Europe."

He sipped his tea. "Where?"

"I don't know."

"Do you have it? The picture?"

"No. Unfortunately, it—no." I toyed with my spoon. "But they were standing on a bridge. A cobblestone bridge. And there was a castle in the background."

"That could be almost anywhere."

The Gatsbys passed our table, the children skipping carelessly, their parents arm-in-arm. All was forgiven.

"Maybe I've been looking at this backward."

He looked over.

"What if the connection to your mother was the woman in the picture, not Skull?"

"You mean the woman and my mother knew each other?"

"Exactly." I brightened. "Maybe they were close friends. And Skull knew it. Maybe he figured your mother could help him track her down. Did she ever talk about her friends in Europe?"

He shook his head. "She rarely talked about her life before the States. That's one of the reasons it's been so hard to find out anything about her. It's as if she built a wall between her life before and after the war."

I drew little circles on the tablecloth with the spoon. "I guess I'm grasping at straws." I sighed.

"My father was sent back to Germany during the war. But you already know that. He died over there, too, but I couldn't really say—"

I stopped drawing. "What did you say?"

"I said, my father was sent—"

"No. The other part."

"That he died over there, but that I—"

I laid the spoon down. "Kurt Weiss didn't die in Germany."

"Of course he did."

"No. Kurt Weiss died here. In Lawndale. At a concert in Douglas Park."

He tipped his head. "What are you talking about?"

"My father was there when it happened."

"That's impossible. My mother said he worked for the OSS. That he came home at the end of the war, but then, because so many Nazis were trying to escape to North and South America, they sent him back for one last mission."

"One last mission?"

"He was supposed to tail a high-ranking Nazi and keep him from slipping across the border. But it all went wrong. Someone double-crossed him, and my father was killed."

I shook my head. "That's not right."

He shifted. "Maybe you'd better tell me what you know."

I summarized what Dad told me. When I finished, he sat very still. I was beginning to think he didn't believe me. "I don't get it," he said, blinking rapidly. His voice was barely above a whisper. "If that's true, why did my mother lie to me?"

I didn't have an answer.

TWENTY-FIVE

I CONSTRUCTION SITE   EXTERIOR   DAY

Fade up from black to a sunbeam dancing on a steel girder. (May need special FX to make sunbeam dance.) Pull back to reveal a crane hoisting the steel girder into the air. Widen out as we see the girder float through the air to the skeletal scaffolding of a modern construction site. As the girder settles on the landing and men in hard hats rush to unhook it, bring up NARRATION.

NARRATOR

Dependable. Durable. Tough. Steel built this country, creating a tradition of strength. And though its form and structure have evolved, the tradition still endures.

Cut to stock footage of steel mill; smokestacks, iron forge, etc. circa 1930s.

NARRATOR (cont.)

Tradition.

Dissolve or morph to modern scene of steel girder.

And progress. The makings of a legacy. The
makings of a leader.

Bring MUSIC UNDER (quiet but authoritative).
Dissolve to scene of Marian Iverson shaking hands
with crowd at campaign event. FADE OUT MUSIC,
BRING UP Marian SOT.

IT NEEDED POLISHING, but I liked it. The legacy part
would appeal to older, male Republicans. But we would
also make it clear Marian had exceeded the past and was
poised to lead in the future. That would appeal to younger
voters and, hopefully, the new constituencies she wanted
to reach.

The squeak of a truck in need of a brake job broke my
concentration, and I watched as the familiar brown truck
stopped in front of the house. UPS doesn't come to my
door much except around the holidays, and usually later
in the day. The energetic driver—they're all impossibly
young, virile, and fit—jumped out of his seat, rummaged
in the back of the truck, and deposited a package at the
front door. Then he rang the bell, skipped back to his
vehicle, and pulled away, all in less than a minute. I was
exhausted.

The return label said Fox Movietone News Library. I
tore open the cardboard packaging. Inside was a video
cassette labeled *March 1942. Slug: Rosie the Riveter.* I
headed toward the VCR, anticipating the thrill of witnessing history as it actually happened, with none of the
shadings or interpretations of time. But as I flipped on the
power, the green luminescent numbers of the clock
flashed one-thirty. Damn. I was late for Marian's interview. I threw the cassette into my bag.

THE SET WAS a two-walled office, minus the desk. On
one wall a fake window covered by curtains cleverly con-

cealed fill lights. Tall, leafy plants were carefully arranged in front, their shadows subtle and flattering. Against the other wall was an oxblood leather sofa, the kind you'd find in a corporate executive's office. But the focal point of the set was an abstract painting done in pastels hanging above the couch. It formed the perfect background, particularly in a close-up. Marian would stand out: the polished, elegant challenger, with just a touch of femininity. I'd asked her to wear a navy jacket. The pastel pallete, combined with the oxblood sofa and her suit, would balance the shot. Tradition but progress.

When I arrived, Marian was in the dressing room, a plastic sheet draped over her, having makeup applied. Roger was pacing the studio, his cell glued to his ear. The three-man crew was tweaking lights and equipment, all of them on headphones that linked them to Mac in the control room.

I sat down on a chair opposite the couch. Although I wouldn't be on camera, one of the crew pinned a mike on me. "Mike check," he said.

I cleared my throat. "Hi Mommy, hi Daddy. I'd like a pony, an ice cream machine, a clown, and . . . an amusement park in my basement."

"That'll do," he said.

"Funny, that's what they said, too."

He started to smirk but then looked behind me.

I twisted around. Marian was headed toward the set, elegant and sophisticated in a navy Chanel suit. Her makeup sparkled and her hair, in a chin-length bob, was perfectly coiffed. A flurry of activity ensued as the crew seated her, pinned a lapel mike onto her jacket, checked her voice level, and tinkered with the lights one more time.

Finally we rolled tape. I'd E-mailed the list of questions to Roger over the weekend, and Marian was clearly prepared. Her responses were articulate, but she managed to pause for just a fraction of a beat before she answered, so she didn't sound rehearsed. Occasionally, after delivering a key message, she transitioned to a brief anecdote. She was witty, too, beginning a discussion of the gender issue with, "When God created human beings, she . . ." then pausing with the timing of George Burns.

When the interview was over, a crew member removed her microphone, "How did I do?" she asked.

"You were perfect," I said. "Witty, articulate, the right balance of professionalism and warmth. It's going to be a tough editing job."

She rose from the couch with a satisfied smile.

Roger appeared at her elbow, and they started across the set. "So what happens from here?" he asked.

"I'll have a finished script to you in a day or two," I said. "With a paper edit of what's already in the can. We can work from that. Oh, by the way, that stock footage I mentioned last week came in. You remember, the Rosie the Riveter footage?"

Marian stopped, Roger nearly bumping her. "Is that the film that you thought might have been taken at the mill?"

"I don't know for sure. I haven't screened it yet."

"Be sure to let me know."

"As a matter of fact, I brought it along."

"Really?" She raised an eyebrow.

"Would you like to see it?"

Roger tapped a finger on his watch crystal. "Marian, you have a meeting with the Lake County Republicans in ten minutes."

"We can be late," she said.

Mac pulled two chairs into a corner and wheeled over a VCR and monitor on a metal stand. Marian sat down. "The date says March 1942," I said, showing her the cassette label. I fed the tape into the VCR and hit Play.

A slew of disclaimers and warnings assured unauthorized users of a spot on the Ten Most Wanted List if the footage was used without permission. Then the swell of a patriotic march broke over the sound track, and the screen faded from black to a grainy black-and-white montage. Soldiers marched in formation, flags fluttered in the breeze. A voice that sounded a lot like Walter Winchell declared that the week just past would prove to be the major turning point in the battle for freedom and democracy against the forces of evil.

According to the narrator, thousands of draftees now in training camps around the country would, in short order, prove to be the undoing of the Axis. We watched as soldiers aimed rifles at targets, squirmed under barbed wire, and scaled chain-link fences. The announcer exhorted us to remember that despite our grief at being separated from our loved ones, their leaders were proud of them. We should be, too.

Marian and I exchanged glances.

The music segued to a lighter tune, and the announcer proclaimed that on the home front, too, the war effort was quickly taking hold. Women in record numbers were filling the shoes of men, working in factories and mills.

The camera cut to a new scene, and we were looking at a sign that read Iverson Steel Works. Marian leaned forward, her elbows on the arms of her chair. A throng of men and women with cheerful smiles and greetings pushed through a turnstile. Some tipped their hard hats to the camera. Most carried lunch boxes and thermos bottles. In the background, ribbons of white steam curled out of tall, skinny smokestacks.

The newsreel cut to interiors of the plant. Machines belched, wheels revolved, belts moved. The camera dollied smoothly from one station to the next, showing the raw power of manufacturing, finally stopping in front of a woman in bib overalls. Although it was a long shot, I could see a face with chiseled features and a mass of blond hair arranged on top. The camera cut to a medium shot. My mouth dropped open.

"My God," I said. "I think that's Lisle Gottlieb."

Marian glanced at me. Then she looked back at the screen. The woman on the screen had the same eyes, the same mouth, the same face I'd seen in Dad's snapshot. But here, in motion, she filled the frame with youth and

eauty. Even in overalls, an aura of glamour surrounded
er. When she looked into the camera, her shy sensuality
t up the screen.

The camera pushed into a close-up of her work. She
vas operating some kind of riveting device, making sure
vets were punched into sheets of steel. It was hard to
ell what was actually being riveted: a truck door, a tank,
ossibly the side of an airplane. Once in a while, she'd
urn her head, as if responding to someone off camera. I
quinted at the screen. The camera pulled back, revealing
 man in suit and tie behind her, smiling broadly.

The camera panned over, and the narrator introduced
'aul Iverson. The stills I'd seen didn't do him justice.
'aller and slimmer than the photos, he was elegantly
ressed and carried himself with the authority of someone
sed to issuing orders. His nose was more prominent here,
is eyes darker. Despite a head of thick white hair, he
ooked to be in his forties. A younger version of David.

As if cued by the Movietone director, Iverson stepped
orward and stood next to Lisle. Both of them smiled into
ne camera while the narrator delivered some pronounce-
nent about the war effort. Iverson draped his arm around
Lisle.

I froze.

It was the way he put his arm around her. It wasn't a
omradely gesture, the boss clapping a worker on the
ack. It was a protective, intimate act, as if he was trying
 shield her from the outside world. Lisle's body lan-
uage confirmed it. Her arm disappeared behind his waist,
er chin dropped, and she shifted closer to him, as if def-
rring to his wishes. The wishes of her man. The wishes
f her lover.

I looked over at Marian, who was studying the screen.
he stole a glance at me. But when she caught me looking
t her, she flicked her eyes back to the screen. The news-
eel moved on to the latest tally of war bonds. I hit Stop.
'or just the briefest moment, neither of us spoke.

Then she nodded, more to herself, it seemed, than to

me. "Fascinating, Ellie. That was fascinating." Something in her manner was off. I couldn't put my finger on it. "What do you think?" she asked.

It's always cold in TV studios to compensate for the lights and equipment, and I rubbed my hands up and down my arms to warm myself. I knew exactly what I thought, but I answered carefully. "I'm sure we can get a few seconds out of it."

"I suppose." She tapped a finger against her chin. "But, you know, I wonder if Roger may be right after all. Perhaps we ought to focus on the present rather than the past. I don't want people to think I'm riding on my father's legacy. Can I think about it?"

"Of course." Was she trying to tell me something?

She gathered her purse and stood up, opening the clasp to rummage inside. With her eyes on her bag, she said casually, "You say you knew that woman?"

I stood up, too. "I think my father knew her. A long time ago. During the war."

"Good heavens. What a small world." Her shoulders were hunched, her muscles tense. Her casual air had vanished. Even the air in the room seemed stiff.

The nerves under my skin jangled, like the discordant notes of a Schoenberg piece.

"How did that happen?"

I answered cautiously. "Oh, it was a family matter."

"I see." She snapped her purse shut and patted my hand, her composure suddenly restored. "Well, thank you for doing such fine research. I don't believe I've ever seen film of my father before."

The chill I felt had nothing to do with the studio air.

I WAS TRYING to figure out how to avoid cooking dinner that evening when the phone rang, and a clipped female voice asked, "Is this the residence of Ellie Foreman?"

"Yes."

"This is Iris Spencer, the librarian from the Rogers Park branch."

Miss Finkel redux. "Yes. I remember." I looked out the window. The late-afternoon sun shimmered through the locust tree, its fronds swaying gently in the breeze.

"I found your number behind the counter. You wanted to talk to Clarence Ramsey."

Boo Boo. "That's right. It was thoughtful of you to remember. But I did—"

She cut me off, her voice quavering. "We got some bad news today. Clarence was shot. About three blocks from here. He's . . . he's in critical condition."

The afternoon sun suddenly turned garish and hard.

"The police believe it was gang related."

I opened my mouth. Nothing came out. I forced out words. "Boo Boo wasn't in a gang."

"It was a drive-by."

Black rimmed the edges of my vision. Through the window I was dimly aware of a small child racing around on a tricycle, followed by another hauling a red wagon. The librarian went on. "I have such little time with them, you see. There's only so much I can do."

I heard the pain in her voice. "You did more for him than you know."

"It's never enough." She drew in a breath.

I asked what hospital he was in.

"Do you expect you'll come for a visit?"

"I . . . I don't know." My head felt light and spongy, too big for my body. I rubbed the back of my neck. I pictured Boo Boo on the computers at the library, tapping into virtual worlds of knowledge. I'd assumed words and books and ideas would somehow gild him, protect him from the life in the 'hood. The roar of an airplane droned overhead. "But when you hear something, could you let me know?"

"Of course."

There was a moment of silence. I broke it with a question. "Do they know who did it? Were there any witnesses?"

"A couple across the street apparently saw a beige or tan car. The police are looking for it."

I gripped the phone so hard that a sharp pain shot through my fingers. "A Cutlass?"

"I'm not sure of the model." There was another moment of silence. "Well, I thought you'd want to know."

"Thank you."

Hanging up, I wrapped my arms around my knees. Ever since I'd taken Skull's cartons, bad things were happening. Ruth Fleishman was dead. My house had been robbed. Now Boo Boo was fighting for his life. And the one link between them was a tan car.

TWENTY-SIX

I STOPPED BY the village florist and sent flowers to the hospital, then went to *shul* to say a *Misheberach*, a blessing. When I got home, there was a message from David Linden, wanting to know whether my father was better and when they could meet. I wasn't much in the mood, but I called Dad, who declared he still wasn't interested.

"Dad, he didn't know that Kurt died in Douglas Park. His mother told him his father was killed on some mission in Europe."

"What are you talking about?"

"David said that according to Lisle, Kurt came home in June of forty-five but left again a short time later. To take a final OSS assignment, she said. Surveillance on some Nazis escaping to South America. It got all screwed up, and Kurt was killed."

"No way. He came back in late July, just a week or so before Hiroshima. Why would she tell him something different?"

I had my suspicions. "I don't know, but he called again today." I looked through the window at the deepening dusk. "Dad, he needs to hear it from you. It would mean a lot."

I heard him sigh through the phone.

"Thank you. I won't forget this."

"What have you gotten me into, Ellie?"

I ignored the question. "Just to give you a heads-up,

Dad, I don't think he knows about you and Lisle. If you know what I mean."

"I know what you mean."

"I love you, Dad."

"I love you, too."

I heard the click as he disconnected. Then I heard another click.

"Dad?" Silence. "You still there?" More silence. First my E-mail. Now the phone. Had I suddenly been sentenced to technology hell? Or was it something else? I frowned and put the receiver back in the cradle.

I WASN'T SURE what to expect when I introduced David to my father in the lobby of The Ritz. I knew Dad would be polite, but it had to be an emotional moment for him. Subdued, almost solemn, he stood at military attention. When he saw David, he took his hand and gazed at him, as if comparing the features on the son's face to his memory of the mother's. Discomfited, I played with my hair. If things had been different, Dad might have been David's stepfather, and I wouldn't even be on the scene. Just as I thought this, Dad gave me a tender smile and brushed his hand across my hair.

David was in khakis today, with a light blue shirt that picked up the contrast between his eyes and white hair. Something stirred inside me. Had Paul Iverson been this handsome? If so, I could understand Lisle's attraction. We sat down in a grouping of upholstered chairs on a Chinese silk carpet. From our angle off the lobby, we had an excellent view of the fountain. Though it was still morning, soft piano music tinkled nearby.

"So," Dad shifted toward David. "Ellie says you trade foreign currency. That must be a lucrative line of work."

"Not as lucrative as you might imagine, sir."

"No?"

Nice touch Dad, I thought.

"Back in the eighties, the spreads were so wide, you

could make good money if you knew what you were doing. But that's all changed now."

"Why is that?" I asked.

"Like everything else, as information has become more available, people see opportunities where they didn't before. There's a lot more competition today." He smiled. "More global players too. Spreads are tighter and profit margins are thinner."

My father nodded. He understood. I didn't.

"Don't get me wrong," David said. "Foreign currencies will always be part of our portfolio. But if a banker's being really honest, he'll tell you the only reason we trade is to service our customers. To help them hedge or finance new ventures."

"I thought the objective was to play the market."

"Not anymore. That's what I'm saying." David leaned forward, his hands on his knees. "Let's say you're Toyota USA, and you know you're going to buy a thousand cars from Toyota Japan six months from now. And let's say the dollar is stronger than the yen."

"Meaning . . ."

"Meaning your dollars will buy more yen than they might six months from now."

"Okay."

"In that case, it would make sense to hedge your yen obligation and lock in the cost of those cars now, rather than waiting six months. That way, you know today the actual cost of your cars out then."

"So I would buy the yen now?"

"Not exactly. You'd contract to take delivery of the yen six months from now, but the price would be fixed today."

"Okay." I sounded tentative.

"See, companies want the security of knowing their actual cost in advance—their cost of goods sold."

"But what if the yen *drops* six months from now?" I said, thinking about Barry's stocks. "Things can go the other way, can't they?"

"Of course."

"So," I said, "in a sense, you're still gambling that the price of yen will go the way you want it to."

He shook his head "No. We aren't speculators. Our clients understand that. What's important to them is knowing the cost of what they've contracted for, before they take possession of it. Foreign currency trading gives them a tool to do that. They're able to lock in the cost— no matter which way the yen goes."

"Sounds simple when you put it that way."

David shrugged.

"But what about that guy in Baltimore—the one who worked for the Irish bank—who lost almost a billion dollars? He was a currency trader, wasn't he?"

"He was trading the bank's money. He made a bad trade and then made it worse by hiding what he did. Then he tried to make it all back before anyone discovered his losses, but it blew up in his face, as it always will, when people fall into that trap."

"So he *was* speculating."

"That's what got him in trouble."

"I don't get it. You just said you don't speculate."

"I don't. What I do is help the bank's customers hedge their foreign currency risks. I'm more of an advisor, in that respect. I don't trade the bank's money."

"But others do."

"That's right."

"Who?"

"My colleagues in the trading group."

I hoped they were better at it than Barry.

A waiter carrying a silver tray drifted over toward us, a question on his face. David waved him away.

"Where'd you study?" my father asked.

"I graduated from the Wharton School, but I learned most of it on the job."

"Philadelphia, you say?"

"And London, Geneva, Tokyo."

Dad notched his eyebrows. "You speak all those languages?"

"God no. I don't even speak German. My mother always talked to me in English."

"That sounds like Lisle." Dad smiled.

David's expression suddenly grew serious. "Mr. Foreman—"

"Call me Jake."

"Is it true what Ellie told me? That my father died here in Chicago?"

Dad's face softened. "In Lawndale," he said gently. "Douglas Park. I was there."

"Jake?" His tongue seemed to trip over the word. "Would you take me there . . . to the place where it happened?"

TWENTY-SEVEN

BY THE TIME we got off the Eisenhower on the West Side, Dad and David were chatting like old friends. As we turned south, Dad rubbed his hands together. He hadn't been this animated in years.

"This is Lawndale, son," he said. "Used to be the heart of Jewish life in Chicago."

We passed scorched buildings and abandoned lots filled with trash, rusty barrels, and in one case, a cardboard appliance box. Lawndale had been ground zero during the riots; forty years later, the scars were still palpable.

"Would you look at that?" Dad cranked down the window as we cruised past a McDonald's. Its sanitized cheerfulness clashed with the detritus of the community. "Miller's pool hall used to be right there." He pointed to the sidewalk in front of the restaurant. "This is where I first met your mother, David. Roosevelt and Kedzie. On a Sunday afternoon."

I slowed so David could take a look. "You met my mother at a pool hall?"

"She was just passing by," Dad said hastily.

I stole a glance in the rearview mirror. David's mirrored shades hid his expression. We continued south on Kedzie to Ogden, where a sign on a large, shabby building said it was the Church of the Lord Jesus Christ. Once upon a time it must have been an elegant addition to the neighborhood, but its cornices and grillwork were now crumbling, and initials in loopy iridescent letters covered the walls.

"This was the Douglas Park Auditorium. Home of the Yiddish Theater. I knew an actress who worked here."

"Skull's girlfriend?" I asked. "The one who was killed by the Nazi Bund officer?"

Dad nodded. I shaded my eyes. The inside walls had collapsed, leaving wooden studs with exposed pipes and wires. Sunbeams danced off shards of glass where windows should have been.

Dad grew more subdued as he directed me to Albany Avenue. We stopped in front of a long, brown brick building with a cross on the front. The sign above said it was the Sacred Heart Home. "It's still here," he breathed. "This used to be the Jewish Orphans Home. Your mother lived here, David, before she moved into Teitelman's."

David leaned his head out the window.

We headed back up to Douglas Boulevard, a broad, four-lane street separated by an island and flanked by leafy, graceful trees. I imagined couples sauntering down the sidewalks years ago, the women in dresses with parasols, children scampering behind.

"Look." My father pointed to a boxy brick building called the Lawndale Community Academy. "This was the Jewish People's Institute. Your mother and I danced on that roof in the summertime."

"You and my mother?" David's voice was laced with doubt.

I grimaced. Dad shouldn't have let that drop.

He must have realized it, too. "Before she met your father," he stammered, "your mother and I . . . we spent some time together."

I stole another glance in the rearview mirror. David's face was blank. "Look across the street, David." I cut in. "That used to be the Hebrew Theological College." I pointed toward a granite building with Doric columns framing the entrance. "We shot it for *Celebrate Chicago*."

"Boys came from all over the Midwest to study here."

Dad picked up on my strategy. "But they moved north twenty-five years ago. Like everyone else." I drove on. "So. Did my daughter tell you what a talented director she is?"

"Producer, Dad, and I told him."

"She tell you who she's working for now?"

"Dad—"

"She's making a video for Marian Iverson," he said proudly. "The one running for the Senate." Dad seemed to have gotten over his antipathy that she was a Republican.

"My mother worked for a man named Iverson," David said. "He owned a steel mill. Is this woman a relation?"

"His daughter," I admitted.

"My mother spoke highly of him. And you're doing a video for his daughter?" His face lit. "What a coincidence."

I turned a corner, thinking about the coincidences that had cropped up in my life: Skull, Lisle Gottlieb, and now the Iverson family. It was all feeling very Jungian.

Dad motioned me to stop in front of a three-story building on Sawyer Street. The Teitelmans. I cut the engine, and Dad got out of the car. He craned his head up to a window on the top floor. When David got out, Dad touched his arm, then pointed. Her room. They both fell silent and peered up.

Back in the car we circled back to Douglas Avenue. As we passed a brick apartment building with white moldings and stately architecture, Dad said, "And this is where your mother moved after your father left for the war."

I slowed. The windows of the four-story building were separated from each other by lots of space, hinting at large rooms with high ceilings. Columns flanked the entrance, and a wrought-iron fence surrounded the property. "This is a far cry from the Orphans Home," I said. "And Teitelman's. How did she afford it?"

"Oh, she knew the owner. We all did. Man by the name of—lemme see—his name was Feld." Dad dipped his head. "He ate in the restaurant from time to time."

"Still—"

"Things were different back then, sweetheart," Dad said. "It was the war. People helped each other out. I'm sure he gave her a deal. What with her husband overseas and all. By the way, son." Dad pulled something out of his wallet, twisted around, and handed it to David. "This is your mother and me and Barney Teitelman in the restaurant. Before we enlisted." David stared at the picture. "Why don't you keep it?"

David looked up. "Really?"

Dad nodded.

"Thank you, Jake." He looked at it again, then slipped it into his pocket.

I headed east on Douglas until it more or less dead-ended and pulled into a parking lot. Once out of the car, we strolled around a man-made pond on paths that were surprisingly free of litter. A profusion of trees and greenery muffled the sounds of the ghetto that surrounded the park. Mothers wheeled baby strollers, children frolicked, and even the men, ragged and probably homeless, seemed pacified by the tranquil surroundings.

As we walked past a carefully tended flower bed, I told them about Fouad and how nicely my own yard was shaping up. "It figures he'd be good with nature and growing things," I said.

"Why is that?" Dad said.

"He's . . . well . . . he's kind of spiritual."

"Fouad." David repeated the name softly. "Is that Arabic?"

"Syrian. Fouad's Muslim."

Dad rubbed his hands together. "Just what a Jewish girl needs."

"He's teaching me how to take care of the garden."

Dad rolled his eyes.

"You wouldn't do that if you knew him, Dad."

He shrugged and kept going. Looming around the bend was an old band shell with a hollowed-out stage. He

slowed near a thicket of trees and bushes opposite the
stage. "This is where it happened." He stopped.

The grass was green, the flowers bloomed, and there
was a lazy buzz from the insects. I pushed through the
trees. Just behind them was a small clearing. Plenty of
room for someone to take cover, stake out their prey, and
shoot. I went back through the bushes, shaking leaves and
brambles off my arm.

Pushing his sunglasses back on his head, David gazed
around, deep in some private world we couldn't share. He
gazed around him as if committing the scene to memory.
Then he looked at my father. "Tell me everything, Jake."
His eyes were tinged with sadness.

"You sure, son?"

He nodded. Even in sorrow, his bearing was dignified,
almost royal. My father took him aside, and they walked
slowly toward the thicket, David staring as if committing
the scene to memory. My father talked, but I couldn't hear
what he said. I didn't want to. David stopped and covered
his eyes with his hand. His jaw worked as he murmured,
"Baruch Dyon Emmes."

"Blessed be the true Judgment," Dad repeated. "Amen."
He put his arm around David.

RACHEL AND I braved the heat and drove up to Uncle
Dan's to check out camp gear. This would be her third
time at sleep-away camp; fortunately, I'd paid the fees
last winter. I was frugal this year, buying only a pair of
hiking boots and a red poncho, which Rachel wore out of
the store. I'd get the rest of her stuff at Target.

Thick, dark clouds massed in the western sky as we
drove home. The leaves on the trees had flipped over, their
pale green bottoms facing up. A brisk wind chased us
inside. As I made dinner, the first drops of rain sizzled on
the street. I closed the windows. A few minutes later, it
was pouring. Forks of lightning singed the sky, and thunder crashed overhead.

Rachel and I were quiet during dinner, as if we had tacitly agreed to let the storm's fury speak for us. She offered to help clean up, which surprised me until I realized she didn't want to be alone. While she stacked the plates in the dishwasher, I made a pot of decaf. Then we camped out in the family room, the rain pounding on the roof. I made sure the door was locked, then crossed the room and lifted the phone off the base.

"What are you doing?" She asked.

"Just making sure it works. You know how these storms are."

"You think the power's going out?" Rachel was still afraid of the dark.

"No way," I gave her my most reassuring smile. "Hey. I'm going to take another look at some stock footage I got for work. You want to watch it with me?"

"No," she said. "I'll read."

"Deal."

She grabbed Harry Potter, and I loaded the cassette into the VCR. As I waited for it to rewind, I worked a finger into my scalp, hoping that maybe I wouldn't see what I'd seen before. Maybe it had just been my imagination, my propensity to make up stories and connections where none existed. Maybe my suspicions would dissipate like the steam rising from my coffee.

But as I watched the scenes of Lisle Gottlieb and Paul Iverson, I saw their body language all over again. How they looked at each other. Reacted to each other. They *were* involved. Intimate. It was all there.

And so was the resemblance between David and Paul Iverson. Both were handsome men with prematurely white hair. Thin, aristocratic noses. Both carried themselves with that almost regal bearing. I grew edgier, and when Iverson, with Lisle at his side, smiled into the camera, I jabbed my thumb on the remote so hard that Rachel jerked her head up.

I snatched the coffee mug and went into to the kitchen. A peal of thunder crashed outside. David Linden was well into his fifties. Which meant that Lisle Gottlieb had to have been pregnant with him when she went to see my father. Yet she raised him to believe Kurt Weiss was his father.

I rinsed the mug in the sink. Lisle had been a busy woman. First my father. Then Kurt Weiss. Then Paul Iverson. Opportunistic, too, moving from the Orphans Home, to a boardinghouse, to a luxury apartment. I reached for the towel. Who was Lisle Gottlieb? Why did she take three lovers in quick succession? Was she that desperate—or lonely?

And what about Skull? Was he in love with her, too? Maybe I was wrong about the picture of the woman on the bridge. Maybe Skull had been one of Lisle's lovers, too; she got around enough. Maybe he was trying to track her down to rekindle their romance.

I dried the mug and put it away. I still had no idea how—or even if—Skull's pursuit of Lisle was related to the theft of his things. If this was a love triangle, quadrangle, or some geometric variant thereof, given all the men who were apparently smitten with Lisle Gottlieb, it still didn't explain who wanted Skull's things badly enough to break into my house.

"MOM?" RACHEL ASKED as I sat on her bed that night.

"Yeah, honey?" The stormed had passed, and moonlight streamed in through the blinds.

"Where's Daddy? Why hasn't he called?"

I chewed my lip. "I don't know."

"Doesn't he know we're worried about him?"

"I think he probably does."

"Do you think he's okay?"

I brushed my hand across her forehead. "I'm sure he is."

"Then why doesn't he call? Doesn't he love us anymore?"

I bent down and nuzzled her neck. "If there's one thing

I do know, it's that your father loves you very much. More than anything else in his life. He must be working on a very important case. I'm sure he'll be in touch as soon as he can."

Her face smoothed out, and she reached her arms around my neck for a hug. Rolling on her side, she cradled her hands under her face. I sat by her side and watched the moonbeams dance on the wall until she was asleep.

TWENTY-EIGHT

LIGHT FROM THE monitors blinked as Hank and I prepared to screen the Midwest Mutual show. The heavy work was over; we were just tweaking. I'd called Barry to give him a piece of my mind, but there was no answer, and I was too angry to leave a message. I settled into a seat in the control room.

Hank clicked the mouse. The blinking lights disappeared; the screen turned black. The plink of a musical note sounded, and a tiny teardrop not much bigger than a pinpoint of light dissolved from black. Behind it a second teardrop appeared, and the soundtrack plinked again. More drops and plinks appeared, until the drops became a trickle, the trickle became a waterfall, and the waterfall a flood. The sound track swelled, too, from plinks to a hum to the sound of crashing waves. When the screen was filled with rushing water, we cut to a teddy bear swirling down a stream. In voice-over we heard a couple bemoaning the loss of their home.

Fifteen minutes later, the closing credits faded to black, and the music ended on cue. Some editors just let the music fade out, but Hank back-times the track so it ends on the last beat.

"It's good," I said.

"Just good?" He looked injured.

"The transitions are smooth, the bites work, and the effects are pure eye candy. You did a great job."

"But . . ."

"No buts. It's better than Karen has any right to expect. But then, she knows that, when you're involved." Hank's face smoothed out. "But next time, we need more glitz." I dangled an imaginary stogie and flicked the ashes on Hank's head. "Star Wars, Armageddon, you know what I mean, baby? The audience'll eat it up."

Hank laced his hands behind his head. "You can take the girl out of Hollywood . . ."

I cuffed him on the shoulder. "On to the Marian Iverson show."

"When do we start?"

I shook my head. "We can screen, maybe tag some footage, but we can't really start cutting until after the Fourth." I told him about the fly-around.

"Groovy. What kind of plane?"

"Oh you know. The kind with two wings and a tail." I looked away. "I hate to fly," I said in a low voice.

"Really?"

"I'm the worst white-knuckler you'll ever meet. I usually have to get drunk before I get on a big plane, and this one is gonna be tiny. I'll be useless by the time we land. If we do."

He laughed. "I guess it won't help to tell you flying is safer than driving. Especially with all the new security stuff."

"Bullshit." I rolled back in my chair. "Everyone knows airplanes are held together with spit and rubber bands."

Hank spread his hands. "I don't believe it. You're not afraid of anything."

Was that his impression of me? "By the way, if you ever tell anyone about this, you will swim with the fishes."

"That's more like it."

The intercom on the phone buzzed. A disembodied voice broke over the intercom. "Hank. Line three for you."

Before I left, Hank fast-forwarded through the Milk Days footage. Armed with a smile, Marian floated from group to group, dispensing a pleasantry or interested look.

Again, I was struck by her composure and how controlled, almost regally, she carried herself. Just like her father. And David Linden.

A MESSAGE FROM my lawyer was waiting for me at home.

"I made some calls about Barry's problem," Pam said when I called her back.

"And?" I twisted the mouse cord around my fingers.

"The situation is a shitload worse than we thought."

I first met Pam Huddleston twenty years ago at a West Side woman's shelter where we both volunteered. I remember how her anger would explode when she saw a battered woman. It still does. "What does that mean, Pam?"

"Let me say, first of all, I don't think you'll be in any trouble." She didn't think? A few weeks ago, she was certain. "But there's some bad news. Barry seems to have disappeared."

"Disappeared? How disappeared?"

"What the fuck do you think I mean? He's gone. Packed his bags and took the last train out of Dodge."

Damn. I should have called after he didn't show on Memorial Day, but my pride didn't let me. If he didn't want us—

"When was the last time you talked to him?"

"Before Memorial Day."

"Well, he's taken a leave of absence from the firm, he sublet his condo, and no one knows where he is. Sounds like a vanishing act to me."

I twisted the mouse cable more tightly. "Why? What's going on?"

"Umm, Ellie, let's back up for a minute." I didn't like the sound of that. "You know Barry owes the Chicago Corp half a million dollars, right?"

"There was a margin call on his stock."

"Right."

"Pam, I thought the whole point of a margin call was to protect everyone so that if the stock tanks, the brokerage sells it, and you only lose what you invested."

"That's the theory. But if the stock falls too far too fast, your account can go negative, and the house loses money, too. They don't like that, so they try to get it back."

"Is that what happened?"

"I'm still trying to get all the details. The problem is that the account was held in both your names—"

"That was a major screw-up by Chicago Corp. They never closed the account."

"Well, actually, they say they did. During the divorce settlement. They say Barry reopened it later on."

"How could he do that? He never asked me to sign—" I shut my mouth. "Pam, Barry may be a lot of things, but he's not that sleazy. I know. I was married to him."

"I remember," she said dryly. "And I'm not so sure I believe the Chicago Corp, either. I think it's possible that they fucked up, and they're just trying to cover their ass. Your former broker retired to Florida a few months after the divorce. Who knows what he was or wasn't doing before he left?"

"What does Barry's new broker say?"

"Well, that's another problem. The guy quit last week. He was hawking the stock and took a huge hit himself. Not to mention all his pissed-off clients."

"Jesus, Pam. This is a mess."

"It is a stinking, god-awful mess. Unfortunately, it won't stop them from trying to recover their money. And since they can't seem to find Barry, they're saying they're going to come after the other fish in the pond—"

"Holy shit, Pam. They're coming after me?"

"Now, calm down, Ellie. Just keep it together, okay? I've already talked to their lawyer. He understands our side."

I stared out the window. The leaves on the locust glittered like sharp blades.

"Ellie, listen to me. It's not that bad," Pam said. "I've

already sent over a set of the records. But I want you to make your own copy, from the set I gave you after the divorce. Are you listening?"

I whimpered.

"Fuck it. Talk to me, Ellie."

"I'm here."

"Good. Now, I want you to make a list of your assets and send it to me. Fax it over today."

"Assets? Pam, the only asset I have is the house. Am I going to lose it?"

"No, Ellie. You're not going to lose it. We will clear all of this up. You had nothing to do with Barry's debts. No court in the country can make you liable for them."

"Then why are we going through all of this?"

"So it never gets that far."

I bit my lip.

"It's a goddammed pain in the ass is all," Pam was saying. "But in the meantime, I want you to be careful."

"Careful how?"

"You're going to be a paragon of financial responsibility. No frivolous spending. No luxuries for a while."

"Like the ones I've indulged in for the past few years?"

"You know what I mean. No big-ticket items. No trips to the beach or the mountains or a spa."

"Don't worry. How long until this is all cleared up?"

"Hard to say. The brokerage might hire a private detective to find Barry if he doesn't show up soon. But cheer up. Things could be worse."

"How?"

"On second thought, forget it. You don't want to go there. Get that list over to me today, okay, hon? And don't worry. We'll beat these fuckers."

I listened to the whine of a lawnmower, the hum of faraway traffic, the call of a crow, until an electronic female voice said, "If you'd like to make a call . . ." I looked down. The phone was still in my hand.

*   *   *

AN HOUR LATER, I zipped through the hardware store, raced through the bank, and charged into the grocery store. Like a tape on fast-forward, I was a blur of activity. Maybe I could outrun my fear.

Years of therapy had reduced my money problem to a simple thesis: Money is power. Power is control. I need control. I don't know where it came from; my parents weren't any more neurotic than anybody else's. Neither were theirs, as far as I know. But the truth is that without the security that money brings, I feel empty inside. Scraped clean. A nonperson. That's probably one of the reasons I married Barry.

I hurried down the shampoo aisle, hunting for Apple Blossom and Honey shampoo, Rachel's favorite. I found the green and gold bottle easily. I was about to toss it in my cart when something made me check the price. Over four dollars. I checked the brand next to it. It was half that. I juggled both bottles in my hand. I put the Apple Blossom and Honey back.

I wheeled the cart to the beverage aisle. The house brand of diet soda was much cheaper than Coke. Resentfully, I grabbed two six-packs and slid them under the cart. I pushed up to the meat counter and studied the cuts of beef, glistening and plump in their plastic wrap. Steak was out of the question. I rolled past.

Then I stopped. Already I was anticipating, accommodating, trying to make ends meet. Why? Barry sure as hell wasn't. He was probably holed up in some beach house or lake cottage, "roughing it" with his Palm, laptop, and DVD. If he didn't play by the rules, why should I? I backed up to the meat counter and picked out the thickest steak I could find. Then I retraced my steps and replaced the house pop with diet Coke.

I rounded the corner to the back of the store. Above me was a mirror that ran the width of the store. Angling down on shoppers, it was an inexpensive security system, designed to show shoppers' activities in each of the aisles. I saw a few kids reflected in the candy aisle, and as I got

near the health and beauty section, a couple debating the
relative merits of first aid sprays. When I reached the
shampoos, I put the cheap brand back and threw Apple
Blossom and Honey in my cart.

Then I passed the cosmetics. I'm always on the lookout
for lavender eye shadow. It hasn't been in fashion for
years, but when you're a forty-something woman with
dark hair and gray eyes, you make the most of what you
have. I slowly scanned the makeup, most of it hanging
from wire racks. I saw dozens of mascaras, eye pencils,
and shadows in all sorts of shades, but no violet.

I bent down to the bottom shelf, and found it sandwiched between blushes and powder. I took it off the rack.
It was exactly what I needed. I checked the price. Almost
five dollars. Too much. I wouldn't scrimp on Rachel's
needs, but mine were another matter. Makeup was a luxury that I didn't need, especially now.

Except it was lavender, and I was all out. I might not
be able to find it anywhere else. It was an investment; it
would last for months. The more I thought about it, the
more I wanted it. I deserved it. Especially now. A familiar
rush kicked in.

I straightened up and looked both ways. I was alone in
the aisle. I looked back at the mirror. I didn't see any blue
smocks, the uniform the store employees wore, but just
to be safe, I turned my back to the mirror. I could get
away with it, but I'd have to act fast. If someone approached from the other end of the aisle, they'd have me
nailed. But I could do it. I could open my leather bag,
pull out my car keys, and slip in the eye shadow at the
same time.

I stared at the makeup in my palm. The fingers of my
other hand closed over my bag. I glanced back at the
mirror. A woman was rounding the corner with a basket,
aiming straight toward me. A rush of conscience struck
me like the slap of a cold shower. Not today. I dropped
the makeup in the cart and headed up to pay.

TWENTY-NINE

A SWEAT-SOAKING HUMIDITY blanketed the air as I drove downtown the next morning. By the time I arrived at Marian's headquarters for a script meeting, my legs were glued to the car seat, and the back of my blouse was slick.

The atmosphere had ratcheted up a few notches since I was last there. Phones rang briskly, fax machines hummed, and eager snippets of conversation swept through the room.

Dory Sanchez looked up and waved at me from her desk. I waved back and headed to the empty office, grateful they'd saved it for me, after all. After freshening up, I pulled out my copy of the script, ready to do battle, when the receptionist appeared at the door, the headphones clamped to her head like a new appendage.

"Call for you, Ellie," she said.

"For me?" She pointed to the black phone on the desk. Who would be calling me here? I hadn't told anyone besides Susan I was working here, and Rachel always called my cell. "Hello?"

"Ellie, it's David Linden." The receptionist retreated to the anteroom. I sat on the edge of my desk, trying to ignore the pleasant shiver that ran through me.

"Well, this is a surprise. How . . . how was the conference?"

"Oh, it was one of those off-the-shelf Andersen workshops. Nothing I didn't know."

"Sorry about that. How's the weather in Philly? Is it as hot as it is here?"

"I wouldn't know. I'm still in Chicago."

My pulse quickened. Stop, I scolded myself.

"I . . . I decided to take some vacation time and stay on for a while. Since you told me . . . since we went down to Lawndale, I've done some thinking. About my father's death. And why my mother never told me about it."

"It had to be a shock."

"It was. But you and your father—well, that's another— At any rate, I've decided to look into his murder. See what I can find. And since I was already here, it seemed like a good idea to extend my stay."

"You've set yourself a tough assignment. It happened nearly sixty years ago."

"I realize that. But I need to know."

"What if the answers aren't what you expect?"

"I'll . . . I'll manage." He paused. "As a matter of fact, that's why I'm calling. You've done this type of research before. I have a couple of ideas, but I'd like to run them by you. If you have the time. Are you by any chance free for lunch?"

Flickers of warmth hopscotched through me. "Um. Sure. I guess so."

"Would it be all right for me to come by?"

"Why don't I meet you? There's a deli not far from here."

"Would it be an imposition if I came by you? I've never seen the inner workings of a campaign."

I hesitated, unsure if I wanted him to associate me with anything political. But I heard the enthusiasm in his voice.

"Okay. Meet me here in half an hour." I gave him the address. "By the way, how did you find me here?"

"Shrewd detective work."

"David . . ."

"I called your house. Your daughter told me."

Marian was still closeted in her office thirty minutes later when the receptionist buzzed I had a guest. As I went out to greet him, I noticed that she hadn't disappeared behind her desk this time but was busily tidying up the reception area, stealing glances at David with a toothy smile. David brightened when he saw me. The receptionist lost her smile.

Leading him around the corner, I allowed myself a small smile. "David, I'm sorry. I thought we'd be finished by now, but we haven't started."

He looked around. "I can wait."

"It could be a while. I hope you brought something to read."

He shrugged. I ushered him into the empty office. Turning around to look for another chair, I saw Dory Sanchez on her way across the room with one.

"Are you always this efficient?" I asked.

She grinned.

I made introductions and listened while she asked the benign questions everyone does when they first meet someone. David answered cheerfully, and they struck up a conversation. I ran a hand through my hair. Dory had a way of drawing out people. Five minutes later, as Dory was still chatting up David, I told myself the twinge I was feeling was silly. Then, a shadow appeared at the door. I cut my eyes. Marian, purse in hand, was watching us.

"I'm so sorry to be late, Ellie dear." Her eyes moved from me to Dory, then to David. Dory tensed, and perhaps because she did, I did, too. Marian stared at David. "And who is this?"

I felt a subtle vibration in the air, some sense that the natural order of things had been disturbed. "This is David Linden. A . . . a friend of mine."

"I see." Marian examined David. Dory watched her watch him. No one spoke. Then she extended her hand. "So nice to meet you, David." He took it.

Marian swiveled her head toward me. "If you're ready, dear," she said crisply, "I'm ready to go over the script." She gave me her back and headed to her office.

* * *

WHEN I EMERGED from Marian's office, Dory was perched on the edge of the desk, her long brown legs dangling over the edge, yakking away to David. When they saw me, she jumped down.

"How did it go?" David asked.

"Not bad." I tossed the file down on the desk. "Just a few revisions."

He gave me a boyish thumbs-up. I smiled in spite of myself.

"Well, I'll be going now," Dory edged around me with a small shrug and stepped through the door. "Good talking to you David." The scent of her perfume, a sexy, tangy smell, trailed behind her.

"Do you still want to have lunch?" I scowled.

David didn't seem to notice. "I'm starved."

As we pushed through the door to the street, a blast of hot, heavy air rolled over us. Trucks and cars crawled past, shimmering waves of heat rising from their surfaces. Pedestrians moved sluggishly as if walking had become an unbearable task. By the time we reached the deli around the corner, the back of my neck was damp.

It was late for lunch—we seemed to be making a habit of late lunches—and the deli was sparsely filled. I inhaled deeply. I've never been able to identify the smell inside a delicatessen—a combination of garlic, onions, and pastrami maybe—but the blend always makes my mouth water. A hostess led us across a black-and-white tiled floor and seated us in a brightly upholstered booth. The muffled play-by-play of a Cubs broadcast, punctuated with an occasional burst of chatter, drifted over us. A waitress in a white blouse and black pants a size too small handed us laminated menus.

Still miffed at the easy camaraderie between Dory and David, I studied the menu. David pushed his shades up on his head and scanned his, too. The waitress returned, balancing plates full of food, drinks, and a silver bucket of pickles on a tray. She deposited the food at the next table, then placed the pickles on ours.

I slumped in my seat, convinced that David would rather be with Dory Sanchez. Who could blame him? She was gorgeous, sexy, and friendly. And I had no claim on him. Even if I did meet him first. And was partly responsible for his decision to stay in Chicago. Ours was just a business relationship. That was fine. It didn't bother me. I wouldn't dignify it by grilling him about her. I folded my hands in my lap.

"So, what were you and Dory talking about?"

He picked up a pickle, sliced it into five pieces, and popped one in his mouth. "I love these," he said. "Don't you?" He speared another chunk and held it out. I took it off his fork. "I haven't told you much about myself, have I?"

I squinted at him. "What do you mean?"

"You know more about my parents than you do about me."

"Well, that's true, but—"

He cut me off. "People like Dory and me don't open up easily."

Dory and me? She *was* a fast worker.

"It turns out we both grew up in foster care."

I stopped chewing.

"About a year after Mother moved to Philadelphia, she married a man named Joseph Linden. I don't remember much about him. When I was about seven, they were both killed in a car accident." His voice was flat, as if he were reporting an approaching cold front, not a life-altering tragedy. "It was winter. There'd been an ice storm, and Philadelphia's got a lot of hills. The car went out of control and skidded off a bridge."

I winced.

"Since I had no relatives in the area—at least none anyone could find—I went into the foster care system. For ten years."

The waitress took our orders, repeated them out loud,

then disappeared. I looked at David, not sure which question to ask first. "How . . . how . . . ?"

"There's this look that foster care kids have. I'd know it a mile away. You kind of look at someone under your lids, hoping they won't notice you looking at them. You don't want to be noticed, see. You just want to get by. Not make waves. Dory has that look. I guess I do, too."

Was that why he wore shades so often? "But you've come so far from . . . from that." I hoped I didn't sound patronizing.

"There was never any question that I would. My mother always told me that I could—no—*would* do anything I wanted. I was special, she said." He let out a sound, more an exhalation of breath than an exclamation. "I believed her. Though I've come to realize she was saying it more for herself than for me."

"What do you mean?"

"I was the proof that the bad guys didn't win. A Jewish boy born after Hitler nearly killed us all . . . I was her victory. The tangible evidence that she, not the Nazis, won. She treated me like a crown prince. Not with material things, of course, because technically, we were poor. But I had unconditional love, and I never wanted for anything." He looked down. "Until she died."

Our meals came. He dug into a roast beef sandwich. I picked at my salad. "I was shuttled to homes all over Pennsylvania for the next ten years," he said after a bite. "Some were good. Some weren't." A muscle in his jaw pulsed. "But I was lucky. I got a full scholarship to Penn State. After a year there, I transferred to U of P. I've been in Philly ever since."

The waitress came over with a pot of coffee. I clamped a hand over my cup, but David nodded, and she filled his cup. He opened two packs of sugar, dumped them in, and stirred. Whatever else Lisle Gottlieb was, I thought, she had been a good mother. Her belief in her son had sustained him through what had to be a lonely, pain-filled adolescence. He had survived. He and Dory.

I pushed my plate away. "So. Tell me what your plans are."

He sipped his coffee. "I thought I'd go to the police and see if I can get the case file on my father. Then maybe see if the detective who worked on it is still alive."

I chewed my lip.

"I know it's a long shot," he said. "But he might have a son or daughter who remembers something."

I shook my head.

"What's wrong?"

"You won't have much luck with the cops."

"Why not?"

"They won't release any information. Especially since the case is technically still open."

"But it's been sixty years."

I shrugged.

"How do you know?"

"A few years ago, I tried to get the file of an unsolved murder for a video I was working on. I went through channels, wrote letters, even pulled a few strings, but I got nowhere. Their rationale was, 'How do we know you're not the perpetrator, or a friend of the perpetrator?' I wasn't, but it didn't make any difference."

David frowned. "Why not?"

"Think about it. What if the file contains a note that the detectives think Mr. Smith killed Mr. Brown, but they don't have the evidence to charge him? If that ever got out, Mr. Smith could sue the police department for defamation. Or his heirs could. Whether or not he was guilty. And these days, you can bet someone would."

"But I don't want to make the information public."

"It doesn't matter." I said. "But hey. Give it a try. Just don't be disappointed."

The waitress hovered nearby; David shook his head, and she disappeared. "I'd also like to track down someone who knew my mother or father," he said. "Aside from your father, that is. Is that friend of your father's—Barney—still alive?"

"He died ten years ago."

"Oh." He sipped his coffee. "Well, maybe I'll try to find someone who worked with my mother at the mill."

I thought about Linda Jorgenson. I should give him her name. I thought about the newsreel with Lisle and Iverson together. I kept my mouth shut.

"I can also try to track down the people my father worked for. Your father said he worked as a delivery boy?"

"That's right," I said.

The lines around his eyes deepened in an unexpected smile. "You know, the picture of my mother is the first thing anyone's ever given me of her. I hope your father knows how much I appreciate it."

"He just might."

"My parents traveled light, you understand, so light I could pack everything they left in one box. In fact, the only thing of my father's I have is a clock."

"A clock?"

"It's a model of a famous clock tower in Prague. The Astronomical Clock. He brought it back from the war." He took another sip of coffee. "It's supposed to be one of the oldest mechanical clocks in Europe, built in the 1400s. The dial shows the revolutions of the sun, the moon, and some stars, and stonemasons added other medallions and figures over the centuries. The Nazis destroyed it during the war, but I understand it's been restored. What I've got is just a cheap copy, of course . . ." His voice trailed off.

I wondered how I'd memorialize my father when the time came. Somehow a Big Band anthology or box of Havanas didn't quite measure up.

"It's odd, though," he went on. "Mother always told me it was valuable. But it's not. I had it appraised; turns out they made hundreds of them during the twenties." He shrugged. "But that doesn't matter."

"I understand."

"Do you really?" He pushed his coffee cup to the edge

of his place setting. "We are different, you and me. You know your father. You have his photos, his things. You can prove he existed. I can't. I've been to Germany. I traced my mother's family, even tracked down one of her neighbors. But I never found out anything about my father. It's as if he and his family never were. I don't even have a picture. The only thing I have is that clock."

The waitress left the check on a little brown tray. I reached for it, and he did, too, and in the process his hand accidentally grazed mine.

"I asked you, remember?" he said, his hand resting on mine for a beat. A flash of heat tore through me. He took the check.

"That's why I want to find out what happened to my father," he went on, as if nothing had happened. "He's part of me. Part of my heritage. I need to know who he was. And what he could have possibly done that would make someone want to kill him. You understand, don't you?"

I was about to say that I did, but then I stopped. Kurt Weiss wasn't his father. Paul Iverson was. What kind of a heritage did that make?

THIRTY

MARIAN HAD LEFT by the time I got back, and the atmosphere was more relaxed. The phones had quieted, the pit bulls lounged at their desks, and even Roger came out to chat. As I went into the empty office to gather my things, Dory broke off from a conversation and headed toward me, a conspiratorial smile on her face.

It struck me that wasn't the attitude that someone with a crush on my lunch date would have. Wouldn't she be more taciturn? Looking at me with narrowed eyes? Hoping I'd shrivel up and melt like the wicked witch? Then again, I've been away from the dating game for a long time; I may not know the cues.

"You have a nice lunch?" she asked.

I eyed her warily. "Very nice, thanks."

"He's absolutely gorgeous."

I shrugged.

"Oh, come on Ellie, don't tell me you haven't noticed." I hoped my face didn't show my pique. "Even I could feel the sparks between you two."

"Sparks?"

"Major sparks. You couldn't keep your eyes off each other. You make a good couple."

I looked up. Maybe I was wrong about her.

"How did you meet him, anyway?"

I leaned against the wall. All was forgiven. I felt a silly smile on my lips. "Oh . . . it's one of those long stories."

She pushed the door closed and hoisted herself up on the desk. "I've got time."

I filled her in, starting with the letter from Ruth Fleishman. I told her about Ben Skulnick, his boxes, and his E-mail account. I told her how I met David, how his mother worked for Iverson Steel, how she knew my father. But I left out the break-in and my suspicions about David's parentage. She nodded and smiled, but when I finished, her face grew serious. "What was the name of that man again?"

"Which man?"

"The one whose E-mail you hacked into."

"I didn't hack into his E-mail. I had his password."

"Right." She paused. "So what was his name?"

"Ben Skulnick."

Her brow furrowed.

"He went by Sinclair, too."

"Skulnick. Sinclair . . ." Her voice trailed off. "Sorry." She pushed off the desk and shot me a sidelong glance. "Who did you say David's father was?"

"His name was Kurt Weiss."

"And he died right after the war?"

"In forty-five. He was gunned down at a concert in Douglas Park."

"And his mother worked for Iverson Steel?"

I nodded.

She started for the door. "Come with me. I want to show you something."

"Dory, I have to get back north. It's getting late."

"It'll only take a minute." She opened the door and walked over to Marian's office. The door was shut. She put her hand on the doorknob.

"What are you doing? You can't just—"

"It's okay. She knows we have to get there sometimes to enter things on her calendar. See?" She twisted the knob, and the door opened. "Roger locks up at night."

I followed her in. She went behind Marian's desk to a set of shelves filled with books and several framed pho-

tographs. Dory reached for one of them and handed it to
me. It was a black-and-white photograph of a man astride
a horse on what looked to be a polo field. He wore a
white shirt, jodhpurs, and shiny leather boots and held a
polo mallet in one hand. The sun gleamed on his white
hair, lighting it up like spun silver. "This is Marian's father," she said. "Paul Iverson."

The man in the photo was David's double. I looked up.
Dory was watching me.

THE AFTERNOON RUSH slowed traffic on the Kennedy.
Sandwiched between a moving van and a yellow school
bus, I nudged the Volvo forward, thinking about Dory.
She knew how much David and Paul Iverson looked alike,
and she wanted me to know it.

But why? What was her stake in all of this? She'd only
just met David, and you couldn't really call *our* relationship a friendship. In fact, I'd considered her the type of
person who tries to assert control by knowing what everyone else is up to. Now I wasn't so sure.

I turned on the radio, uneasily punching the buttons on
the console. Random bits of noise spilled out: the twang
of a country tune, a man barking in Spanish, two beats of
a base guitar. I settled on one of the all-news stations.

". . . latest poll by the *Chicago Sun-Times* ranks Marian
Iverson eight percentage points in front of her challenger,
downstate Democrat Frank Clayton . . ."

Marian. Her reaction to David had been just as peculiar.
Unnatural, now that I thought about it. I was certain she
noticed the similarity between David and her father, but,
unlike Dory, she didn't say a word about it. That was
strange. If a man showed up looking as much like my
father as David, I'd be curious. At the very least, I'd say
something, maybe show him the picture of my father. I
might even quiz him about his family, in the remote
chance he was a long-lost cousin.

But Marian didn't do any of those things. After a brief,

awkward moment, she proceeded to ignore the situation. Pretended it wasn't happening. Exactly what she did when we screened the Movietone newsreel. I flashed back to the newsreel of Iverson and Lisle. Their casual intimacy, the way their bodies almost touched. David Linden had to be the son of Paul Iverson and Lisle Gottlieb, and Marian knew it. Why did she pretend otherwise?

I went over the chronology. Germany surrendered in the spring of '45, and American soldiers started trickling back to the States by June. Kurt Weiss came back in July, Dad said. At which point he and Lisle picked up where they'd left off. By all accounts, whatever was between Lisle and Paul Iverson ended. A few scant weeks later, Kurt was murdered. Then a week or so after that, Lisle showed up at my father's, claiming to be pregnant with Kurt's child.

I braked sharply, narrowing missing the van in front of me. The timing was the proof. Today, with home pregnancy tests, you know if you're pregnant within a few days of conception, but back then it took longer—at least six or eight weeks. Lisle announced her pregnancy less than two weeks after Kurt died. But he'd only been home a few weeks at most. Which meant she was already pregnant when he came home. Lisle had lied.

In a way, it was understandable. Abortions were expensive then, difficult to obtain, and dangerous. She may have felt she didn't have any options. Paul Iverson wouldn't be the type to drop everything simply because his mistress—his Jewish mistress—became pregnant. He probably slipped a few C-notes off his roll of bills and told her to take care of the problem herself. Don't call me, sweetheart; I'll call you.

I edged into the left lane and came abreast of the moving van. The heat had glued my clothes to the seat, and my skirt was hiked high on my thighs. The van driver ogled me as we inched up the Edens. Not much has changed, I thought darkly.

THIRTY-ONE

THE NEXT DAY dawned bright and clear. A fresh breeze swept away the sultry air, and the sun threw shafts of gold across the floor. I brewed a perfect pot of coffee, watered the flowers, and went for a walk with Susan. We hiked over to the bike path, a ribbon of narrow asphalt that wound through the forest preserve. Dappled sun flickered through the dense shade, and the cushion of leaves under our feet was spongy.

I'd already told Dory Sanchez about David, so I filled Susan in, figuring she'd be thrilled that after four years I was finally showing an interest in the opposite sex. I giggled as I related our meeting at The Ritz.

"So we like him, do we?" She smiled enigmatically.

"Yes. But there's a problem."

"There always is."

I told her about his resemblance to Paul Iverson and my suspicions about his parentage. Susan slowed her pace. "Are we talking about Marian Iverson's father? The woman you're working for?"

I plucked a wildflower from the edge of the path. "Yes."

"Ellie, how do you do this?"

"Do what?" I twirled the flower stem.

"How do you get yourself into these . . . these situations?" She circled her hands in the air. "Where everything is connected and turns back on itself?" She looked at me. "There's some kind of theory about that, isn't there?"

"Probably the gravitational pull of Jewish geography." She threw me a puzzled look. "An elemental force known to connect people, places, and things throughout the world." I laughed. "No. More like the universe."

Susan arched an eyebrow. She had it down to an art.

"Don't sell it short. David's trying to find his roots, and his mother lived in Lawndale. It used to be a Jewish neighborhood."

"But Iverson's mill wasn't in Lawndale."

"Women came from all over to work at the mill during the war." I shrugged. "But what David is looking into happened in Lawndale."

"His father's murder."

"The man he thinks is his father."

"So what are you doing to help?"

"Nothing."

"Why not? You do that kind of thing. You're good at it."

A cloud of tiny gnats hovered above my head. I waved a hand, and they immediately dispersed. "How can I, knowing what I do?"

She faced me. "How can you not? You're the one who got him to Chicago in the first place."

"Not really." I hesitated. "He came for that conference."

"Nice try."

I threw the flower down and picked up my pace. "Susan, don't make me feel guiltier than I already do. I can't help him."

"Why not?"

I picked up my pace. "David grew up idolizing Kurt Weiss. Not only as his father, but also as a war hero. I already shocked him once by telling him that Kurt died here, not in some trench in Europe. I can't tell him the rest. It would rip him apart."

"But he's searching for the truth."

"I don't have the truth. All I've got is a gut feeling, a

few seconds of a newsreel, and a series of suspicious events. I need more proof."

"All the more reason to find it."

We ducked under a low branch hanging over the footpath. "It's . . . it's not my place."

"Since when have you ever worried about propriety?" She bristled. "Ellie, you've already found out more about his family in a few weeks than he has in fifty years."

"What if he can't face the truth?"

"So now you're sitting in judgment of what he can or can't accept? From what you told me about his life, he's already faced plenty."

"Maybe." I shot her a look. "Anyway, I've got other issues to deal with."

The thing about Susan is that she always knows when to back off. "So, what's going on with Barry?"

I told her about Barry's disappearing act. "No one knows where he is, and I'm worried. I'm beginning to think I should get someone to find him."

"You mean a private detective?"

I shrugged. "Pam said the brokerage might hire someone. But I don't know. What if he's in trouble?"

"Barry can handle himself."

"Half a million in the hole is a lot to handle." I jammed my hands in my pocket. "Don't get me wrong. I'm eternally grateful that I don't have to live with him anymore, but he is the father of my child. For her sake, I hope he hasn't done anything crazy—"

"Crazy?"

"Like—" I froze.

Susan stopped, too. "What?" My heart started to jitterbug in my chest. "Ellie, are you okay?"

"No, no. It's not me."

"What?"

"I just thought of something. About Kurt Weiss."

"David's father." She corrected herself. "The one he thinks is his father."

I nodded. "Remember I told you Kurt came home from the war and was killed a few weeks later?"

"Yes."

"I just remembered something. Paul Iverson died around the same time. A heart attack, the articles said. That's what Marian said, too. But someone else told me he committed suicide."

"Paul Iverson committed suicide? Who told you that?"

"A woman who's kind of the resident historian of the steel industry in Chicago. She said everyone knew he killed himself, but the family wanted to put a respectable face on it. So they let out that he died of a heart attack."

Susan searched my face. "I don't get it. Why would a successful tycoon, a man with everything, even a mistress on the side, blow his brains out?"

"Good question."

"You trust this woman? This historian?"

"I have no reason not to."

"It sounds fishy."

"Not necessarily. A suicide wasn't the kind of thing you wanted to broadcast back then."

Susan shrugged.

"If you're hinting that she has an ax to grind, I don't see it," I said. "She seems pretty credible."

We rounded a bend on the bicycle path. I heard the hushed sound of traffic from the expressway. Susan threw her shoulders back and, with a determined tilt of her chin, picked up the pace for the home stretch.

"You know," I said, a few paces behind her, "yesterday, David asked me what his father did that made someone want to kill him. What if it wasn't what Kurt Weiss did? What if it was what he had?" Susan slowed. "Kurt had Lisle Gottlieb," I went on. "Paul Iverson didn't. He lost Lisle—and possibly his unborn child—to Kurt. And then Kurt was murdered."

"And then Iverson killed himself." Susan finished.

We walked in step with each other. Neither of us said anything.

"You're right about one thing," she said finally.

"What's that?"

"You're going to need proof."

THIRTY-TWO

I'S BECAUSE OF Rick Feld that I no longer cringe at the thought of a root canal. Not because of the classic rock music that flows out of hidden speakers on his walls. Or the picture of a young Robert Redford hanging at chair level. Or the special goggles that let you watch a video while he drills into your mouth. Rick's skillful. And he gives great drugs.

But I wasn't camped out at his office the next morning for a procedure.

After Rachel went to sleep, I tried to figure out how to prove that Lisle and Paul had an affair. Where had they gone for their trysts? I didn't think there were many hotels on the East Side near the steel mill; at least none that Paul Iverson would have felt comfortable in. I couldn't see Lisle bringing Paul Iverson to her room at the Teitelmans' either. Too many prying eyes. Where would they have gone to consummate their relationship? I walked from room to room, trying to focus my thoughts. It was nearly midnight when it came to me. I called Dad.

"Ellie, do you know what time it is?"

"You weren't asleep, were you?

"No, but—"

"I'm sorry, Dad, but I need to know something. Whatever happened to Feld, the man who owned the apartment building Lisle moved into?"

"Lisle again?" He sighed. "What now?"

"What happened to the man who rented her the apartment on Douglas Avenue? You said his name was Feld."

"I got no idea." The strains of a clarinet played softly in the background. "But let me ask Marv. His family used to own real estate down there. I'll call you back tomorrow."

I was brewing coffee the next morning when Dad called back. "Feld died a long time ago, but Marv thinks there's a son up in Northbrook. A dentist or something."

"Not Rick Feld, the root canal guy." See what I mean about Jewish geography?

Which was why I was at Rick's office before it opened, without an appointment.

From his toys you might expect Rick Feld to be hip and New Age with Levi's, sandals, and a Hawaiian shirt under his white coat. Or maybe the gold chain type with designer shoes and buffed nails. He was neither. In his midsixties, Rick was small enough for a jockey, though he claimed to have been a crew coxswain in college. What little hair was left was short, gray, and curly. But he was a cheerful man, and the twinkle in his eye said he still enjoyed a good joke.

His nurse ushered me into a small back room where Rick was hunched over his computer, his white medical jacket bathed in the glow of the monitor. Colorful graphics and lots of text splashed across the screen.

"Good morning, Rick," I said.

He jerked his head up. "Ellie," he said in a startled voice. "Do we have an appointment?"

Shaking my head, I peered at the monitor. He quickly closed the file. A flush crept up his neck.

A porn site, I figured. "I'm sorry," I said. "That's none of my business."

He glanced at the monitor, then back to me. "Actually," he cleared his throat. "I was reading." His face was cherry red.

"Reading?"

"There's this science fiction site with free stories on it. It's not bad." He shrugged. "I log on when I get a minute."

So much for prurient inclinations. I grinned. "Sorry to intrude, but I wanted to ask you a question about your father."

He logged off. "What about him?"

"He owned property in Lawndale at one time, didn't he?"

"Yes. We lived there until my sister was born."

"Do you by any chance remember an apartment building on Douglas Avenue? A red-brick, four-story place with columns in the front?"

"That's where we lived."

My heart machine-gunned in my chest. "You're kidding."

"Until we moved to Skokie."

"Rick, can we set up the goggles? I want to show you something."

"No problem." We moved to a small cabinet in one of the treatment rooms. "What's this all about?" He flipped the power switch on a VCR, then picked up a pair of goggles that looked like sunglasses without the frames. A pair of earphones lay beside them.

"It's a long story." I dug out the video of the newsreel and slipped it into the cradle. I'd cued it to the scenes of Iverson and Lisle before I left home.

He offered me the goggles.

"No. You watch it," I said. "Tell me if you recognize any of the people you're looking at."

"Is there sound?"

"No. Well there is, but you don't need to listen to it."

He plugged the goggles into a slim silver box attached to the VCR and put them over his head. He pushed the Play button on the VCR, looking like something out of a Jules Verne novel. He raised his head, and his mouth started to twitch. Then his mouth opened. A few seconds later, he took the goggles off.

"This is amazing. Where did you get it?" He handed me back the goggles.

I looked through them. On the right, just at eye level,

was a tiny screen, no more than an inch square. I could just make out scenes from the newsreel running in miniature but perfect proportion. "Do you recognize them?"

"I sure do. They rented an apartment in the building."

"They?" I laid the goggles back on the VCR and pushed Stop.

"The guy with the white hair. And the blond. They lived upstairs."

"Both of them?"

Rick nodded. "I used to play Allies and Axis with Tommy Steinberg in front of the building. I remember that man's hair. We decided he must be a magician or a wizard or something. He came in and out with her all the time."

"All the time'?"

"They left in the morning. They came back at night. They left the next morning."

I tightened my jaw. "So he lived there?"

"That's what I said, Ellie." Rick angled his head. "So, what's the deal? Who is that guy?"

"Paul Iverson."

"The steel magnate?"

I nodded.

"I always knew he was someone important."

"How long did they live there together?"

His eyes wandered around the room. He shook his head. "I don't know. I was only about six or seven, you know. Hey, wait. I do remember." His face brightened. "He was there during D day. I remember that. I was outside with Tommy, and they came up the walk, both of them laughing and smiling, and he said something like, "This is a day to remember, sonny. A very important day." I remember I ran inside and asked my father what he meant."

I nodded, trying to suppress the mix of emotions roiling my stomach.

THIRTY-THREE

FOUAD'S DODGE RAM was parked in the driveway when I got back that afternoon.

"Ellie, hello. I'm glad to see you," he said, coming around from the front. "There is a slight problem."

I followed him to the yews at the front of the house. He shook a few branches. Sprinkles of tan bristles fell to the ground. "Spider mites," he said. "They've infested the yews. If we don't do something, you will lose them."

"Great." I said, unable to summon up much enthusiasm for gardening. "What do we do?"

"We can spray them with Dursban or diazanon. I have both. Come."

"Isn't diazanon what you use on grubs?" I said as we walked to his pickup.

"That's correct." He dropped the back panel.

"That's powerful poison."

He hoisted himself into the bed of the truck where a wheelbarrow, bags of peat moss, hoses, and a complement of garden tools crowded together, all partially covered by a tarp. Throwing off the tarp, he rummaged around, eventually locating his backpack sprayer. As he pulled it out, I noticed two long brown objects wedged against the side of the bed. He saw me looking at them and quickly covered them with the tarp.

"Fouad, what are you doing with guns in your truck?"

He checked to see if anyone had seen us. "I hunt."

"I didn't know this was hunting season."

He looked down. "It is not. I am moving them."

I waited.

He sighed. "I am not supposed to own them without a FOID card, so I keep them hidden."

I pointed. "If that's what you call hidden, I'd consider finding a new spot."

He jumped out of the pickup and slipped his arms into the straps of the sprayer.

I eyed him curiously. The idea that Fouad would consciously break the law seemed ludicrous. "Why don't you apply for the card?"

He heaved the sprayer onto his back.

"Fouad?"

His mouth was thin and tight. "I had the card. It was not renewed."

We started to walk back to the yews. "Why not?"

He hesitated. "When I first came to this country, I lived in Skokie. I did not know the customs. Or the legal system. I was here only two months when my roommate was arrested for stealing a television set. The police caught him in my car. He had borrowed it. Even though I was not involved, the police did not believe me. The man in the store said he saw two boys." He stopped walking. "I did not have money enough to hire a lawyer, but my roommate said his lawyer would represent me, too. I thought it would be good. He was Syrian, you see? Like me." He smiled helplessly. "The lawyer got my roommate off, but not me."

"What happened?"

"Since it was a first offense, and there were disagreements between some of the witnesses, I did not go to jail. I received community service. And probation." He took the sprayer off his back and attached a hose to it. "Of course, that was thirty years ago."

"And you've had a card since then."

"Yes. But you see, the rules have recently changed. Before, only convictions within five years of the application were grounds for rejection. But now any conviction, at any time can be a problem."

"That doesn't seem fair. Can't you explain?"

"I tried." He shrugged. "But they do not believe me."

"Why not?"

"What is my name, Ellie? Where am I from?"

A finger of anger slid down my spine. In America, it's not supposed to matter if your name isn't Smith or Jones, if you're a law-abiding citizen. "How do you do it, Fouad? How do you maintain your equanimity?"

He smiled. "The Koran says, 'I do not control for myself any harm, or any benefit except what Allah please.' I try to yield to the will of my God." He pointed the hose of the sprayer toward the yews. "And," his eyes twinkled, "I keep the guns hidden in my truck."

We were spraying the yews when a red Honda cruised around the corner and stopped at the curb. The drivers-side door opened, and David uncurled himself from the seat. He was wearing light khakis, a turquoise shirt, and loafers without socks. Raising his sunglasses off his eyes, he started across the grass toward me. His hair glinted in the sun.

A visceral ping shot through me, and I took a few steps toward him. We stopped a few feet away from each other. With Pavlovian smiles on our faces. Time stood still.

Fouad cleared his throat, and at the same time, Rachel bounded out of the house. "Mom, did you see my—" She stopped when she saw David. I watched as she slowly sized him up, her eyes taking in his clothes, his white hair, his smile.

"Rachel," I said, "this is David Linden. David, this is Rachel. And Fouad Al Hamra, my friend."

Rachel sidled up, gave him her hand, and snuck a look at me. "Hi."

"Hi, Rachel." He took her hand and kept it in his for a beat. Then he turned to Fouad and shook his, too. He took his sunglasses off his head. "I was in the area," he said. "I've been trying to find a woman who worked at Iverson's. She lives in Mount Prospect." Mount Prospect is a few villages west. "But it seems she moved into a nursing home a few months ago . . ." His voice trailed off. He folded his sunglasses and stuffed them in his shirt pocket.

I couldn't stop smiling. Neither could he. "Tell you what. You and Rachel go inside while I finish up with Fouad. Then I'll make some iced tea. Rachel, make sure he feels at home."

Rachel tossed her head importantly.

I watched them go, then turned to Fouad. He was smiling, too. Dammit. Couldn't anybody do anything but smile?

"You do not need to be here, Ellie," he said. "I can finish up."

"No, I want to help."

As we sprayed, the tinkle of the piano floated out the window. Rachel never touches the piano during the summer, but she was playing the piece she'd learned for her recital. When the piece was over, I heard the occasional plink of a chord. I came inside and washed my hands. David and Rachel were on the piano bench, their heads bent over the keys.

"The arpeggio, with its sets of thirds and fourths, is just a series of numbers," David was saying. "What they call a mathematical progression."

Rachel turned a puzzled face toward him. "What do you mean?"

"There are rules about what chords follow other chords, how different melodies are supposed to be combined, right?"

She nodded.

"It's no accident. There's a simple numerical interval or ratio between beautiful sounds—they're related to each other. Like this." He played a chord in G major.

"What about this?" She played a G-minor chord.

"Same thing," he smiled. "All you did was change the ratio on the bottom third."

She studied the keys. "Two whole steps to one and a half."

"You're pretty quick."

She beamed.

"Music and mathematics are closely related. In fact, they say that playing an instrument can make you better at math."

Her face turned skeptical.

"It's true. Scientists are finding that music and brain wave activity are built on the same kinds of patterns."

"You're just saying that so I'll practice more."

He laughed. "Can't put one past you, can I?"

I slipped into the kitchen and made a pitcher of iced tea, then carried it into the family room. "Who wants some?"

Rachel whispered to David. They both looked up. "Uh, Mom? We have an idea."

"That sounds dangerous."

"We're both kind of hungry," David said. "How about if I take you both to dinner?"

"Dinner?" I grinned. "You said the magic word."

He winked at Rachel.

THIRTY-FOUR

I SHOWERED AND threw on a pair of slacks and a blue top that makes me look like I actually have a neck. We piled into David's car and drove to the Italian Gardens, a small restaurant with a statue of Venus de Milo in a fountain out front. Rachel pulled out a penny and flipped the coin into the fountain. It bounced off Venus's torso and plopped into a shallow pool glittering with other pennies and an occasional dime.

"Don't you want to know what I wished for?" She edged toward the door.

"If you tell me," I said, "it won't come true."

Her eyes flitted from me to David. My cheeks got hot.

A wave of garlic eddied out as we stepped in. The place was crowded, the tables covered with red-and-white checked cloths and candles in small woven baskets, layers of hardened wax dribbling down their sides. Most of the tables were filled. Accordion music spilled out of speakers.

The maître d' sat us near a saltwater aquarium filled with tropical fish. Bursts of yellow, blue, and orange glinted through the glass. I'd been a regular here after Barry and I separated. One night, after I'd had too much to drink, Vincenzo, the owner, made a pass at me. Nothing happened; he'd had more to drink than me. A few days later, he confessed it was just as well. Fish were his real passion. They didn't talk back, and they didn't care if he respected them in the morning.

The bluish light from the tank lit our menus as a waitress took our drink orders. Rachel asked for a Coke, and David ordered a bottle of Sassicaia, a Tuscan wine which he said was better than Chianti. I saw approval on the waitress's face.

Rachel inherited my mother's Southern charm, a trait that apparently skipped me, because she chattered away, peppering David with questions about Philadelphia, cheese steaks, and the Liberty Bell. Then she moved on to parlor tricks. We were going to play a game, she announced.

"Here's how it works." Her blue eyes brimmed with authority. "You have to think of things that go together like 'pen and ink,' 'milk and honey,' things like that. We go around the table really fast, and the person who can't think of anything is out. Okay?"

"Okay," David nodded.

I dreaded what was coming. I can't think on demand. I'd make a lousy quiz show contestant.

"I'll go first," Rachel said. "Jack and Jill." She smiled triumphantly. "Now you." She pointed to David.

"Black and blue," David said without missing a beat.

Four eyes gazed at me. Oh God. Now he'll see how lame I am. My eyes darted around the room. Saved. "Salt and pepper," I said in relief.

Rachel curled her lip. A trace of mother-daughter competition, perhaps? "Birds and the bees," she declared.

"Romeo and Juliet," David said.

"Uh, uh, the Jets and the Sharks," I said.

"Show and tell." Rachel was pretty good at this.

"Bonnie and Clyde." So was David.

My turn again. I stared at the fake stucco patterns that swirled across the ceiling. I drew a blank. "Um—"

"Come on, Mom."

"Redford and Newman," I blurted out.

"What?" Rachel drew herself up. "Who are they?"

"Two guys who were in a couple of movies together."

David looked at his plate. His mouth twitched. Rachel

caught it. "You're out," she said imperiously.

I shrugged.

David laughed. "Don't feel bad. I was hanging on by my fingernails."

"Come on, guys. Let's do it again," Rachel said with the confidence of someone who knows she's going to win. Thankfully, the waitress interrupted with our meal. Rachel and I debated whether she should use a knife and fork with her pizza or pick it up in her fingers. I lost.

AS WE WALKED back to the car, two searchlights swung back and forth in a wide arc, piercing the night sky. I wondered who or what was lost, relieved for once it wasn't me. When we got home, Rachel made a pretense of yawning and went upstairs.

I found a bottle of amaretto, two brandy snifters, and carried them into the family room. I poured and handed one to David. In the back of my mind, I knew I had to tell him about Paul Iverson and his mother. But I didn't want to break the spell. Like Scarlett, I'd think about it tomorrow.

David rotated the glass in his hand. Shafts of light shot through the amber liquid, and patterns of tawny light danced across his hand.

"Nice effect," I settled down on the couch next to him.

"How would you do this in video?"

"Smoke and mirrors," I said.

He smiled through half-closed eyes. I was aware that our bodies were close together. I drained my amaretto. His hand rested just inches from mine. He covered it with his and lifted it to his lips. I shivered. He pressed his mouth against my wrist. Something inside me swelled up. He slid my hand around his neck and drew me close. His lips grazed my neck, my cheeks, and stopped at my mouth. I tasted the amaretto on his tongue and wondered if he tasted it on mine. I wrapped my arms around his neck. His kisses grew urgent, and his tongue sought out mine. His fingers stroked the side of my face. I slid down on my back. He moved on top of me. I smelled the faint scent of soap behind his ears. His hands left my face, caressed my neck, my shoulders, my breasts. I trembled, feeling his weight press down on me.

Then, abruptly, I felt space between us. I opened my eyes. He had pulled away. My breath was coming in short gasps. "What?" I whispered hoarsely.

He shook his head and moved to the edge of the sofa, where he dragged himself to a sitting position. "I'm sorry."

The back of my eyes ached. I tried to steady my breathing. "What is it?"

"It's not you. I . . . I—"

"Is there someone else?"

He didn't answer. His silence was proof enough. I stood up. So did he.

"Well," I said slowly, "I guess that's it." I saw regret on his face, as if he wanted to say something. I raised a finger to his lips. "No," I whispered. "Don't apologize. It's all right."

But it wasn't.

I walked him to the door. The cicadas had already started to chirr. When I was young, the serenade of the cicadas at dusk was the first sign that summer was finite. That the sweet, languid days would eventually end. Since then, their song has always sounded bittersweet.

I went to bed and burrowed under the sheets, feeling the empty space next to me. Images of David drifted into my mind. His thick white hair. Smooth skin dusted with gold. The way his jaw worked when he was upset. I would probably never see him again.

I closed my eyes and raised my T-shirt. I put my hands on my breasts and stroked my nipples. My fingers moved in tiny circles, caressing the skin around them. My back arched under the sheet. My hands glided down to my abdomen. His hands. Then lower. They stayed there until my breath came in short little gasps and a soft moan escaped my lips. The cicadas sang. The bed was still empty.

THIRTY-FIVE

RACHEL AND I loaded her two duffels, sleeping bag, and backpack in the car and headed off to Wisconsin. Just past the state line, the scenery changed from suburban sprawl to farmland, and we smelled grass overlaid with manure. Clumps of blue wildflowers mixed freely with Queen Anne's lace at the side of the road. We drove through small towns with church spires on one corner and bare-chested bikers with flag bandanas on another. The Heart-land.

Rachel didn't talk much, preferring to pop her gum. But a few miles from camp, she said, "I like David."

"I think the feeling's mutual."

She looked over. "Are you going to see him again?"

"I don't know."

She nodded, as if she knew not to push it.

Silver Lake Camp was the kind of place I wished I had gone to. Nestled beside a small lake, the camp had a heated pool, a climbing wall, all the requisite land sports, and horses. Rachel had begged me to let her take riding lessons, and I said okay. Never having ridden myself, I missed out on that sexual-awakening thing that makes young girls obsess over horses. Maybe Rachel would tell me about it.

As we hauled her bags into her cabin, another camper and a woman were already inside. The camper, a plump little girl with long black hair, was trying to unpack her duffel. The woman, who I assumed was her mother, was blond and rail thin. Wearing a halter top, shorts, and three-inch sandals, she watched her daughter struggle with the duffel bag without lifting a finger to help.

The two girls checked each other out. Rachel introduced herself, and then, digging into her backpack, asked if the other girl wanted to listen to music. The girl, whose name was Emily, nodded. Rachel unpacked her speakers from her duffel, and set them on the lower cot of a bunk bed. Seconds later, Brittany Spears blasted through the walls of the cabin. The girls started to sing.

Meanwhile Emily's blond mother, her roots noticeably darker than the rest of her hair, struck up a conversation. Within five minutes I knew she was divorced from Emily's father, wintered in West Palm, spent summers abroad with her European boyfriend, and had a son on a camping trip in Alaska.

I watched the girls out of the corner of my eye. Rachel unpacked her toilet articles, took out two Q-Tips, and proceeded to stick them up her nose. That brought peals of laughter from Emily.

"Rachel," I said, "get the Q-Tips out of your nose."

A barrage of giggles from Emily. Rachel made a face and took them out. Emily's mother's nattered on about a shopping trip in Geneva, where she'd picked up the gold that glittered around her neck and wrist. Rachel and Emily were now smoking pretend cigarettes, holding the Q-Tips between their fingers and blowing imaginary smoke rings in the air.

When Emily's mother saw them, her eyes widened and she immediately launched into a five-minute sermon on the dangers of smoking. The girls dropped the Q-Tips on the floor and lapsed into stony silence. Emily's mother turned toward me with a look of satisfaction.

"One must never miss an opportunity to parent."

I smiled weakly.

After hugging and kissing Rachel a few times, I hit the road. As I roared down the ribbon of concrete, I cranked up the radio. "Thunder Road" blasted from the speakers, the wind whistled through my hair, and for one timeless moment it was as if the past thirty years hadn't happened. I was young and free, my life yet uncharted, unlimited opportunities ahead. I could go anywhere, do anything, be whatever I wanted. Then the song ended, and I was back in the present, with the accumulated weight of mistakes, disappointments, and self-recriminations on my shoulders.

It was dark when I got home. Tired and gritty with highway dust, I was looking forward to a glass of wine and a hot bath. As I passed through the kitchen, the red light on the answering machine blinked. I hit Replay.

"Ellie, This is Dory Sanchez. I need to talk to you. Please call me."

I called the number she left, but there was no answer, and no machine picked up. The other message was from my lawyer, Pam Huddleston. "Ellie, call me as soon as possible. It doesn't matter what time."

I reached her at home.

"Ellie, I'm glad you called," Pam said. "Listen, sit down. The Chicago Corp is filing suit against both you and Barry to recover their money. They say they're going to file an injunction to seize your assets."

I didn't say anything.

"Are you there?"

"Yes."

"They've hired a private investigator to find Barry. But if they can't find him, they're saying they expect you to pay the whole thing. You'll get the summons tomorrow."

THIRTY-SIX

I DIDN'T SLEEP much that night. It was steamy out the next morning, but I huddled in my bathrobe. When the summons arrived, I took it, signed my name, and threw it on the kitchen table.

I watched the sun glaze the locust tree leaf by leaf. Money is power. Power is control. I was going to have a lot less of both very soon. Though I despise conspicuous consumption and feel vastly superior to people like Emily's mother who practice it, at that moment, I would have gladly traded my life for hers. To sail through life with a brazen disregard for prudence, with the certainty that money was an ever-renewing resource, seemed like a luxury I'd never know.

Not that I hadn't tried. If you're not careful, you can start to confuse wants with needs. You can start to think you are entitled to money and the things it can buy. Particularly when the rest of your life is a void and you're living a half-life of anger, disappointment, and stress.

At first it was never anything that cost a lot; a candy bar, a greeting card, a pen. I wanted them. I deserved them. I was entitled. So I stole them. After about a year of petty shoplifting, I saw a blouse in a department store. A sheer lemony tank, it was the kind of top that would look great with either pants or a skirt. I tried it on in the dressing room; it was a perfect fit. I was about to take it out to the counter and pay when it hit me. I was alone, the saleswoman was nowhere in sight. I could do it. I could get away with it. I dropped the blouse into my bag.

I remember the smell of new clothes, the weave of the store carpeting as I hurried to the revolving doors. I also remember the sharp cry of the saleswoman as she shouted "Shoplifter!" the feel of the guard's hand on my arm, the shocked faces of other shoppers.

I offered to pay double for it, but it didn't work. The cops took me down to the station, their strained civility failing to mask their scorn. I sat riveted to the chair, afraid that if I got up, I would be thrown in a cell and never come out. Then Barry arrived, and a half hour later, the charges were mysteriously dropped.

The memory of that shame was a powerful deterrent. I joined a twelve-step program. I made progress. I tried to develop a rational relationship with money. I got divorced.

But now I owed half a million dollars. I'd have to file for bankruptcy. I'd lose the house. And that was just for starters. Barry wouldn't rescue me this time. In fact, he'd left me holding the bag. This must be just retribution. God's payback. I got dressed and watered the flowers, wondering how much time I had left in the house.

IT ONLY TOOK twenty minutes to get to the Iverson estate that afternoon. I drove past the house and parked by a small bridge. The heat had intensified since morning; the back of my shirt was wet. A motorboat somewhere on the lake whined in the distance, the engine of the Volvo ticked. Otherwise, it was still.

I stretched my arms over the railing. A forested ravine lay beneath me. At the bottom, a skinny stream of water flowed out toward the lake. Partway down the steep hill was a structure, half hidden behind a woodsy tangle of trees. I squinted. It was a brick cistern, about eight feet in diameter, built on top of a stone base. Butterflies hovered around it.

I was wrong about Paul Iverson. I'd assumed Lisle was just a plaything for him, someone to have his way with on sultry afternoons. I'd imagined Lisle, blond hair framing her pretty head, lounging seductively on the bed in her slip, watching Iverson pull on his clothes for the trip back to Lake Forest. He would have dropped a trinket on the bed for her, planted a kiss on her cheek, and headed out, a satisfied smile on his lips. She would have dashed to the window and watched him stroll to his chauffered car, counting the days and hours until he pulled her off the assembly line again.

But if what Rick Feld said was true, Paul Iverson was living with Lisle Gottlieb. What started as a casual affair, something to while away time, had turned into a consuming passion.

I could see it. First he finds himself spending more and more time with her, unable to muster the will to leave. Then he realizes that he's fallen in love with her. Finally, he comes to believe that living with her, possessing her, seeding her with his child, are the only things that could possibly matter in life. Besotted, he abandons his wife, his house, and his family, believing only Lisle can satiate him, fill the void in his heart he hadn't known was there.

But then, one day, she unexpectedly rejects him. Leaves him for another man. Snatches away their unborn child. Without warning, the lifeline he has come to depend on, as critical for his survival as air or water or food, has been ripped out of his hands. The powerful steel magnate, defeated by the girl on the line.

A motor revved and wheels screeched behind me. I whipped around just in time to see a car peel out of the Iversons' driveway. As I stared at the retreating vehicle, a knot of fear twisted my stomach. It was a tan Cutlass, with two figures inside. I frantically searched for a license plate, but the car was moving too fast. I watched it grow small and disappear, a dull roaring in my ears. I was scheduled to interview Marian's mother. Paul Iverson's wife. How did they know I was here?

A few hundred yards to my left, the road ended in two

stone pillars. A sign between the pillars read Lake Forest Cemetery.

INSIDE, THE HEAVY wood door seemed to seal off the outside world. I felt as if I'd stepped into another realm, another time. A maid in a black-and-white uniform led me through the dark hall into the drawing room. I hadn't noticed the cathedral ceiling, elegant moldings, or antique furniture at the fund-raiser. They made an impression now.

Frances Iverson reclined on a brocade sofa, a cup of tea in her hand. Her wheelchair was pushed against the wall. Despite the cobalt blue of her dressing gown, her skin was ashen, and the hand holding the teacup looked like veined marble. A silver tea service on a mahogany table held an assortment of scones, tiny sandwiches, and pots of jam.

"Thank you for agreeing to do the interview, Mrs. Iverson."

A pair of raised eyebrows was her response. "A mother's duty, I'm told." Her voice was coarse, as if age had stripped away all vestiges of her gender. She put the teacup down and allowed me to shake her hand. Her skin felt like crepe paper. She gestured for me to sit in an empty chair. The seat was warm.

Despite heavy drapes, the western sun poured through at an angle, hitting me in the face. I raised my hand to block it. Either she didn't notice my discomfort, or she wanted it that way. Her eyes were pools of indifference. "My daughter says I'm to answer all your questions."

"That's why I came a few minutes early. I thought we could go over the questions." I snuck a look at her. "Mrs. Iverson, before we begin, I need to ask you. Did you just have some visitors?"

Her brows knit together. "Visitors?"

"Two men. Driving a tan Cutlass?"

"I wouldn't know." She flicked her wrist. "It's possible. There's always someone doing something around here.

Landscapers. Repairmen. So much upkeep. I really ought to find a smaller place." Rousing herself, she reached for a silver bell on a mahoghany table. "Let's ask Justine."

"Oh, don't bother. It's not important."

"Are you sure?"

I shook my head.

"As you will. Now, please have some tea." She smiled and poured me a cup. "And don't pass up these scones. We make them ourselves." As I bit into it, her smile widened. "I'm glad you're not one of those women who pick at their food."

I put the scone back on the saucer. "Marian said you weren't looking forward to this."

"I've always considered the press intrusive. And sensational."

"I'm not with the press." I thought she'd known that. "I'm producing a campaign video about your daughter. A favorable one."

Raising her chin, she looked down her nose at me. She was a tough sell. Unless she was trying to intimidate me. I forged ahead. "One of the things I'd like to get on tape are your recollections of Marian as a little girl. Particularly any anecdotes you recall."

"Anecdotes? Let me see." She studied her tea service, then launched into a story about Marian learning to ride a horse. How she fell off but fearlessly got back on. Perhaps sensing my lack of response, she smiled again, her cheeks disappearing in a sea of wrinkles. "That won't do?"

"Well—"

"You're right. It's much too patrician." She leaned forward and patted my hand, the same way Marian did. "Give me some time. I'll come up with something more appropriate."

Sunlight glinted on a group of photographs on a marble mantle. "We're also going to need some photos of Marian when she was young." I motioned. "May I look?"

"Of course."

I wandered over. In one of the silver frames, a young Frances and Paul Iverson were seated next to each other. Paul's hair was already white, but, in his dark tailored suit and white shirt, he was striking. Frances had been an attractive woman, too, with blond hair, a pronounced chin, and a slim figure. Marian took after her. The children posed in front of them: young Marian, in a lacy white dress, and her brother, in bow tie and knickers.

I picked up another photo of Paul Iverson. It was the same shot that Marian had in her office. Frances watched me look at it. "That was taken right after Paul and I met. On the polo grounds. You should have seen him on a horse."

I turned.

"Cantering up and down the field like a knight in shining armor. Of course, he was a little rough around the edges." She paused. "But we were young. We had time." A wistful smile played around her mouth.

"Could I borrow these? I'll scan them in and get them back to you."

"I'll have Justine bring you a box." She lifted a silver bell on the tray.

"No need." I took the two photos over to my bag. "I'll just put them in here." I slid them carefully inside. "Marian told me about your son's death. I'm so sorry." Her lips drew together in a tight, grim line. "Who ran the mill between the time your husband died and Gordon came in?"

She looked up. "We put together a consortium. A triumvirate, actually. Management selected an executive, the union suggested someone—"

"The union?"

"Well, the union officials."

"Was the mayor's father still shop steward?"

"I believe so. He was a help. They kept us going until Gordon was groomed."

I checked my watch. Mac was late. Okay, Susan, this one's for you. I sat down. The sun's rays had shifted away from my face. "Mrs. Iverson, I heard a rumor the other day. I'd like to run it by you."

"What's that?"

"The rumor is that your husband didn't die of a heart attack but took his own life."

She didn't move for a moment. Then she unfolded the blanket and draped it over her legs. Something unpleasant glinted in her eyes. "Who told you that?"

"A woman who owns a small mill on the East Side."

She nodded, more for her benefit, it seemed, than mine. "I've heard that story before. It seems to resurface every few years." She picked up her teacup. "I suppose there will always be rumors about people who are successful, charismatic, or in some other way distinguished. That's what I mean about the press."

"Mrs. Iverson, your response won't go into the video."

She sipped her tea. "Then why do you care?"

I looked at her. "Marian said he died of a heart attack. The articles I read say that, too. But I wondered. I wouldn't want to say something . . . inappropriate."

She breathed out a sigh. "Marian was a little girl when Paul died. She barely understood the concept of death. She kept asking when her daddy was coming back. She thought he was on a business trip."

The doorbell rang. Mac and the crew had arrived. "So it is true?" I asked in a low voice.

She set down the teacup. "My husband passed well before his time. It was a tragedy for all of us."

She lifted a cucumber sandwich from the tray. Patches of satin on the brocade sofa gleamed in the sun.

THIRTY-SEVEN

HEADING HOME AFTER the interview, I sped past a blur of signs, stores, and parking lots on Skokie Boulevard. In corporate doublespeak a nondenial is considered a tacit confirmation of fact. Exactly what Frances Iverson gave me.

I ran a hand through my hair. Iverson and Lisle had an affair, starting late in '42, give or take a few months. She moved to Douglas Avenue shortly after that, and a year later, in '44 if Rick Feld was right, Iverson moved in. By '45 she was pregnant. Then Kurt came home from the war. Lisle broke up with Iverson, Kurt was murdered, Iverson killed himself.

Was Paul Iverson involved in Kurt Weiss's death? Did he kill Kurt in a jealous rage, and then, unable to deal with his crime, kill himself? It had started as a crazy, far-fetched theory, but now I wasn't so sure.

Turning south on Sunset Ridge Road, I rolled down the window. Hot air shot across the front seat. I rolled it up again. That might explain why the Iverson family circulated the story about a heart attack. The family didn't want even a breath of scandal, however softly it was whispered, to be associated with the name of Paul Iverson.

It would also explain why Marian clung to the pretense. The idea that the father of the leading candidate for the Illinois Senate might be involved, however indirectly, in the sordid murder of a GI could be damaging. Irresistible fodder for the press. It might not cause a major scandal, but it would be good copy for a day or two. It might even trigger a dip in the polls. It made sense to prevaricate.

I turned onto Happ Road, the sun behind the trees. No wonder Marian was becoming tense around me. I was on her payroll, supposedly a loyal employee. Yet I'd unearthed film that hinted of an illicit affair between her father and another woman. I'd even flaunted David, the product of that relationship, in her face. She was probably wondering whose side I was on. And what I planned to do with the information.

She and I needed to have a quiet little talk. She needed to know I wouldn't betray her. No Judas reporter me. I would never make that information public. I pulled into the driveway, pleased with my strategy. It was the right thing to do.

Opening the garage door with the remote, I remembered the tan car. Clearly someone was stalking me, keeping close tabs, but not closing in. Why? What did they want? And why was the seat of the chair in Frances's living room warm? I climbed out of the car, feeling like I was skidding on ice, about to smash into oncoming traffic.

"HOW'S RACHEL?"

"David?"

"Did she get off okay?"

"Fine." Why was he calling? His behavior the other night had been pretty definitive. "She's already faxed me twice. She wants to come home."

"No."

I laughed. "Not to worry. She's right on schedule."

"Excuse me?"

"For the first couple of days, I always get tearful faxes and letters demanding I drop everything and bring her home. Then, after a week or so, I only hear from her when she wants gum, CDs, or money."

"Oh." Silence.

Okay. Small talk's over. I've done my part.

"Ellie, I . . . I've been doing some research since we last talked, and I wanted to get together. There are some things I'd like to go over with you. I could come by."

So I can risk another rejection? I don't think so.

"You were right, you know," he was saying. "The police weren't very cooperative. But I got a lead in spite of them."

"A lead?" He sounded like a detective.

"I went downtown to the library to look over old newspapers, thinking I might find some mention of the murder. I must have scrolled through hours of microfilm, but other than a couple of lines in the *Daily News*, there was nothing. Then I happened to strike up a conversation with one of the librarians, and she gave me the name of this woman who's supposed to be an expert on the history of the steel mills in Chicago. Her name is Jorgenson. I'm going to call her."

Shit. If he hooked up with her, he might find out about his mother and the newsreel. And Paul—"How, uh, interesting. But, uh, what do you think she can tell you? Your father didn't have anything to do with the steel industry."

"No, but my mother did. And this woman might be able to put me in touch with someone from Iverson's who knew her. Who knows what they might remember?"

Who knew indeed? I groped for something to say. "Do . . . do you really think anyone from that time is still alive?"

"Of course. They'd only be about as old as your father, no more."

"I suppose." I chewed my lip. Weak. Very weak. "But . . . is that really the best use of your time?"

"You wouldn't do it that way?" He sounded uncertain.

Actually, that's exactly how I'd do it. "It seems like you're hunting for a needle in a haystack. I'm not sure I'd waste my time. Or the woman's." I sighed audibly. "But then, what do I know?"

"A lot. You were right about the police," he said

thoughtfully. "I'll think about it. So, what about it? Can we get together?"

"David, I have to get up early tomorrow to fly downstate. How about the day after?"

"Oh." He sounded disappointed. "Sure. I'll call you."

As we hung up, I heard another click on the line, but it barely penetrated my guilt. I'd lied, dissembled, and tried to manipulate a man I cared about. I was wrong about one thing. Judas was my middle name.

I CALLED DAD to tell him where I'd be. There was no answer. He was probably out with the guys. I left a message.

THIRTY-EIGHT

THE ROAR OF the engine stung my ears. Patches of color flashed past the window. The ground tore away from us, and we hurtled into the air. I squeezed my eyes shut, waiting for the fiery plunge to earth. Instead, we lifted straight up. I opened my eyes. The plane was banking over the lake.

The sound of the engine changed from a hardworking drone to a hum. My stomach lurched to my chest. Now we would fall out of the sky. We hit a bump, and the plane lifted, as if soaring over a bubble. I waited for the corresponding drop. It didn't come.

A flat, tinny voice broke through my terror. "Are you all right?"

I'd almost forgotten Mac was strapped in next to me. I gulped recycled air.

"Nice takeoff." He grinned.

Through the window I saw buildings the size of doll-houses, cars that crawled like ants. I looked the other way. Marian and Roger were crammed into the first row of the ten-seat Cessna. Stephen Lamont was next, sitting next to a young woman I'd never seen before. Roger introduced her as his assistant, but it wasn't Dory Sanchez. In fact, the only word to describe this girl-woman with blond hair and a button nose was *perky*. Mac and I were behind them, Mac's crew behind us. Lamont and the assistant were into an animated conversation, and I heard Marian laugh from the front. Everyone except me seemed calm. If they knew they were going to die, they were hiding it well.

We landed in Carbondale, "the best small city in Illinois," according to a poster at the airport. At one time, the town, situated near the state's southern border, had been a shipping hub for the transport of coal and fruit. Now it was known as the home of Southern Illinois University.

An advance team from the Republicans of Jackson County met us at the gate. As we left the air-conditioned chill of the tiny terminal to pile into cars, waves of heat eddied over us. Four hundred miles south of Chicago, we were closer to Kentucky than Wisconsin. I didn't mind; I was grateful to be alive.

Outside the city we turned into the Shawnee National Forest and Giant City State Park. The whine of the air-conditioning eased as the shade from a thousand maples, firs, and oaks cooled the air. Surrounded by enormous sandstone bluffs, Giant City got its name from a portion of the forest where huge rock formations mimic walls, streets, and alleys so precisely that they resemble a city made of stone. Climbers come from all over the Midwest to scale the rocks, though the Southern alums I know insist you have to be stoned to enjoy it.

The cars wound past woodland trails, fishing ponds, and scenic lookout points, ending at the center of the park where a lodge occupied a clearing. Adjoining it was a sheltered swimming pool. A podium festooned with red-white-and-blue draping stood in front of the lodge, and over a dozen tables covered with red-and-white checked cloths were lined up on the grass.

More than two hundred people had already gathered. As Marian's car rolled to a stop, I heard a smattering of applause. She stepped out and was immediately escorted inside to freshen up. Roger and his new assistant buzzed around the crowd. I followed Mac, but he waved me off.

"I've got it covered, Ellie. Go commune with nature

and get yourself centered. I'll let you know when we're ready."

Still queasy from the flight, I wandered toward the edge of the clearing, looking back on the scene in long shot. A bench on one side of the tables groaned with tubs of potato salad, drinks, and trays of fried chicken. On the other side a trio of musicians in striped shirts and straw hats plucked a banjo, guitar, and bass. The scent of chicken mingled with woodland pines.

I grabbed a soda from one of the tubs and rolled the cold can over my forehead. I didn't want to shoot more video of enthusiastic crowds and patriotic speeches. I wanted to disappear down one of the trails, drink in the cool quiet of the woods, and plan how to broach the Paul Iverson issue with Marian.

Instead, I slowly worked my way back toward the crowd. Stephen Lamont and Roger had their heads together. Lamont hadn't mentioned his proposed story on the video since Milk Days. I didn't want to remind him. Veering in the opposite direction, I introduced myself to a blowsy brunette in a flag shirt, red shorts, and heavy makeup. She turned out to be the wife of the chairman of the Jackson County Republicans, and she complimented me on how smart we were to choose Carbondale for a visit, given that Southern Republicans were so influential in Springfield. I sipped my soda, swallowing a grimace at being lumped in with the "we's." I was a hired hand, not one of the team.

While the flag lady confided that her husband, in line for a gubernatorial appointment, was checking out real estate in Springfield, I spotted Roger and Lamont heading my way. Roger crooked his finger at me. "Excuse me," I said, almost grateful, and trotted over like one of the team.

"Ellie." Roger draped an arm around my shoulder, "Didn't you tell us you were doing research on Marian's father?"

"Uh, yeah. A little. Why?"

"Lamont's looking into Marian's background." He

waved a finger. "You two should hook up together."

"All I did was download some articles," I turned to Lamont. "I'm sure you already have them. About the labor unions, mostly." I shrugged, as if to apologize for wasting his time. Lamont stroked his beard.

"Didn't you track down a newsreel with Marian's father in it?" Roger said.

I rolled the empty pop can between my hand, stalling for time. I had the story Lamont was searching for. The candidate's father: a philanderer who fathered a child out of wedlock and then took his own life after his mistress's husband was murdered. It was sordid. Sensational. Lamont would be all over it. I answered cautiously. "I found a few seconds of footage. Sandwiched between some stories about war bonds."

"Listen, babe. Make sure he sees whatever you got, okay?" Roger squeezed my shoulder.

"Sure." I backed away. "Babe."

Roger dropped his arm. Lamont smiled.

I wasn't paying for the footage. It belonged to Marian, and if she wanted Lamont to see it, I couldn't stand in his way. I could hope he wouldn't pick up on the Lisle-Iverson relationship, but given that he was a professional observer, I wasn't optimistic.

Roger's new aide interrupted us. "They're ready for Marian," she said, pronouncing Marian's name almost reverently. As she headed back toward the podium, hips swaying, Roger studied her ass. He licked his lips unconsciously, and then, as if just remembering I was there, bit down.

"Where's Dory?" I asked.

Irritation flashed across his face. "She . . . she left."

"Left what? The campaign?"

He nodded.

"When? Why?"

He hesitated. "She . . . we decided she really wasn't cut out for campaign work."

I frowned, unable to hide my dismay. "I got the impression she was doing a great job."

"No. She wasn't." He started after Ms. Perky, his curt tone indicating the subject was closed. Halfway across the lawn, he turned around. "Ellie, speaking of labor, Marian's doing a rally on Labor Day downtown. There's gonna be a fund-raiser at the Palmer House the night before, and she wants to show the video at it. We'll rent large screens and put them all around the ballroom. Terrific, huh?"

MARIAN'S SPEECH WAS mercifully short. Once it was in the can and we'd shot cutaways, Mac wrapped up. I called Dad. He still didn't answer. I felt a twinge of concern. I didn't like not knowing where he was. I ducked inside to the lodge.

I'd expected a rustic, rough-hewn decor, maybe with sandstone walls and quarry tile floor. But the carpeted hallways, gift shop, and nondescript bar were just like every other hotel on the rubber chicken circuit. I padded down the hall, looking for the ladies' room, and stopped at a closed door. I twisted it open and found a large parlor with a parquet floor and small groupings of furniture artfully placed around the room. A fireplace was at one end of the room, a bar at the other. A few tables had checkers and backgammon sets on them.

I wandered in, scanning the perimeter for the ladies' room but quickly realized I'd opened the wrong door. I was about to back out when a familiar voice stopped me. I glanced over my shoulder. Marian stood in the corridor, talking in low tones to a man whose back was to me.

"I told you never to approach me." Her stage whisper was laced with tension.

"That's unacceptable," the man replied. "We have business to discuss."

"Not here. Not now."

"You're in no position to dictate terms."

Her shoulders heaved. She started toward the door. 'You've got one minute. In here."

My breath caught in my throat. She would see me in less than two seconds. Though I had no idea who she was talking to, I instinctively knew that would be a mistake. Reflex kicked in, and I raced to the far end of the room. Hoping that my gym shoes muffled the sound of my feet, I threw myself behind the bar just as the door swung open.

"Why are you here?" Marian's voice was harsh. "No one must ever see us together."

"I came to inform you of recent events," the man replied.

"I don't want to know." Marian's voice was louder, more distinct.

Propped on my hands and knees, my muscles tightened. Please God, don't let them walk to this end of the room. Footsteps clacked on the parquet floor. Toward me. Another set of footsteps followed with a heavier, slower tread.

"You must. Labor Day will be here sooner than you think." His voice grew closer. Too close. "We've moved the operation, and we need to ramp up quickly."

A beat of silence. "Why?"

"Minneapolis was sloppy. They made mistakes. We won't."

More heels sounded on the floor. The faint trace of Chanel # 5 drifted over me. Marian was just on the other side of the bar. All she had to do was lean over, and she'd see me.

"This is none of my concern. I've said that before, and I'm telling you—" Her voice was so clear she might as well be whispering in my ear. I squeezed my eyes shut.

"Our supplies are already in place. We've infiltrated a construction site in the Loop. Right across the street. We're stowing equipment there."

Silence. Then, "Why are you telling me this?" But her voice wasn't quite as distinct. Had she turned around?

"You will be protected. You will receive instructions."

"You came all the way down here to tell me that?"

"There's another matter. The girl. She must be dealt with."

"No." Her voice was determined. And less muffled. She had turned back in my direction. I held my breath.

"We've respected your wishes up until now."

"She is my employee."

"She's getting too close. It's become dangerous."

"And whose fault is that?"

"It was always unfinished business. Old business. We need to take corrective action."

"I can't allow it. I . . . I'm fond of her."

"Your humanity becomes you. But, as I said, you're not in a position to dictate terms." More silence. "There will be a time—quite soon—we will want you to disappear. Up to Door County. The country house. You will stay for a long weekend."

"It's the middle of the campaign. I can't do that."

"You've been working hard. You need a break. Before the home stretch between Labor Day and November. People will understand."

Another silence. Then, "Keep me out of it." I heard the click of her heels against the wood floor. Retreating.

The man's voice dropped. "We will. You just keep collecting those votes."

"Wait here five minutes after I go." Her voice was like ice. "And for God's sake, don't let anyone see you." The door squeaked and then thumped shut.

I let out my breath but didn't move. What if the man decided to explore the room while he waited? What if he got thirsty and needed a drink? I stared at the sink behind the bar. A small mirror above it, which I hadn't noticed before, angled out to the room. A chair scraped against the floor, and I heard a soft thud as a body sank into it. I craned my neck. If I could raise my field of vision a few inches, I might be able to see who it was.

I heard the buzz of the crowd, a few loud laughs, the band's dogged rendition of "Dueling Banjos." Quietly

unching into a crouch, I lifted up and caught a glimpse
of the man's profile in the mirror: slicked-back blond hair
and a sparse mustache. It couldn't be. But it was. I ducked
back down, my pulse thundering in my ears.

Then I heard footsteps. Receding. The door opened and
closed. I counted out fifty more seconds and slowly stood
up. I was alone. I drew in a breath and shuffled awkwardly
to the door. Trying to be as quiet as possible, I slipped
into the corridor.

Where I stumbled into Stephen Lamont.

"Jesus Christ." I backed off as if I'd singed my fingers
in a flame. "You just scared the shit out of me. What are
you doing here?"

His eyes narrowed. "Maybe I should ask you the same
thing." He pointed to the room. "You were in there,
weren't you?"

I glanced at the door, then glared at Lamont. What did
he know? "So?"

"Marian came out of this room a few minutes ago."

I wrapped my arms around myself to try to stop the
shaking. Put on a front. Don't show fear.

"I was in the lobby buying gum. She walked past me.
Coming from this direction."

Looking around, I motioned to the ladies' room sign.
"Couldn't follow her in, huh?"

"Nice try." He eyed me suspiciously. "Why were you
meeting with her?"

"It wasn't me." Shit. It slipped out.

"Then who was it?"

He didn't know. "You know something, Lamont? I
have a feeling if she wanted you to know, she'd tell you
herself." I started to edge around him, but he stepped in
front of me, blocking my path.

"I can keep digging, and eventually I'll find out who
she met with, but it would a lot easier if you told me."
He put a patronizing hand on my shoulder. "It'll save me
a lot of time and effort and you the frustration of won-

dering what I know. You're gonna run back to Wolinsky and tell him I'm on to something, anyway. You're part of the inner circle."

I shook off his arm, annoyed but at the same time surprised he thought I had that kind of clout. Then I remembered he was a reporter. "If you're fishing, try a different lake. I'm just a hired hand."

"Bingo." He pointed a finger at my chest. "You see things."

I pointed a finger back at him. "Do you always think something subversive is going on, or is it just a job requirement?"

He held up his hand and ticked off his fingers. "Marian had a meeting that wasn't on the schedule. No press. No media. No Wolinsky. But you were there." He hesitated. "And I hear things."

"What things?"

He shook his head.

"Come on, Lamont. You're too shrewd to let that drop without a reason."

"So tell me."

"Tell you what?"

"Tell me who's sending me anonymous E-mails."

I stared at him.

"No names. No IDs. No return paths. Just one-line notes."

"Which say?"

"That I should take a closer look at the Iverson campaign."

I felt an uneasy twinge. "Someone's sending you mail?"

"They are."

"It's probably the other side. A dirty trick or something."

"You think so?"

"You can't think it's me."

He raised an eyebrow.

"Lamont, even if I did know something, how can you think I'd spill my guts to you?"

He crossed his arms over his chest. "You know something? You're probably right. I'll ask Marian who you and she were meeting with. She's been pretty open with me, and even if she isn't, her reaction will be interesting."

He had to be bluffing. He couldn't do that. She'd know I was eavesdropping.

He watched me carefully. "Then again, there could be something else you can help me with." He smiled innocently. "That woman, the Hispanic one? I don't see her around."

"You mean Dory Sanchez?"

"That's the one. What happened to her?"

I bit the inside of my mouth. Maybe he figured out I wasn't supposed to be in that meeting. Maybe he saw me wander into the room by mistake and used that knowledge, playing me, manipulating me right where he wanted. Either I told him what he wanted to know, or he'd tell Marian I was spying on her. He had me, and we both knew it.

"She's been let go," I said in a low voice.

"When?"

"A few days ago."

"Why?"

"I don't know. But if it gets out—"

"Not to worry." He shoved his hands in his pockets. "I'm one of the good guys, Ellie Foreman. The question is, are you?"

WHILE MAC LOADED the gear on the return flight, Lamont grabbed the seat next to me. Glowering, I thought about switching seats, but Ms. Perky had deposited herself next to Mac's sound man, and the only seat left was next to Roger. I burrowed into my seat.

But Lamont didn't pump me on the return trip. Surprisingly pleasant and talkative, he regaled me with back-room stories about the mayor and a city council member considered to be his nemesis. Though I knew it was just another tactic—if bullying doesn't work, try charm—it still rattled me when Marian turned around and saw us with our heads together. I didn't like what I saw on her face.

The only saving grace was that I didn't think about my fear of flying on the way back. How could I be concerned about that when the man she'd been meeting with was Jeremiah Gibbs?

THIRTY-NINE

MY MESSAGE MACHINE was blinking when I walked in the door. Pam called to say she'd received a letter from the Chicago Corp lawyers. Despite the summons, we might be able to work something out. I should call her right away. There was also a message from Mac. I'd sent him an E-mail with the editing schedule, but all he got was a garbled page with my name on the return path. Would I please send it again? I made a note to call my ISP; this was the second or third time my E-mail had been acting up. Then a thin, reedy voice came on the machine.

"Ellie. This is Marv. Your father's friend? Look, swee-tie, I don't want you to worry, but . . ."

I stiffened.

"Jake, I mean, your dad is okay. They're just keeping him for observation, and . . ."

I didn't listen to the rest. When Dad's phone didn't answer, I called the home. Twenty minutes later, I walked into Evanston Hospital.

I hadn't been there in several years, and the remodeled lobby, with its modern sculpture, recessed lighting, and block benches, resembled a museum more than a hospital. They needn't have bothered. Death sucks, no matter how prettily you dress it up. My mother died at Evanston. From pancreatic cancer.

The woman at the information desk said my father was on the fifth floor. The blue and yellow arrows that used to line the floors had been replaced with neutral carpeting and new linoleum, but the walls still reverberated with deep silence. I'd spent a month here, helplessly watching the life seep out of my mother. I'd vowed never to come back.

The fifth-floor nurse's station was depressingly familiar, as if it had been transplanted from the oncology ward. Cheerful paneling covered the desk, and there was abstract art on the walls, but the files held the same charts, the patient board listed the same names. Even the diet Coke can on the counter was the same. A nurse with precise, exotic Asian features frowned at her monitor as she typed.

"Excuse me. I'm looking for Jake Foreman."

The woman looked up. "Down the hall. Fifty-one ten." She threw me a smile. Everyone here was so polite and solicitous. So goddamned caring.

Dad was sitting up in bed watching TV, one side of his face swathed in bandages. His skin looked pasty and fragile, but he was sipping through a straw on the other side of his mouth. I wanted to cry and throw my arms around him. Instead I said, "I go away for a few hours, I don't even leave the state, and look what happens."

His eyes brightened, and he tried to smile. I saw him wince.

I ran across the room, knelt down, and buried my head in the crook of his arm. Tears stung my eyes. "Oh Daddy, are you all right? I was so scared."

He brushed his hand over my head. "I'm all right, sweetheart. I'm all right."

"What happened?" I said between sniffs.

"Someone tried to mug me in an alley last night."

"Oh, my God."

"We were going to see a movie. The new Danny DeVito one. It got great reviews. The other guys went last weekend and told us we hadda see it. So Marv and I went to see the late show. He drove—he still has a license—and he let me off at the end of the block while he looked for a parking spot." He zapped the remote. "So there I was, minding my own business, about fifty feet from an alley, when these two goons grabbed me and forced me into it."

"What did they do?"

"What do you think they did? They tried to beat me up."

I delicately touched the side of his head. "Looks like they made some headway."

"Ha." He leaned over and opened the drawer of the bedside table. "They didn't count on this." He pulled out a can of mace.

My mouth opened. "How long have you had that?"

"Honey," he croaked, "I've had this for years. Never leave home without it."

"Did you try to fight them off?"

"I did fight them off." His spine straightened. "Don't ask me how, 'cause I still can't really tell you, but somehow, as I was going down, I managed to pull that sucker out of my pocket, and I started spraying." He chuckled through his grimace. "The guy in front of me dropped like a rock, and the other guy—well, I guess he got scared—because he dropped his hold."

"What did you do?"

"What any sane person would do. I got up, stumbled out of the alley, and screamed like hell. Of course, by the time the cops came, they were long gone."

He looked inordinately pleased with himself. I wound my arms around his waist. "Dad, do you know how close you came to—I mean, my God, you could have been killed."

"It takes more than two punks to stop Jake Foreman."

His bravado notwithstanding, I started to tear up again.

"Sweetheart," he crooned. "Stop crying. I'm going to be fine. It's just a bump on my *keppe*."

I shook my head.

"What is it?"

"There were two guys right? Did one of them have a fishing hat?"

He angled his head. "Maybe. Some kind of hat."

"The other—did he have a ponytail?"

His eyes narrowed. "Why?"

I bit my lip. "You were attacked because of me. It's my fault."

"You? Now I know—" He stopped. "How do you figure that?"

"There are a few things I need to tell you."

I plumped his pillows, smoothed out his sheet, and let it all spill out. The break-in. The theft of Skull's things. Boo Boo. The tan Cutlass. I told him about showing Marian the Movietone newsreel, her mounting uneasiness with me, her strange reaction to David, her meeting with Jeremiah Gibbs.

When I finished, he steepled his hands in front of him. The veins on his forehead protruded. "Is that everything?"

I nodded, relieved that someone besides me finally knew it all. "Someone's going after all the people who knew Skull. You knew him in Lawndale."

"Why? What do they want?"

"I don't know. But whatever it is, it's apparently worth killing for."

"And you think it's Marian and this Gibbs character?"

"I'm not sure. If it weren't for the fact that we know Skull was trying to find Lisle, I'd say there were two different situations."

He ran his tongue over his lip. "I don't like it. I want you to quit working for this woman."

"Dad, I've got to finish the video."

"Ellie, this is your life we're talking about. Who the hell cares about a goddamned movie?"

"But she's already paid me."

"So let her sue."

"Dad, listen to me. Why would Marian Iverson be coming after me in a tan Cutlass? She doesn't need to. She sees me all the time."

"But this Gibbs' person was talking to her about eliminating you. How much more proof do you need?"

I didn't answer.

"I'm a tough old bird, Ellie. But you. You should make yourself scarce. Stay out of sight. Especially Marian's. Until we can figure out what to do."

"I can't. I have responsibilities."

"Your responsibilities are to me. And your daughter. You need to keep yourself alive."

I didn't have a comeback.

FORTY

AFTER A MOSTLY sleepless night, I cut across the yard at dawn. The grass, still wet and slick from dew, chilled my bare feet. I looked both ways down the street. No one was there. I grabbed the paper. Lamont had filed an innocuous story about Giant City. Back inside, I brewed coffee and made a decision. A compromise of sorts, for Dad. I would finish editing the tape at Mac's; I wouldn't go downtown. That would take two or three days. Then I'd regroup and figure out what to do.

I was rinsing my cup in the sink when a red Honda roared around the corner. David parked and climbed out, casually dressed in jeans and a green T-shirt. My pulse started to pick up. I opened the door before he knocked.

"How was your trip?"

"Fine," I lied, stepping outside. "Until I got home." I explained about my father.

Shock swept across his face. "What can I do?"

"Nothing."

I considered telling him about the men in the Cutlass. But David didn't know anything about Skull, except for exchanging a brief E-mail. He didn't need to be worried.

"Is he still in the hospital?"

"They're keeping him another day." I walked over to uncoil the hose. "Really. He's okay."

He nodded. An awkward silence followed. Then, "I went down to the steel mill the other day."

"Iverson's?"

"Yesterday. It was surrounded by a chain-link fence. But I climbed over and poked around. Looked through some windows."

I turned on the hose, imagining him crawling through dirt and dust, a little boy exploring forbidden territory. I almost smiled.

"It was strange, you know. I almost thought I sensed my mother's presence. Being in the same place she'd spent so much time." His cheeks were flushed, and his eyes glowed. I had to look away. "Iverson must have been some businessman to build the place from the ground up." He stepped over the hose. "You've been looking into him. What was he like?"

I waved the hose over the impatiens. "I don't know. Sort of a twentieth-century robber baron, if you ask me." I adjusted the spray of water.

"Do you have any pictures of him?"

I tightened my grip on the hose. "You know, I don't think I do." Why was he asking me questions? Why was he here at all? He'd made it clear what kind of relationship he wanted—or didn't want—from me. I don't do "friends" well. He should go back to Philadelphia. I looked up. "David, there's—"

As if he sensed my thoughts, he interrupted me. "Ellie. That's not the reason I'm here."

Here it comes. The girlfriend. The fiancée.

"I want to explain about the other night."

I looked away. "You don't have to."

"Yes. I do. There isn't anybody else, Ellie."

I froze.

"It's just that, well, I'm a middle-aged man. I never expected to meet someone like you at this point in my life. And with all this attention on my roots and my parents, I was afraid to trust—oh God, this is hard . . ."

The hose spat water on the dirt.

"Your father. Your daughter. You attract people. It's as if they're the moths and you're the flame. You create a sense of family around you."

"I don't—"

"Let me finish. It's not just your father. Or your daughter. Even your gardener—"

"He's my friend."

"That's what I mean. You turn everyone into family. And I . . . I want to be part of it."

My heart thumped furiously.

"But I was—I mean—after what happened between your father and my mother, I was—"

"You know about them?"

"When a man loves a woman, it's hard to disguise it. It was all over your father's face. That's why I left the other night. I didn't know how you felt about it. Whether you cared. I was afraid."

The water from the hose pooled around the impatiens and the runoff spilled across the front step. I bent down and turned off the water. "Let me understand. You were afraid how I might react then, but now you're not?"

"I'm terrified. But I decided if there was a chance—any chance you had feelings for me—despite what happened with our parents—I'd take it."

Goose bumps danced on my arms. I went to front door, opened it, and held out my hand. He took it and followed me in.

FORTY-ONE

BY EVENING, WE were both starved. At least I was. I threw on his T-shirt and scrounged in the refrigerator. With Rachel gone, the choices were limited.

As I cracked eggs into a bowl, I heard his step on the stairs. I turned around. He was wearing pants but no shirt, and the hard cut of his muscles made me groan with desire. As if reading my mind, he drew me into his arms. I traced the line of his neck with my finger, remembering the feel of his body on mine. How we touched each other gently at first, then more insistently. How we found our rhythm quickly but made sure to go slow. How we came together at the peak of passion, and then did it all over again.

"I hope eggs are okay," I turned to the stove. "It's all I have."

"Eggs are perfect." He nuzzled my neck from behind.

A shiver ran through me, and I arched into him. "You keep doing that, there won't be any eggs."

"You win." He dropped his arms. "I'm hungry."

I took out English muffins and put them in the toaster. Then I got silverware out of the drawer. As I was setting the table, he grabbed my hand. Smiling, I flicked my eyes over, but when our eyes met, my smile faded. His face was shadowed in sorrow.

"What's wrong?" He didn't say anything. "David?"

He shook his head. "Nothing. Forget it."

My stomach started to churn. "You can't do that." I

withdrew my wrist. He still didn't say anything. "David, this isn't the way it works. We're supposed to talk to each other. Communicate."

"Okay." He nodded. "Okay." He twisted around in the chair. "Why didn't you tell me the truth about Linda Jorgenson?"

I froze. "Who?"

"Linda Jorgenson. The woman who knows the history of Chicago steel companies."

I turned back to the stove and poured the eggs into the skillet. "What are you talking about?"

"Remember when you waved me off the police? And told me they wouldn't be much help?"

"I was right, wasn't I?"

"But not about Linda Jorgenson." I pushed the spatula through the eggs. "You knew I got her name at the library. When we finally connected, she said someone else had called her about Iverson recently. A woman. Who was making a film for his daughter's campaign."

I blinked.

"Here's a woman who might have valuable information about my mother, and you'd talked to her. But you never mentioned her to me. In fact, you tried to talk me out of calling her. I just want to know why."

I kept my mouth shut.

"Communicate, Ellie. Isn't that the way it's supposed to work?"

Beads of sweat broke out on my forehead.

"You know I've been looking for answers to my past. I thought I could trust you to help me."

"You wouldn't understand." My voice sounded small and puny.

His voice was quiet, not accusatory. "If I thought that, I would never have brought it up."

I turned away. Why was he being so reasonable? He knew I'd lied to him, deceived him, and yet he made passionate love to me. What was wrong with him?

"Ellie, I'm not angry. I just want to—"

"Why not?" I spun around. "Why aren't you angry?" How dare he treat me so well? "Who are you David Linden? Are you always this forgiving? This blind to people's faults? Or"—I waved the spatula—"are you so desperate to be accepted that you'll overlook anything a woman does?"

He flinched.

"I'm sorry," I mumbled. "That was out of line."

But he was already out of his seat, pushing the chair under the table. "I thought we'd be able to talk about this reasonably. But I see I made a mistake. You're someone I wanted to get close to. I've never done that before. Maybe now I know why."

"Damn you." I hacked the spatula through the the eggs, which had turned rubbery and dry. "Damn you, David Linden."

He turned away from me, his face sad but calm. Somehow, his coolness, his rational control made my temper spike. Fuck him and his patronizing attitude. "Well, maybe it's not so strange." I brandished the spatula. "Considering Lisle Gottlieb was your mother."

"What?"

Shit. I picked up the skillet, intending to scrape the eggs into the disposal. But I forgot it was hot. It dropped from my hands and it clattered to the floor. "Damn it to hell."

He stepped back into the kitchen. "What did you say?"

"Forget it. I didn't say anything." I yanked on the cold water and stuck my singed fingers under the spigot.

Suddenly David was in back of me, swinging me around to face him. The cords on his neck were taut, and his grip on my arm was strong. His eyes glanced at the skillet and then my fingers, as if making sure I wasn't hurt. Then, "What do you mean, 'considering Lisle Gottlieb was my mother'?"

I tried to shrink from his touch. "Nothing. I was angry."

His jaw worked, all his coolness and composure gone. "There's something you're not telling me. What is it?"

I felt a sick twisting in my stomach. "You don't want to know."

"Ellie. If you have information about my family, anything at all, you have to tell me." He shook me. "You have to."

I heard the refrigerator motor kick on, smelled the butter from the skillet. He was clutching my arms. I choked back a sob. "I didn't want it to happen this way. I don't want to hurt you."

The look in his eyes said it was too late. I went into the family room. He followed me in. I dug the Movietone newsreel out of my bag.

"This is a newsreel from the forties. About Rosie the Riveter. Your mother is on this tape," I said. "So is Paul Iverson." I tried to look the other way, but his face swam before me. "Your mother had an affair with Paul Iverson. During the war. While Kurt was overseas."

His eyes narrowed. Disbelief spread across his face.

"They lived together in an apartment in Lawndale." I paused. "She got pregnant, David. Kurt Weiss isn't your father. Paul Iverson is." I handed him the tape. "It's all here. You look exactly like him."

His sharp intake of breath was the only sound in the room. He stared at the tape in his hand, then studied my face. I looked away, not trusting myself to go on.

"There's more, isn't there?"

Tears rolled down my cheeks.

"Tell me all of it," he said hoarsely. "Now."

"Your mother left Iverson at the end of the war and went back to Kurt," I whispered. "A week or so later, Iverson killed himself."

He waited.

"But before he did, I think he killed Kurt Weiss."

FORTY-TWO

A HIGH, THIN cloud layer leached the color out of the sky the next morning. I called David's hotel room as soon as I woke up, but there was no answer. Feeling heavy and dull, I dragged myself to a meeting with Pam Huddleston.

She said we'd bought ourselves some time. The papers she'd sent over supported our position that the account had been closed during the divorce proceedings and that I had no knowledge of any new activity on Barry's part. Pam had convinced the Chicago Corp to wait until their PI found Barry before proceeding further. A continuance would be filed.

After the meeting I stopped off at Mac's, where we recorded a scratch track for the video. I'd hire a professional narrator for the finished version, but I hadn't decided on a female or male voice. For now, my voice would do.

When we'd finished laying down the track, Hank and I screened the Giant City footage. Mac had shot plenty of B-roll. We had cheering crowds, smiling faces, and colorful shots of Americana. Hank and I discussed the pacing. We were aiming for the illusion of momentum, success, maybe even a feeling of inevitability. We listened to library music that would reinforce those themes, and he promised to have a rough cut by the following week. I left him paging through the logs.

I picked up Dad at the hospital and took him home, then got Chinese takeout for dinner. When he fell asleep

on his chair, I quietly let myself out. Back home, I called
The Ritz again. This time I asked for the front desk. David
had checked out. I tried him at his office, but it was after
five on the East Coast, and he wasn't there. I called his
home; his machine picked up. My heart skipped a beat
just hearing his voice.

"David, it's me." I cleared my throat. "I . . . I wouldn't
blame you if you never speak to me again. There's no
excuse for what I did. I could tell you I'm under a lot of
stress. That I'm panicked about half a million dollars that
my ex-husband lost in the stock market. That I don't know
how to tell Marian Iverson about her father. Your father.
That I'm still spooked about my father. And a break-in at
my house. And a kid who was shot in a drive-by a few
weeks ago. I should have told you about all of this a long
time ago. But I wasn't sure. And I didn't know how,
and . . . well . . . it doesn't matter now. It doesn't excuse
the fact that I lied. Or the pain that I've caused you. I'm
sorry. I hope you can forgive me."

I hung up and looked at the phone. Noise from the TV
in the family room spilled into the kitchen. A commercial
for an appliance store was already hawking a big Labor
Day blowout sale. I flashed back to Jeremiah Gibbs at
Giant Park. He'd been talking about Labor Day. The blue
light from the television threw strobelike shadows across
the room. I tried to remember what he said. Something
about the base of operations having been moved. His people infiltrating a construction site in the Loop. The phone
rang. I jumped.

"Hello."

"David," I breathed.

Silence.

"Are you okay?"

"Oh, sure, Ellie. Drop a bomb on me any time, and a
few hours later, I'm just peachy."

"I didn't want it to happen like that."

A harsh sound came out of his throat. "You were right
about one thing. We look alike."

"You watched the tape."

He laughed bitterly. "Like father, like son." More silence. "I wasn't going to call you. I never wanted to hear from you again." His voice was tight. "But goddammit, Ellie, you're the only person who understands." An anguished sob escaped. "These are my parents, Ellie. My family."

I squeezed my lips together, longing to see him, to touch him, to smooth the hair off his forehead. "I wish I was there. I'd do anything to help."

He cleared his throat. More silence. When he spoke again, his voice was calmer. "There may be something."

"Anything."

"When I got home, I started going through everything that had a connection to my father. I wanted to prove you were wrong. That it wasn't true." He took a breath. "I started to fiddle around with his clock. You remember. The one I told you about?"

"The one from Prague?"

"Right." He cleared his throat again. He sounded stronger. "I was staring at this thing for an hour, and suddenly I saw a hairline crack circling the face of the clock. You know, around the hands. I'd never noticed it before. So I got a putty knife and started working it back and forth. A few minutes later, I got it off. There was something inside."

"Inside the clock?"

"It's a report. Some kind of document. Ten or so pages, all folded up. I'm not sure what it says. It's written in German. But there's a cover letter with it addressed to Heinrich Himmler and two other Germans."

"Himmler?" I whispered. "The Nazi? That's crazy. How can that be?"

"You think I know? But that's not what stopped me." He hesitated. "There was a fourth name on the letter."

"Who?"

"Iverson."

"Paul Iverson? You have a document that's addressed to him and Himmler, too?"

"Yes."

"Is there a date on it?"

"Nineteen forty-four."

Iverson didn't enlist, and he wasn't drafted. He was home, making sure the mill produced tanks and planes for the Allies. So, what was his name doing on a German document from 1944 along with one of Hitler's most trusted aides?

"I called my assistant at the bank. Her mother's German. She's going to read it and give me a translation."

"Did you make a copy of it?"

"Ellie, give me some credit." A beat of silence followed. "That's why I'm calling." Another beat. "I want to fax it to you."

"Me? Why?"

"Well," he said slowly, "you work for Marian Iverson. I want you to show it to her. Maybe she knows what it means."

I swiveled around in the chair. My feet hit the floor with a thud. "That's not a good idea."

I heard defiance in his voice. "Why not?"

I groped for words. I couldn't go to Marian Iverson with this. Not now. Not ever. And I'd promised my father to stay away from her. On the other hand, my relationship with David was so precarious that if I refused to help him, he'd walk out of my life—forever.

"David, what am I going to say? Uh, Marian, could you please take a look at this? I don't know what it means, but maybe you do? By the way, I got it from your half brother. You didn't know you had one? Well, guess what?"

His voice grew icy. "Is your opinion of me really that low?"

Shit. Me and my mouth.

"I expect complete discretion on your part. Until we—I know more about my birth father, Marian shouldn't know anything about me." I imagined him scowling into the phone. "Perhaps you're the wrong person to do this." His voice was cold, professional. Like the first time we'd talked.

I remembered our lovemaking. The way our bodies fit together. The thrill of his mouth, his skin, his taste. The way he filled me up. This was a test. My last chance. He was waiting for my answer. A knot of anxiety thickened my throat.

"Okay," I whispered. "Fax it to me tomorrow."

FORTY-THREE

"GLAD YOU'RE HERE." Roger popped his head into my office at campaign headquarters the next day.

Against my better judgment, I'd come downtown. I rationalized that I'd only be there a few minutes. Just enough time to feel out Marian. See where she stood. What could happen in broad daylight, anyway, the place buzzing with people?

"Let's go over some due dates. You're planning to finish up when?"

"We should be done a couple of days after we lay down the track."

"Right. I ran the voice tapes by Marian. She's thinking about them." I nodded. "No problem having it ready by Labor Day weekend?" I shook my head. "Good. At least you're under control."

"Excuse me?"

"Nothing." His forehead puckered and his fingers made Captain Queeg circles. "You happen to hear from Lamont recently?"

An uneasy feeling slid around inside me. "Why?"

"I can't seem to reach him. He said he was going to run a big story about Marian over Labor Day weekend." Roger made a noise. "Oh well. I wonder why Marian said to check with you?"

I hiked my shoulders. "You tried the *Trib*?"

"He's not around. Not at home, either."

After he left, I wondered why Marian thought I would

:now Lamont's whereabouts. Then I remembered the
light back from Giant City. She'd been watching us, and
he didn't look particularly happy. I headed to the bath-
oom. My uneasiness grew. I was naive to think I could
roach David's document with her. There was no way.

With just two stalls, the ladies' room was small, but
he soft, recessed light was a nice change from the fluor-
scent bulbs that usually make my face look washed out.
finished my business and was running a comb through
ny hair when a key twisted in the lock. It was Marian.

"Ellie, dear." She smiled brightly as she came through
he door. "I was just thinking about you."

"Oh." My smile was cautious.

"Yes. I'm so anxious to see the video. Roger tells me
:'s just wonderful."

Roger hadn't been near the editing room. "Thanks."

She bent over the sink and started washing her hands.

"Marian," I said, "could I talk to you about some-
hing?" What was I doing?

She caught my reflection in the mirror. "Certainly." Her
xpression was curious.

"Its . . . it's about your father."

"Yes?"

Suddenly a key jingled in the lock, and the receptionist
alked in, her headphones capping her ears. When she
aw us, she pulled them off and smiled cheerfully. Marian
miled back. The girl edged around me and entered one
f the stalls. Marian reached for a paper towel.

"Could we talk in your office?" I asked.

She dried her hands and balled up the towel. "Oh dear,
was just off to a meeting at the Drake."

"What about tomorrow?" I asked.

She threw the towel in the waste bin. "Frankly, I was
oping to sneak off for a few days."

"You're going away?"

"Roger tells me it's probably the last opportunity I'll
ave before November. Full steam ahead, you know. I
ought I'd go up to Door County."

I nodded.

"Of course, if it's very important . . ." She smiled regretfully. "Perhaps in an hour or so . . ."

"No, it can wait."

She patted my hand. "Thank you." She sailed through the door.

Back at my desk, I gathered up my papers. It was time to leave. As fast as I could. I was just starting out the door when the phone trilled.

"Ellie, it's David." The pleasant shiver that ran through me was short-lived. "Ellie, something bad happened."

My stomach tightened.

"The woman I gave the letter to . . ." He hesitated.

"The one who was going to give it to her mother?"

"Janine. My assistant. She was mugged on her way home from work tonight. She's dead. The police just left."

I gasped.

"Someone ambushed her when she was walking down Market Street. They pulled her into an alley. They . . . they shot her."

"Oh, God."

"Ellie, listen to me. Whoever killed her took the document."

"What?"

"When she left the bank, she was carrying it in a manila folder. It wasn't on her when the police found her."

Feeling my knees go weak, I stared through my door. Western light poured in through the mottled glass of the windows, scattering sunbeams like jewels. I whispered, "But David, the only people who knew about it were you and me."

"I know." A swell of air brushed through the phone line, like the surf of a faraway ocean. "Ellie? I want you to be very careful."

"But I'm seven hundred miles away."

There was a pause. "I faxed it to you this morning."

A shadow blocked the light outside my office. Maria walked by.

                    *   *   *

THREADED MY way through streets clogged with traffic.
hough the AC was blasting, my hands felt clammy. No-
ody was supposed to know about that document. David
ad just found it, and I hadn't told anyone. The sun hit
y face as I turned up LaSalle, but storm clouds billowed
nderneath. I turned on the radio, but the noise was flat
nd tinny. I snapped it off. The traffic lights were out
long LaSalle, and cops blew whistles at streams of pe-
estrians and then motorists, to the annoyance of both but
ssing of neither.

Maybe Janine's death was a tragic mistake. A horrible
ut random death in the *Grand Guignol* tradition. Right.
s I swung onto Lake Shore Drive, the sun disappeared.
heets of gray water dusted with whitecaps bobbed on my
ght. Angry clouds loomed above.

At home I ran up to my office and grabbed the sheets
f paper poking out of the fax. I studied the signature on
e letter. Between a fold in the paper, the scrawled pen-
anship, and the degradation caused by the transmission,
e name was barely legible, but it looked like Josef Men-
le. I stiffened.

Mengele was infamous. A Nazi's Nazi. An ambitious
octor who rose through Hitler's ranks, and who, as com-
andant of Auschwitz, conducted medical experiments so
scene and barbarous that even today people are reluc-
nt to discuss them.

This had to be a sick joke. I called David. He picked
the first ring.

"I got it." I fumbled with the papers. "This is—there
ust be some mistake."

"You saw the signature."

"It's wrong. It's got to be."

"Ellie," He cut me off. "Did you tell anyone else about
is?"

"No one," I whispered. "You?"

"Just you. And Janine." Then, "Maybe I should fly out I don't like what I'm thinking."

"No." I was surprised by my vehemence. "Stay where you are. See what the police say. I'll call you tomorrow."

We hung up. I was about to replace the receiver when I heard a click on the line.

"Hello?" No response. "Is someone there?"

Nothing.

Suddenly I knew what the clicks on my phone were Quills of fear tickled my skin. I carefully replaced th phone in its cradle. Someone else knew about the report Someone who wanted it badly enough to kill for it. Now David had one copy, I had another, and whoever was tapping my phone knew it.

FORTY-FOUR

OTHER THAN WHATEVER was under the bandage that now replaced the dressing, my father had made a remarkable recovery. His eyes were clear, his voice strong, his color good. He put on his reading glasses and looked at the report. I sat on his couch, watching the play of light from a streetlight seep through the blinds. When he looked up, the half-frames of his glasses slipped down his nose.

"Where did you get this?"

"David faxed it to me."

"You know who Mengele was?"

I nodded.

His lips curled in disgust. "Thousands of Jews died unspeakable deaths at his hands. And not just at Auschwitz. He had associates at Birkenau and Dachau. That's who Sigmund Rauscher is."

"What about Clauberg?" They were the other two names on the document.

"He was Mengele's assistant at Auschwitz." Sounds thumped on the window. Fat drops of rain slapped against the glass. "They were monsters, Ellie. Torturing prisoners for days with agonizing tests and procedures. Dissecting their bodies like frogs. Freezing them in vats of icy water. Pouring chemicals in their eyes to change the color. Suffocating others in high-altitude experiments. And the twins . . ." He swallowed hard. "The things he did to those twins—"

"Stop." I covered my ears with my hands.

Dad waited.

"What . . . what does it say?"

"My German's pretty rough, but it seems to be thanking people who helped support their efforts. Something about working toward the same goals. Sharing the results of their research." He paused. "It's looks like Iverson was bankrolling Mengele."

He looked up, saw my expression. "Don't be so shocked. Plenty of Americans thought Hitler had a good idea. Lindbergh, Coughlin, Henry Ford—Christ, Ellie, even Joe Kennedy." He sniffed. "But Iverson apparently went farther than they did." He refolded the letter, his face grim. "David found this, you say?"

"In a clock that Kurt brought back from Prague."

Dad arched an eyebrow.

"Why? What's so significant about Prague?"

"Prague was a gateway to Eastern Europe for the Allies. It had enormous strategic importance. Much of the intelligence from the Resistance and the underground came through Prague. Even though it was occupied. Kurt may have gotten this from an informant."

"Skull?"

He eyed me. "Why? What's happened?"

I told him about David's assistant.

"Why didn't you tell me before?"

"I just found out."

He squeezed his eyes shut, as if he was weary. When he opened them, fatigue lines showed in the corners. Was he thinking that so little had changed in sixty years? That the same hates and fears still drive human behavior? That history can and does, despite our best efforts, repeat itself?

"Who else knows you have this?" He asked quietly.

"The wrong people."

There was no outburst. Or anger. "You're not going home. It's too dangerous."

"Dad—"

"No discussion. You'll bunk here."

I sank down on the couch and glanced at the phone.

should call David. As if sensing my thoughts, Dad said. "He should be careful, too."

I nodded. "He's dealing with a lot of issues right now."

He ran his finger along the edges of the document. "One of them being the fact that he's the spitting image of Paul Iverson?"

I stared at him. "How did you know?"

"It isn't hard to figure out if you know what Iverson looked like. And then, after you asked about Feld . . ."

"You knew about their apartment?"

A bittersweet smile played around his mouth. "There was no way Lisle could have afforded that place on a riveter's salary."

"You never said anything."

He shrugged. "It wasn't my business."

My heart went out to him. "Well, at least that explains why Iverson killed Kurt."

Dad frowned. "What do you mean?"

"He couldn't let Kurt tell Lisle that the man she'd been living with for over a year was bankrolling Mengele, especially after he'd started helping Jews emigrate to Palestine. Lisle would have been appalled to find out he was playing both ends against the middle. Plus, if Kurt was out of the way, Iverson might have thought he could get her back. So he killed him."

Dad stroked his chin with his fingers. "Maybe. But why commit suicide afterward?"

I was improvising. "Maybe Kurt told Lisle about Iverson's activities before he was killed, and when she confronted Iverson about it, he couldn't handle the guilt."

I got the feeling Dad wasn't convinced. "What does David say?"

"We haven't talked it through."

"You need to."

I bit my lip. "I want to. But I can't call from here. They could be tapping your phone, too. And my cell is out of juice."

He tried to cut in, but I overrode him. "There's a pay phone at the drugstore. I'll be back."

I DIDN'T NOTICE the headlights at first. The storm had strengthened, but Walgreen's was only a block from Dad's, so I didn't turn on the rear wiper. But as I swung into the parking lot, I realized a car was riding my tail. I slowed as I got to the parking slots at the rear of the building. The car behind me slowed, too. I checked the rearview mirror, but the rain caught the glare from the headlights, and I saw nothing but droplets of sparkling water.

I eased my foot off the brake and circled the lot. The car behind me did, too. I headed back out to Golf Road and turned west. So did the headlights. I turned left at the light.

Gross Point Road unravels through Skokie like a strand of wool. Though it generally heads southwest, it occasionally banks and curls around commercial storefronts, small apartment buildings, and other squat structures. In some spots it's almost four lanes; in others it narrows to two. Rain lashed the windshield, blinding me to the road, and the wind threatened to shove me out of my lane. I tried to hug the center line, but it flashed in and out of sight with the swing of the wipers, like a yellow beacon on turbulent seas.

Checking the rearview mirror again, I saw the headlights still behind me. I stepped on the gas. All at once, the Volvo bounced against something, and I lurched forward. Fear skittered around in me. The car bounced back and skidded into the center lane. I eased into the skid and managed to gain control. I must have driven up on the curb. Shaking, I checked the speedometer. Nearly fifty.

The windshield was steamy with condensation. I wiped my sleeve against the glass. An intersection was up ahead. But the discs of light behind me grew brighter and larger. They were closing in. I slammed my foot on the gas.

As the intersection loomed closer, the light changed from green to yellow. A truck at the cross street was waiting for the light to change. I couldn't brake. I blasted my horn and jerked the wheel to the right. The Volvo swerved and shuddered, veering into another skid. The truck filled the windshield. My tires screeched. I heard myself scream. Then, somehow, the Volvo gained purchase and bucked forward. It lunged through the intersection, avoiding the truck by inches. I heard the angry blare of the trucker's horn.

I turned down a dark, deserted street. I didn't recognize any landmarks, and there were no street signs or lights. Finally, a low, wide structure set back from the road emerged on the left. Another one appeared on the right. A dim light on one of the buildings illuminated a halo of raindrops. Warehouses or factories. I was in the industrial backwoods of Skokie, maybe Niles.

I checked the rearview mirror. The headlights were gone. Taking my foot off the gas, I allowed myself to breathe. I'd lost them. Now all I had to do was figure out how to get out of here. I relaxed my grip on the wheel. The road dead-ended ahead. As I reached the end of the street, I turned left and gasped.

A car was parked broadside, blocking my path, its headlights shining. I slammed into reverse, maneuvering back the way I'd come. The car blocking my path turned in a smooth arc and followed me. I jerked the Volvo and turned left into a driveway. This time the Volvo, as if saying it had enough, skidded right, hit the curb, and stopped. I gunned the engine and felt tires spinning, but nothing moved. I gunned the engine again. The car bucked but stayed where it was.

I flung open the car door and jumped out. I was in an empty parking lot surrounded by a chain-link fence. A hundred yards away was a one-story warehouse. I started to run. Rain pelted my skin like stones, splattering in my eyes, blurring my vision. A car door slammed. I looked over my shoulder. Someone was chasing me, their head bent against the rain.

I careened across the parking lot. Out of my peripheral vision, I saw the building ahead. I tried to run parallel to it, but thirty feet down it angled sharply, and a wing cut off my access. I was trapped. I ducked my head and threw my body against the wall, my hands clawing the surface, as if I could magically rapelle up its side. Footsteps sloshed on the wet surface behind me. I tried to melt into the wall. A pair of hands gripped my shoulders.

FORTY-FIVE

DORY SANCHEZ SPUN me around. Though her clothes and hair were sopping wet, her expression was as intense as brushfire. We stood beneath an overhang at the back entrance of the factory, the dark partially offset by a halogen light affixed to the wall. Beside Dory was a man who looked familiar.

As Dory moved in and out of the light, her face alternately pale and shadowed, I thought I saw the hint of a smile. "You move fast when you want to."

Panting, I leaned against the factory wall to steady myself. Every muscle in my body twitched. "You almost killed me, Dory."

"We had no other way to contact you." No apology. No excuse.

"Jesus." I peered toward the Volvo. "I've got to go back to the car. The motor's still running. It's stuck on something."

"No." She turned to the man. "Raoul, you go." He nodded and sprinted toward the car. I recognized him then: Raoul Iglesias, head of Latinos for a Better Order. LABOR. Dory turned back and drew out a pack of Marlboros. She offered it to me.

"I haven't smoked in fifteen years," I said. She held the pack out. I took one.

She took out a match, struck it several times, threw it down in disgust. She tried another. I cupped my hands around hers. The match caught. We touched our cigarettes to the flame.

"You never called back." I took a drag of the Marlboro.

"I couldn't." She inhaled deeply and blew out a stream of smoke. "Your phone is tapped."

I nodded.

Her eyes registered surprise, as if she hadn't expected me to know. "You've been watched."

"I know."

Again, a flicker of surprise. "How much do you know?"

"I'm just starting to piece things together."

Raoul rejoined us and handed me the keys. "Your car is fine. It was mud. It is free now."

I nodded my thanks and shoved the keys in my pocket. Dory flicked her cigarette away as if she were suddenly impatient with it. "Do you remember when your friend David came to the office?" I nodded. "And I showed you the picture of Marian's father?"

"Yes." I took another drag off my cigarette.

"David's name was in an E-mail I came across at the office."

"David's? At the office?"

She gave me a speculative look. "It was a message written to Marian."

"From who?"

"The Church of the Covenant."

Jeremiah Gibbs. A chill ran through me. "What did it say?"

"The message said they were aware of developments and that they would take the necessary actions."

"What developments?"

"It's not hard to figure out." At my puzzled glance, she went on. "Marian may be many things, but she is not stupid. It's pretty obvious how much David resembles her father."

I stared at the embers of my cigarette, orange and round and speckled. The Movietone newsreel. Marian's reaction. She *did* know about her father's affair. Which meant she knew who Kurt was. And that her father had murdered him. I ground the cigarette out with my foot. She couldn't allow that to get out. A scandal would threaten her campaign. So she'd turned to Gibbs.

I had to warn David. I spun around, about to sprint to the car, but Raoul grabbed me in a hammerlock and pinned my arms.

"Let me go." I hissed, thrashing. "I've got—"

Dory placed her hands on my shoulders. "Ellie, wait."

The weight of her hands and the need in her voice stopped me. I sagged against Raoul. "Who are you? What do you want?"

Dory studied me, then nodded to Raoul. He dropped his hold.

"About eight months ago," he said, "a man came to work for us at LABOR. He was one of those people who seem to appear out of nowhere and are satisfied doing menial jobs. An errand boy. He said he was from the part of Mexico that borders Belize. Near the Mayan rain forest." Raoul looked past me. "We soon learned that he was a mole."

"A mole? How?"

"Certain activities we had been planning were suddenly . . . interfered with." He waved an arm. "We were trying to rent space in Wicker Park for an office. We were close to an agreement; the next day, we found out the space had been unexpectedly rented." He looked at me. "We were planning a surprise demonstration against a company that was harassing a Latina. Suddenly, the case was quietly disposed of. After a few more incidents, we started paying more attention to our people. We discovered that our rain forest friend was a plant."

"How?"

"We found a check in his apartment. The signature on the check was Iverson's."

I sucked in a breath.

Raoul went on. "We decided not to confront him at first. We wanted to see how far he would go." He shifted.

"But the stakes changed when Marian Iverson announced for the Senate. Especially after she voiced her friendship for Latinos. We knew there was a disconnect somewhere. We were afraid that if Marian Iverson was elected, LABOR's problems would become far more serious than lost office space." I looked over at Dory. "That is why Dory volunteered to go to work for her. To find out what was going on."

"My brother and Raoul are close friends," she said, but the way they exchanged glances made it clear the friendship didn't stop with the brother.

"You've been spying on Marian?"

"We must know what her role is. She is a powerful politician."

"What have you found?"

"As you may know, we have called for a counterdemonstration to the Labor Day rally," Raoul said. "The one she will be appearing at with the mayor." I remembered the news reports. "A large crowd of Latinos will come to Daley Plaza to protest for higher wages, more promotions, more contracts for city business." He paused. "We suspect that someone—perhaps Gibbs or his agents—will try to sabotage us at that rally. Something is planned, something that will embarrass or discredit us."

"A disruption that will be blamed on LABOR?"

"Dory has found correspondence to that effect."

"Correspondence?"

"More E-mails."

"From Gibbs?"

"No. These have no return path."

I knew it was possible to cloak your identity in cyberspace. But who would do that? And for what reason? "Hold on," I said. "Have you been hacking into Marian's E-mail?"

Dory shrugged.

I burst out laughing.

She smiled sheepishly.

Raoul looked bewildered. "What is so funny?"

I remembered how she'd needled me about Skull's E-mail and shook my head. A fresh wall of rain slammed across the parking lot. The light on the wall of the factory sputtered. We retreated further under the overhang.

"What did you find?" I asked.

"We're not sure," Dory said. "The references are veiled. Maybe a spontaneous riot. Or some other type of violence."

"But Marian needs your votes. Why would she deliberately alienate you? That's political suicide."

"LABOR is a small group of Latinos," Raoul said. "Some say we do not represent the majority." His eyes narrowed. "Listen. The only way she will suffer politically is if it is proven she arranged it. Orchestrated it. We don't think that's the case."

"I don't get it. You discover the possibility of sabotage through her E-mail, but you don't think she's involved?"

Dory lit another cigarette. The match threw long shadows across her face. "Someone else is orchestrating it."

"Gibbs."

"No," Raoul said. "Gibbs is too small. It's someone with unlimited money and resources and expertise. Someone who can plan a civil disturbance and make it appear spontaneous."

I stared at Raoul, then Dory. Suddenly an image of Giant Park flew into my mind.

"You may be right."

Raoul looked over.

"Marian met secretly with Gibbs."

His eyes widened.

"At Giant Park. Over the Fourth of July." I explained how I'd overheard their conversation. "He talked about some operation. She seemed to know what it was."

"What kind of operation?"

"I don't know. But it's been moved from Minneapolis to here."

"Minneapolis?" Raoul said. "What else did you hear?"

I thought back to their conversation while I was hiding

behind the bar. "A construction site. He said his people
had infiltrated a construction site in the Loop."

Moving to the edge of the overhang, Raoul slapped his
fist against his palm. Then he turned around. His tone was
cold. "It's a bomb. They are planning to explode a bomb
at the rally. And they will say we did it."

Horror swept across Dory's face.

"Yes," he said. "Don't you remember? The FBI arrested terrorists in Minneapolis earlier this summer. They
found a bomb. Built by a white separatist organization.
With ties to Gibbs's group." Raoul clenched his fist.
"They're going to do the same thing here."

"I just remembered something else," I cut in. "Gibbs
told her that Minneapolis was sloppy. They made mistakes. He said he wouldn't."

He raised his fist in the air. "That's it."

"No." Dory's jaw tightened. "Gibbs plans marches, not
bombs. He is just the front man. He may be involved, but
he is not the leader."

I scowled. "If it's not Gibbs, it has to be Marian."

Dory shook her head.

"Why not? She could be siphoning off campaign funds
for him."

"Politicians never give money away," Dory said. "They
take it. And I saw the books when I was there. There
were no unexplained expenses."

"So, it's some other neo-Nazi group."

"Perhaps. But if we are to stop them, we need to find
out who." She looked at me.

Goose bumps prickled my skin. I started to back away,
but Raoul blocked me.

"We need you."

"I can't."

"You can," Dory said. "And you must. Come with me.
Tomorrow night."

"Where?"

"To the office. To go through her correspondence."

"You want me to break into campaign headquarters?
With you?"

"I have a key. And I know her password."

"Oh. That makes it all right."

"The pieces are there. We can put them together. Then we can take action."

Action? What action? I shook my head. "You go."

"I don't work there anymore. You do."

"What do I say if we get caught?"

"You are working late."

"In Marian's office?"

Dory shrugged. "There are ways to handle it."

"And where will you be . . . if somebody comes?"

"Raoul will be downstairs. He will warn us. I will hide."

"No," I said emphatically. "It's crazy. Marian's too smart to keep anything incriminating lying around."

"Arrogance breeds carelessness. I found the message about David, didn't I?"

Wet concrete glistened in the light. My sandals and feet were soaked, and the rain had seeped through my shirt. I would start to smell soon, that damp, earthy, mildewed smell.

I thought about Marian. And David. And the document with Iverson's name on it. Did Marian know about that, too? A sour taste rose in my throat. Maybe it wasn't just Kurt's murder she was trying to cover up.

I told them about the document. As I explained, Dory moved closer to Raoul. "I've got to warn David."

"But you are in danger, too."

"I can take care of myself."

"Can you?" Dory said. "Listen to me. Here's what will happen. Marian will call you. She will say she wants to see you. Meet with you. But it won't be downtown. It will be someplace remote. Perhaps out of state."

Marian was leaving for Door County tomorrow. On Jeremiah Gibbs's orders. "I won't return her call. I won't meet her."

"You think that will stop them? They broke into your house. Shot the boy at the library. Attacked your father. They probably killed Skulnick as well."

My head jerked up. "But he died of a heart attack."

"There are chemicals that simulate heart attacks. Easily available, if you know where to look." She planted her hands on her hips. "And you're forgetting one other thing."

"What?"

"You have a daughter at camp."

I went rigid. My voice cracked. "They wouldn't."

"Are you sure?"

FORTY-SIX

I CALLED DAVID from the drugstore, but there was no answer. I didn't leave a message. I picked up a toothbrush and took it to the checkout counter. The withering look from the sales clerk unnerved me; I hadn't even thought about shoplifting. I understood when I checked myself in the mirror. Unkempt, wet, and scruffy, I looked like something from one of those teenage slasher movies.

"Where were you?" Dad scolded when he opened the door. "I was about to call the police." His eyes narrowed. "You're soaking wet."

I toweled off and told him what Dory and Raoul had said. When I finished, Dad let go of the sofa bed he'd been making up and disappeared into the bedroom. The half-folded mattress stayed open, its foot poised in the air. I heard drawers open and close. He came back in with an automatic pistol in one hand and a box of bullets in the other. I watched as loaded the Colt. After he attached the clip, he laid it on the hassock of the chair and went back to making the bed.

I stepped around the hassock, carefully avoiding the gun. "Dad, do you think Skull knew about the report?"

He bent over a pillowcase.

"Do you suppose he was the one who got it to Kurt in the first place? He was working with the Resistance. Kurt was with the OSS. Could they have known each other in Europe?"

"That would be a hell of a coincidence." He straightened up. "But even if they did, I don't know how you'd prove it. They're both dead."

"We know Skull was looking for Lisle. And that he was on borrowed time. He told Boo Boo if they caught him, they'd take him out. And it wasn't just Lisle. He was making inquiries all over the place. Boo Boo said he even wrote the CIA. Maybe he was trying to confirm the report . . . the one he gave Kurt all those years before."

Dad started to nod. "It's possible."

"And if Marian or Gibbs knew that's what he was doing, it would explain a lot."

"Meaning they killed him because Skull knew Paul Iverson was financing Mengele."

"Yes. But they might not have known whether he actually had the report or not. Which was why they had to steal his things. And eliminate anyone else who might have known about it."

"Including me?"

I nodded.

"I don't know," my father said. "Even if Skull knew Marian's father collaborated with the Nazis, why kill him?"

"How could she let that get out? It would destroy her at the polls."

Dad shook his head. "These things aren't such deeply held secrets anymore. Ford, General Motors, Bayer. They've all admitted similar things, and they're doing fine. True, it would have been embarrassing, but it might not have been a deal-breaker. Remember, this was her father. Not her. She could distance herself from him. Tell everyone how abhorrent it was. How different she is."

I pitched the towel on the floor of the linen closet. "If she's so different, why was she meeting with Jeremiah Gibbs?"

My father's gaze went to the gun. "I don't know."

*   *   *

COLORLESS FRAGMENTS OF dreams led me to the edge
of sleep and then back again. I woke up fatigued and still
tense. Dad snored gently in his chair. The gun lay on the
floor. Thinking David might have called, I got up quietly
and dug my cell out of my bag. Then I remembered it
was out of juice.

I tiptoed into the bathroom and splashed cold water on
my face. Suddenly a face appeared in the mirror behind
me. I jumped before I realized it was Dad. His eyes were
bloodshot, and gray stubble covered his face. I touched
his cheek with my hand.

After washing up, he went into the kitchen and took
out a bowl. Then flour. Milk. Eggs. When I was little, he
used to make pancakes on special occasions. Not the thick
Aunt Jemima kind. His were delicate thin, light golden
crepes rolled up and filled with jam, with powdered sugar
on top.

I didn't think I was hungry, but I wolfed down four
crepes. And two cups of coffee. After clearing the table,
I gathered my things and put the fax in my bag.

"What do you think you're doing?"

"I can't stay here. I've already put you in too much
danger."

"Where are you going?"

"I've got to put the document in a safe place. And I
have to warn David—"

"Ellie—" He stopped. He must have known it was useless to argue. He picked up the Colt off the floor. "Take
this with you."

I gulped. "I don't know how to use it. I'd screw it up."

He motioned me over. Releasing the clip, he showed
me how to load the magazine, move the slide, and cham-
ber a round. Then he showed me how to aim through the
sights. I placed it gingerly in my bag. "If I don't hear
from you by tonight, I'm calling the police."

I kissed him and slipped out the door.

FORTY-SEVEN

IT HAD STOPPED raining when I turned onto my block. My eyes were on the move for anything that didn't belong. Outside the garage door, I listened for noises. Nothing. I took the stairs two at a time. In the kitchen, the answering machine blinked.

David's voice cut through the silence. "I'll be there this afternoon. Leave a message where I can find you."

Damn it. If anyone was listening, and I knew they were, they'd know where he was headed. I erased the message.

I showered, dressed in jeans and a T-shirt, and went down to the kitchen. Rummaging inside the cabinet, I pulled out a plastic bag and carefully slipped the fax inside, securing the bag with a twist-tie. Then I went outside. Dark clouds still roiled the sky, threatening a new downpour. My eyes roved the grass, the locust tree, the beds of impatiens under the evergreens. Near the back of the flowerbed at the base of the house was a window well, covered with a semicircular disk of plastic. Partially obscured by the yews, I'd almost forgotten it was there.

I stepped carefully between the flowers, mud caking my shoes, and wedged myself against the window well. Trying to avoid the sharp bristles of the yews, I leaned over and struggled to raise the lid. At the bottom of a five-foot drop was a layer of gravel mixed with years of accumulated lawn detritus: leaves, twigs, and grass in various stages of decomposition. I took a quick look around, then jumped into the pit.

The window had been painted shut well before we moved in, and a series of cobwebs, some more recent than others, filmed the glass. I tried not to brush up against them as I scraped a layer of stones and leaves to one side. Then I crouched down, dropped the plastic bag in the empty space, and covered it back up. When I was satisfied it looked natural, I braced my arms on the ground and hoisted myself back up. Again I checked the yard and the street in front. No one. I replaced the cover and went back inside.

I scraped the mud off my shoes, then made a circuit of the house. Empty and quiet, the house had an expectant hush, as if waiting for the command to start the activity of living again. I tiptoed upstairs and booted up the computer, its clicks and beeps piercing the silence. Opening a search engine, I requested images of Prague. Within seconds, a digital contact sheet of twelve tiny pictures appeared on the screen. I scrolled down castles, government buildings, even the clock tower David had told me about. I jumped to another page.

A shot on the third page stopped me. Captioned "Prague: Charles Bridge," the photo was a long shot of a cobblestone bridge. I clicked on the thumbnail, and a larger version came into view. In the background was a castle set high on a hill. In between the bridge and the castle were a group of buildings, some of them with red roofs.

The text beside the photo explained it was the Charles Bridge and the castle of Hradcany. Originally built in the Middle Ages, the castle had been expanded over the centuries by various emperors and princes. Now it towered over the city, a monument to the Austro-Hungarian Empire. The bridge in front of it, with baroque statues of saints flanking its sides, was built in 1342, but its wood structure dated back to 900 A.D.

A buzz skimmed every nerve in my body. I knew this bridge. Though this was a long shot, and the one I'd seen was a medium shot, it was the same location. It was the bridge Skull was standing on in the snapshot at Ruth's. Skull, a woman, and a baby. With a castle in the background.

I saved the picture and turned on my printer. Skull had been in Prague during the war. Kurt was, too. This was more than a Jungian coincidence. I hit Print. The printer lurched and sucked in a piece of paper.

As the picture was spitting out, a fresh batch of rain sheeted down. I closed the windows. Forks of lightning singed the sky, and thunder crashed overhead. Hail pelted the roof. The lights flickered once. Twice. Then they snapped out. The monitor went dark, the printer stopped, and the house fell into silence, all its clicks, hums, and vibrations eerily still.

I went downstairs and threw open the junk drawer in the kitchen. I'd never replaced the flashlight that had been smashed during the break-in. I was mentally cursing myself for procrastinating when a thump cracked the silence.

I froze, my arm extended over the drawer. Another thump. And some rustles. Outside. I peered through the window. A fork of lightning sputtered, flooding the lawn with light. The yard looked empty. Then I heard a clank, as if metal was scraping against concrete under the window. Too close to the house to be seen. I flattened myself against the wall. I shouldn't have come home. I should have listened to Dory.

The gun. If I could make it to my bag, I could defend myself. Where the hell had I put it? In the family room. I looked into the hall. I needed seven steps to get to it. I told myself to move. Nothing happened.

More thumps. Terror broke my paralysis, and I raced into the family room. Grabbing my bag, I pulled out the Colt. I crept to the door and released the safety, raising the gun to chest level. My breath came shallow and fast. I peered out of the eyehole.

Fouad stood dripping on the doorstep.

I sagged in relief and threw open the door, but when

he saw the Colt in my hand, he jumped back, and his hands shot into the air.

As something metallic clanked on the concrete, a new ripple of fear surged through me. How did Fouad know I was here? What had just dropped onto the concrete? Had I just thrown open the door to my enemy? I kept a tight grip on the Colt. "What are you doing here?"

"I got caught in the storm." He edged closer to the wheelbarrow. I tensed. "I knocked, but you didn't answer the door."

"I didn't hear you."

He yanked a thumb. "I tried to wait it out in the truck, but my windows do not close. When I saw you shut your windows, I knew you were home." The storm was so loud he was shouting. The water streaming down had plastered his clothes to his body.

My eyes darted to the metal object that dropped to the ground. Squinting through the rain, I made out a pair of pruning shears.

I relaxed. "Come in." I put the safety on the Colt and laid it on the hall table.

He followed me in. I fetched a towel, which he ran over his head, face, and arms, then draped around his neck. His eyes fixed on the gun. "You are in trouble, Ellie."

I looked at the floor.

"Is it your ex-husband?"

"No."

"Your daughter?"

I shook my head, feeling a pang of longing for Rachel.

"Your new friend?"

I saw the concern etched on his face.

"How can I help?"

"You can't. I shouldn't even be here."

"This is big trouble."

I nodded.

"You cannot tell me?"

"It has to do with the woman I'm working for."

He raised an eyebrow. "The hosta woman? In Lake Forest?"

"Yes." I was surprised he'd remembered.

"You must wait until the storm passes." I looked outside. Curtains of rain lashed the lawn. Wind rattled the windows. We went into the kitchen and sat down.

We were on our second cup of coffee when the phone trilled. I knew I shouldn't answer it. It could be Marian. Or Roger. But what if it was David? I stared at the phone. It continued to ring. An eternity passed. Finally, my machine picked up.

"Ellie, it's Roger. I'm calling for Marian. She needs to meet with you. She says it's important. Please call her."

The machine clicked off, and the message light blinked. Fouad and I exchanged glances.

FORTY-EIGHT

BY DUSK, THE rain tapered off, but a sticky film of humidity hung in the air. I parked in back of Walgreen's near Dad's. Five minutes later, a blue Chevy turned in and circled the lot, slowing as it came abreast of the Volvo. Dory was driving. Raoul opened the door, and I climbed into the back. She pulled out and turned east. Both of them were in dark clothes. Dory's hair, pulled back with a band, was hidden under a baseball cap.

"You were right," I said. "Marian called. She wanted to meet with me."

"You didn't call her back?"

"No."

"You see? You have been watched. Your home. Your phone. Even your E-mail."

"My E-mail, too?" Dory nodded. I remembered the garbled messages that never got through to Karen and Mac. They had been thorough.

We cruised down Ridge Road through Evanston. Like Oak Park, Bronxville, and Bethesda, border towns are often more livable than the cities they adjoin.

"Why me? Why did you recruit me to help you?"

Dory met my eyes in the mirror. "It was partly this Skulnick business. The way you talked about him. Something was odd. And then, when David looked exactly like Marian's father, and I saw Marian's reaction, I knew something was going on."

"You saw it, too."

"I tried to warn you." I recalled when she showed me
the picture of Paul Iverson in Marian's office. "But we
didn't know how much you knew until I got the call from
Stephen Lamont."

"Lamont?" I leaned forward. "You're working with Lamont?"

She sidestepped the question. "When I left the campaign, the public, sanitized version was that I resigned
But Lamont knew I'd been fired. He wouldn't say how
he knew, but I got enough out of him to realize it came
from you."

I frowned. "That wasn't intentional. He manipulated me
into it."

"Isn't that what they're supposed to do? He's not bad
you know. For a reporter."

"If you can tolerate the species. Roger's looking for
him, by the way. He seems to have disappeared."

Raoul cleared his throat. "He's on assignment."

"For you?"

"For himself, mostly."

"He told me someone's been E-mailing him," I said
"Anonymously. Telling him to look closely into Marian's
campaign. Any idea who that might be?"

Raoul smiled. "Don't worry. He's safe."

"I'm sure of that." I turned to Dory. "Is that why you
left the campaign?"

She gripped the wheel. "No. It was Wolinsky. He pres
sured me to sleep with him, but I wouldn't." I flashed on
an image of Dory outside Marian's hotel room in Rock
ford, her face spasming between fury and anguish. Raou
reached for her hand.

I leaned against the back of the seat.

WHEN I OPENED my eyes, we were on Michigan Avenue
During the day, the strip of road between Oak Stree
Beach and the Conrad Hilton is brash, bright, and confi
dent. But when night falls, the street devolves. Figure

slip in and out of shadows, cars creep by, strangers prowl back alleys. Away from the pools of light, a sinister, more primitive force lurks the streets, linking passion and danger in a macabre dance. Demonstrators at the '68 convention were beaten up near here; Andrew Cunanan stalked his prey close by.

Dory and Raoul were talking in low voices.

I yawned.

"Good," Raoul said into the rearview mirror. "We're almost there."

I stretched my arms. "I'm still wondering about something. Did Marian hire me because of my skill or because she had to keep me close?"

"I don't know," Dory said. "But it goes to the heart of the matter. Who was—who is—in control." She twisted around. "I can tell you this much. When the subject of a video first came up, Roger thought of you right away. Without any prompting."

I looked out the window as we headed east on Superior. "So it was totally serendipitous that I went to work for her in the first place?"

Dory shrugged.

Another Jungian coincidence.

FORTY-NINE

AT THE OUTDOOR parking lot, a stooped old man with a toothless grin took our money and wished us a good evening. As we walked the two blocks to the River North office, patches of fog drifted past us, their smoky tendrils dissipating on contact. Raoul retreated to the Italian restaurant next door. He would wait outside. If anyone went into the building, he'd call Dory's cell, let it ring twice, and hang up.

Dory's key opened the outer door, and we quietly entered the narrow lobby. The building wasn't big enough to warrant a security guard, but a sign advised us that the alarm system was connected to the Eighteenth Precinct. I hadn't noticed it before. The small, rickety elevator deposited us on the third floor.

I tried to swallow my fear. If I hadn't thought Rachel might be in danger, I would never have let myself get talked into this. "Are you sure we should—"

Raising a finger to her lips, Dory slipped her key into the lock. It turned easily, but the door squeaked as we stepped through. I heard it latch behind her. Just inside the door on the wall was an electronic keypad. Dory opened it, tapped in four digits, and a red light turned to green. She blew out her breath. I'd never noticed the alarm. How did she know they hadn't changed the code since she left? An uneasy feeling swept through me.

The reception area was shrouded in darkness and, except for the tick of the clock, it was still. A car passed below, its radio blaring heavy metal. A pair of white head-phones lay on the marble-topped desk. We rounded the corner. Light from streetlamps poured through the large, patterned windows, spilling distorted fleur-de-lis shadows across the floor. As we circumvented the pit and passed Roger's office, Dory scowled.

Marian's office was a few feet away. The door was closed. Dory pulled another key out of her pocket, fit the key into the lock, and opened the door. A dark expanse stretched out. I let my eyes get accustomed to the absence of light, and gradually, shapes dissolved out of black. At one end of the room was Marian's round conference table, chairs, and the sofa. At the other end was her desk, her computer monitor on top. Dory glided over to the hard drive underneath.

The machine whined as it cranked up. A moment later, a blue glow washed over everything. I walked over, aware that precious minutes were slipping away. Finally, the cur-sor changed from an hourglass to an arrow. Dory clicked on Marian's E-mail, which promptly asked for her pass-word.

Dory typed in the letters S-T-E-E-L, and the program opened. Over a hundred messages appeared in her in box. Either Marian never deleted anything, or she got more fan mail than a rock star. Dory and I scanned the list, looking for anything with the words *Gibbs* or *Covenant* or *Church* in the return address.

We had almost reached the bottom of the list when I pointed to an entry: admin@covenant.org. Dory opened it, and we read the first few lines. It was a request for more information about Marian's domestic policies. Im-personal and bland, it was soliciting the type of infor-mation many organizations do when they evaluate which candidates to support. Dory and I traded glances. She mo-tioned to the printer. Raoul said to print out anything we found. I turned it on.

As the printer whined, she kept scrolling. At the bottom of the page was another E-mail from Covenant. She started to open it, but the printer stopped, and she reached for the paper. She was about to stuff it in her bag when a noise outside the door made me freeze.

Dory jerked her head around, angling her head to listen. A squeak sounded. Someone was opening the outer door. Panic shot across her face.

"Someone's coming. We're fucked. Get out!" She hissed. She raced to the door, and her outline disappeared.

I grabbed the paper from the printer, just as light from the reception area flooded the big room. There was no time to get out or to shut down the computer. I threw myself under the desk next to a warren of crossed cords and wires. The wires were attached to a power strip with a glowing orange light on one end. I flipped the master switch on the power strip. Everything went dark. And quiet.

Except for the steps thudding across the floor.

I held my breath, fear piercing my skin like a sharp blade. Who was out there? Where had Dory gone? It flashed through my mind that the office alarm code had in fact been changed, but Dory hadn't realized it. Maybe it had been programmed to accept the old code and simultaneously trigger an alarm. Which meant that they might have suspected her all along. Maybe they'd tripped the alarm to trap her.

More footsteps tramped across the floor. The sounds of a struggle echoed through the walls. Grunts, definitely male. A voice hissing, "Fucking bitch!" Then a groan, this time female. I looked around wildly. There were no panels covering the sides of the desk. Whoever it was would spot me as soon as they looked into Marian's office. I thought about climbing out the window, but it was covered with bars. There was no room behind the couch and no closet in the room. I pulled out the Colt, crawled out from under the desk, and ran to the door, throwing myself behind it.

From the other room, I heard more scuffles, and then what sounded like a swift exhalation of breath. Another rustle. A thud. Then silence. Was it over? Were they leaving? Seconds later, two muffled cracks split the air. Oh God. I released the safety on the Colt. More footsteps. Headed toward Marian's office.

All at once the door banged into my face and crushed me against the wall. Pain ripped across my nose. I sagged down the side of the wall, a wave of dizziness washing over me. The Colt clattered to the floor. I covered my face with my hands, feeling something warm and sticky and metallic smelling. A pair of arms dragged me out from behind the door, whipped me around, and threw me against the wall.

I tried to get my wind, but something solid and hard hit me from behind. My knees buckled, and I fell sideways to the floor. I tried to break the fall with my hand. A sharp pain snaked up my wrist. I groaned, trying to shift back on my haunches, but a heavy weight slammed down on top of me. Something pushed my face into the floor. I felt hot breath on my cheek, and a gravelly voice hissed in my ear.

"Don't even think about it, bitch." My tongue tasted dust and grit. I smelled rancid body odor. "Get the cuffs."

Another voice grunted. Footsteps sounded to my right. Black rubber-soled shoes filled my field of vision, and the weight on my back shifted. Someone pulled my right hand then my left behind my back. Pain sluiced through me. I heard a click, felt cold metal banding my wrists. Then something else stabbed the small of my back. A gun?

Sour cigarette breath strafed my face. "You get up now, nice and easy, and walk to the elevator. Got it?" Someone grabbed my hair and pulled it away from my face. Spasms of pain tore through my scalp. "Got it?" He pulled tighter. My head felt raw. "Tell me you got it."

I moaned.

"Good." The throbbing around my head eased. I felt a prod as something hard was thrust deep into my back. "Just in case."

Someone else grabbed my shoulders and pulled me up. I stumbled forward, losing my balance. Rough hands clutched me and broke my fall. I took a tentative step, then tried to collapse and melt the way I'd been taught during the '60s.

The jab in my back deepened. "You do that again, I'll shoot you with your own gun." The Colt. I tried to twist around. The jab got deeper. A shove pushed me out of Marian's office. Beyond the door, between Marian and Roger's office, a dark form lay motionless on the floor. Dory. Bitter anger welled up in me. Where was Raoul? What happened?

They shoved me into the elevator, facing me against the back wall. As the door closed, someone threw a blindfold around me and pulled it tight across my nose. The rush of blood prompted a new wave of dizziness. A wad of what tasted like cardboard was stuffed into my mouth, forcing my tongue back against my throat. I gagged. Someone stretched tape across my mouth. The elevator door opened again, and I was pushed through the hall.

Hinges squeaked against metal. I'd never used the back door to the building, but I knew it led to a makeshift parking lot off the alley; Marian and Roger parked there. The door closed, and we were outside. I breathed in air scented with garlic.

A car door opened, and I was thrown in, falling sideways against the backseat. The door slammed. I heard murmurs outside. Then it was still. I wriggled on the backseat, trying to gain purchase, but the upholstery was too slippery. After what seemed like a long time, the doors of the car opened, and the springs under the front seat squeaked.

"You get rid of her?" It was the gravelly voice.

"Yup." A second voice replied. Not as deep. Reedy.

"What about the other spic?"

"I left him at the Dumpster."

Raoul. A wave of nausea threatened to choke me. Doors slammed. The engine gunned. The car swung around. I rolled on my side, lurching back and forth on the seat. Finally, the car accelerated in a straight line, and I became more or less stationary.

The ride was a blend of stale cigarette smoke, weed, and the acid smell of violence. Facedown on the seat, every bump was a fresh slice of pain. My left cheek rubbed against a patch of rough tape, probably used to repair a tear in the upholstery.

"Fire me up one," the rough voice said. A few seconds passed. "Now, asshole."

I heard the click of a lighter being depressed. The air filled with cigarette smoke. Someone exhaled. "You must always think ahead, Burl. Anticipate. And prepare for it."

"I'm doing that, Eugene. I am."

"Fuck you are. You haven't learned anything since the goddam dog."

Dog?

"I took care of it, didn't I?"

"Yeah, but it was your mistake that got us into this in first place. You should have known the old lady was taking the mutt for a walk."

Bruno. And Ruth Fleishman.

"If we hadn't gone back to finish them off . . ." his voice trailed off.

"But we fixed it, Eugene. Didn't we?"

A grunt was the response.

"It'll end up okay, once she's out of the way, won't it?"

"Here. You keep this."

"A Colt? Hey, thanks."

The men lapsed into silence.

I tried to breathe normally but couldn't gulp down enough air. The gag reflex kicked in again. I made mewling noises in the back of my throat. Surely they would take pity on me.

"If I hear another sound from you, bitch, I'll do you right here. Just like your *amiga.*"

So much for pity. I tried small breaths through my nose. Gradually, the tension in my throat eased. I tried to count in an effort to keep track of time, but I couldn't get past eight. Was Dory really dead? What about Raoul? Where were we going?

The car slowed and made a turn. I had no idea how much time had passed, but I could tell from the uneven road we were off the highway. After a few more turns, tires crunched on gravel, and we came to a stop. The car doors opened. Hands pulled at me, and I stumbled forward. I smelled fresh-cut grass and heard the quiet slap of waves.

FIFTY

IMAGES FLEW PAST my eyes, like flashing lights on a carousel, but I knew my mind was playing tricks on me. I was curled up in a dark, silent place. The blindfold was on and I was still cuffed, my wrists now chafed and raw. I had no idea how much time had passed, but I felt the tape on my mouth. My jaw was stiff, and my lips and throat were parched.

Feet shuffled outside. I heard a key inserted into a lock. The door opened.

"Rise and shine." A harsh voice. Gravel Mouth. Eugene.

I tried to swing my legs and sit up but lost my balance. My right cheek and side slammed against a cold, hard surface. I saw stars.

"Clumsy bitch, ain't she." The other voice from the car.

A pair of hands grabbed me, pulled me up. Again I tumbled, but the hands caught me and pushed me forward. Something cold and hard pressed against my cheek.

"Do you know what this is?" Gravel Mouth.

I shook my head.

Another prod stabbed my cheek. "It's my Glock," he said. "And Burl has the Colt."

I didn't move.

He ripped the tape off my mouth. Pain stung my lips and skin. I whimpered.

"What did I tell you?" He jabbed the Glock into the side of my head. My lips throbbed like someone had poured alcohol on an open sore. I gulped down air.

We clacked down an uncarpeted hall, linoleum proba
bly. Someone gripped my arm and pushed me up a fligh
of stairs. I counted thirteen steps.

Upstairs it felt warmer. I had been in a basement.
turned toward the person gripping my arms.

"Water?" I croaked hoarsely.

"I told you not say anything." It was Gravel Mouth.

"Please . . ." I begged.

"Shit." Then, "Give her a fucking glass of water, Burl."

Footsteps. Water gushing from a faucet. A glass bein
filled, the trickle changing from hollow to full. I coul
have cried in gratitude. More footsteps, then someon
slipped the glass between my lips. I opened them eagerly
I smelled the slight chlorine odor. My mouth sang wit
anticipation.

"Not so fast, bitch." The reedy voice. "Give us wha
we want, we'll give you what you want." The glass wa
snatched away. The water drained into the sink. I hear
laughter.

"Damn, Burl," the gravelly voice chuckled. "You d
learn."

A buzzer sounded. Loud. Flat.

"Let's go." The blindfold was pulled off my head
Blinding light blasted my eyes, and with it sharp pain.
squeezed my eyes shut. After a while I slowly cracke
my lids. A man with beady eyes and a ponytail stood i
front of me. I'd seen him before. Driving a tan Cutlass.

He pushed me through the door.

FIFTY-ONE

WEARING WHITE LINEN slacks, a silk shirt, and looking very much the gentleman of leisure, Jeremiah Gibbs lounged on the Iversons' brocade sofa. Night hugged the windows, and several table lamps glowed. Pinching the barrel of the Glock against my neck, Gravel Mouth shoved me into a tufted chair. A pitcher of water sat on the mahogany table in front of it. I eyed it jealously.

Stroking his blond mustache with two fingers, Gibbs studied me for what seemed like a long time. He poured a glass of water. Ice cubes plopped into it. My throat was on fire. My mouth opened. Gibbs motioned to Gravel Mouth. "Give it to her."

Taking the glass, the man thrust it between my lips and turned it up at a sharp angle. I gagged, and the water sloshed down my chin, my chest, soaking my shirt and jeans.

"Eugene. Be careful. Those are expensive carpets." Gibbs rose and grabbed the glass, raised it to my lips, and gently tipped it into my mouth. I drank greedily.

"Good breeding is a thing of the past, isn't it, Ellie?"

He removed the glass, and our eyes met. I looked away. He set the glass back on the table.

"We, on the other hand, know what good manners are." He sat down. "But breaking and entering?" He chided, airily waving a hand. "*Them*—well, we know how *they* are. But you? You should have known better." He squared his shoulders, and his face grew cold. "Did you really think we wouldn't change the alarm? Or that you'd find anything we didn't want you to?"

I tried to speak.

"What?"

I whispered hoarsely. "David?"

"Yes. We will deal with him. When he arrives."

My head jerked up.

"Yes. We know he's on his way."

"My phone. You've been—"

He flashed me a modest smile. "Your E-mail, too."

"You tried to kill my father." I heard rage in my voice.

He ran a hand through his hair. "Strong guy for his age. And fast. He was lucky. We'll get him, of course. In time."

"Leave him alone. You've got me."

"Sorry. He knows too much."

"What? What does he know that I don't?"

He raised a finger to his lips. "You'll find out. 'Patience is bitter, but its fruit is sweet.' " He paused, as if waiting for me to praise his intellectual pretense. "Aristotle."

I tried not to react, but I wondered where he had learned that. Was he the kind of loner who hung out at the library as a kid? Didn't psychopaths often start out like that? Suddenly, the memory of another kid at a library passed through me. "You shot Boo Boo. He's an innocent."

He shrugged. "He was helping Skulnick at the library. Who knew what he knew? And—before you ask—yes. The old lady—Fleishman. She was in our way. But she did give us your name. Which made catching up with you a lot easier." He fingered the silk collar of his shirt. "You've been a busy woman. And, until now, quite resourceful. My compliments. Hacking into Skulnick's E-mail was good. Likewise getting past me at Giant Park."

I glared at him.

He folded his arms across his chest, all business now. "We know you found the document. You and your boyriend. The question is, who else knows about it, Ellie? That's what you must tell us."

I eyed him steadily.

"Don't be a hero. It doesn't suit you. Does Lamont know?"

I kept my mouth shut.

"You'd be wise to tell me." He yanked a thumb toward Gravel Mouth.

I shook my head.

"Oh Ellie." He nodded to Gravel Mouth. "I thought you had more sense."

Keeping the Glock at my neck, Gravel Mouth sidestepped around to the front and extracted a Swiss Army Knife from his pocket. Flicking it open, he used the gun barrel to raise my T-shirt and slashed a line across my right breast. I screamed as hot, searing pain shot through me. Bright red blood bubbled up through the incision. I started to collapse, but Gravel Mouth caught me and shoved me back in the chair. A red mist of pain rolled over me, and my head lolled to the side. A mixture of horror and fascination registered on Gibbs's face, as if he was witnessing a gruesome accident and couldn't look away. He licked his lips.

"Well, Ellie?" He leaned forward, his voice deep and hoarse, as if he were sexually aroused. "What does Lamont know?"

"I don't know." I wheezed.

"You've been working together, haven't you?"

"No."

"Don't lie to me."

I tried to move my head to the other side, but I couldn't.

Again Gibbs nodded. Gravel Mouth set the gun down and grabbed my T-shirt, bunching it at my neck. His hand dropped to my left breast, and squeezing it like a grapefruit, he slashed it with the knife. Blood spurted, and I slumped to the floor. Once again he hoisted me up and pushed me back on the chair. The pain lashed my skin,

clanged in my ears, made my entire body throb. I gulped
down air, trying not to pass out.

Gibbs rose and came closer to me, his breath quick and
shallow. I tried to shrink back. "You are proving to be a
problem, Ellie."

"I warned you." A new voice came from behind me.
Deep. Barely female. I twisted around. Frances Iverson
was at the door.

I gasped.

"Frances." Gibbs smiled. "How lovely to see you this
evening."

Frances slowly wheeled herself into the room. Lifting
a gnarled hand off the giant wheels, she motioned to the
table. Gibbs poured her a glass of water. She drank half
of it, then handed it back.

"I told you she would cause problems." She sniffed.
"We should never have waited."

"We're handling it now," Gibbs replied.

Gravel Mouth spoke up. "Burl's got her car. You still
want to run it over the bridge?"

Gibbs held up his palm. "A few minutes."

I buckled in the chair.

"I am sorry, Ellie. Marian was very fond of you. In
fact, that's why you're still alive. She persuaded us not to
harm you. But now, of course, we don't have a choice."

The presence of pain is so overwhelming, demanding
so much from the brain, that the remaining neurons sometimes compensate and perform amazing feats. Thought
patterns are clarified. Previously obscure connections
emerge. Maybe because I was fighting the pain so fiercely
the rest of my brain freed itself up. I swiveled toward
Frances. "It was your name on the letter. Not your husband's."

"I told you not to underestimate her." She set the brake
and sank back in her wheelchair.

Gravel Mouth broke in. "Ma'am, with all due respect
we're running out of time."

Warm, sticky blood clung to my T-shirt. My breasts

throbbed with pain. I was weak and dizzy. Part of me wanted to curl up on the floor in a fetal position. Give up. Let it end. But the pain wouldn't release me. Keep them talking, it prodded me. Stall for time. I opened my mouth, my lips dry and cracked. "Why?" I croaked. "I don't understand."

Frances appraised me with a neutral expression, then shot a look at Gravel Mouth. "She's entitled." She propped her arms on her chair. "Many patriotic Americans . . . people with means . . . good people . . . believed in Hitler. And his ideas. Separate the wheat from the chaff. The leaders from the led. It made sense. There will always be some who are superior. My father, Henry Ford, the Coughlins, they all saw the wisdom of this thinking. Hitler merely accelerated the process." She shot me an ironic smile.

"Interestingly, our quarrel was not with the Jews. At least, not at first. You were smart. Useful. For us, it has always been the coloreds. The browns, the blacks. The yellows. They are the problem. They breed like rabbits. Overpopulate the world. Consume precious resources." She tossed her head. "We knew that even before the war."

"Before World War Two?"

"Of course."

"But . . . but you were just a young woman."

"A young woman with polio. Confined to a wheel-chair."

Keep going, the pain said. "Polio?"

"My parents searched the world for a cure. There was none, but that didn't stop them. They took me to every spa, every sanitorium, even though our hopes were flimsy." Her eyes grew dense and smoky. "It was in Switzerland, during the thirties, that we met a handsome, ambitious young doctor. He was studying genetics in Frankfurt. My father owned a pharmaceutical company, so we had much in common. This doctor couldn't cure me, but we 'bonded,' as you young people say. We listened. We learned. We liked what he said."

"Mengele." I breathed.

"A few years later, he began to research the concept of the master race. First while he fought with the Waffen SS, then through his experiments at Auschwitz. Unfortunately, though, his funding was cut back. Hitler had other priorities: the military, the Einsatzgruppen, the camps. That's when Mengele remembered the rich American with the crippled daughter. By then, of course, the rich man had died, and his daughter inherited his firm."

"You financed Mengele."

The smile deepened. "Not at first. I was wary. The concept of the master race was appealing. Tantalizing. But so unrealistic. How could it be done? How much would it cost? How long would it take? And I was busy with the children, busy being Paul Iverson's wife."

"But you did it anyway. The sterilizations. The torture. The killings. It was your doing."

Her smile faded, and her eyes turned into pools of steel. "Do you know what it's like to have your husband leave you for a whore?"

Lisle.

"He was besotted with her. Bought her clothes, paid for her apartment, even gave money to her causes. And she manipulated him. Used him. The proof of it was that as soon as Weiss came home, she ran back to his bed like a jackrabbit."

Her eyes softened, and for an instant, filled with pity. "Paul was a fool." Then the steely look came back. "He started to respect, admire Jews. The others, too. He even came to believe the people we knew, our family and friends, were wrong. And then, when he started to give money . . ." A brittle look suffused her face. "It wasn't acceptable."

"So you retaliated by bankrolling Mengele."

"The concept had merit. It still does. The war may be over, but the problems are not. We have a moral responsibility to continue. Quietly. In our laboratories. And now, of course, we are light-years beyond Mengele."

Recombinant DNA. Designer genes. I pushed the images out of my mind. How could her family . . . how could her husband have condoned it? Paul Iverson was a decent man. With a defined sense of justice. How could he have lived with a woman who . . . Unless . . . "Paul didn't know," I said suddenly. "He didn't know you were financing Mengele."

"That is correct."

"Then, how . . . why . . . who . . ." I reached, trying to unwind the skeins of the past. She financed Mengele. Mengele sent her reports. Paul Iverson didn't know. But someone else did. Someone who saw the reports. Or copies of them. The report David found in the clock. "Kurt Weiss. He had the report."

She arched an eyebrow. "He got it from Skulnick."

Skull and Kurt. Together. They had known each other.

"Skull's woman slept with a German courier, I'm told. She lifted the report from his pouch."

The woman with Skull. In the snapshot.

A bitter smile crossed her face. "Skulnick turned it over to Weiss. But Weiss never passed it through channels." She took another sip of water. "Instead, he confronted Paul with it after the war."

I heard the whine of a broken muffler outside. My eyes flicked to Gibbs, then Frances. They didn't seem to notice. I sat up straighter.

"Paul assured Weiss he would look into it. He rushed home and demanded an explanation. When I told him, he said we were through. That he was going to divorce me." She gazed at the French doors, shrouded in white tulle against the night. "I laughed in his face. I said it didn't matter. He had already lost the whore. 'After Weiss shows her the Iverson name on the report,' I said, 'she won't believe anything you say.' Paul said I was wrong. He would beg her to forgive him. And spend the rest of his life atoning for my sins."

She smoothed out her robe, a dark but shiny material. "I was right, of course. She cut him off. Oh, Paul tried to win her back. But she wouldn't see him. Then, after Weiss met his untimely death, it was finished. Paul knew the whore would blame him."

"Untimely death? But I thought—"

"It was an ugly time. The news about the camps was just starting to come out. People were appalled. We would have been ruined."

A heart-chilling terror slapped me. "You killed Weiss." She gave me a curt nod. "And Paul couldn't live with it. Knowing Lisle would think *he* did it."

"As I said, he was a fool."

"So he took his own life."

"So it seemed."

I bent my head. So it seemed? "No. It's not possible. He was your husband."

She shrugged. "A heart attack. Perhaps a suicide. You must understand. He was threatening to expose us. The company. The research. We couldn't allow that."

A car door slammed. My pulse started to race.

"What was that?" Alarm flickered across Gibbs's face.

"Burl. Get in here," Gravel Mouth shouted. The man in the fishing hat appeared. "Go see who's outside."

"Sure thing, Eugene."

Gibbs fidgeted in his chair. I had to keep them talking. Especially if who I thought was outside, in fact, was. But after taking another sip of water, Frances grew quiet. Shit. Think, Ellie. I cleared my throat, willing away the pain.

"How did you know that Skull became active again, after so many years in prison?"

"Good question, my dear." Frances spread her hands. "We have allies. Friends. In powerful positions. They alerted us."

I frowned. What friends? What positions? Then it came to me. Skull had been E-mailing the CIA. "The CIA?"

"There are many—in the highest levels of the public and private sectors—who still believe as we do. Particularly now."

"Now?"

"Isn't it obvious? Society has coarsened. We have lost all sense of order. Rage and violence are the rule. A child cannot even go to school in safety."

Gibbs picked up the thread. "So many inequities still exist. Fine young men lose jobs to minorities because of affirmative action. Food stamps and welfare subsidize the shiftless. Money is wasted on diversity programs that do nothing but institutionalize mediocrity. Millions of dollars are lost to economic development projects that themselves become slums."

My brain refused to complete the circuits. I felt as if I had stepped through a warped looking glass where black was white, bad was good, and fascists were the saviors of society.

"Carl von Clausewitz," Frances said, "probably the finest theoretician to ever write about warfare, said, 'To secure peace is to prepare for war.' We have been preparing." Her eyes slanted sideways. "My young, able friend understands the new technology. His associates are my arms and legs, so to speak." She chuckled. "I provide the strategic thinking and—"

"The money."

The darkness closed in, pressing in on us as if it were alive. I tried to wiggle my fingers, but they were numb. I thought of Dory and Raoul. "A bomb at a Labor Day demonstration is part of the strategy?"

Frances pressed her hands together. "A war cannot be fought on one front alone."

"You're inciting chaos. Civil disorder and anarchy."

"We are accelerating what already exists."

"You're orchestrating it so others will be blamed."

"The masses are restless and undisciplined."

"In order to save the world, you're destroying it first."

"Isn't that the essence of true revolution? What happened sixty years ago was just the prologue. We are in the fight of our lives."

"You're not fighting a war," I said. "You're financing terrorism."

"Semantics." Frances waved a hand. "Only afterward will people see the need for structure and order. A firm guiding hand. To lead them out of the storm."

"Marian."

Frances smiled. "Perhaps."

"But she's the reason you're . . . she's an integral part of this." I stopped. My voice was a strangled whisper. Maybe she wasn't.

Frances anticipated my question. "She may think she isn't. She's spent years modeling herself after her father, trying to convince herself she is nothing like me. But she's a politician. Survival is a powerful motivator. In time, I expect her to embrace her responsibilities."

"And if she doesn't?"

"If she doesn't, well . . ." She met my eyes with a small smile.

The sounds of a scuffle broke through from outside.

Gravel Mouth sprinted to the window. "Burl?" There was no response. Pushing the curtains aside, he peered out into the night. "Burl?" Still nothing. Wheeling around, he pointed the gun at my chest.

"What are you doing?" Gibbs leaped out of his chair.

"I'm finishing the job." He pulled back the slide. "Then, I'm going—"

"No," Gibbs screamed, cutting him off. "We can't risk the bullets. Or gunshot wounds. We need an accident. The car over the bridge is better." His eyes blazed. "Give me the gun."

"There's no time—"

"Give it to me."

Gravel Mouth hesitated, his eyes darting from Gibbs to Frances.

"Do what he says, Eugene," Frances commanded. "Get your equipment." Her eyes were cold, her voice deadly calm.

Reluctantly, Gravel Mouth handed Gibbs the Glock and bent over a canvas bag I hadn't noticed before. I thought about rushing Gibbs. If I were fast enough, I might reach

im before he fired. Or he might miss. But my arms were
till cuffed behind me, and I couldn't stand up without
help. Think, I screamed to myself. Think how to stall. But
was groggy, and I wanted to go to sleep. I forced myself
o pull against the cuffs. They sliced into my skin, paining
me awake.

"Lamont knows," I lied. "His story will be running in
orty-eight hours."

"You'll say anything at this point."

My lips cracked. "Are you sure?"

Gibbs narrowed his eyes. Gravel Mouth hurried back,
arrying a syringe filled with a clear liquid. "I'm ready."

"Do it." Gibbs nodded.

FIFTY-TWO

GRAVEL MOUTH CLOSED in on me. He fumbled with my T-shirt with his free hand, but the folds of cotton, which had helped stanch the flow of blood, were stiff and sticky. I shrank back in the chair, my eyes level with the Nike logo on his shirt. I had one chance left. I swung my knees up as high and fast and far as I could. They hit him in the groin.

His eyes filled with something fierce and ugly. Balling his hand into a fist, he slammed it into my head. The side of my face exploded with pain. I collapsed sideways, gasping for air. He caught me as I fell to the floor and threw me back on the chair. I sprawled against the seat, my chin on my chest.

Seizing my right breast, he squeezed as hard as he could. Fresh blood spurted out of the cut. I screamed. Tears sprang to my eyes, and a new wave of light headedness washed over me. But somewhere, in the recesses of my consciousness, I knew I had to keep fighting. Even if it was only symbolic.

My mouth was parched. My throat was tight. I coughed, summoning up a clump of spittle from somewhere. I let it fly. It landed on Gravel Mouth's cheek. He didn't wipe it off, but his eyes narrowed. Releasing my breast, he straddled me and slammed himself down on my thighs. I felt myself cramp. He positioned his thumb on the plunger, ejected a drop or two of fluid, and drew back the syringe.

But before he could act, a flash lit up the deep blue of the drawing room, followed by a tremendous explosion. The glass panels of the French doors shattered. Shards of glass blew out across the room. Gravel Mouth fell off my thighs and out of sight.

A series of images and sounds strafed the room. Gravel Mouth writhing on the floor, screaming, most of his head down off. Blood and pink brain matter splattered on the rugs. Frances screaming, hands on her head, horror on her face. David aiming a shotgun. Gibbs pointing the Glock, not at David, but behind me.

A crack. Another flash, not as bright, from the muzzle of the pistol. I heard a scream. It was me. I heard a curse. It was Gibbs. I twisted around. Fouad was crumpled on the floor, his rifle at his feet. I swung around. Gibbs was slumped on the sofa, his body limp, a stream of red blood staining his silk shirt. The Glock was on the floor. I looked at David. He lowered the shotgun.

FIFTY-THREE

FOUAD MADE IT to the hospital in time. Gibbs didn't.
Neither did Gravel Mouth. They found Burl unconsciou[s]
on the ground at the back door. Fouad or David, I neve[r]
found out who, had whacked him over the head with [a]
shovel. They dressed my wounds in the ER; I neede[d]
stitches. They took David to the Lake Forest police sta[-]
tion. I never saw him. They took Frances there, too. Davi[d]
apparently left a few hours later. Frances didn't.

My father cabbed up to the hospital and took me hom[e.]
By afternoon, two FBI agents in a nondescript blue ca[r]
showed up at the house. I told them what I knew and du[g]
out the report from the window well. By evening, paper[s]
were prepared, charging Frances with multiple homicide[s,]
including those of Kurt Weiss, Paul Iverson, Ben Skul[-]
nick, Ruth Fleishman, and Dory Sanchez. Burl Greenma[n]
was arraigned for the murders of Skull and Dory. The[y]
picked up Marian in Door County.

The Feds raided a construction site across from Dale[y]
Plaza, where they found fertilizer, fuses, and blastin[g]
caps. Had the ANFO bomb they were constructing ex[-]
ploded, they claimed, hundreds—maybe thousands o[f]
people—would have died. The Feds prepared charges o[f]
terrorism against Frances, Greenman, and Marian. Maria[n]
withdrew from the race.

A team of local police and FBI officers searched th[e]
Iverson estate, the offices of the Church of the Covenan[t,]
and Marian's campaign office, where they confiscate[d]

omputers, files, and hard copy documents. After repeated
questioning, it was decided that Roger Wolinsky didn't
know anything, and he promptly left the state. They found
a cache of assault rifles, machine guns, and hand grenades
n the cistern, which they traced back to Eugene, an active
member of Aryan Nation.

They also found a beige metal tackle box. It had been
opened, possibly with a crowbar, police said. Inside was
a snapshot of Skull, a woman, and a baby on a bridge in
Prague. There was also a scrap of paper with two names
scrawled on it: Magda and Kasia Panchuk and an address
n the Ukraine. Two faded yellow newspaper articles were
inside, too: a paragraph from the *Daily News* about the
fatal shooting of a veteran in Douglas Park, and a more
extensive article about the death of Paul Iverson. Finally,
there was an address book belonging to someone named
Peter Schultz. He turned out to be the head of the German-
American Bund in Chicago during the '30s. Frances Iverson's name and number were in his book.

Frances admitted everything under questioning. I
wanted to believe that she was overwhelmed with re-
morse, but I knew her confession was precipitated by ego.
Her grand plan might be in tatters, but she wanted the
world to know how close she'd come.

With her confession, the past piece of the puzzle fell
into place. Just after Kurt was killed, she'd had a visitor,
she said. Ben Skulnick came to see her in Lake Forest.
He knew Kurt Weiss, he knew about the Mengele document and he knew she, not Paul, had killed Kurt. When
she asked him how he knew, he showed her the address
book with her name in it, which he'd lifted off the body
of Peter Schultz after he killed him back in Lawndale. It
wasn't conclusive proof, he told her, but he vowed to
spend the rest of his life searching for more.

But Frances trumped him. Prevailing on the judge at
Skull's trial, she made sure that Skull got a life sentence
and made it clear his daughter's life would be at risk if
he continued his efforts from prison. With that done, she

assumed she was out of danger. Until he was released, and a letter from a friend at the CIA warned them a man named Sinclair was making inquiries about declassified Nazi documents. It didn't take long to connect Sinclair with Skulnick, and when they did, she ordered Gibbs and his associates to eliminate him.

When the press avalanche began, I gave Stephen Lamont an exclusive and referred all calls to him. His reporting turned into a monthlong series, and he's been on Larry King twice. The rumor is he's moving to New York.

The Republicans put up another candidate, but no one expects him to win, and the Democrats are already crowing about having two senators from Illinois.

I visited Fouad in the hospital. It was a close call, but the surgeons successfully removed fragments of a nine-millimeter bullet from his chest. A quarter inch more would have killed him. By some miracle, Raoul survived, too, despite two stomach wounds. His brother is planning to hold the protest on Labor Day in his and Dory's honor. And the librarian from Rogers Park called to say Boo Boo had made remarkable progress and would be going home next week.

I went to *shul* the next weekend and said a *Misheberach* for Fouad, Raoul, and, of course, Boo Boo. Then I said *Kaddish* for Ruth, Dory, and Janine. That evening, I said it again for Skull and Kurt.

MY BRUISES AND wounds turned purple, then yellow, then slowly started to heal. One evening, Susan made me go for a walk. The air hummed with crickets and cicadas, and the breeze hinted at cooler nights ahead. The sun dipped below the trees, shooting glints of gold across our faces.

"This Skull . . . he was a hero, wasn't he?" Susan said.

"Yes, he was. But there are lots of heroes in this story."

I flexed my wrists to relieve the stiffness. "Skull. Kurt. Iverson. Even Lisle."

"Paul Iverson? How?"

"His only mistake was falling in love with Lisle."

"You thought that's why he killed Kurt."

"I was wrong. He changed when he fell in love with her. He wanted to do the right thing. But he was up against powerful forces—"

"His wife."

"A monster." I shivered. "In a way, he made the ulti- mate trade-off. His life for Kurt's."

Susan raised an eyebrow. "And Lisle? How was she a hero?"

"Lisle saw an opportunity to do something good. Avenge the Nazis, honor her family's memory."

"By having an affair with Iverson?"

"No. She took up with him because she was alone and scared. She didn't know if Kurt was coming back. She might have assumed he was already dead. Iverson was rich and powerful. And crazy about her. I figure she made a quid pro quo with herself." Susan looked puzzled. "If she could persuade Iverson to help Jews escape the Nazis, she'd consent to being his mistress."

We were passing the church.

"Do you know the story of Esther?"

Susan shook her head.

"Esther, a Jew, married King Ahasuerus. He wasn't Jewish, and he didn't know Esther was. But one of the king's advisors, an evil man named Haman, did know. Haman, being the wicked man that he was, convinced the king to kill all the Jews. But when Esther found out about the plan, she went to the king, admitted she was a Jew, and begged her husband to revoke the order. He did, and killed Haman instead. Esther saved her people from geno- cide."

"It's a nice story." Susan frowned. "But to what end? What did all that heroism accomplish? Were any of them better off? Most of your 'heroes' suffered tragic deaths.

Frances Iverson is alive. There's still hate and violence and evil in the world. What's changed?"

I didn't have an answer. We made our way down Happ Road.

"I know it's crazy," I said, "but I almost feel sorry for Marian." Susan looked at me. "She was trapped . . . caught between forces she couldn't control."

"Come on, Ellie. She knew who and what her mother was. She made her choice, and then she lost control."

"That doesn't mean she approved."

"She went along. It's the same thing. I'm not sure you can ever escape your heritage."

"You don't believe in redemption?"

"Do you?"

I didn't answer.

She changed the subject. "How did Fouad know you were in Lake Forest?"

That I could answer. "When David flew out from Philadelphia, he came to the house. I had just left, but Fouad was still there. Fouad told him I was in trouble, and they both decided to stick around. When I never showed up, they called Dad, and he told them what he knew. Fouad did the rest."

"How?"

"The flowers."

"Huh?" Susan cocked her head.

"I'd told him a while back that the woman I was working for owned an estate on the lake in Lake Forest. With a lawn covered by hosta and impatiens. Fouad found it."

"At two in the morning?"

"The floodlights were on."

"Clever. So, have you spoken to David?"

The drone of a faraway truck spiked and faded away. "He won't return my calls."

We kept walking.

"She almost did it, you know. Two perfect murders, made to look like heart attacks. Four more to cover them up. And Marian was building a power base. Her appeal was broad. Deep. She had the mayor eating out of her hand."

"And you."

"And me." I hung my head. "Her own Leni Riefenstahl."

Susan slapped at a mosquito. "There's still one thing I want to know."

"What's that?"

"Did Frances Iverson kill out of principle? Or rage that she'd been dumped for another woman?"

FIFTY-FOUR

I PICKED RACHEL up from camp the next day. It had only been four weeks, but she looked tan, healthy, and tall. On the way home, I told her as much as I thought she could handle. That night we went out to celebrate her homecoming; we slept late the next day. I was pulling weeds when a battered Plymouth stopped at the curb. Rachel, who'd been listening to music inside, tore off her headphones and streaked out the door.

"Daddy!" Rachel shrieked and threw her arms around her father.

"Sweetikins." He showered her with hugs and kisses. As usual, he looked great in pressed khakis and a blue shirt. I smoothed out my rumpled shorts, waiting for a Pavlovian pang. It didn't ping.

"Hello, Ellie." He pried himself away from Rachel.

"Hello, Barry. Long time no see."

He didn't say anything. I scratched my cheek. It wasn't like him to let one of my zingers get by.

"I came by to see Rachel. And . . ." He hesitated. "To thank you."

"Thank me? What for?"

"For what you did."

I frowned.

"The loan."

"What loan?"

"Your banker, David Linden. He helped arrange a loan with terms I can live with."

Shivers rippled my stomach. "He did what?"

"Ellie, come one. I know you set it up. He told me."

"David Linden arranged a loan to cover your stock losses?"

"He brought the papers out from Philadelphia."

"He's here? In Chicago?"

"I just signed the papers at The Ritz."

Rachel and I exchanged a glance. "Barry, you're taking Rachel, aren't you?"

"Uh . . . I hadn't planned—"

I ran upstairs, shedding my gardening clothes. "Make sure she cleans her room."

I FLEW DOWN the highway. The hum of the engine skimmed every nerve in my body. I parked half a block from the hotel and charged into the elevator. As it ascended, I tapped my foot impatiently. Why was it so damn slow? When I got to the lobby, I dashed for the house phone.

He picked up on the second ring.

"Where are you?" My breath was coming in short little puffs.

"Sixteen twelve."

The elevator took too much time. I stepped off at sixteen. A door opened at the end of the hall. David stood framed in the light. I broke into a jog.

I stopped a foot away and spread my hands. "Why did you do it?"

"To thank you."

"To thank me? I should be thanking you. You saved my life."

He shrugged. "Then I guess we're even. You helped me find what I've been searching for my whole life."

My hands fell to my sides. "Does that mean you're okay with it? Paul Iverson, that is?"

"Paul Iverson was a decent, moral man. He tried to do what was right." He smiled. "So did Kurt Weiss, who will always be as much my father as Paul Iverson." He reached for my hand, wincing when he saw the scab on my wrist. "And the woman they loved, my mother, was as principled as they were. All three of them believed in something bigger than themselves. And acted on it." He traced tiny lines on the back of my hand. "I'm honored and humbled to have that as my legacy."

His face swam in front of me. I couldn't stop blinking. He tipped my chin up with his hand. "You gave me my past, Ellie. And now, if you'll let me, I want to give you my future."

He drew me inside and closed the door.

EPILOGUE

THE CAFÉ IN *downtown Odessa was a few blocks from the Potemkin stairway. Like other spots in this Black Sea port, its tile floors and stucco walls had a Mediterranean feel.*

Two men sat at a table playing chess, their glasses half filled with thick, dark coffee. A woman, smartly dressed in a tailored blue suit, sat at another. Her short hair was flecked with gray, but the dazzling blue of her eyes hinted at the beauty she'd been in her youth.

Our interpreter, a young blond who asked several times if we could send her some American CDs, approached her. Smiling hesitantly, the woman craned her neck in our direction. I extended my hand. David followed suit. Our interpreter translated.

"I am Kasia Wojnilow. I have been eager to meet you."

"We have, too," David said.

We sat down and ordered drinks. When they came, Kasia told us her story. She had lived in the Ukraine all her life but moved to Odessa when she became a grandmother. Moving her bottle of pale yellow soda to one side, she rummaged in a straw bag and drew out pictures of three robust children, two girls and a boy.

"And you?" She opened her palm toward us.

I took out my picture of Rachel and handed it over. She pointed to Rachel's eyes and then to mine. We smiled.

"Family is the most important thing." The vertical line

between her brows deepened. "I never knew my parents. They died during the war."

"Your mother's name was Magda Panchuk?" I asked. She nodded.

David pulled out the snapshot of Skull, the woman, and the baby. "Is this your mother?"

She inspected the picture. When she looked up, her eyes were wet.

"The man in the picture is your father. His name was Ben Skulnick. He was a hero. A war hero," I said.

Her eyes flickered with pride.

"How did your mother die?" I asked.

Kasia's back straightened. "She worked for the Resistance. Behind enemy lines. She was trying to pass information to the Allies when she was caught. They killed her. I was still a baby. I went to live with my aunt. In Kiev."

"Kasia," David said, "Let's order a round of schnapps. We have a story to tell you."